"I do find the idea of beautiful men making love erotic. . . I just perceive sex as an act of worship. The worship of life. Sex is a mysterious thing, and therefore, to me, magical. . . If you cast off the inhibited distaste in which our society has shrouded sexuality, then the idea of two beings joining together physically to create energy and pleasure, if not new life, is the weirdest form of magic."
— Storm Constantine, interviewed in *Ex Cathedra*

"She keeps a special place in her heart for those slat-ribbed, kohl-eyed boys. And their boyfriends. . . Storm's love for her characters, their love and lust for one another, and her celebration of their beauty fairly drips from her pages."
— Poppy Z Brite

"I've dreamed of the sensuous, secret-shrouded lands of antiquity, where the nights are filled with perfume and the tantalising slither of silk against skin. In these places, the incubi and the succubae of the imagination wake up and walk."
— Storm Constantine, from her "Introduction"

". . . combines the best qualities of Jacobean tragedy with a steamy male sexuality in a setting like something out of 1001 Nights."
— *Locus*

FICTION BY STORM CONSTANTINE

The Enchantments of Flesh and Spirit (1987)
The Bewitchments of Love and Hate (1988)
The Fulfilments of Fate and Desire (1989)
The Monstrous Regiment (1989)
Aleph (1991)
Hermetech (1991)
Burying the Shadow (1992)
Sign for the Sacred (1993) *
Calenture (1994) *
Stalking Tender Prey (1995)
Scenting Hallowed Blood (1996)
Stealing Sacred Fire (1997)
Three Heralds of the Storm (1997)
The Oracle Lips (1999)
Thin Air (1999)
Sea Dragon Heir (1999)
Thorn Boy (1999) *
Crown of Silence (2000)
Silverheart with Michael Moorcock (2001)
The Way of Light (2001)

NON-FICTION BY STORM CONSTANTINE

The Inward Revolution with Deborah Benstead (1998)
Bast and Sekhmet: Eyes of Ra with Eloise Coquino (2000)
Egyptian Birth Signs (2002)

* available from Stark House Press

Storm Constantine

The Thorn Boy

And other Dreams of Dark Desire

With a New Introduction by the Author

Stark House Press
Eureka, 2002

THE THORN BOY AND OTHER DREAMS OF DARK DESIRE

Published by Stark House Press
1945 P Street, Eureka, CA 95501, USA
griffins@northcoast.com

ISBN: 0-9667848-4-7

Text set in Garamond #3 and Franklin Gothic
Heads set in Cherries Black
Interior layout by Kevin Fox
Copy editing & proofreading by Gregory Shepard
Cover design by Mark Shepard
Cover art by Campbell Shepard

PUBLISHER'S NOTE

First Stark House Press Edition: December 2002

0 9 8 7 6 5 4 3 2 1

The Storm Constantine Information Service:
44 White Way
Kidlington
Oxon OX5 2XA
England
E-mail: peverel@aol.com

Table of Contents

Introduction

Quite often, I write stories as presents for friends, and several of the pieces in this collection fall into that category.

The first, 'The Thorn Boy', was originally created as a birthday present for Eloise Coquio, and I produced it as a self-published booklet in an extremely limited edition – one for Lou and one for me.

'Spinning for Gold', 'Nothing Child', 'Living with the Angel' and 'The True Destiny of the Heir to Emiraldra' are reinterpretations of old fairy stories. These were written in the late Eighties for a gay male friend of mine, and are retold with his fantasies in mind. ('The Heart of Fairen De'ath' was also part of this sequence, but as the story is due to be published soon in a separate collection, I have omitted it here.)

After a visit to Australia, where I met the publishers from Eidolon Publications, 'The Thorn Boy' appeared as a novella from them in 1999. I rewrote and expanded it greatly for publication. It quickly went out of print and is now one of the most sought-after of my books by collectors. Greg Shepard had distributed the book in the States and he suggested that his family's publishing company, Stark House, should republish the story. There is still a big demand for the book, and to make it even more collectible, Greg and I decided that we should include other stories, both previously published and unpublished, set in the same world, that of 'Sea Dragon Heir', 'Crown of Silence' and 'The Way of Light', collectively known as the 'Chronicles of Magravandias'.

Even though the Magravandias trilogy was published fairly recently, I've written stories set in its world for a long time. 'Spinning for Gold' and its companion stories were written while I was still involved in producing the first Wraeththu book. As such, they can be viewed as juvenilia, although I have re-edited them for this collection.

Over the years, I've set other stories in the same world, in particular involving the land of Mewt, which is a fantasy interpretation of Ancient Egypt. Three of these later stories have been published before, in various anthologies and magazines. For one of them, 'Night's Damozel', I collaborated with Eloise Coquio. Although I did most of the writing, we came up with the plot between us. 'The Island of Desire' is an unpublished story I began writing about five years ago. For some reason I never got around to finishing it, but have now completed it to include in this collection.

If there is a theme that links these stories, other than a shared world, it has to be that of the darker aspects of desire and how, when we indulge our passions, there can be unpredictable results. Most of the stories involve the protagonist lusting after a character who is in some way 'other', alien or bizarre. The compelling allure of 'otherness' leads the protagonists into shadowy dangerous territory, where sometimes their lives, if not their souls, are put in jeopardy. Often the landscape of the tales is almost like a character itself. I've dreamed of the sensuous, secret-shrouded lands of antiquity, where the nights are filled with perfume and the tantalising slither of silk against skin. In these places, the incubi and the succubae of the imagination wake up and walk. This book can be seen as a travelogue of the exotic landscape of the imagined realm. Travellers tales.

Storm Constantine
August 2002

The Thorn Boy

This story is mentioned by one of the characters in the second book of the Magravandias trilogy, 'The Crown of Silence'. It is regarded, during the time in which the trilogy is set, to be an early legend of that world. I wrote 'The Thorn Boy' a long time before I even thought of the idea for the Magravandias books, but when I came to write the trilogy, found I wanted to set it in the imagined world I'd created for several of my early stories. I wanted, in particular, to explore the land of Mewt in more detail.

Originally, this piece was written as a birthday present for a friend, but I expanded it considerably for its first publication by Eidolon Publications in Australia. I saw it as the first of a series of linked stories. Each story would feature a 'Wonder' of this imagined world, an astounding edifice of some kind. The 'Wonder' in 'Thorn Boy' is Phasmagore, the temple of the goddess Challis Hespereth. I saw this as a gargantuan hollow statue of the goddess, the head of which would be lost in the clouds. Inside it was a warren of chambers, shrines and corridors. Strangely enough, I read recently that somewhere in India an enormous statue of Buddha is being built, along roughly the same lines. Another of these Wonders features in the story 'Blue Flame of a Candle' (published in The Oracle Lips collection, Stark House, 1999), and that is the Pyramid of Mipacanthus.

I see this story as a tragedy, but with a hopeful resolution. I certainly don't think Darien's story is by any means finished, and one day hope to continue it.

The first time I saw him he hung screaming in the clutch of two white-sheathed knights. They had prised him from the corpse of Harakhte, the dead, enemy Khan, brought him straight from the battlefield to present to the king. Now, his skin was lathered with the sweat of fear and the dead warrior lord's blood.

The Khan's boy; a prize of war. He had been a slave to Harakhte; why now did he wail the lament for the lost and the loved?

He was almost naked, his young, slim body filigreed with cuts and bruises. The blood of his dead lord mingled on his skin with his own. A muddied plait of fairish hair hung to the back of his thighs. It was impossible to tell whether his face was beautiful or not, because it was disfigured by the grimaces of grief. The knights, in their thin, milky scales of armour, held him as if he were an animal. They paid no heed to his screams, but then most of his exclamations were in Mewtish; a foreign, incomprehensible tongue.

King Alofel sat beneath his canopy of white muslin, which was fringed with gold. They had brought for him a throne, all the way from the palace in Tarnax. I knelt beside it, looking at the Khan's boy, my heart full of disdain and hate and, even then, the more subtle atrocity of envy.

The King summoned his chief concubine, Porfarryah, who accompanied him everywhere, even to the brink of death. She too was clad in scales of white, but she never lifted a sword. Alofel would not allow it, and I think that secretly she must have been grateful, although she swore she was equal to any man in strength and valour.

Alofel gestured with distaste at the captive and spoke to his concubine. 'Have someone make the boy comfortable, and see to his wounds.'

As Porfarryah bowed her head, she caught my eye. We had long been conspirators; it was essential at court. Queen Mallory was dangerous. Full of envy for those who usurped her place in her husband's bed, she reigned over a clutch of gossiping cabals. We had to keep our wits about us.

The boy continued to wail his ghastly requiem. I could tell it offended Alofel's ears, which enjoyed only the tinkle of faint music, the play of the fountains on his marbled terraces, the sweet voices of love. 'Is there nothing we can do to calm him?' Alofel asked his company, and Porfarryah gestured for the herbalist's assistant to come to her.

Presently, the herbalist himself came swaying between the ice-coloured hangings of the tents, bearing a box of dark metal. At the sight of him, the boy screeched only louder. I put my hands over my ears and closed my eyes, feeling, with satisfaction, the brief pressure of the King's fingers upon my head. Then, I heard a series of strangled, terrible sounds and had to open my eyes, even though I was not that eager to see. The herbalist had inserted a row of medicinal thorns into the flesh of the boy's chest, beneath his rib-cage, designed to bring a floating euphoria to his mind. For one endless moment, his eyes met mine. I shrank before his pain and bewilderment, suffused with an unbearable sense of pity. This was most unlike me, and I felt uncomfortable with it. Pity translated to despising in my heart. Presently, his noise subsided and he hung there, limply, his breath sobbing, his head lolling.

I felt the King's relief. It brightened the air. 'Good,' he said. 'Now we must be charitable.'

They dragged the boy away, his feet trailing in the churned dust as if his ankles were broken. I felt an absurd sense of anger for the way he'd affected me, and again caught Porfarryah's eye. We sneered in complicity, and I thought the matter closed.

I had been with the royal army for three months, for my lord, King Alofel, had ordered my presence. I had no love of war. Noblemen who once had glided about the court, talking in hushed voices of high and philosophical ideas, now relished wallowing in the blood. They even seemed to take pleasure in their own injuries, boasting about the fires at night of the hurts they had received and inflicted.

The King, my Lord, as ever an acetic presence, commented little. He rode silently among his men, never courting danger, but never shying from it. His sword flashed redly with the rest of them, but I knew he took no pleasure in it. It was his duty as guardian of the land, nothing more.

Mewt is a hot, arid country, and we had harried the Khan to the foot-hills of Sessalia; a crop of unforgiving, rocky spikes where water and food were scarce. Here, the war had been ended. It had begun over a dispute concerning the xandrite mines in the mountains of Lorgh Hash that swept down into both our countries from Elatine. Cos and Mewt each claimed ownership of the mines—although technically they must belong to Elatine. The meek Elatinians, however, would side with whoever seemed strongest and never dare to claim ownership themselves. Harakhte, the Khan of Mewt, recently-crowned, young and ambitious had decided to end the centuries of bickering. The answer was simple. The mines belonged by sacred law to the holy land of Mewt. Naturally, the Cossics objected to this and what began as a territorial skirmish escalated into full-scale combat. Allies from other lands were recruited, and the fighting ranged long and bloody throughout the reaches of two years. Now, it was ended, and Harakhte lay dead, taken by an arrow through the throat—which unhorsed him—followed by a barrage of dismembering sword-thrusts. There would be little left to display to his grieving people. His armies had lost heart after his death, and soon a puppet lord would sit upon the Bull Throne in Mewt. People speculated that Alofel would woo Menefer, the younger brother of Harakhte—it was rumoured he could be bought. Harakhte's remains had been placed in a regal sarcophagus by the conquering king and delivered to the generals of Mewt along with praises for Harakhte's courage. A strong party of our own generals and their men accompanied the sarcophagus, surrounding a slyness of Cossic advisors, who would arrange the new government.

I did not see the Khan's boy again until we reached home, the city of Tarnax, capital of Cos. I rode behind the army on the beautiful white pony that the King had given to me for my last birthday. At my side, Porfarryah sat astride a lean, black destrier. Citizens lined the street and keened in our victory, throwing us flowers, lucky coins and painted feathers bound with ribbons. The atmosphere was intoxicating. I was glad to be home.

The Queen waited on a balcony of the palace. Its balustrade was draped with golden tapestries and garlands of flowers. She was surrounded by a horde of young concubines—all of whom she loathed—and the three little princes, two of which were her own children.

There was only one Queen, but she resented having to share her husband. In her country, Kings were allowed only one woman, officially. Theirs had been a marriage of convenience, a mating of land rather than souls. Of course, she loved Alofel, for who could not? He was a slim, tall man, with a flag of bright gold hair, and a noble face. When he spoke, his voice was quiet. He gave the illusion of feyness, but everyone was aware of his power and his strength. I, as his favourite, knew him the most intimately. He would confide things to me he would never speak of to Porfarryah or her sisters. Sensitive to how this state of affairs could provoke trouble for me, from the day of my arrival at court, I had curried favour with the women. I counted all of the concubines as my friends, and we were united in our suspicion and dislike of the queen.

More importantly, I had ingratiated myself with several members of the King's Council, which on my seventeenth birthday had resulted in me being voted into an honorary seat. The position was not secure, and although I could speak whenever I wished, there were only certain, inconsequential matters on which I was allowed to vote. I could be removed at any time, should I fall from the king's favour. Still, I had strong allies among the Council, for they knew I had Alofel's ear, at times when he was most amenable. Mallory too had friends on the Council, and occasionally official meetings were little more than a game of wits. The Queen wanted to have her own place there, but Alofel would never grant her that wish. I do not think he was concerned about her having more power, but rather that he was a traditional man, and expected his wife to enact the domestic role played by generations of royal women before her. Under other circumstances, I might have supported her ambitions. Despite our mutual animosity, I admired her strength and intelligence and recognised that, given a free rein, she would have been an asset to Cos' government. Still, even if there was grudging respect between us, there was no chance of alliance or friendship.

Our party entered under the great arch of the palace and ahead of us, the sky was dominated by the monstrous temple of Challis Hespereth, queen of heaven and earth, mother of all the gods. The fane was constructed as a titanic likeness of its deity. Clouds of vividly-coloured birds circled the mass of stone, released from on high by rejoicing priests and priestesses. The army had veered off towards the barracks, so only the members of the royal household who had accompanied the King on campaign, and his generals and advisors, were left in the group. Once the soaring gates had closed behind us, we all dismounted and a crowd of stable-boys and servants ran up to attend to our mounts and our luggage. Porfarryah complained of thirst.

There would be a formal reception to welcome home the King, but first we would all repair to our chambers to refresh ourselves in private and bathe away the stains of travel and war.

Porfarryah and I walked into the palace together, past the knot of grieving ladies who had realised, by now, that their husbands were not among those who had returned home.

The palace is white, but its great halls at ground level are very dark inside. Dark and cool, their grey flagstone floors covered in red carpets. The love I felt for the palace was physical. I looked about me at the familiar, massive marble columns, grey in the gloom, the glint of old gold, where gigantic urns stood on plinths among the columns, the sweep of stairs with their thousands of shallow steps, swaying this way and that towards the galleries on the first floor. Muted white, dull gold and deepest crimson; these are the colours of the halls of Tarnax. The air smelled sweet and clean, as if fresh hay had been strewn everywhere. It was the odour of a special incense, blended in the monasteries in the hills behind the city.

I had chambers on the third floor, high above the city. It was where all the King's concubines and favourites lived. He had other boys, apart from me, but he used their services rarely, preferring to lend them out to visiting dignitaries and ambassadors from other lands. Subservient lords were forever sending their beautiful sons and daughters as gifts for the King. Some, he partook of only once, out of politeness and quite often, they eventually ended up in the household of some Duke or another. Alofel didn't like to think of any of his people being bored and the life of a concubine must necessarily be one of relaxation. Also, those whom the King ignored could only enjoy low status among their ranks, so it was for the best that some were moved on. Porfarryah and I were privileged, but we did not make the mistake of believing our positions were secure. At any time, another girl or boy could come to the palace and take Alofel's eye, if not his heart. Sometimes, when we thought it expedient, we had resorted to poison. Not murder, but something more subtle, that destroyed good looks and slurred the speech, made the body smell foul. Alofel only liked beautiful things.

'He will call for you tonight,' Porfarryah said and we walked slowly to the third floor.

'No, for you,' I said. It was a ritual between us, for in truth, we could never guess. The only certainty was that it would be one or the other of us, at least for an hour. Then the Queen might have him, if she was lucky. After that, a lesser concubine, when he was tired, or a boy with whose own pleasure Alofel was not concerned.

As we mounted the final steps to the third floor, a host of downy girls in floating gowns of pale colours came running down the corridor. They virtually dragged us onto the landing, covering us with kisses, wrapping us in their soft, perfumed arms. 'Tell us stories! Did you see the battles? Were you ever in danger?' Later, we would have to gratify their curiosity, but for now, we pleaded tiredness and were able to escape to our own chambers.

I bathed and dressed myself with care, attended by my servant, Wezling. Just as he was finishing arranging my hair, a messenger came to the chamber door. 'The King has asked for your attendance,' I was told. This was unusual. It was not the hour when my art was required.

I presented myself at the royal apartment and was ushered into the King's presence. He received me in his sitting-room, a place where we had often dallied in erotic play. It was a comfortable room, swathed in draperies, cool in summertime, warm in winter. The King wore only his dressing-robe and was standing up. I sensed that something was bothering him and prostrated myself with extra diligence.

'Rise, Darien,' he told me. 'There is something you must do for me.'

I gestured widely with my arms to indicate I would do all within my humble power to accommodate his desires.

'Akaten,' he said. 'This night, he will attend my bedchamber, but it would please me if you would sit with him after the servants have made him ready. His state of mind is skittish. Sit with him until the banquet is over. You should miss only half an hour or so of merriment.'

At first, I was at a loss for the name Akaten meant nothing to me. Of course, I nodded vigorously and declared that it would be my pleasure to do this thing. Inside, I was perturbed that this unknown person had taken the place of Porfarryah or myself. It was a departure from routine and I was immediately suspicious of it. Had some lord sent the thing we feared at last; a beauty to command the eyes of the King?

'My squire will come for you at the appointed time,' Alofel said. 'I would be grateful if you could attempt to assuage Akaten's fears. You are a gentle boy, Darien. I'm sure he will trust you.'

Trust me? I fought down a surge of anger. 'Is he familiar with palace procedure, my lord?' I enquired delicately. 'That is, how long has he been resident here?'

Alofel looked at me blankly for a moment, then enlightenment dawned. 'It is the Khan's boy,' he said.

I felt a wing of doom brush the palace roof.

I confided my fears to Porfarryah as soon as possible, even going to her chamber before the reception began. She listened with complete attention, the pupils of her dark eyes wide with a potential for attack. 'Be observant,' she advised. 'Talk to him, befriend him. We must take care. This Akaten is a king's boy too. He will match you in art. Alofel was touched by his loyalty to his dead lord. It took them some minutes to disengage him from the corpse. I heard only an hour ago, that he attempted suicide on the journey back from Mewt. Alofel himself stopped the blood, and sat by the boy's bedside for half the night. It is unsettling that the king's body-servants felt the need to keep quiet about this.'

I shook my head, aghast. 'I am troubled. I don't deny it.' Never before had such information been kept from me. Usually, Alofel's servants fell over themselves in their haste to pass me morsels of gossip.

Porfarryah brushed my fears aside with a careless gesture of her hand. 'A minor inconvenience, I'm sure. Let Alofel have his fun attempting to woo a boy who looks upon him as a murderer. It will not last. Chances are he'll throw himself from the palace roof at the first opportunity!'

Torches burned low on the walls as I followed the King's squire to the royal chambers. I was not sad to leave the banquet, for my evening had been poisoned by the thought of this thorn that had come to embed itself in Alofel's flesh. I was not stupid in my jealousy, for I knew the boy, Akaten, had not designed the circumstance. I suspected he would be indifferent to it, but his indifference was irrelevant. He existed, he was a potential threat. I would be a friend to him, for now.

The squire left me in the antechamber to the king's bedroom. Here, I examined myself in a mirror on the wall to check I looked my best. Then I opened the final door as quietly as possible, so as to give myself a few moments' private scrutiny of the rival before he was made aware of my presence.

The windows were open to the night, admitting the perfumes of the summer city, and the lilting chime of music from the banqueting-hall. Climbing vines had crept into the room, festooned with fleshy, blue flowers that smelled of spring rain: mingvolvus; the creeping lover of the god,

Tantanphuel. Akaten was there beside the window, his knees pressed against the sill. The King's chamber was on an upper floor of the palace; it was eight stories to the gardens below. If a body should fall from that window, its flight would be impeded by the stone arms of caryatids and gargoyles, or else impaled. I could see him thinking of his own death, and he was achingly lovely as he did so: the archetype of all the boys ever loved by kings. His hair, unbound, flowed down him like a veil; the colour of dark honey. His eye, in profile, was slightly slanted, its cat-like shape accentuated by a kiss of kohl. They had dressed him in a simple tabard and leggings. His ribs were bare at the sides, showing a tawny swatch of flesh, a braid of rib and muscle. He was effeminate in his beauty, but also intensely masculine. There was little softness of line about him. I watched him, transfixed.

He mounted the sill.

I could let him fall and none would be the wiser. In a moment, I could go into the outer chambers, seek the squire and complain there was no one within the bedroom. Then a search would be made, inside and out, and a shattered body would be found among the roses.

He shook upon the broad slab of marble, crouching down. He did not want to kill himself, and yet he did. How would I feel in his position? If a king other than Alofel took me to his bed? I realised I would not care. If it meant I would survive, I would kiss anyone, open my body for any man.

One moment, I was standing by the door, the next I found myself by the window, Akaten's upper arms in my grip. I pulled him back. He uttered a dull, dismal sound; relief and regret.

'Don't be foolish!' I said and turned him round. We were much of a height, and perhaps around the same age, nineteen years. He would not look at me.

I half led, half dragged him to the canopied bed, and made him sit down on it. He had begun to weep, silently, his body shuddering to his chest-deep sobs, tears running freely down his still face. He wept as a woman might, or a prideless barbarian. I'd heard stories of how Harakhte had wept publicly before his army when certain of his favourites had been killed on the battlefield. Alofel would never shed tears in the company of others.

Feeling impatient and strangely vexed, I poured the boy some wine from the flagon that stood waiting for the king's hand beside the bed.

'Drink this.' I was surprised that he took it. He drank it down in one long gulp, then wiped his face and handed the goblet back to me. Still, he would not meet my eye.

'Are you afraid?' I asked him. Perhaps he could not speak our language.

He looked at me then. 'Afraid? No. Not of what you think.' He spoke Cossic fluently, beautifully accented with a hint of Mewtish. In his eyes, I did not see weakness but a quiet, if saddened, strength.

'You were Harakhte's slave, now you are Alofel's. What's the difference? Act temperately and your life will continue much as before.' I don't know why I proffered this advice, for I wanted him to be miserable enough to brave the fall to the garden.

He looked at me steadily. 'The man I loved is dead,' he said, and then added with scorn, 'Do you really believe I wish to give myself to the one who slaughtered him?'

I felt only disdain. People such as Akaten and I could never be the lovers of kings. We were baubles, ornaments, to be discarded at will. Where did love come into it? Of course, I adored Alofel as my sovereign, but I did not rely on his love in return. That would only be asking for heartache. I handed Akaten a cloth. 'Wipe your face. The king will be here shortly.'

He looked at the cloth as if he'd never seen one before, then applied it with dignity to his eyes.

'It can be of short duration,' I said, 'if you know how to arouse him. If he thinks you require pleasuring, he will take his time. To avoid this, after the first kiss, raise and offer yourself to him. He will understand. He is not a cruel man.'

Akaten looked at me, as if stunned. 'Why tell me this?' he asked. 'Who are you?'

'A member of the household,' I answered. 'The king has a large retinue of concubines and boys. We are a community of sorts. We look out for one another.'

'I was Harakhte's only lover,' he told me. 'besides his queen.'

I shrugged. 'Customs vary.' In truth, I scorned his sentiments.

He wound the cloth around his fingers. 'I remember you,' he said. 'Your hair was very black in the sunlight, your skin very white. You looked strange to me, like a ghost. When they tortured me, you were there.'

'When they tortured you?' I was confused for a moment, then laughed. 'If you mean when they put the thorns in your flesh, that was meant to soothe you. The herbalist did it.'

'A strange way to soothe,' he said. 'You enjoyed watching it.'

'I did not!' My voice rang out too loudly.

He smiled and shrugged, pushed his hair off his face. 'I don't care. It

doesn't matter. Not now. Back there, at Alofel's camp, I thought you were
the Dark Messenger come to lead me from life. Now here you are again.'

There was a fatalistic tone to his voice. Death was not far from his
mind. I realised, or convinced myself, that Alofel might hold me responsible should anything happen to this creature before he took his pleasure. I
sat down beside him on the bed. 'Come now,' I said in a gentle voice,
'surely your Khan would not want you to suffer. Be strong for him, for his
memory. Endure this night, then carry on living. I should imagine that is
what he would have wanted.'

Akaten regarded me coolly. 'You have no idea what Harakhte would
have wanted. Don't patronise me.'

I shrugged uneasily. 'I'm not. I just think your situation isn't as bad as
you think.'

He narrowed his eyes. 'What is this to you? I don't think you care
about anyone but yourself.'

His unsettlingly astute remarks made my heart beat faster. 'You are
simply a stranger to our ways,' I said airily. 'What you perceive as indifference is no more than courtly behaviour. We adhere to strict protocols.'

He smiled. 'You are lying. Still, at least you spared the time to try
and comfort me. You did not have to come. I understand it does not rest
easy with you.'

His attitude was beginning to irritate me. This barbarian could know
nothing of the way I felt or conducted myself. Neither did he realise that
I had no choice in the matter of being there with him. I gritted my teeth
and grinned at him. 'It is the least I can do.'

'What is your name?' he asked me.

'Darien.'

He nodded. 'I have heard of you! Alofel's famous, beautiful catamite.'

My teeth were pressed together so hard I thought my jaw would break.
'I am a member of Alofel's household,' I managed to respond. 'Second only
to the queen.' This, of course, was not entirely true.

'You are like me,' he answered. 'Only you have never cared for the one
who owns you.' He frowned and looked around the great bedroom. 'What
place will I have in this royal house?'

I too had been wondering about that. The best I could hope for was
that he'd end up in the harem of one of Alofel's friends. I wriggled my
shoulders. 'You will be looked after. No one of your beauty would ever be
abused in Tarnax.'

'How comforting,' he said. 'Perhaps I will choose the windowsill after
all.' I knew then that he had decided to live.

I would have given much to have lingered in the king's chambers that night; concealed behind a curtain, lurking beneath the bed. I wanted to see the outcome of his taking of Akaten. I did not feel jealous, surprisingly, but weirdly aroused by the thought of Alofel's long, sensitive hands removing Akaten's garments, smoothing his tawny skin. As I prepared myself for bed, I thought about how I might turn all the conflicting thoughts and feelings I had for the Khan's boy into an amusing anecdote for Porfarryah. Occasionally, in private, we swapped lewd stories. I could almost hear her delighted shrieks of laughter as I described what I imagined Alofel might do to Akaten.

That night I dreamed of him as I'd first seen him, struggling in the hold of his captors. Only he was not bloody and dirty, but dressed in clean, white linen and crowned with purple flowers. I knelt in the dust before him, at the feet of the king. Alofel was talking about how Akaten would be brought to his bedchamber that evening, but that I would have to take his place. 'You must use my sword,' Alofel said, and I knew then that I had to execute the Khan's boy.

'But I want his head now,' I said, speaking far more firmly than I would dare in waking life. 'Give it to me, my lord, upon a bed of lilies.'

'He wants *your* head!' Alofel said, smiling. 'And he will have it.'

I felt disorientated, aware I had no control over the situation. I could not remember what I should say next. And then the executioner came striding through the flapping tents, clad in scarlet silk. Akaten was pushed to his knees, his hair hanging forward to pool on the ground before him. I saw his pale neck, and the knobs of spine and gristle. Would it be my head that fell in the dust when the fatal stroke was delivered?

I awoke before the sword fell, my groin pounding with desire and the echo of Akaten's screams ringing like temple bells in my ears.

Discomforted, I went out in the dawn, to walk in the palace garden. My thoughts were tortured by memories of my dream, and the events of the night before. Had Alofel dismissed Akaten immediately his pleasure was taken, or did the foreign boy slumber still in the chamber of the king, his honey hair fanned by the swaying canopies? I thought of him lying there, on his back, his torso naked above the coverlet which hid the most delicious secrets. I imagined his tawny skin, the scent of him in sleep. This vivid image disturbed me. I knew desire when it assailed me, but generally my interests always veered towards men of power and status. Never a servant like myself, and certainly not a slave. As I walked through the mists of the garden, surrounded by the ghost-calls of drowsy peacocks,

I fantasised making a request of Alofel; not for Akaten's head, but for his immeasurable self. Would the king grant me that favour? I could say that Wezling was incompetent, and that I needed a further attendant. My servant's ineptitude was already a joke about the palace. But perhaps Alofel was already ensnared by the interloper's charms and would jealously keep Akaten to himself.

Even as I thought these things, my face burned with shame. I dreaded Porfarryah discovering my feelings. It was senseless. All based on a short time in his company and a lurid dream. Was I mad?

There is a saying: in dreams the heart speaks truly.

The temple loomed out of the morning mist ahead of me, the fane of Challis Hespereth. Her earthly abode was called Phasmagore, and it was a wonder of the world. Its construction had begun during the reign of mad King Missiker, four hundred years ago—only a mad-man could have conceived it—and had been completed when Missiker's grand-son, Tastuel, had held the throne. Phasmagore was monstrous, a towering mass of stone that shadowed the land around it. It was a statue of Challis Hespereth of cyclopean size. Her hollow, seated body concealed a labyrinth of chambers, tunnels and royal tombs, while her high crown housed observatories and the school of astronomy. Some days, the goddess' face seemed to sneer down from the clouds, while at other times, her countenance was benign and tranquil. Today, it was invisible, just a dark blue shadow in the sky.

I felt confused and anxious, as my feet led me towards her. It was some time since I'd visited the temple. Now, I needed to make penance, to speak with the goddess in the manner she demanded of her sons. All the way, Akaten's face swam before my inner eye. I felt sickened and excited, as if my steps led to the arms of a cherished lover. I knew they did not. My feelings were inexplicable and wayward, and the strange, disorientating flavour of my dream lingered in my mind. I sensed that only doom lay in the future of my yearning. In the dark halls of Challis Hespereth's holy house I could purge the sentiments that gripped my mind. I would offer myself unto her, cleanse myself of the hunger that had come to hang like a hag upon my heart. Never in my life had desire attacked me so quickly and so thoroughly. I thought it was unclean, a disease of the soul.

Soon, the temple filled the sky before me. I reached the giant toes and began to climb the perilous steps that were carved into the folds of her robe. The ascent was long, and I paused at several of the terraces, cut into the goddess' calves, where temple acolytes sold refreshment. By the time I marched over the hills of the divine knees, the sun was high in the sky, and my spirits had lifted a little. I walked along the plateau of her thighs, towards the mountain of her body. Many other worshippers travelled beside me, and some came hollow-eyed towards us; those who had spent a night in the fane, drunk on narcotic juices, dreaming for the goddess, and making the sacred offerings.

I would have been missed at the palace by now. Porfarryah would be looking for me, eager for news of the previous night's events. I did not care. I dreaded facing Porfarryah's knowing glance, feeling as if my guilty thoughts were emblazoned across my face.

At midday, I began the descent down the wide stair-case that led to the temple portal, which was situated at the statue's groin. This last stage of the journey was short in comparison to the rest, and soon I entered through the wide-flung doors into the soft, perfumed gloom of Phasmagore. Here, ghost-footed priestesses, drifted by in robes of soft, russet muslin, swinging censers on the air, which unfurled ribbons of silvery-green smoke. White-skinned priests, clad in indigo robes that left one half of their chests bare, stood on guard before all the doorways, their eyes rimmed in black and the dark, serpentine tattoos of their calling crawling across their arms.

At the doorway to the Shrine of Bestowing, I paused to burn a pinch of incense at a huge brass font that was filled with smouldering coals. Many travellers from far lands came to visit Phasmagore, but only the natives of Tarnax would ever pass beyond this threshold. It was a shrine accessible only to young men and boys. Women had their own secrets chambers elsewhere within the complex. At fourteen, I had been initiated into the secrets hidden within the shrine, and knew that I would not be able to sample them for ever. Only the young and beautiful passed into the Shrine of Bestowing to offer the goddess the most precious gifts. It had been some time since I'd visited this place, and I approached it now as I had the last time; with excitement and fear. Two silent priests stood before the entrance, as still as if they were carved from milky marble. They did not challenge my approach.

The shrine's portal was hung with a tunnel of grey, swaying voile, which seemed to lift of its own volition as I stepped into it. Presently, I was surrounded by the whispering fabric, guided forward only by the gaps that appeared in the rearing veils. I was never sure whether I would find pleasure or pain beyond the grey, whether I would give or receive benediction. Eventually, the veils disgorged me with a final flutter into a small, dimly-lit chamber that was thick with the smoke of benzoin resin. A voluptuous priestess sat cross-legged on a stone bench by the wall, fanning herself with a palm frond, not to keep cool, I thought, so much as to enable her to breathe. She appeared slightly bored, clad in diaphanous trousers of voluminous black muslin, her round belly encrusted with jewels. The nipples of her heavy breasts were pierced by rings of gold and she wore a golden bone through her nose.

I knelt before her, and touched my forehead to the cool flag-stones beneath her seat. 'Sister, I come to make an offering.'

The priestess tapped me with her palm frond. 'Rise, supplicant.'

I looked up at her and got to my feet. She took a sugared pastille from a dish on her left side and held it out to me. Bowing my head, I accepted it and placed it upon my tongue. The priestess nodded once, and pointed with her palm to a stone seat on the opposite side of room. Then she produced an hourglass from among the folds of her trousers, turned it over and set it upon the floor. I went to the slab and sat down. In silence, we watched the sands glitter through the waist of glass, and the pastille dissolved inside my mouth, the sugary taste subsiding to bitterness. The priestess sighed occasionally, and continued to fan herself with the frond. I felt the room grow larger around me, and heard the deep echoes reverberating throughout the vast temple complex. I heard cries and moans, ululations of delight and the softest whimpers of terror. The incense smoke began to take on forms before my eyes; twisting phantoms with yawning faces, spectral fingers raised to their silent mouths. My heart was beating fast, and I shifted on the stone. I could hear the hiss of the sand in the hourglass now.

As the last grains sifted through, the priestess gestured for me to rise. I was unsteady on my feet, unsure whether to laugh or scream and run from the chamber.

'Give yourself in entirety,' murmured the priestess.

I bowed uncertainly, nearly slumping to the floor and the doors to the inner chamber swung open with a sound of grinding metal. It was too late to turn back.

Beyond the portal, all was in near darkness. I stumbled inside and the doors ground shut behind me. For a while, I sat on the floor, trying to clear my head, but the secrets of the pastille had occluded my senses. We took the drug to rid ourselves of earthly inhibition, to enable ourselves to make the sacred offerings without restraint. I could hear the low, urgent throb of drums in a chamber nearby and the wail of dancers as they made their spiralling devotions. Perhaps it was a troupe of lithe warriors, spinning round, pleasuring themselves for Challis Hespereth with quick fingers, so that their seed would fall upon her revered altars. My sex grew hot and thick at the thought of this image.

There seemed to be no one with me in the room. In that case, I would have to wait. Sometimes, if many had come to make an offering, the act of worship would take place here. But no feet approached me through the smoke. After a while, I got up and wandered further into the darkness, feeling with my hands for the yielding touch of flesh. Instead, my fingers encountered stone, and the incense smoke parted with my breath to reveal the wicked smile of Challis Hespereth in her wildest aspect. Here was no patrician goddess clad in acres of robes. She sat naked upon a plinth, gesturing for her worshippers to come to her, to learn the arcana of her hidden knowledge. She was fashioned of gleaming, dark green stone, her breasts nibbed with gold leaf. Her hair was a Medusan coil between them. I pressed my lips to her outstretched fingers, which were tipped with scarlet lacquer. In my befuddled state, it seemed she blinked and nodded in approval, gestured for me to pass on to the deepest chambers.

I entered a narrow passageway, and here the light was orange, the ceiling low. The sounds of the drums had faded. I ducked into the first of many oval doorways, and found the chamber beyond it empty. To advertise my presence, I unfastened the brocaded curtain that was hooked to the wall inside the door. An oil lamp flickered on the floor, and I went to sit beside it, upon a heap of cushions that smelled of musk and sweat and sweet resin. A statue of Challis Hespereth, with gleaming rubies for eyes, reclined upon a pedestal nearby. There was quiet hunger in her carved expression. I sat beside her with a straight back, the soles of my feet pressed together, my hands gripping my ankles. I was conscious of the idol's patient stare, then my spine and the heavy pressure of my hair upon my back through the fabric of my silk shirt. Who would the goddess bring to me?

There were footsteps in the corridor beyond the curtain, furtive and cautious. Just the sound of them struck desire in my loins, and I felt my blood raise the spear of manhood towards my belly. I heard the scape of a soft shoe and then the curtain was lifted by a single hand. I saw the long slim arm and the dark shape of the body, a tumble of loose hair that fell around him like a frayed cloak. He brought a breeze with him that worried the flame of the lamp, and sent shadows of laughter across the face of the goddess. If I looked hard at her now, would her stone body sit up to pay attention? He let the curtain fall and stood before me in the room, golden in the light of the lamp. I felt my blood chill in my veins, freezing my engorged prick to ice. What illusion was this? He looked too much like Akaten, dressed in the tunic and leggings I had last seen him in, his hair unbound over his chest. I knew the effects of the pastille, and how it could warp the senses, but this flagrant manifestation of my desires was too much to bear. I must have made a sound, scrambled to my feet, but then his hand was upon my arm, and it seemed the lamplight illumined only his eyes, which were golden brown.

'Peace,' he said, and the single word contained all the stillness of the world.

Despite what my eyes told me, this could not be Akaten. He was too calm and confident, and in his demeanour seemed so much older. Also, no hysterical foreigner with tear-stained cheeks would ever pass into this shrine.

'Forgive me,' I said. 'You seemed familiar.' I should not have spoken, for the words of the mundane world did not belong in this place. Also, it was impertinent to refer to the fact we might have met beyond the temple. What happened here was secret and must be forgotten once a worshipper left the shrine.

He put a single, straight finger to his lips and smiled. I closed my eyes and leaned into his embrace. I felt as if this stranger knew me intimately. He was no earthly creature, but a son of Challis Hespereth herself, old with the wisdom of gods. He pushed me gently back onto the cushions and as I fell, I heard the sibilant slide of panels being opened in the walls, where priestesses would observe our devotions. He did not want to hurt me, nor me him. It was pleasure alone we sought, and we ventured along its many avenues. My body became nothing more than a delirious nerve of erotic energy. We were one creature, vibrating with the force of creation. Beyond the walls, the priestesses chanted in time to our rhythm, until the room was filled with a spinning cone of sexual power. Our congress was violent, but I was beyond feeling pain. I wanted to leave my seed inside him, his mouth or his body, but I orgasmed as he speared me, a jet of liquid pearl streaming from my body across the floor. Then he withdrew and pulled my head to his groin. I could smell myself upon him. He was slimed with mucus, unguent and traces of blood. Challis Hespereth demanded great sacrifice, but I am naturally fastidious and felt this was giving too much. In vain, I tried to free myself. He was too strong, his fingers were entangled in my damp hair, and he forced himself between my lips. I was almost swooning, half sickened, half eager, and sucked the salt bitterness of our mingled essences, until he filled my mouth with his seed. It seemed to last an eternity and I was afraid I would choke. But then he took my face in his hands, and freed himself. Kneeling before him, I pressed my head against his stomach, gulping for breath, inhaling the strong, musky scent of his flesh and our communion. I felt I had passed beyond some threshold of understanding and experience. We had taken the right path and he had wholly intuited the way to it.

I had my hands curled around his buttocks, my fingers digging deeply into his muscles. His whole body was shaking. I heard him mutter beneath his breath and he pushed me away, but not with cruelty. I sensed he regretted that final act of our devotion, and felt he'd abused me. Shame for his abandoned behaviour had come upon him. It happened often, and was part of the penance. He stumbled blindly towards the doorway, gathering up his discarded garments. I wanted to call him back, speak to him, even though it was forbidden. In my eyes, he was still Akaten. I needed to tell him he had not offended me or hurt me, but even though I dared to whisper, 'Don't leave!' he did not pause. When the curtain fell, I knelt upon the floor of the shrine, my clothes spread about me, my hands plunged between my knees. My vision was blurred by gritty light. My whole body throbbed in memory of his heartbeat.

This visit to the shrine had not purged me at all, but quite the opposite. I had lived my desire and it had, in my heart, turned to aching, unquenchable need.

How I managed to maintain a cool mien when I returned to the palace I cannot explain. The walk from the gardens and through the lower floors was a nightmare. People stopped me to chat idly, and their voices were claws across my mind. It seemed to take an age to reach my quarters.

As I had anticipated, Porfarryah had been worried by my absence, then suffused with curiosity when I returned. She sought me out in my chamber. 'Are you ill, Darien? You look feverish? Shall I order a sherbet for you?'

I felt so nauseous and peculiar, I just wanted her, my dearest friend, to leave me alone. When she clucked around me in concern, tears welled in my eyes.

'What has happened, Darien? What's wrong? Where have you been all day?'

I clung to her and wept, not just for release, but to stem her questions.

She stroked my hair for a while, then said softly, 'Are you worried about the Khan's boy?'

My heart seemed to convulse in my breast. Was the cause of my suffering so evident? I made a muffled sound against her hair.

'There's nothing to worry about,' she said. 'Alofel has had his pleasure. Now he will lose interest.'

My panic subsided. I pulled away a little. 'Have you seen him, the Khan's boy?'

She looked down at me tenderly, stroked my face. 'No, but one of the king's servants spoke to me briefly. The foreigner did not sleep with the king, and near dawn asked to be escorted to the temple to worship. He has yet to return.'

'What?'

Porfarryah's eyes widened at the wildness in my voice. 'It's not that unusual. The Mewts worship Ma-ten-waya, Lady of the Rivers, and she is an aspect of Challis Hespereth.'

'No, no!' I cried. 'It can't be! It's impossible!'

Porfarryah looked frightened by my hysterical outburst. 'What is it, Darien? What's impossible?'

'I went to the temple as well,' I blurted. 'To the inner chambers...' I wanted to confess to her so badly, if only so that she could assuage my fears. But I knew I could not divulge the religious secrets of men to a woman. I would have to bear the consequences of her revelation alone. It couldn't have been Akaten in the shrine. I was filled with a weird mixture of gratitude and revulsion.

Porfarryah shook her head in confusion. 'So, what happened there?'

'I thought I saw Akaten,' I gabbled. 'I thought Alofel had... already bestowed privileges. If the foreigner has been allowed into the inner shrines, it might mean that Alofel intends to grant him status within the household.'

Porfarryah smiled. 'Don't be ridiculous! You're imagining things, Darien. This boy is not a threat to you. He would only be allowed access to the outer chambers. You should know that. If you thought you saw someone that looked like him, it was because the idea of him ousting you was playing on your mind.'

'Yes, you're right,' I said. 'I'm sorry.'

Porfarryah shook her head. 'I've never seen you like this. Regain control, Darien. It's not like you to be afraid or weak.'

Afraid and weak. That was exactly how I felt, and it was an alien experience for me.

Alofel did not call for my presence, and that night, I writhed sleeplessly on my damp, hot bed, with the taste of the shrine visitor in my mouth, the scent of him on my skin. I wanted to believe he had been a complete stranger, yet at the same time I yearned for him to have been Akaten. I wanted the Khan's boy to appear in my chamber, tell me he had been thinking about me. I wanted to demand his head on a bed of lilies. Hate and love: were they the same thing? Had anyone else ever felt this way?

The following morning I came across one of the king's body-servants, Lazuel, as he carried Alofel's dirty linen to the laundry. Naturally, I stopped him to ask for information, offering my own snippet beforehand to enhance his mood for gossip.

'I hear the Khan's boy visited the temple yesterday. That request must be a first for a captive of war!'

Lazuel rolled his eyes. 'I know about that. There are many firsts occurring in the chambers of the king!'

Dread seized me, but I managed to smile. 'Such as? I understand Alofel did not keep the boy with him the entire night.'

Lazuel put down his basket and folded his arms. 'Well, the lovely Akaten did not *sleep* with the king the other night, but this was because they stayed up together until dawn! I took the precaution of concealing myself in one of the dressing-rooms, just in case Alofel needed me, but spent a sleepless night. I overheard much of interest.'

'Indeed! Tell me about it.'

'I will, for I think you should know. First of all, for several hours, they took a light meal together and talked. I managed to overhear Alofel asking many questions about the Khan. It's clear that Harakhte fascinates Alofel. He was especially insistent upon knowing about Harakhte's relationship with his people. Akaten said that many would kill themselves when they learned of the Khan's death. Ordinary people in the street! It's quite unbelievable. I think the boy must have been exaggerating, but Alofel didn't seem to think so. The foreigner spoke so freely about Harakhte's marvellous attributes, I thought the king would call for his guards and a sword to silence the insolent tongue! But no. He seemed oblivious to the snide criticisms. Perhaps he did not hear the words, but saw only the lips.'

'What has happened to the famous grief then?' I asked sourly. 'The boy conversed well for a person who only days ago was slashing at his wrists.'

Lazuel pulled a wry face. 'Quite so. At the beginning of the conversation, the Mewt's voice was dull and sad, but after an hour or so our little foreigner appeared to relax in the king's company. He brightened up considerably, and even told a few comic tales about certain Mewtish dignitaries. The strangest thing is, I heard Alofel laughing. Have you ever heard that?'

I shrugged uncomfortably. In truth, Alofel was not a person disposed to displays of hilarity, confining proof of his amusement to gentle smiles.

'Yes, he laughed,' Lazuel said, nodding. 'I have never heard him so informal. Then, the worst thing happened.'

'What?'

Lazuel looked to left and right, then leaned closer towards me. 'The king never took his pleasure! After the boy's clever tales, Alofel must have decided it was time to sample the goods. Before a single finger met flesh, Akaten began to weep and lament, having no doubt drunk too much wine and coughed up too many memories. It was incredible. He thanked Alofel for his courtesy—the impudence of it!—and then begged to be killed. He does not want to live now the Khan is dead, and cannot bear the thought of another man touching him. As you can imagine, Alofel was perturbed by this behaviour. Here comes the order for the guards now, I thought, but again, no. At this point, I felt I had no choice but to peer through the curtains. Alofel took the boy in his arms and told him not to be afraid— the only time he would take him to the royal bed was if Akaten himself desired it. Can you imagine that?'

I couldn't. 'What else happened?' My mouth was so dry I could barely speak. I wanted to ask whether my name was mentioned, but feared Lazuel making his own deductions.

'Nothing much. Alofel spoke about life, honour and duty, and how we must all learn to live with grief. Akaten asked for permission to visit the temple, in order to perform the rites of mourning, and it was granted. He returned in the evening, and last night slept alone in the room that Alofel has provided for him. There is a rumour that rich clothes and jewellery were sent to this room.'

I could no longer hide my shock and dismay. 'What you have told me is incredible. I don't know what to say.'

'Darien, it is all too bizarre. I have never heard anyone, even of high rank, behave so informally with the king. Displays of emotion, weeping and laughing: the antics of an unmannered brute! But the strange thing is, Alofel seemed to like it.'

I shrugged uncomfortably. 'Perhaps he was amused by the novelty of the situation.'

Lazuel nodded. 'This is possible, although I'd be a liar if I said I agreed with you.' He looked at me with sympathy. 'I fear there will be disruption. What will you do?'

I shook my head. 'I don't know... It seems there is little I can do.' In comparison to Akaten, who could make Alofel laugh and relax, I felt insubstantial and empty. The thought of resorting to poison against such an enemy was dangerous. Alofel might be more inclined to investigate should something happen to someone who had attracted his attention so much.

Lazuel touched my arm. 'You can be sure the king's staff support you. We don't want foreigners mucking up our routines.'

I spent the remainder of the day in a delirium of nervous anxiety, comforted by Porfarryah, who was equally alarmed by what had happened. In
the evening, when the king's squire came softly to request my presence in
the royal chambers, I was convinced it was so that Alofel could tell me he
was sending me away. Hastily, I brushed out my hair and applied pale
powder to my hectic cheeks. Still, my mirror told me I looked far from my
best.

The man who greeted me in Alofel's quarters was a stranger, someone
who looked like the king, but whose character was completely different.
He was animated, his movements sudden. His eyes were alight. 'Darien,'
he said. 'I need to talk to you.'

I could barely speak, and bowed stiffly. Alofel seemed oblivious of my
appearance.

'Sit down,' he said.

I perched on the edge of a brocaded chair and knotted my hands in my
lap to disguise the fact that they were shaking. Alofel stood staring down
at me, an expression of contemplation on his face. I did not want him to
look at me, sure he was making certain comparisons and finding me wanting.

'Darien, answer a question for me,' he said. 'I would like to know
whether you are happy.'

I looked up at him in surprise. 'I beg your pardon, my lord? Happy?
About what?'

'I want to know whether you are happy in your position here at court
as my favourite.'

I blushed. 'Yes, of course.' The question was absurd.

He shook his head. 'No, I don't think you quite understand me. What
I mean is, if you had the choice, would you be here at all? You were sent
here from your parents' estate and have been forced to give up all title to
your inheritance. You did not come here of your own free will.'

'My lord, I am honoured to serve you. Whatever else my life might
once have held is no longer relevant to me.' I was terrified, convinced
Akaten had said something to him about me. 'And if anyone claims otherwise, they lie!' Normally, such a forward remark would earn severe discipline, but Alofel ignored the tone of my outburst.

'I do not question your loyalty, Darien, but I have been thinking. I
never wooed you. I simply took you. You did not come to my bed in desire
but in subjection. Is it right for me to keep you here, perhaps against your
will, to use your body as I please?'

'You are the king!' I whispered, horrified. 'It is your right to do as you please.' Taking advantage of his strange mood, I asked a direct, if timidly-voiced, question. 'My lord, is it that you no longer want me here?'

He reached to touch my face. 'I will always want you here, Darien. Although I have never spoken of it, you have soothed me when I've been distressed a thousand times. I have never wanted any boy here regularly in my chambers but you...'

Until now, I appended silently. I looked into his eyes and formed this thought within them. Unable to hold my gaze, he turned away. I did not like what had happened to him. It seemed as if a peculiar disease had taken hold of his mind, and I hoped sincerely he'd not behaved this way with anyone but me. I could only speak frankly. 'It seems something has come to this court that is causing a strange disturbance. I know my traditional place, and there is no question of me resenting it. My lord, I am distressed that you do not seem to be yourself. Is there anything I can do to help?'

He turned and looked at me again, his eyes once more filled with a weird inner light. 'I feel as if the last fifteen years have fallen from my body, as if a mask of iron has fallen from my eyes. This should not distress you, Darien. Please don't worry about it.' His gaze became distant. 'Today, I smelled the lost perfumes of childhood summers in the air. In the garden, it was as if all the flowers and the trees had become more colourful and vibrant. Sounds assailed my ears from every side like music; the call of birds, the mutter of servants, the hiss of wind in the leaves...'

Oh, Sweet Challis, I thought. He is in love.

Alofel adopted a posture of deep thought, his right hand cupping his jaw. After a while, he said, 'I can guess what you are thinking. That Akaten is responsible for the way I feel. And you are right!'

I swallowed nervously, waiting for the axe to fall.

Alofel began pacing up and down. 'I don't want you to feel concerned for your position. It is important to me that you befriend, Akaten.'

'What?' I couldn't help the exclamation. Alofel had truly lost his senses. Where was the calm, contained man of only a couple of days before? How could one person affect him so much? It was outrageous.

'I am still concerned for his state of mind, and have discussed it with my physicians. We think it expedient that Akaten is kept euphoric until such time as the sharpest edge of his grief has become blunt. There is a risk he might try to take his life.'

Good, I thought. 'My lord, what do you think I can do to help this situation? Such excesses of emotion are alien to me.'

The comment was unwise, and I noticed Alofel's wry glance when I'd uttered it. 'I can understand that Akaten's ways must seem uncouth to you, but if you spent some time in his company, I have no doubt you would warm to him. He spoke highly of the way you comforted him on his first night here.'

I knew for a fact that Alofel's court would not approve of these developments. He was charging blindly towards circumstances of embarrassment and humiliation. Bewitched by beauty! How could he be so weak? I felt that all I could do was comply with his wishes for the time being, in the hope of somehow ameliorating the situation. 'I will of course obey your command, my lord.'

'It is not a command, but a request,' Alofel answered, and when he looked at me, I sensed he was wondering whether, if ever anything should happen to him, I would want only to die as well. The answer of course was no, but I hoped he didn't realise that.

As I walked back to my rooms, I considered how confused the king must be feeling. He had enjoyed Akaten's romantic tales of Harakhte, and wanted me to be like a Mewtish boy, a lover who could not bear the thought of life without him. Legends spoke of how favourites took their life upon the battlefield, to die beside their fallen kings, but they were legends that came from other lands, not ours. Did Alofel believe that if I were Akaten's friend, his attitude towards his king would rub off on me? Or was it just that he trusted me to care for his new possession, and would keep it safe until he felt the time was right to take what he so sorely wanted?

The following day, reluctantly obeying Alofel's injunction, I went to visit Akaten in his rooms. My feelings too were utterly confused. I was filled with excitement at the prospect of seeing him, but also harboured feelings of outrage and envy.

I found him out on the terrace, playing with a puppy—perhaps another gift. He was sitting on the marble tiles, his long legs sprawled out, his hair plaited loosely down his back. He looked up when his attendant announced my arrival, and my heart stilled for a moment. I felt as if I'd known him for many years. We had held each other intimately. I wanted to go to him, take him in my arms, begin our conversation with a kiss. But at the same time, my mind told my heart not to be foolish. This foreign creature was not the one who had come to me in the Shrine of Bestowing. My addled brain had provided that image.

'Hello again,' he said. His voice was slightly slurred, and I could see that the pupils of his eyes were large. His senses, clearly, were not his own. 'You look more like the Servant of Death than before.'

I walked towards him, maintaining an outward semblance of dignity. 'King Alofel wants us to be friends.' He must have heard the coldness in my voice.

For a moment, he ignored me, dragging his hair across the marble to make the puppy frolic, laughing softly like a hiccuping lunatic. Then, he looked up again. 'So, here you are, an obedient slave.' He sounded drunk, and even threw out his arms. 'Would you care for refreshment? The people here bring me anything I ask for.'

I folded my arms and sighed through my nose. He was smiling at me. I did not like the thought that he might be aware of my discomfort and disapproval. Something snapped inside me. 'I don't like what you are doing, Khan's boy. You think you can cause trouble here in Cos. Is this your revenge for your master's death? You might be able to fool Alofel, but I can see through you. Don't believe that everyone here is bewitched by you. I will fight you, every inch of the way.'

'Fight me,' he echoed, and put his head on one side, then laughed and put up his fists before his face. 'Are you suggesting physical combat?'

I would not let him unnerve me. 'If necessary.'

He grinned, as if my threats meant nothing to him, then got unsteadily to his feet. He walked in a zig-zag to the balustrade with the puppy cavorting round his ankles, and there leaned down on the stone, staring out towards the misty bulk of Phasmagore.

I stood awkwardly for a few moments, then went to stand beside him. Gazing upon the temple made me feel hot and anxious, but I felt compelled to do so.

'We have wonders in Mewt too,' Akaten said, and now his voice had become more steady, 'but the temple of Challis here is perhaps more splendid.'

I managed to expel a choked laugh. 'Really! I thought you believed everything Cossic to be inferior to anything Mewtish.'

He glanced at me sideways. 'No, I mean it. The temple is wondrous. I went there yesterday, and it left me... breathless.'

I held his gaze for a moment, and felt the heat come to my face. Once again, I was unsure whether the stranger in the shrine had really been him or not. If it had been, this cool posturing now was senseless, but if not, I risked making a complete fool of myself.

'What's the matter?' he asked me. 'Your deathly face has become almost alive, or is that a blush?'

'I thought I saw you in the temple yesterday,' I said.

He shrugged, yawned and dragged his hands over his face. 'Perhaps you did, but it is a massive place, so it would have been a remarkable coincidence if we'd bumped into one another there.'

Despite the narcotics in his body, he was too composed to have been my ephemeral lover. If we'd truly shared that experience, there was no way he could be so dispassionate now, but I had to be convinced. 'Are you sure we did not meet at the temple?'

He shook his head. 'I can't remember. Everything's so... muddled. I wanted only the solace of the goddess and to make my farewells to my love.'

'Please try to remember.' I was aghast at myself for my persistence.

Akaten frowned. 'Why are you so concerned about it? Were you doing something there that you shouldn't?'

Was he laughing at me? I wished I could be certain about him, one way or the other. 'I never do anything I shouldn't,' I said lightly. 'I was mistaken about you. It's of no consequence.'

We went to sit upon cushions, and his attendants brought us wine and sweetmeats. I could not force food down my throat, but sipped the wine cautiously. All the time, he watched me, blinking. Was that amusement in his clouded eyes? 'You no longer seem grieved,' I said, hoping to puncture his good humour. I watched with satisfaction as his face dropped.

'I will always grieve,' he answered. 'It is beyond your comprehension.'

I almost pitied him. He looked utterly bewildered, his mind fogged by the philtres he'd been given. 'You are still young,' I remarked, biting into a sickly sweet. 'And the human spirit can be remarkably elastic.'

He shrugged, still frowning. 'Harakhte once said to me that life is a dynamic process and constantly throws new challenges into our path. I'm not sure what I'm supposed to do now.' He shook his head, then looked at me. 'Must I live? Is that what he would have wanted?'

'You'll live,' I said. 'It is our instinct to survive.'

'But *here*? In Cos?'

I sighed. 'You have no choice.'

He drank some wine. 'No.'

So began my care-taking of the Khan's boy. During the first weeks, the king did not see Akaten once, but often asked me of his progress. I kept my answers vague; enough to satisfy without giving too much information. Alofel seemed pleased with that. He trusted me.

I knew I would have to be careful and keep a check on both my jealousy and my wayward desire. I was still unsure of what Alofel was planning. The implications of Akaten's presence in the palace were at best unsettling. My feelings were torn.

Akaten was very ill, I could see that. At times, demented with grief, he would throw himself against my unyielding body to pour out his misery. Only the most inhuman creature could resist such pathetic, childish appeals for comfort. I put my arms about him as a brother, and felt nothing but pity for him.

Then there were the occasions when the herbal liquors in his blood made him almost coquettish. This was when I hated and desired him most. He would laugh uncontrollably at nothing, dance to unheard music and complain of unbearable itching in his lungs and head. To soothe him, I began to read aloud to him. At first, the sound of my voice appeared to irritate him, but then, as I kept my pitch low, he would relax and lie upon the cushions by my feet with eyes half open like a corpse.

One day, I read to Akaten a story of love. It was about an ill-favoured poet who desired a blind boy. The story was hackneyed and it was no surprise that the boy found the poet's words beautiful and did not care he had a warty face. However, as I read, I felt emotion rise within me. "As I recited my ode to him, his white eyes stared at the clouds. I knew he could not see me, would never see me. If I was silent, I might not exist..." It seemed too pertinent, and I stopped reading.

At my feet, Akaten opened his eyes. 'Don't stop. Your voice is soothing.'

I did not want him to look at me. 'It's a vapid tale.' I threw the book onto the floor. 'Tomorrow, I'll bring something better.'

Akaten looked at his hands, which were laced on his stomach. Gazing at him, I realised he seemed more composed, less confused than he had been. 'I liked the story,' he said.

'You can't mean that!' I forced a laugh. 'How are you feeling today?'

He tilted back his head on the cushions and looked at me. 'Things seem more real today. I think the palace torturers have decreased my dose of poison.'

'And how do you feel about that?'

He wrinkled his nose. 'I don't know. I don't really feel anything. It's odd.'

'Do you still want to die?'

He was silent for a moment, and my heart seemed to pause, waiting for the answer.

'Darien, I realise now that you spoke sense to me that first night, when you pulled me off the windowsill. I must thank you for it. If you hadn't come to me, I might well be dead now and, you are right, Harakhte would not have wanted that. He was never selfish or cruel.'

'I had no choice but to come,' I said coldly.

'I know that,' he replied. 'But you could have let me fall.' He squirmed round to lie on his belly, chin resting in his hands. 'I expect you sometimes wish you had.'

I looked back at him. His sensitivity unsettled me. 'I am the king's servant and he wishes you to be well again. My feelings are irrelevant.'

Akaten reached out and touched one of my feet. 'Darien, that is not true. I dare to think that once you hated me, but now you have come to like me a little. I have never wished you ill. I am here by an accident of fate.'

I wanted to reach out and touch his face, but resisted. A voice in my mind nagged that I must still be cautious. In his place, I would want to make a friend of the king's favourite, but only as a safety measure. 'Fate is capricious,' I said. 'We both know that.'

He shook his head. 'Darien, something has happened between us. Can't you feel it?'

I felt as if the sky had fractured. 'What?'

He looked at me. 'I can't explain...' He kneeled before me and took my arms in his hands. 'I want us to be friends. I need a friend. I am afraid. You are the only stable thing in my life now.'

My whole body had become rigid. I wanted to pull away from him, sure he was playing with me, but wanting to believe he spoke without guile. 'I will do whatever the king asks of me. Yes, we shall be friends.'

He closed his eyes and shook his head, as if in pain. 'No! Be my friend because you want to, not because your king has given an order.'

I looked at him, a hopelessly enchanting vision of masculine beauty. 'Why?'

'We have happened to one another,' he said, and with those words invoked all the confusion of the abyss into my staggering mind.

I had not thought of my lover of the temple for weeks, but now the unsettling images came back to me in chilling, glorious clarity.

The next few days are fragmented in my memory now. I spent so much time in Akaten's company, Porfarryah began to complain. She asked me if I was sleeping with him, and I answered that I was not, which was true. Akaten made no overture towards me in that sense, and there was no way I would make such a move myself. At night, I dreamed of him, and sometimes the dreams were mildly erotic, but by the end of the week, I had managed to convince myself once more that I had not met Akaten in the temple.

Twice in that week, I went to Alofel's quarters at night. On the second occasion, he quizzed me in more detail about my friendship with the Khan's boy. I confessed that we had now got to know one another, and that, yes, I had warmed to Akaten. This remark thoroughly aroused the king, who then subjected me to exquisite lovemaking. I could not complain about that, although it amused me to imagine that as we acted out our fantasies upon each other, we were both thinking of our Mewtish visitor.

One night, I lay upon my bed, drowsing in the hot, perfumed air. All my windows were thrown open, and the cries of owls filled my room. Akaten and I had been out riding that afternoon, even though the weather was really too warm for the horses' comfort. An armed guard had accompanied us, for Alofel still did not trust Akaten not to try and escape. I myself was unsure whether he'd take the opportunity if it arose. As we'd dismounted from our steaming mounts in the shadowed stable-yard, Akaten had stroked my hair. He had offered no explanation for the caress and had walked away from me before I could speak or respond. Afterwards, I considered that the gesture had been too pre-meditated. I suspected he knew all about my feelings for him and liked to pull my strings. He was never far from my thoughts.

As I lay there, idly stroking myself, a knock came at the door. Hastily, I covered myself with a sheet. The hour was late. Who would come knocking at this time of the night? I suppose I knew even then who it was. 'Come in,' I said, and Akaten opened the door. I was unable to speak, although the question, 'what are you doing here?' churned round my mind.

'Are you tired?' he asked me, venturing into the moonlight that streamed through my window.

'Why?'

He shrugged. 'I want to walk in the garden, and as you are my official friend, I thought I'd call for you on the way.'

'It is very late,' I said.

'And the night is beautiful. Come on. Don't be tiresome. Why lie here awake when the moon calls us?'

'Wait outside the door,' I said. 'I must dress.'

He raised one eyebrow, but complied with my words.

As we padded silently through the darkened halls of the palace, I wondered how Akaten had escaped his vigilant attendants. His position in the household was still tenuous. Technically, he was an enemy captive, who should not be allowed to wander around unsupervised.

We roamed across the lawns, beneath the spreading branches of the trees. Peacocks drowsed on the grass, their folded tails trailing in the early dew. Akaten went to one of the trees and leaned back against it, gazing up through the sighing branches. So far, we had spoken little.

'So, tell me, how did you escape?' I asked him.

He put his head on side to look at me. 'Easily. I climbed the vines on the terrace wall up to the roof.'

I could not help laughing. 'A precarious climb! You were lucky you weren't killed!'

He smiled. 'No, Darien, that wouldn't have happened. Tonight, there is magic in the air.'

My laugh turned into a sneer. 'Is there?'

He shook his head and looked at me. 'You are so unimaginative.'

'Hardly,' I answered dryly. If only he knew!

'You're never anything but formal. It diminishes your attractions.' He didn't wait for me to respond to that, but began to walk around the tree, touching it with one hand. 'It must be the way you've been trained, or brainwashed. It's such a waste. I like to imagine you with tangled hair and dirt on your face. Then you would be more real.'

Indignation hardened my heart. 'I am very real, Akaten. More so than you can imagine.'

'No, you are a dream.'

I thought he seemed intoxicated as if he'd been drinking or smoking hemp. The conversation itself had taken on a dream-like quality. He seemed fragile and fey. Perhaps they had increased his dose of herbals again. Impulsively, I reached out and grabbed hold of his arm, stopped him circuiting the tree. He leaned his side against me, his head hanging forward. 'What do you want of me?' I hissed. 'What is this game?'

'The game of life,' he answered. 'I thought you knew.'

'Look at me!' I said.

He did so, blinking. I wanted to hit him, to kiss him.

'Akaten, what are you doing?'

He ran his fingers down both sides of my face. 'I don't know. I just wanted to walk with you.'

This was what I wanted. It had to be, and yet, my insecurities flood my mind. I should have taken him in my arms then, but a cruel spirit took hold of me. I desired him, yet in my confusion wanted to hurt him. My words were unforgivable. 'Think of your dead Khan!' I shook his arm.

'Only a short while ago, you wanted to die for him. What's this all about now? How can you be so fickle?'

He pulled away from my hold, rubbing the flesh where I had touched him. 'Don't, Darien! Don't say that!' I saw his shoulders move. I heard him weep.

'What do you expect?'

He turned on me then, angrily palming away his tears. 'Expect? Understanding. Was I so mistaken about you? I expect comfort, warmth. I always believed that's what friends were for.'

His anger pierced my heart more than his grief could ever do. 'Are we really friends, Akaten? You see life as a simple process, but it is not.'

He sighed, all the rage drained out of him. He was not a creature disposed to anger. 'My life before seems unreal. I can hardly remember living it. Sometimes I think someone only told me about it. It's hard to recall how I felt.' He laughed uncertainly, clawed his fingers through his hair. 'It was the philtres they gave me. I think they did something to me, something permanent.' He laughed. 'Akaten is dead. Yes, that's it!'

I disliked the gleam in his eyes. It seemed dangerous, a return to the territory of self-destructive grief, despite his words of feeling nothing. 'Take hold of yourself,' I said. 'You sound mad.'

He was still laughing, and staggered away from me to lean his forehead against the tree. I saw his long fingers flexing against the bark. I went to him and put my hands on his shoulders. 'What am I doing here?' he murmured. 'What's happening to me?'

I turned him round. His eyes were black, full of pain. I could resist no longer, and wound my arms around him. 'Akaten, you have suffered, and it takes time to get over that. You mind was dulled, yes, but it was for your own safety.'

'I am destroyed by grief,' he said, ignoring my remarks, 'and that is why I'm so confused. If I loved Harakhte above all others, why do I want you?'

I couldn't answer, but pulled him closer, expelling a groan of need. He could be no more confused than I.

'Yes,' Akaten murmured, as if coming to a decision, and then we were kissing in the night-shadow of the branches. A voice whispered in my head, You've come home, *come home*...

After some minutes, Akaten broke away from me. 'Water,' he said. 'I need to be near water.'

I took his arm and led him towards the lakes. He staggered at my side, his fingers digging into my flesh. I took him to a place where thick evergreens shrouded the edge of the water, and here we sat down. Akaten took off his shoes and put his feet into the lake. White birds stood sleeping around us, like statues.

'Can we swim?' Akaten said.

I shuddered. 'No! This place is not for swimming. It's full of weeds and mud.'

Akaten sighed. 'I should have known you'd say that.' He got to his feet and began to undress himself.

'Don't,' I said. 'You'll regret it.'

'Perhaps.' He stood before me unashamedly naked. 'Come with me, Darien. Be daring.' Without waiting to see whether I'd comply or not, he stepped into the water and began to wade out to where it became deeper. I watched him splashing around, wondering how long it would take for the guards to hear him and come investigating. I was thinking about whether he'd come back to my rooms, whether we could make love.

Presently, he came back to the bank and lay shivering beside me, his skin striped with slimy weed. 'That was wonderful,' he said. 'You should have joined me.'

'Your teeth are chattering,' I replied. 'Perhaps we should go back now.'

He smiled, and stroked my thigh with his damp fingers. 'No, Darien, if you want me, you must have me here.'

I remember uttering an anguished cry, and throwing myself against him, taking his cold, wet body in my arms. His shuddered in my embrace with silent laughter, wound his legs around my own. 'Take me, Darien!' he said. 'With Alofel, you have to be a dutiful boy, but I want you to be a man for me.'

'And how would you behave with Alofel?' I couldn't resist asking.

'He waits for me to ask for his love,' Akaten replied. 'He will wait a long time.'

'Don't ever go to him,' I said harshly. 'If you do...' I couldn't finish. I meant that I did not want to have to look upon him as a rival, someone against whom I would eventually have to take action.

'Give me a reason not to,' Akaten said and pulled my face towards his own.

We are all so many people; a hundred burgeoning personalities confined within a single body. I am weak, I am strong. I am afraid, I am courageous. I am a vessel, I am the fluid that fills it. Akaten was languorous beneath me, and I was not the person who had swooned in the arms of the stranger in the shrine. I felt powerful, twice as tall, capable of anything, but entirely tender. My lovemaking was as gentle as the dew falling around us. When I slid into him, he opened for me like a flower. He was a lily on the water, and I rode him slowly, so slowly, to the shore.

From that moment, we became one. In the days that followed, we never spoke of love, although I was sure that was what I felt for Akaten. From a young age, I had been trained to suppress my feelings, and never to speak of them. Therefore, I had no way of knowing whether Akaten returned my feelings, or was simply comforted by our closeness. I was obsessed by him, wanted to *be* him, be absorbed by his flesh, sucked into his mind, so that we would be utterly inseparable.

We tried to keep our alliance private, but it is impossible to keep secrets in the palace, and soon it was common knowledge that we spent most of our nights together. I was unsure as to how Alofel would react to this news when it finally came to his ears, but he never mentioned it to me, and his attitude towards me remained unchanged, even though he must have known I left his bed at midnight to go to Akaten's chambers.

Alofel continued to shower Akaten with presents and now, because it was obvious that Akaten was no longer stricken, Alofel commanded his presence. Every day, in the late afternoon, my lover would go to the king's rooms and talk with him for over an hour. Several nights a week, they ate their evening meal together. I did not feel jealous exactly, but could not entirely eradicate the sense of unease that these visits conjured within me.

Porfarryah was scathing of my relationship with the foreigner, and I felt myself cooling towards her. Our friendship became brittle and fragile, although we were careful not to let it break entirely. We still needed to be allies at court.

The summer passed like a hazy dream. I can still recall the flavour of it; the endless days in the garden when Akaten would gaze at me smiling, his long eyes hooded with promise, and the hot nights when we lay together in the moonlight, our sweat fusing our bodies together, wrapped in the heavy perfume of night-blooming flowers and sexual musk. I should have known that nothing ever remains the same. As Harakhte had once said to Akaten, life is a dynamic process and change is inevitable.

The Mewts had accepted their Cossic conquerors only grudgingly, and Alofel's advisors had been busy constructing a new government in Mewt, and making promises to the people in order to keep them tractable. Near the end of the summer, when the gardens were baked dry and the lakes almost rancid, a delegation of Mewts came to Tarnax to engage in talks with the king. Among them was Menefer, the younger brother of the Khan, whom Alofel had installed as his puppet governor in Mewt and needed to keep sweet. Alofel had taken advantage of a family feud. He had learned that Menefer and Harakhte had had their problems. Perhaps recognising some ignoble trait within his brother, Harakhte had never given him status within the army or the government. Now, Menefer was being offered the throne of Mewt, but there was a cost.

Akaten was disturbed by Menefer's presence in the palace, and kept himself hidden. He told me that Alofel should not underestimate Menefer. Whatever grudges might have existed between him and Harakhte, his loyalties would still lie more with the dead than with the conquerors. 'Menefer has had to learn to survive,' Akaten told me.

I would not let the implication slip. 'Did Harakhte treat him badly?'

'They hated each other as much as they loved each other. The relationship was complex. You'd have had to witness it to understand.'

I guessed that he thought his dead lover's brother would consider him a traitor, because he had slipped into life at Tarnax so readily. I hoped the visit would not be protracted.

The Mewts have an almost holy regard for beautiful boys beloved of kings, and Alofel was aware of this. Mewtish folklore was plump with tales about the mysterious, sacrosanct relationship of male lovers, whereas the Cossics were far more casual about these liaisons. Most Cossic noblemen had wives and boys, but there was really little distinction between them. So, in order to demonstrate to the Mewts that we Cossics were equally capable of homo-spiritual relationships, Alofel decreed that while our visitors remained at court, I must be present at all state functions, silent and enigmatic at his side. No mention was made of Akaten putting in an appearance; an arrangement that suited everyone, except perhaps the Mewts. The situation amused me, because I knew that both sides regarded the other to be barbarians.

One night, soon after the Mewts' arrival, a banquet was held in honour of the visitors, and Cossic dignitaries from around the land were invited to attend. Alofel wanted me beside him on the top table, much to the chagrin of Queen Mallory, whose place I temporarily usurped. She knew that the Mewts would note how far down the table she'd been placed. This was unprecedented. In public, when the queen was present, I was never seated closer to the king than her. At the time, I did wonder whether Alofel was doing rather too much to please our visitors. I had no love for Mallory, but we were not Mewts. We had our own traditions, and should stick with them.

Menefer was a striking individual, honey-dark of hair and skin like Akaten. His demeanour was courteous, he had a dry wit and a quick intelligence. He was clearly wary of Alofel, and would only commit himself to plans that he deemed were designed to help his people. Honour, beauty and intelligence; a sickeningly noble combination of traits. I found it hard to credit that Harakhte had refused this man a place at his side. It pained me to hear that Menefer was considered but a shadow of his dead brother. How could Akaten love me if this were true? I was a pampered plaything, pale and thin; a sickle moon to the memory of Mewt's slaughtered sun king.

We sat down to eat at sunset, I at the head of the table next to Alofel, with Menefer on his other side. Further down the board, Queen Mallory sat glaring at us from among her company of women.

Menefer complimented Alofel on the gracious hall, the wine, the food, the efficient service of the servants. Then his eyes turned to me. 'And your companion delights the eye, a moon child. I have never beheld a youth so pale and lovely. Such magic must refresh your very soul.'

Alofel smiled thinly, perhaps sensing in which direction the conversation was about to head. 'Ah yes. Darien is my consolation.'

I bit into a bitter fruit, mistrust coursing throughout my body, and smiled rather coldly at the Mewt.

'There is one matter,' Menefer began delicately, 'which has been causing consternation at home.'

'Yes?' Beneath the table, Alofel's thigh pressed gently against my own in warning. I returned the pressure. We were both suspicious.

Menefer touched his mouth with his fingertips, made an abrupt gesture. 'It concerns my brother's lover, Akaten.'

Silence fell. I detected ears around the table tuning into the conversation. Alofel said nothing, but waited for Menefer to continue.

The Mewt fixed Alofel with wide, guileless eyes. 'The truth is, my lord, we want him back.'

Alofel laughed politely. 'That is a matter to be discussed with my advisors.'

Menefer blinked slowly and shook his head. 'No. With you. I understand why you want him near you, but Akaten is a legend in our country. The people feel he is a prisoner of war and that, to promote good feeling between our countries, he should be released. My brother is dead, but Akaten still lives. The people want to honour him. He must come home.'

Alofel took in a long, deep breath through his nose. His fingers tapped the tablecloth with dangerous economy of movement. 'I do not want to get into dispute,' he said. 'This is not the time nor the place. Again, I feel this is something that our diplomats should discuss.'

Menefer leaned back in his seat, shrugged. 'I must warn you I am unprepared to leave here without him. My people would be very disappointed in me if I did.' He gestured languidly. 'I have a reputation to live up to—my brother's. You want and need me to be your hand in Mewt, but you must give me weapons and power. Give me Akaten, to return to his people, and their respect for me will be enhanced. I will be honest. Not everyone in Mewt is happy that I am here now. Some still talk of resistance and war.'

Alofel was now severely distressed by Menefer's words. He knew, and I knew, that Menefer spoke with sincerity and sense. We should return the Khan's boy; it would be seen as a magnanimous gesture and help kindle warmth towards Cos. But unfortunately, emotions were involved, and good sense is rarely seen in their company. Also, there was the matter of what Akaten himself would feel about the suggestion. His true thoughts remained a secret to both Alofel and myself, but I sensed he would feel uncomfortable being honoured in Mewt when he had accepted the gifts of Harakhte's conqueror, and shared a bed with a Cossic lover. As I sat there, trying to maintain an outward cool, I began to wonder whether Akaten was secretly pining for his home, for his people. Was his apparent acceptance of his position in Cos simply a device to ensure survival? As the silence thickened around the top table, Menefer made a frantic appeal, perhaps his undoing.

'My lord king, we have dozens of youths such as Akaten at the Mewtish court. You may have your pick of them, but I beg you to be lenient concerning my request.'

Alofel fixed Menefer with a stern, disapproving eye, and I could see that the Mewt realised immediately that he had overstepped propriety. Alofel smiled, a dreadful sight. 'My dear Menefer, I assure you I have the pick of any desirable young creatures here in Cos. Akaten is a symbol of my victory, a spoil of war, if you like. I could have had him slaughtered on the field beside your brother, but chose to bring him back to Tarnax only because he was a prominent member of the Khan's household. If your queen had been present in the camp, I would have brought her home as well and added her to my house of women. I cannot help but suspect that you would have accepted *that* circumstance with less fuss. If, by some freak chance, your brother had been in my position, he would have done the same as I did. Mewt is my country now, and while I appreciate the wisdom of making conciliatory gestures towards my conquered people, I will not be insulted in my own house, nor be bullied into making gestures against my will. The matter is ended. I would be grateful if you did not mention it again.' He smiled and took a grape from a silver dish before him. 'After all, you have a number of ambitious cousins who would happily take your place as regent of Mewt.'

Menefer had gone pale beneath his honeyed skin. I saw his throat convulse. Perhaps he was thinking about how his esteemed brother would have handled this discussion differently, and emerged from its conclusion with more spoils in his hands. Too late now.

The banquet proceeded with a less informal atmosphere than before. I sensed Alofel was now eager to leave the company. Menefer had offended him. Also, I knew that he was enamoured of Akaten, and nothing would convince him to give the boy up. It was fortunate that he had a battery of excuses to present to the Mewt rather than risk exposing the truth. If Menefer knew of Alofel's feelings, the balance of power in this subtle game would shift considerably.

As everyone stood to leave the table and proceed to the halls of music for entertainment that would drift on towards the dawn, Alofel made a discreet series of signals to me. Understanding their meaning, I nodded briefly, and when my absence would not be noticed, quietly left the shining halls and made my way to the council offices, which were on the same floor. Alofel came to me shortly.

'You are close to Akaten,' he said bluntly, as soon as the door was closed behind him. 'Is there any risk he might collude with Menefer? You can be sure that, before he leaves this court, the Mewt will somehow manage to get a message to the boy. These people are as slippery as greased rats.'

'I don't know, my lord,' I answered truthfully. 'I doubt I can tell you anything about Akaten and his feelings of which you're unaware.'

He nodded thoughtfully. 'Be vigilant, Darien. I cannot risk an incident which might cause embarrassment. You must understand that if Akaten were found to be in league with Menefer, in any way, I'd have no choice but to take punitive action. Perhaps it would be best if you could advise Akaten of this, but as subtly as you can.'

I bowed. 'I will, my lord.'

'Good. Now, return to the party ahead of me. Speak kindly to the Mewts. These celebrations are in their honour, after all.'

He held out his hand and I pressed the royal seal on his ring to my brow. He reached out and laid his hand on my head. 'Dear Darien, your beauty and your kindness paves my path before me. Do not for one moment think that I underestimate all that you are doing for me.'

I hid the cynicism in my eyes, lowered my lashes modestly. 'My whole life is yours, my lord.'

I should have been more concerned about how determined Alofel was to keep Akaten in Cos and also his mistaken belief that I had befriended Akaten in an attempt to sway his feelings towards Alofel, but at the time, I was just grateful for such a powerful ally. Alofel clearly had no idea how deep my feelings ran, but that was perhaps because the depth of his own love blinded him to the possibility. The thought of Akaten being sent away filled me with a sick dread. If I had to kill Menefer to prevent that happening, I would.

Later, near dawn, I went to Akaten's chambers. I found him asleep on the terrace, with the sounds of merriment drifting up from below. An empty flagon lay on its side beside him, next to a cup still half full of wine. He was wearing only a belted robe of soft, dark material, which hung open to reveal his thighs and shoulders, tantalisingly clasped at the waist to hide the fruit of his body. A night breeze had made a dune of fallen petals along my beloved's side. His hair was spread out on the tiles, and his puppy lay curled upon it. Merely the sight of him engorged my lust. I fell to my knees beside him, ran my hands over his cool skin. The puppy awoke and scampered off, his claws ticking against the tiles. Akaten murmured something and shifted slightly in his deep, intoxicated sleep. My fingers slipped free the knot of his belt and I pulled aside the cloth. His prick was thick and hard, against his belly, his balls tight against his body. Perhaps he dreamed of me. Feverishly, I disrobed myself, knowing I was about to steal something precious and divine. My belly burned inside me. Naked, I knelt beside him once more, loosed my hair so that it fell in inky waves onto his skin. I lowered my head to his groin, lightly kissed his fragrant balls, the steely shaft of him. Still he did not wake. Lightly, I took him in my mouth and sucked him softly. His hands twitched against the tiles; he sighed. His hips moved rhythmically beneath me. Oh, my beautiful one, you cannot want to leave me. I am your incubus, your nemesis. You must love me.

I raised myself and straddled his body, impaled myself upon him slowly. The tides of sleep drew back from the shores of his consciousness. I sensed his mind drifting up to wakefulness. Still half dreaming, he reached up to me, gripped my waist. His face was partly hidden by a swatch of hair, but I could see he was smiling, his eyes still closed. We moved together languorously, until his hunger became great. Then he reared up in one fluid movement and pushed me backwards without severing our connection, manoeuvring himself onto his knees. I curled my legs high around him, feeling as if he drove against my heart. He was powerful, dominant, and in my heart and mind I was taken back to that delirious time in Phasmagore. My lover of the shrine had returned to me! It *had* been Akaten! As this realisation crashed through me, I cried out in euphoric release, pushing my heels against the sky. He reached between us for my prick, aiding my orgasm, and presently I felt him convulse within me. He fell upon me, sought my mouth with his own, filling me with his tongue which was bittersweet with the taste of red wine. I began to weep, suffused with a sense of eternal joy and repletion.

Then Akaten sighed deeply and stroked my face. 'Harakhte,' he murmured, and my heart contracted in agony. I realised he had never truly awoken.

It was impossible for me to sleep, but I could not leave him. For the remainder of the night, I lay beneath him, with his gentle snores in my ears. When he finally awoke, I expected him to be surprised I was there, but he merely blinked at me sleepily and smiled. 'Darien, I'm glad you came to me.'

I could not be entirely warm towards him. 'You were dead drunk. Does the presence of Menefer cause you so much pain?'

His eyes clouded at my sharp tone. He sat up and looked away. 'I have betrayed my people,' he said, then got to his feet. I watched him as he donned his discarded robe.

'You betray me by saying such things,' I said.

He glanced at me as he pulled his belt across his belly. 'I know,' he said. 'This is hard for me, Darien. Please try to understand.'

'Menefer wants you,' I said harshly. 'How do you feel about that?'

He looked puzzled. 'What do you mean?'

'Last night, he virtually demanded that Alofel deliver you into his hands. Is that what you want?'

He shook his head. 'No, of course not. I could never give myself to him. That would be more of a betrayal to Harakhte than sleeping with you, or Alofel, for that matter.'

'So much for your elastic feelings,' I snapped. 'Only a few short months ago, you were eager to bypass the stage of mourning by slipping into my bed. Now, you talk of betrayal and...' I couldn't help myself. '...utter *his* name while you're making love to me. You're not over him, Akaten! Why lie to me? You're using me to make life easier for yourself! Why don't you just go back to Mewt with Menefer? There is a tomb there for you to wank over! Or, perhaps in Menefer's bed, you can pretend your beloved is still alive. They look alike, I believe.'

Akaten's face was inscrutable. I hated myself for what I was saying, but misery and jealousy pushed aside all considerations of sense and propriety.

'I will always love him,' Akaten said in an even voice. 'I thought you knew this.' He stalked with dignity into his chambers.

I lay back on the cold tiles and cursed myself. What was I doing? In my stupidity, I had revealed that Akaten had a means to return to his country. What I had not revealed was that Alofel would never allow it to happen.

Presently, I collected myself enough to dress and follow Akaten into the palace. I found him in his dining room, seated on the floor by a low table, his attendants arranging dishes of food before him. Tears ran uncontrollably down his face, which his staff studiously ignored. I ordered the servants out, and sat down beside him.

'I'm sorry.'

He shook his head. 'There is no need. You're probably right.'

That was not what I wanted to hear. I took his hands in my own. 'Akaten, don't say that. We've had a delirious summer together. I know you've been happy.'

He tore his hands from my grip. 'No! I've been a shallow, selfish fool! Darien, I know you care very deeply for me, and I've enjoyed basking in that, but part of me is still on that battlefield, senseless with grief and wandering blindly like a ghost. I dream of him! I see his face among the crowds at court. At night, his voice speaks to me sadly from the shadows while you sleep! You have been my solace, my exorcism, but perhaps my place is beside his tomb, celibate and faithful. I must speak to Alofel.' He shook his head in confusion. 'I must go home.'

'No!' I leapt to my feet. 'You're talking nonsense! Emotional rubbish! I won't let you do it!'

'Why?' He looked up at me with anguished eyes. 'Do you really want me, Darien? I can never give you what you want. I'm only here because Alofel thinks that, one day, I shall give myself to him. It won't happen! If Menefer wants me, and is persistent, eventually Alofel will tire of his useless wooing and cast me aside. Neither you or I will have any say in that.'

My heart was beating so fast I could barely think. Its thunder deadened my thoughts. 'Akaten, you have a life. Live it. Returning to Mewt is a ridiculous thing to do. You'll hate yourself for it eventually. I can heal you, but Menefer will only open your wounds—forever. Will he respect your wishes to be celibate? I think not. Each time he takes you to his bed, you'll think of Harakhte, and while fantasy might soothe you for a while, each morning will bring guilt. One stage of your life, though sweet, is over. You've been given another chance. Don't be a fool. Take it!'

Akaten put his hands over his face and bowed his head. I heard him murmur, 'Help me, Darien.'

I put my arms around him, kissed his hair. 'My love, I am here for you. Always. Yes, I am jealous of Harakhte, and always will be, but content with whatever you can give me. I could not live without you now.'

'I'm not worth this!' he said, but relaxed against me.

'Oh, you are!' I told him hotly. 'In the temple of Challis Hespereth, you came to me, whether in body or spirit. You called to me, and I answered.'

He looked at me. 'I don't understand... Tell me.'

At last, I told him everything.

He listened, wide-eyed, and when I had finished speaking, shook his head. 'That could not have been me,' but his expression was furtive.

'It was!' I insisted.

He took my face in his hands. 'I know how much you want to believe that, Darien, but it would be unfair of me to say that I was that person in the shrine.'

'But you said yourself you can't remember what happened in Phasmagore.'

'I'd remember that!' he said. 'No, we must be realistic. Our relationship is based on earthly things, but even so it is precious to me. This summer, you have saved my sanity a hundred times.' He leaned forward and kissed me.

'I love you,' I told him, the first time I had ever uttered those words to anyone. 'But so does Alofel. We must be careful and use his feelings to protect you from Menefer.'

'Are you suggesting I give in to Alofel's need?'

I shook my head with passion. 'No! He would monopolise you, and then I'd have nothing. All I meant was that it must be made clear to him you don't want to leave here.'

Akaten looked troubled. 'I will do as you think best,' he said, although I could tell part of him still wondered whether he should return to Mewt and live a life of isolated grief.

The next day, I reported to Alofel that Akaten had no desire to return home, hardening my heart to the joy this news brought to his face.

'It may be,' I said coolly, 'that Menefer will have to hear this from

Akaten himself before he believes it.' Part of me was still bruised from hearing the Khan's name on Akaten's lips in the heat of passion, and I felt he deserved at least a little discomfort.

Alofel nodded. 'This is true. How does Akaten feel about facing Harakhte's brother?'

I shrugged. 'I'm sure he can be persuaded.'

'Then make sure he is.'

Akaten was, as I'd anticipated, far from overjoyed by this development. When I went to him, later that morning, and informed him what he must do, he flung himself around the room in a panic. 'I cannot! No! It must not be!'

Sprawled in a chair, I watched his confusion. 'Alofel wants this proof from you and so do I.'

He paused in his wild pacing and stared at me with round eyes. 'You profess to love me, yet you'd force me to endure this?'

'See reason,' I said casually. 'It is all a game, and this is merely another move. Think of your own survival. Alofel has granted you his protection. There is nothing to fear.'

Akaten shook his head. I knew what he feared most: the diluted image of Harakhte's face before him, etched onto the younger brother's features. He dreaded a resurgence of grief and shame and anguish. I was unsure why I wanted him to go through it, but I did.

'There is nothing left for you in Mewt,' I said. 'Your life is here now, a fresh, new start. You fear Alofel casting you aside? He won't. Eventually, he will grant you status, and perhaps a house of your own. He will give you anything you ask for.'

'And will you share this house with me?' He sneered. 'I am not a fool, Darien. We both know our place. My future here is precarious, unless I give myself to your king. We are owned creatures, without free will. Our affair is as ephemeral as this summer. How can it last? And when it is ended for us, what will become of me then?'

I was silent for a moment. 'You underestimate your influence with the king.'

He raised his eyebrows. 'If I speak to Menefer as you desire, then I'll be at Alofel's mercy.'

'You believed yourself to be so before Menefer arrived, so what difference will that make?'

Akaten shook his head. 'Darien, I think you have a cruel streak within you.'

'It is the streak which ensures survival. Learn its colour.'

His eyes hardened. 'Very well. But remember, you instructed me.'

Akaten was presented to Menefer in the Council Chamber. Golden morning sunlight streamed in through the high windows, dust caught like the ghosts of thoughts in its rays. Prudently, Alofel was not present, but three members of the Council and myself were in attendance.

Menefer was seated among his entourage, but stood up when Akaten came into the room. His face—I could hardly bear to look at it. Admiration, relief, joy.

'You are safe,' Menefer said, as if until that moment, he had believed Akaten had been killed or else incarcerated in some dungeon pit.

Akaten's face was pinched, although his frown could not eclipse his natural beauty. He nodded. 'Yes.'

'We have all been concerned for you.' Menefer went towards him and Akaten took a step back.

'I have been treated very well, with every consideration.'

Menefer's face began to cloud, as if he intuited what was to come. In a quiet voice, he said, 'I mean to take you home.'

Akaten lifted his head. His eyes were dry, his voice surprisingly firm. 'I cannot, Lord Menefer, return with you.'

Menefer's people all began to mutter and stir upon their seats. Menefer silenced them with a raised hand. 'You can,' he said, 'if you ask for it. King Alofel told me this himself. It is why we are here now.'

Akaten shook his head. 'I cannot.'

'What have they done to you?' Menefer demanded. 'What threats have been made?'

It was the turn of my people now, to stir uncomfortably.

'None,' Akaten said, 'but I will not go back with you.'

'Why?' Implications filled that simple, softly-spoken word.

'My life is here now,' Akaten said. 'Harakhte is dead. There is nothing for me to return to.'

'Your people,' Menefer said quietly, treacherously. 'You have a responsibility.'

'No one has the right to ask anything of me. I was devoted to Harakhte, you know that, but he is no more.'

Menefer shook his head in disbelief. 'Are you saying that you *want* to stay here?'

'Yes.'

Menefer laughed, incredulous. 'Then you are not the person I believed you to be! Has the wealth of Cos seduced you, or its murdering king?'

Perhaps only I could see how Menefer's words were wounding Akaten. He did not flinch or stumble over his words, but his pain seemed like a visible aura to me. 'Alofel has been kind to me. I wish to forget the past. I will remain here.'

There was silence for a moment, a terrible silence. Then Menefer released a string of insults. 'You are a whore! Unworthy of honour! In Mewt, your name shall be erased from all Harakhte's monuments, where once they waited for your blessing! I am only relieved my brother cannot witness your treachery!' With these words, he spat in Akaten's face and stalked from the room, his entourage hurrying behind him.

Akaten stood in a ray of sunlight, his head bowed. He looked shrunken, ill. For a moment, a shadow passed across my mind. Then I went to him, put my arms around him, and he allowed me to lead him from the room.

After this, relations with the Mewts cooled considerably, and only two days later, they rode away from Tarnax, leaving Alofel's government in a state of consternation. They feared trouble would follow the Mewts' departure, and more than one councillor confided to me that perhaps it would have been better if Menefer had been granted his wish. I tried to allay their anxieties, and reminded them that Akaten was indeed a spoil of war and that to relinquish him would perhaps have had worse consequences than keeping him at Tarnax. Mewt must know its position; a conquered country. It could not stamp its foot, make demands, and expect to have them granted.

Alofel appeared unconcerned, his steady eyes daring anyone to comment on the wisdom of his actions. I am quite sure a lot was murmured behind his back.

Queen Mallory did not shrink from making her sentiments known. I found out very quickly what she had to say about the situation. There were accusations that Akaten was a spy of Menefer's, that the performance in the Council Chamber had been a premeditated act, designed to lull Alofel's suspicions. Menefer might once have felt resentful of Harakhte, and coveted the throne, but now that he had it, had rediscovered his patriotism, and even now plotted to evict our army from his country. Akaten knew this and had resolved to remain in Tarnax in order to gather information. I even heard one rumour that Akaten would kill Alofel in his sleep, given the chance.

Perhaps Mallory was astute about Menefer, but I gave no credence to her claims that Akaten was part of any plot. I knew that what irked her more than anything was the fact that Alofel had true affection to give to

Akaten. I, and the other concubines, were tolerated because Mallory thought we meant little more to Alofel than his favourite dogs. We were an unavoidable nuisance. But, as I had, Mallory sensed that Akaten could be something more. We all knew that Harakhte had granted Akaten status above the queen of Mewt. Mallory, no doubt, feared the same happening here. In her eyes, she already had to make too many concessions to whores and catamites. She had allies in her smear campaign, for there were still many who would have liked to see Akaten shipped back to Mewt.

The king himself stepped in to end the intrigue. He summoned the entire court, not to the Council Chamber, but to the Hall of Judging, where decisions over the gravest matters of state were made. Here Alofel made a statement. He said that any accusations made against Akaten, were in effect made against the Crown, since Alofel himself had decreed Akaten would remain in Tarnax. Speaking plainly, he stated that if any more ill-founded rumours came to his ears, he would discover the identity of the perpetrator and punish them severely, whoever they were. This was a public humiliation for Mallory, because everyone was aware towards whom the threats were directed. Mallory and Alofel had never been in dispute before. I knew that he respected her and was often lenient in his treatment of his spirited consort, but this time she had underestimated his feelings and had gone too far. I knew that Akaten had made a dangerous enemy, but was confident that Alofel's love would shield him.

I had protected Akaten from the malicious gossip as best I could, although after Menefer's departure, he seemed in such a daze, he was incapable of noticing any hostile nuances around him. He had become introverted, troubled. I understood the trauma he'd been through, but trusted I could heal his troubled spirits. He did not seem to harbour any ill-feeling towards me for my part in his trials, and I took this at face value. His beauty, however, became haunted. Occasionally, he would start at nothing, and stare at empty corners of the room. Sometimes, I awoke in the dead of night to find him pacing up and down beside our bed, mumbling in Mewtish under his breath. He always responded to my voice and came silently to my side, curling up against me, but we no longer seem to communicate in the way we had. He would not articulate his fears, no matter how I cajoled him. Occasionally, he would refuse to eat for days at a time, and became feverish, but again, he obeyed my injunctions without argument, and sipped the herbal concoctions I procured for him from the palace apothecary. During this time, my lust for him became inflamed, and I forced myself upon him at every opportunity. Wearily, he submitted himself to my demands, a passive lover whose eyes were clouded. I realise now

I was stupid, and did not heed the signs. I should have pressed him to speak to me, forced him to voice his anger, for it was there. All the time. Unspoken.

Alofel commented a couple of times on Akaten's apparent preoccupation, and seemed to hold me personally responsible for his episodes of vagueness and delirium. Patiently, I shouldered these criticisms with many apologies, continuing to dose Akaten with potent elixirs and smother him with affection. It seemed, eventually, to work. Never again did I hear Harakhte's name upon his lips.

The summer cracked and dried the land, heading towards a change of season. As the nights cooled slightly, Akaten seemed to settle down. His behaviour became less eccentric, his smile rested easier on his face. Although the country of Mewt might have dropped off the face of the earth, for all mention he made of it, we did begin to converse freely once more. About nothing, really.

One night, he initiated our lovemaking himself, and I was filled with relief. Alofel stopped complaining, and once more took delight in Akaten's daily company. Akaten himself seemed to derive more pleasure from his conversations with the king. He would return from the royal apartments with a spring in his step and try to tell me about what they discussed. I had no interest at all in their conversations, and responded only in monosyllables. Sometimes, I caught Akaten regarding me wryly as I snapped some dismissive remark at him, but I was stupid enough to pay it no heed. Queen Mallory's waspish comments about Akaten lost their sting. Nobody believed now that he was a threat to national security. He was no longer referred to as the Khan's boy, or even 'the Mewt'.

Akaten generally returned from the royal chambers several hours before I could expect the king's summons, but as time went on, and the colours of the garden changed to brazen gold, the time between our visits to Alofel grew less and less, until one evening I found myself passing Akaten on the stairs outside Alofel's rooms. I paused, a little surprised. 'It must have been a long conversation today.'

'Not as long as yours will be, surely!' he answered, rather coldly.

I shrugged and made to pass him. 'I will see you later.' He let me kiss him on the cheek, but made no move to return it. Clearly, my sharp remark had offended him, but I had no fear I couldn't cajole him out of his bad humour later on.

The next evening, I received no summons from the king, but that was not unusual. I did not expect him to call for me every night, and looked forward to a relaxing evening on the terrace with my beloved. I had the servants prepare a sumptuous supper for us and went out to wait in the starlight. Soon, it would be too cold to eat outdoors at night. The Cossic summers and autumns were long, but once winter marched in, the transition was brief and brutal.

I went to stand against the balustrade, wrapped in a light cloak. Akaten's puppy licked his paws on the tiles beside me. Presently, I became ill at ease. Akaten was very late. Where was he? I went to where the supper lay waiting for us, and poured myself a cup of wine. Once this was consumed, I drank another, then another. After that, I must have dozed for a while.

It was the laughter that woke me. I sat up, with the echo of a dream in my head, some memory of when Akaten and I had first made love beside the lake. My mouth was dry, my head muzzy with the heavy wine. Then I realised the laughter was real, that I recognised it, and that it came from the garden below.

In a daze I flew to the balustrade and looked over. I saw Akaten running across the yellow lawns, which were bleached in moonlight. He ran between the dappled shadows of the trees, scattering peacocks before him. I thought at first he'd gone utterly mad and was about to call out to him, because my voice always seemed to bring him back to his senses. Then I realised he was not alone. Another figure pursued him, someone who also laughed. Akaten dodged around the trees, his hair swinging. My heart, which at first seemed to have lurched unbidden to my mouth, now sank to the very pit of my belly. It was Alofel who was running and laughing with Akaten in the garden.

I was incensed at once. How dare he! What was this game, when he should be here with me? My fingers curled around the stone beneath my hands. Akaten spun around on the seared grass, leading Alofel a hectic dance. I saw the king's hands lash out to grab the spinning boy, always clutching at nothing. Then, as I blinked, he caught up and took Akaten in his arms. Akaten did not try to break away but stood there, motionless. His arms went about Alofel's neck. They stared at one another for a few moments, then kissed.

The heat of my anger chilled within me. I was made of ice. I was winter.

I don't know how I endured that long night. Tears blurred my vision before I saw them leave the garden. I crouched against the balustrade, shuddering with cold. At some point, I must have fallen asleep, for when I opened my eyes again, it was morning. The puppy had eaten all of our supper, and scraps were spread about the scattered plates. After a moment's stunned contemplation of this forlorn sight, I collected myself and jumped to my feet. I did not want Akaten to find me in this state, and hurried back to my own rarely-used rooms, past Akaten's curious servants who were already seeing to breakfast.

The air in my bedroom was stale, and I threw open the window. Then I bathed myself with care, and tidied my appearance. Wezling fussed around me, sensing my distress, but too polite to comment on it.

Akaten appeared about an hour later, sauntering into my rooms with a smile on his face, as if nothing had happened. The moment I saw him, an arrow of pure hate lanced up through my body, but it was feathered with bewilderment and grief. Never had I loved him more.

His smiled faltered. 'Good morning, Darien. You seem in bad spirits.'

I wanted to shout and accuse, but realised the folly of it. Only honesty would do. 'You forgot our appointment last night.'

He frowned a little. 'Oh, were we supposed to be doing something?'

'Only the same as we have done every night for months.' I fixed him with a steady stare.

He had the audacity to return my gaze with unfaltering eyes. 'I did not come back from the king's chambers. So what? Most nights I am left waiting alone for you.'

I did not bother to remind him that I always came to him eventually. 'I saw you in the garden.'

His gaze flickered only slightly. 'Did you?' He bent to investigate my breakfast, which lay mostly untouched on the low table before me.

'Yes. So you have betrayed me and given yourself to him!'

He looked up at me. 'Darien, cast your mind back to the day when you told me I must speak to Menefer. You have taught me well. I am merely ensuring my own survival. Didn't you tell me to do that? Why are you so distressed?'

'You kissed him!'

'Yes.'

'And what else besides?'

Akaten sighed. 'It was just a kiss, Darien. A game. Most nights, you give yourself to him. You have no right to accuse me.'

'But I have no feelings for him. It means nothing. It's my job.'

He shrugged. 'I know.' Then he reached out and put his hand on my knee. 'Oh, don't be angry. It's senseless. Alofel knows the way I feel, but I have to give him *something* in return for his tolerance and generosity. If you and I want to remain together, it's essential. Come now, change your face. I'm here now.'

I wanted to believe him and allowed myself to be convinced. I blotted from my mind the memory of their laughter, the pause before the kiss which must have meant so much. Even now, I have no doubt that Akaten was merely putting on a performance designed to please Alofel, but he had deliberately advanced their relationship, allowed things to happen that would only encourage Alofel's obsession. During those moments on the lawn had Akaten thought once of me? It was unlikely. Yet every time I went to Alofel's bed, I dreamed of him. It was the only thing that made the experience bearable.

Alofel did not summon me for two days, and I began to worry. Akaten assuaged my fears, saying that the king was unwell. 'Don't fret. He'll call for you soon. What's the matter? Are you missing him?'

His teasing scored my heart.

On the third evening, a royal servant came to summon me, and I believed that all must be well. Alofel did seem rather frail and distant, but treated me kindly, and afterwards, gave me a present—a jewelled pin for my jacket.

Things progressed in this fashion for a couple of weeks. Akaten spent more time with king, but took care to return to me each evening. Or, at least I *supposed* he took care. Perhaps it was just coincidence. Representatives from a noble family were visiting the palace, so Alofel might not have had as much time as usual for amorous dalliances.

Then one night, Akaten did not make an appearance. I was waiting for him in his chambers, and we had definitely agreed to be together that night. It was one of the girls' birthdays, and a party would take place in the women's quarters. We had planned to go there together. By the tenth hour of the night, an hour after the party had started, Akaten had still not come back from the king. Seething with suspicions, I wrapped myself in a dark cloak and crouched upon his balcony to watch the garden, although it was unlikely they'd wander out there now. The autumn rains had started, and each evening the lawns were soaked. After over an hour of huddling in the depressing drizzle, I went back into his rooms. I paced around, lifting objects—all of which were presents from the king—my head afire with torturing thoughts. Porfarryah's face swam before my inner eye; her hard expression, the words, 'He will *damage* you, Darien. Take care.' Servants bustled invisibly in the rooms around me, their ears tuned to my frantic movements. I sensed their delighted whispers, the exchange of intriguing information, which had no doubt already fluttered its way into the women's quarters, spicing up the conversation at the party. It felt as if the whole palace was buzzing with gossip about me. I could imagine what was being said: I had been betrayed. Akaten had used me in a scheme to take my place at Alofel's side. I had been fooled by love and beauty. Soon, I might be sent to the court of some lesser nobleman, because my continued, useless presence in the palace would be an affront to Alofel's sensibilities.

Then Akaten would lounge like a great tawny cat in my place, his exotic face wreathed in an enigmatic smile.

I could stand it no longer.

My feet seemed to drag my agonised mind out of Akaten's rooms. I walked slowly, and with purpose, towards the chambers of the king. Around me, the echoing halls seemed immeasurably high. Banners of gold and purple swayed in a distant breeze, miles over my head. I seemed to shoot out my body to hang among their dusty folds and look down at the small figure striding along the ancient corridors, his cloak blown out around him like dark wings, his head surrounded by a halo of black flames.

The journey through the palace seemed endless. I was dazed, perplexed by the eternal flights of shallow steps that made me feel like a tiny, crawling creature negotiating a fallen pack of cards. From every shadowed corner, rampant stone lions and gryphons leered down at me with lolling tongues. Ancient swords clashed upon the walls around me. I walked in a sick delirium, my mouth full of the taste of blood and shit, a cruel reminder of my lover of the shrine, who might or might not have been Akaten. If it had been, how apt his actions now seemed. He had forced me to taste myself, the most bitter gall of my inner being, and now I retched upon it, again and again.

Then the final flight of stairs were before me: smooth grey stone, carpeted with velvety red plush. Motionless guards stood to attention before the great doors that led to the reception room of the royal chambers. I heard clarions blare, and the howls of victory. I heard the stamp of many horses.

One of the guards shifted position a little as I approached. Usually, I was escorted to these rooms and never came alone.

'It's all right,' I said, laying a feverish hand on his armoured arm. 'I am expected. Akaten and the king.'

The guard peered down at me suspiciously through the translucent scales of his visor. He looked like a legendary bird, wings furled at his back. But it was only the shift of draperies against the wall.

The second guard said, 'Let the boy in,' and by the secret tone of his voice, I knew he did not care whether I was expected or not. These were *my* people. They would stand behind me.

I inclined my head to him as I passed through the doors. For a brief time, I wondered whether I would ever come out again.

I passed through the dimly-lit rooms like a phantom, drifting through skeins of woody incense smoke. Luck was with me, for I came across none of Alofel's staff. Then, at the door to his bedchamber, his steward Capronel appeared from a side door. The steward's eyes almost fell from his head when he saw me. He rushed forward and took hold of my arms.

'What are you *doing* here?' he hissed.

'Let me go,' I said calmly.

He shook his head, speaking in an urgent whisper. 'I can't, Darien. You must know that I can't.'

I tried to prise myself from his grip and spoke in a low, clear voice. 'I have to *see*, Capronel. Please, let me see. I'm not going to do anything rash, but I have to know. My future is at stake.'

'What is the point of seeing?' he asked sadly. 'It was inevitable. Come, let me take you back to your rooms. I will find Porfarryah...'

'No!' Because I knew I was on the point of being marched out of the royal chambers, I summoned all of my strength, and broke free of Capronel's hold. I threw myself at the doors ahead of me, flung them wide.

The room was low-lit by guttering candles. The lovers were sprawled on the wide bed, among the tangled sheets, apparently well-sated. Akaten lay on his back, his head resting on Alofel's lap. He held a goblet of wine upright on his chest, while the king played with his shawl of hair. Akaten was talking, gesturing with his free hand. Alofel gazed down at him like a moonstruck doe. My arrival interrupted their conversation, and both of them looked towards the door. Alofel didn't seem to recognise me at first, probably because it didn't occur to him I'd have the audacity to walk in on him, but Akaten knew me straight away. His expression was unreadable. I wanted to think it was shock, but mostly I think it was empty.

'Darien,' Alofel said eventually. His voice held the beginning of censure. Before he could call for his guards, I slammed the doors shut quickly. I had seen what I'd come here to see. Behind me, Capronel made an anguished sound, half scolding, half sympathetic. I brushed away his fluttering hands and went back the way I had come.

I could have gone to Porfarryah; she would have been pleased and relieved to see me, and for my sake, would have kept any smug sense of vindication from her manner and voice. But I could face no one. I went back to my rooms and drank myself unconscious, waiting for the knock of doom upon my door.

By morning, the entire palace must have known what had happened, because Capronel would have told everyone. I had never experienced the feelings that surged through my body. Such anger, such indignation, such pain. I had no idea what Alofel would do, but guessed he would not let the matter pass. I had acted above my station, as if I were his equal, bursting into his private room like a scorned lover. At the very least, I could expect a beating, but what I feared most was dismissal, exile to the house of an ancient nobleman. At any moment, the guards would come. I paced my chamber, trying to think, to plan.

The hour for breakfast had nearly passed, and no guards had arrived to drag me off into custody. Perhaps Akaten had appealed to Alofel on my behalf. Perhaps they were waiting to see what *I'd* do. After all, Alofel would have been aware I had my allies at court. I half expected Porfarryah to show her face, but she did not. I even harboured a small, sickening desire for Akaten to come to me, but even as I longed for it, I knew I was destined to be disappointed.

I could go to one of my friends on the Council and speak to them in confidence. I could make provisions for an exile I could bear. If I made a dignified retreat, Alofel would be unlikely to oppose it, because to do so would attract more attention to the situation. Yes, this would be the safest course. I knew exactly from whom I could expect sympathy and aid. But these things would not give me what I desired most: revenge. I resolved, in my unfamiliar agony, to take a risk.

I donned my smartest, blackest clothes and brushed my hair until it gleamed like jet. I put earrings of obsidian into my ears, and brushed the skin around my eyes with a kiss of charcoal. My mirror showed me the image of an aloof young man of glacial beauty. I was a black and white creature; even my lips were without colour, and my eyes were the darkest grey. It was as I desired.

Once my preparations were finished, I called for Wezling and ordered him to precede me to the women's quarters. Only servants were about at that hour, but I was conscious of the way they avoided my eyes as I approached. Once I had passed they would look back at me and whisper.

Wezling hopped around outside the swan-relief doors to the concubines' apartments, but I did not pause. Surprised, he jumped ahead of me. 'Excuse me, sir, but where are we going? You said the women's quarters...'

'Of the queen,' I answered.

He said nothing more.

Guards stood on duty before Mallory's chambers, as they did before Alofel's, but her quarters were more modest and were not approached by a flight of steps. This area of the palace was very feminine, light and airy. There were no impending grey stones, no heavy banners of dark, funereal colours, but gauzy cream curtains, and tiles of polished white marble. Pretty green birds sang and fluttered in enormous cages that hung from the ceiling. The incense here was of mimosa, jasmine and rose.

Wezling bowed to the guards and requested that the queen's steward be summoned. After a few minutes, a tall youth in saffron livery presented himself before us. Orlando. He was entirely a creature of Mallory's and despised me utterly. I, after all, was the favourite of the king, while he was relegated to the service of the queen. No doubt he thought enough of himself to believe he was more worthy of Alofel's attention than I. I disliked his small, full lips, and the indistinct colour of his hair, although by many his looks were considered incomparable. He glanced at Wezling and beyond him. His mouth turned down into a sneer when he saw me standing there upon the rose-coloured carpet, a spectre in black. He did not bother to address my servant.

'What do you want?'

'Good morning, Orlando. Be so kind as to tell the queen I wish to speak with her.'

He laughed in incredulity. 'What? Do you really think she will oblige you?'

I refused to return his rudeness; my voice was mild. 'Yes. When she hears what I have to say.'

'Which is?'

'That is my business and Queen Mallory's. I will not discuss it with her underlings.'

Orlando flared his nostrils. 'You needn't think that just because you've lost the king's favour, you can come sniffing round here, hoping Her Majesty will take pity on you. She won't. You're finished, Darien, and not before time.'

I sighed patiently. 'Orlando, I have no interest in your opinions. Tell the queen I am here, and that I must speak to her. It is for her benefit as much as mine. And let me tell you now, if you continue to be obstructive, to the point where the queen does not learn the information I have to give her, she will not look kindly upon you at all.'

He hesitated a moment, and I could almost see his dim brain trying to invent some new insults. Clearly, none were forthcoming, because he dismissed me from his attention and stalked back into the royal apartments. I

looked at Wezling's mortified face and smiled gently. I felt my power
coming back to me. It filled the fibres of my body with crimson fire.

I knew that the queen would not be able to resist finding out what I
had to say, although she did keep me waiting outside her quarters for over
an hour. She sent no one to invite me into the reception chamber, where I
might have waited in more comfort. Still, these affronts did not bother
me. I understood why she felt I deserved them.

Eventually, Orlando reappeared and ordered me inside. 'You're lucky,'
he said. 'She's curious.'

I smiled politely and followed him into the queen's morning room.
She sat beneath the window at her breakfast table, being fussed over by a
gang of maids and boy-servants. She had clearly come recently from her
bath, because she wore only a belted gown, and the room reeked of lilac-
scented body powder. I realised this was the closest I had ever come to her.
Mallory was an imposing sight; very tall, and although not in the slightest
given to fat, a statuesque and heavy-boned creature. Her heavy ash-blond
hair fell over her shoulders and curled down into the ripe cleavage of her
powder-spotted bosom. She wore no make-up, other than a scrawl of black
over each plucked eyebrow. Her lips, like mine, were unusually pale.

'Well, well,' she drawled as I entered the room. 'What have we here?
A little black imp, I believe!' All her menials tittered at the joke.

I bowed low. 'Thank you for granting me an audience, Your Majesty.
I would speak to you alone.'

Mallory lifted a huge strawberry from a porcelain dish before her, dipped
it into an avalanche of white sugar heaped in a bowl nearby, and popped it
into her mouth. She chewed thoughtfully as she looked at me. 'I wonder
what you could have to tell me that I might find interesting.'

'It concerns a matter of mutual anxiety.'

She smiled and took another strawberry, twirling it in her fingers before her lips. 'But, Darien, I don't feel anxious,' she said and bit into the
fruit.

'I would very much like to speak to you in private.'

She stared at me, chewing. Her gaze was inscrutable, although I could
tell she was delighted I was there. She swallowed, and for a few moments,
glanced around herself scornfully, as if appraising her staff, who all gawped
at her like eager puppies. Then, she sniffed. 'Very well. Out. All of you!
Scamper off now!'

Once they had all departed in a flustered and disgruntled throng, I
bowed again. 'Thank you, Your Majesty.'

Mallory raised a hand at me dismissively. 'Oh, don't come that with me. We both know where we stand. Now, I suppose you want my help because Alofel is glutting himself on Mewtish meat.'

I told her then what had happened the previous night.

When I had finished speaking, she twitched her nose and drew her finger through the sugar, licked it. 'I can't understand why you think I might have the slightest interest in your plight, or even what I could do about it. It has long been ground into me I have no influence over my husband's carnal affairs.'

'I am not looking for help,' I replied, 'but a partner.'

Mallory laughed fiercely. 'What?' Sobering, she shook her head. 'Oh, Darien, Darien, I believe I might be dreaming. Do not take me for a fool.'

'That is the last thing I would ever take you for,' I said. 'I never have.'

'Flattery now, eh?' She took another fruit, nibbled it thoughtfully, pointed at me with it. 'Let us face facts. You have been a thorn in my mattress for years. You strut around as if you were his wife, not I. You and that slut, Porfarryah. If you are in pain now, I applaud it.'

'Your Majesty, I enact my role in this palace as you enact yours. I understand your vexation, but the way things are is really not my fault.'

'Perhaps not, but you're the one asking for my aid, not Alofel. I have to admit, I'm aghast you have the impertinence to present yourself here. Has love brought you to this grovelling state, sweet Darien?'

'Not love,' I said. 'Something you understand, I think. Revenge.'

Mallory laughed again. 'It makes no difference to me whether you or the Mewt wave your backsides in Alofel's face. I have no desire to help you or conspire with you. Whatever happens, my life will still be littered with impudent strumpets.'

I dared not feel defeated. 'Your Majesty, the presence of the Mewt is a threat to all. Much as it seems distasteful to you, we should close ranks over this interloper, otherwise we could all be out in the cold.'

Mallory raised an eyebrow. 'Really? Explain.'

I sauntered to her table and she watched in silence as I helped myself to a strawberry. 'You know as well as I how Akaten was regarded in Mewt. As Alofel's favourite, he may well wheedle similar favours here. If I am a thorn in your mattress, he will be a cage of briars around you.' I paused and chewed the strawberry. 'Alofel loves Akaten. That is common knowledge. Love makes people stupid. They desire to please.'

Mallory shook her head. 'Alofel is a creature of tradition. He would not dare to make too many changes. He would be opposed.'

I took a deep breath. 'Naturally, and it would damage him in the eyes of the court. Perhaps we have a duty to address this situation. Look, I could have approached members of the Council about this, but despite our mutual feelings, I came to you. Why? Because I know this is your territory. You are the only person in this establishment capable of dealing with the Mewt.'

Mallory regarded me keenly for a while. 'Well, these are words I never expected to hear.' She rolled a strawberry around in the sugar. 'Maybe, just maybe, I could be of assistance. However, I will not come from this empty-handed.'

'I would not expect you to. What are your terms?'

'As you have implied, you have friends among the Councillors. You must speak to them. Before this matter can proceed any further, I want your promise that you will arrange for your council seat to be passed to me.'

It took some effort to conceal my surprise. 'That may be difficult, Your Majesty.'

'Oh well. You may leave, then. The matter is closed.'

'There would have to be a vote.'

'I know. But for your allies, my friends would have swayed the vote a long time ago.'

I realised then she had been waiting for a moment such as this. In her patience, some instinct had advised her it would come. Once I was dismissed from Alofel's side, my seat would be lost in any case. I had nothing to lose. 'Very well. I will do as you ask.'

'Good. Do it now, and return to me with news. Then we shall talk.'

It was not an easy task. Some of the councillors were extremely wary of Mallory, a queen who showed more interest in affairs of state than was considered demure. I had to remind my council friends of favours I had granted them, words whispered to the king that had advanced their various, personal causes. One particular duke, Ferdinand, spoke plainly that morning.

'Darien, yours was ever a thin pole to balance upon. Now you have fallen. What use are you to any of us now? I admire and respect you, but for my own safety I should stand back and observe as you bleed and struggle with your broken bones.'

'I know too much,' I answered. 'You won't let the fall cripple me.'

I saw him mull over, then, the things I had done for him in the past, and how the details of his affairs, brought to light, would cause him discomfort.

'You are Cossic,' I said in a kinder tone. 'Surely you would prefer Mallory beside you on the council rather than Akaten?'

'That would not happen!' he said.

I shrugged. 'Akaten will not help you. He does not understand the machinery of the court. Mallory as an ally, however, could be of use.'

Ferdinand shook his head. 'You want blood, don't you,' he said.

I smiled. 'I have been treated badly, betrayed and used. Blood is the least I desire.'

By noon, I had persuaded all but two of my allies to vote for Mallory. It was the majority she needed. In truth, I think most of the councillors realised that as they would be losing me, they might as well attempt to woo the queen. I knew she wouldn't be as amenable as I had been, and was forced to exaggerate a little concerning this, but if they paid whatever price she demanded, they might still claw back some clandestine influence over the king.

The next time I presented myself at Mallory's door, I was allowed entrance immediately. She saw me once more in her salon, now dressed in a robe of soft, heather-coloured silk. I gave her a list of names, beside which I had secured some signatures. The next time the council met, they would have to vote in someone to replace me. Now, that would be Mallory. Alofel might not like it, but he'd be aware his position was delicate at present and would not put up a fight.

Mallory nodded and smiled and sat down at her table. She laced her hands in her lap. 'Now then, Darien, take a seat. We will have an informal discussion.'

She pursed her mouth in thought, then spoke. 'You've been sharing the Mewt's bed for months, and many unfettered remarks pass back and forth across the pillows of love. I think it's time you began to remember a few.'

'Perhaps you could help jog my memory.'

'Of course. Well, I don't believe for a moment that Akaten has lost his love for the dead Khan, or his country.'

'He has not. Harakhte's name was ever upon his lips in moments of intimacy.'

She nodded. 'Good. Menefer too is not what Alofel thinks. Cossics do not understand Mewts. They ascribe to them the morals and values of Cos. This is a grave mistake. I am not Cossic, and I can appreciate the Mewtish mind only too well. The Cossic nobleman is a thinker; honourable, loyal and traditional, but he keeps emotion in check. Challis Hespereth demands sex as a sacrifice, not love. The Mewt, on the other hand, is a passionate individual; he *feels*. Love to him is all; it is his god. He would die for it. Emotion leads people to act irrationally, as we have seen here over the matter of Akaten.'

'This much is obvious,' I said, unsure of where she was heading.

She raised a hand to silence me. 'Whatever Menefer thought of Harakhte in life, he will not dishonour his memory in death. Alofel and his councillors look down upon the Mewts, see them as fiery barbarians, who will act impulsively, but who do not have the strategic wit or discipline to win a war. Wrong. Menefer will bide his time, but will eventually raise an army against Cos. Harakhte brought prosperity to Mewt. He was the beginning of a new age, and consequently his death is a bigger blow to the people than the Cossics realise.

'Think about this. If Alofel were to die in battle, Cos would mourn and then crown his heir as king. The young monarch would be accorded as much loyalty and honour as his father. *This has not happened in Mewt.* Harakhte has been deified in death. When the time comes for war—and it will—Harakhte's face will adorn the banners of the Mewtish forces. They will march to war led by love. Let us now come closer to home. Akaten was Harakhte's beloved. And he is here, in Tarnax, in the midst of Mewt's enemies.'

'I see.'

'Yes. I have voiced these thoughts to my friends on the Council, but they are too arrogant to believe Mewt can ever be a threat now that Harakhte is gone. What they fail to perceive is that Harakhte is not gone. He is more powerful now than ever.'

'Knowing this, it seems preposterous that Harakhte's beloved should be so close to the king.'

'Indeed. Now, think, what did Akaten say to you when his guard was down.'

I thought for a few moments. 'Now that you've reminded me, I recall he did speak passionately for his country's freedom.'

'And when Menefer came here—what was Akaten's excuse for remaining in Cos?'

'Well, he told me that he loved me and could not leave me. I was blinded by emotion at the time and did not question...'

Mallory interrupted me. 'No, Darien, that is not what he said. Think again.'

I did. 'Akaten said he had a duty to remain here. I asked him what he meant by that and he spoke of trying to persuade Alofel to be lenient with his people.'

'Yes, that makes sense,' Mallory said. 'You would, of course, have believed that.'

I nodded. 'Yes.'

Mallory took in a long breath. 'However, should you spread any tales about the court, people will merely believe you are fabricating because you have been ousted. It's doubtful they'll give you any credence.'

I sighed. 'That is most likely true.'

'Hmm.' She tapped her lips with pale fingers. 'You must be prepared to wait, Darien. We cannot act immediately.'

'I will wait for as long as it takes. However, my position here is tenuous. I may be sent away.'

Mallory smiled. 'I have not been idle while you've been badgering your allies. I have learned that Alofel intends to punish you with disdain. He is furious you had the effrontery to barge into his rooms last night and has discovered the cause of your jealousy. You sought to own something he thinks is his. You deluded him. He sees it as a gross betrayal. I think he would have sent you packing, but it seems that the Mewt, despite having revealed the details of your relationship, spoke out for you at the last moment and begged Alofel for leniency. Whether this is a blessing or not, only you can decide. When you return to your apartments, you will find they have been stripped of your possessions, which have been moved to a room in the quarters of the other boys Alofel has at his disposal. You are demoted, Darien, and will pleasure the king's guests as he sees fit.'

I had known something like this would happen, but it still shocked me to hear it. I went entirely numb. Mallory laughed softly. 'At one time, I believed you had the upper hand, but at least, as queen, I could never suffer the ignominy you must suffer now.'

I put my head in my hands. I should have let Akaten return to Mewt with Menefer. I had been so foolish, so blind. Now, he had destroyed me.

'Pull yourself together,' Mallory said. 'I could wash my hands of you now, because I have what I want. No one will support you. But, we made a deal and I will stand by it. You might be of use to me in the future.'

As far as Alofel was concerned I might have simply dropped out of existence. I was no longer allowed access to areas of the palace where before I had roamed freely. The door to the king's wing, along with those to my old apartments, would remain closed to me. Forever. As for Akaten, I did not see him. He made no move to contact me and I had no idea of his thoughts or feelings.

In my new quarters, the other boys took delight in humiliating me. I had once lorded it over them; now I was easy game. As winter breathed its chill across the land, so I became frozen—externally. I spoke to no one. Even my former servant, Wezling, was above me now. Perhaps he served Akaten. At times, when dignitaries came to court, I and the other boys would be herded into a salon, and the men could take their pick. My peers often made sure the visitors knew who I was, what I had been, and for this reason I was chosen regularly. I did not care. I might as well be dead. Clearly, those who used my body thought this too as they grunted and heaved upon me. It did not matter to them.

Once, in the early days, Porfarryah came to my rooms. The grief that filled her eyes, the pity: I could not bear it. She held out her hands to me, but I turned away. In my heart, I was screaming for comfort, but I could not allow myself to take it.

'He takes no one now,' she said huskily. 'Akaten is the only one. We are all redundant.'

Just the sound of her voice conjured tears in my eyes. I did not want to hear her words, perceiving them as complaints rather than sympathy. She, after all, had not been stripped of her privileges. 'I want you to go,' I said.

'Darien...' She did not stay long to argue, and left without clawing another word from me.

I hid from everyone the fiery pain within me. The other boys thought I was strong and cold, untouched by and disdainful of their taunts, but in truth I was a flabby, gasping thing, shocked and bereaved. The small cruelties of catamites could mean nothing to me, because of the immense cruelty I had suffered at the hands of love. I nursed the wounds a tiger had made, while mosquitoes buzzed around my head and lapped at my blood. I could not understand how a human being could feel as I felt. It was, after all, inhuman.

At night, alone, I indulged myself in terrible fantasies of reconciliation and vengeance. Sometimes, I imagined Akaten and myself fleeing the country, finding sanctuary in Mewt. I loved him then. At other times, I visualised Alofel realising the folly of his ways and begging my forgiveness. I would demand that Akaten be killed. And it would be done.

Occasionally, I would remember—as a memory of a memory—that time in the temple of Challis Hespereth. Was the goddess punishing me now for profaning the rite? If Akaten had not come to me there, it had been his ghost, the potential of his destructive power.

Winter was hard, and spring came slowly, but there was no rebirth within me. I received a summons from the queen, and was taken to her apartments, even though the lust for vengeance seemed futile now. Akaten was unassailable, Alofel unreachable. Mallory did not see me herself, but entrusted Orlando to interview me. To his credit, he was neither condescending nor smug, but cool and business-like. I was not a person to be envied now. He told me to be ready and that the queen would call for my assistance soon. That was all.

Returning to the boys' quarters, I realised that great wheels had begun to turn, but it was difficult to glean any satisfaction from that.

Paranoia breeds the fear of conspiracy, and once in its grip, plots and connivances are perceived everywhere. It began, quite slowly, with a single event. A village on the border of Mewt was burned. It was an inconsequential village, of no value, but its demise was a message whose meaning could not be mistaken. Rumours, and finally reports, came thick and fast after that. Mewt terrorists were making attacks on Cossic citizens. Menefer, when confronted, protested firmly he had no knowledge of these events and even promised to investigate the matter in order to quell it. Perhaps he spoke with sincerity. Perhaps it was some other force creating skirmishes among the border villages. We shall never know. I heard that Menefer was worried though. His position was not yet strong enough for revolution and war.

Then, a more serious attack occurred. One of the king's companies, collecting tithes from a remote town was ambushed. No one was killed, but all the tithes were stolen. Those who were attacked attested that their assailants wore Mewtish garb, but that their faces were concealed. Information must be leaking out from the palace. As one, all eyes turned towards the royal apartments.

Another delegation of diplomats were sent to Mewt, this time under greater guard, and the occupying army was enlarged. Menefer would be very worried now. To this point, I had not realised how deadly Mallory could be, and even believed her hand was not behind these events. I realised I must be wrong. Some of Mallory's creatures were among the delegation to Mewt. They brought back astounding news. I was not surprised that Menefer was prepared to sacrifice Akaten, but astounded that he claimed his officials had uncovered an underground resistance movement in Mewt. Akaten, apparently, was its figurehead. Documents appeared, letters that connected Akaten's name with terrorist activities taking place in Cossic territory. I have no doubt that if there were any terrorists, they didn't know a word of Mewtish. Mallory, in some way, had coerced or threatened Menefer.

The time came when Mallory's plans came to fruition. The government was convened and evidence presented. Alofel, who was present, listened to the accusations with a blank expression. His word superseded all others, but he was no fool, and would not, ultimately, risk his neck or reputation because of a lover. I wanted to keep myself in the background, and had no desire to attend the meetings, but Mallory insisted I was present. I stood behind her servants in the gallery, high above the governmental chamber.

I witnessed the moment when Alofel, defeated, ordered his guards to take Akaten into custody. Even then, the king did not falter, no shred of emotion crossed his face. I thought about how he must have assured Akaten constantly that he was safe, that the king's word would protect him. Did either of them guess who was behind it all?

My future had been wholly concentrated on revenge, but now I had achieved it, everything seemed grey and vague. I would never be Alofel's favourite again. Mallory was a cold, indifferent patron. I sent word to her, asking if she could arrange for me to be sent back to my parents' estate, but she refused. I remembered that she had once told me I might be of use to her in the future. She intended to keep me at court, just in case.

At night, I lay alone in my new bed, but could not weep. My heart condensed slowly into a kind of numbness. Men took my body, my contemporaries tormented me, but strangely, it no longer seemed to matter. I felt as if my existence had ceased, and that what lived on in my body was just a ghost, devoid of thought or feeling.

On the day of Akaten's sentencing, Mallory again insisted that I should be present. One of Orlando's underlings brought me a message. I would be collected by one of the queen's servants at the appointed hour.

Everyone met in the Hall of Judgement—I had never seen the galleries so packed with curious faces. I stood once more among Mallory's lesser staff, high on her private balcony. I felt light-headed and slightly nauseous. The chamber tilted before my eyes.

Alofel sat on his throne, surrounded by his advisers. His face looked like it was carved of stone, but I thought I could see the bewilderment and horror beneath his facade. He was wondering, as I was, how all this had happened, how it had got so out of control. Now, he had supreme power over life and death, yet no power at all. Things were expected of him. He must perform. At the end of all things, he must be king before he could be a man. The crown must take precedence over love.

Akaten was brought in, his hands bound before him. As I looked at him, a shred of emotion came back to me. For a moment, my heart seemed to squeeze itself of blood, but I forced myself not to look away. He looked small between his guards, and so thin. His hair was a dusty rag down his back. Someone read out the charges and then announced that Akaten had been found guilty of treason, of plotting against the king's life. He did not stir himself to contest these accusations. How can anyone believe it? I thought. Look at him. He's pathetic.

Then Alofel spoke: 'Akaten, the sentence of the crown is this. You will be taken from this place, unto the executioner's yard, and there offer up your life in penance for your crimes.'

Akaten raised his head then. I could not see his face, but I did not envy Alofel having to look at it. 'You are all barbarians,' Akaten said. 'You have abused me, and my people will not forget this.'

Alofel made a curt gesture with one hand. 'Take him away.'

Akaten struggled a little as the guards attempted to turn him round. Perhaps at that moment he realised he was about to die. I saw his eyes frantically scanning the gallery. I knew what he was looking for. I wanted to run but was held fast in the press of curious bodies.

Akaten saw me among the crowd. Our eyes locked. His face was that of a lunatic, without reason or feeling. He uttered a string of obscenities in Mewtish, among which I recognised my name. Then the guards began to drag him from the hall.

'Darien!' he screamed. 'You have cursed yourself! It was me in the shrine! It was me! Now you send me to my death! The goddess will not forgive you!'

I could not move. Mallory's people all looked at me with interest, perhaps expecting me to make some last retort. But I could do nothing. Mallory, leaning forward in her seat at the front of the balcony, did not even turn her head to glance at me.

The echo of Akaten's wails resounded around the chamber for several minutes. Alofel stared at the doors through which he'd passed. I realised then that within minutes the person I loved beyond all others would be dead. The axe would fall. His perfect head would be severed from his body. I could not bear it.

The pieces of the body would be shipped back to Mewt. I wandered around in a daze, barely able to recognise face that I knew. Even the boys kept their distance from me, watching me with morbid interest, but realising the sport of taunting me would no longer satisfy them. I was broken now,

truly broken, not even allowed the dignity of retreat. The palace, which I
had loved, became the realm of hell.

One day, Porfarryah sought me out. Perhaps she felt concern for me,
or like all the others, only curiosity. 'You should have poisoned him when
you had the chance,' she said.

'Yes...' I sighed.

'I can't bear this,' she said.

I glanced at her. 'It could easily have been you.'

'I know.'

So she visited me regularly, attempting to revive the friendship we had
once had. I think she was superstitious about what had happened to me,
and sought to appease the gods by trying to help me. But she could not. I
no longer had the strength even to appreciate her gesture.

Some weeks after Akaten's execution, I asked permission from the keeper
of the harem to visit Phasmagore. I needed the solace of the temple, the
quiet wisdom of the priestesses, and did not intend to visit the inner chambers. Porfarryah accompanied me and we went to make offerings in one of
the shrines together, a gift of twisted flowers laid upon an altar. Tourists
thronged around us. I stared at the inscrutable countenance of the goddess,
robed and chaste in her nimbus of incense, and said to Porfarryah, 'I have to
go to the Shrine of Bestowing.'

She looked at me anxiously. 'Darien, wait. Leave it a while.'

I shook my head. 'No. Now.'

'I will wait at the portal for you,' she said.

When I entered into the tunnel of veils at the entrance to the shrine, it
was as if I'd stepped back in time. Dreamily, I hoped that by doing this, I
could somehow erase all that had happened over the last few months. When
I came out again, I would find myself in early summer, and Akaten would
just have arrived at the palace.

It seemed that it was the same priestess sitting fanning herself with a
palm frond in the antechamber. She gave me the pastille and I swallowed
it. Everything happened just the same. I went out into the darkness,
swallowed by the thick shrouds of scented smoke. I found myself face to
face with the naked goddess, who gestured for me to pass onwards. I went
into a small chamber and sat there upon the cushions, waiting for the one
who would come to me.

A shape appeared in the doorway, limned against the light. All around
me, a thousand panels slid back in the walls. He came towards me and I
stood up. Yes, it was happening, the magic of the shrine was working. I

held out my arms to him, murmured his name. *Come to me, come to me.* He did so.

I could only see his eyes, which were lit by a band of light. 'Darien,' he said. 'Don't you know that I will always be here waiting for you.'

I took his face in my hands. 'Beloved. Peace.'

I leaned forward to kiss him, but he crumpled before me. I was confused, for I still held his head between my hands. Then I realised. A body lay at my feet, its severed neck gouting blood. I held only a head in my hands, a head whose mouth murmured, 'Kiss me, Darien, kiss me!'

I began to scream, and flung the head away from me. It hit the wall and then rolled across the floor, its accusing eyes still staring up into my face. 'But you love me,' it said.

I remember nothing more.

That was three years ago. The severe decline I suffered after my visit to the shrine meant that I could no longer live at court. Visiting dignitaries had no desire to bed a gibbering lunatic, even if he had once been the favourite of the king. The keeper of the harem, who had some mercy, arranged for me to be cared for in a monastery, in the hills above Tarnax. I was ill for a long time, and my sanity returned to me only slowly. I was hidden away, an embarrassment, forgotten by all. I was lucky. Yes. I could have lived out my days in the palace as a shunned nobody, an outcast. Here, at least, I have found a kind of peace.

These days, I think to myself, *but I am still a young man.* Is this all my life is to be? I could run away, no one would stop me, but where to?

Now, I work as a servant in the garden and the kitchens of the monastery. It suits me, for I do not need to talk to anyone except to discuss my duties. The monks are kind, but they know I am not like them. I have no faith. Challis Hespereth chose to champion Akaten; me she despises. Some weeks ago, I spoke to the Abbot here, and told him my story. I needed his opinion. He nodded slowly, then told me that he believed I had hallucinated in the shrine, my guilt and fear had driven me insane. I know this is probably correct, but another, less rational part of me still doubts. Throughout my relationship with Akaten, I had wanted to know whether or not he'd been the one who'd come to me in the shrine, and only at the end did he admit to it, when it was too late.

Or perhaps that was a lie.

Yesterday, I went down to the city for only the second time since I began my retreat here. I went to the market to shop for spices, and there walked among the people, envious of their lives. There is a well there, right in the middle of all the busy stalls. I was thirsty and walked up to it. A man was standing beside it, drinking from the metal cup that the well-tender had given him. My heart convulsed. At that precise moment, the man noticed me. Our eyes met, and I saw the shock in his expression.

He could not have been much older than myself. His skin was tawny-gold, and his long hair hung nearly to his thighs, confined at his neck.

We knew each other instantly. It was not Akaten. This man looked nothing like him. I realise that now.

What happens within the temple is sacred and secret, not be discussed once the devotions are completed. We must forget what happens there. But still, I may return to the market soon, and he will be there, waiting. I know it.

Spinning for Gold

This story is the first of a sequence I wrote for a gay male friend of mine while I was still creating the first Wraeththu book 'The Enchantments of Flesh and Spirit'. My friend was feeling low at the time, so I wrote these pieces to cheer him up. They are retellings of old fairy stories, with a gay theme, this one being my interpretation of 'Rumpelstiltskin'. In folklore, you acquire power over supernatural creatures, in particular goblins and fairies, when you learn their true names. Another version of this story can be found in the Scottish folk tale, 'Whoopity Stoorie'.

'Spinning for Gold,' is set in the land of Cos, and its king is called Ashalan, as he is in the Magravandias trilogy, but this is a distant ancestor of that character. If the Magravandias stories are set in an Alternate Victorian Age, then these fairy tales are in the Medieval Age of that world.

This story and its two 'sequels', 'The Nothing Child' and 'Living with the Angel', can be seen as different chapters of the same tale.

In the land of Cos, many years ago, an important master miller lived beside a deep-flowing river. Widowed when his two children were very young, he had acquired along with his wealth a tendency to drink and gamble rather more than was advisable. So much so, that quite often, his son, Jadrin, and his daughter, Amberina, would lie trembling in their beds at night, waiting for the drunken homecoming of their father, for it was not unknown for him to behave irrationally under the influence of liquor. Sometimes, frenzied at not being able to find the whereabouts of his pipe or tobacco pouch, he would attack the furniture and even any household pets or servants who were too slow to move from his path. Having said that, however, he was not on the whole a cruel father. To be fair, his faults were merely the children of his grief, which had never healed completely, and in the faces of his son and daughter, he could often see the eyes of his dead, beautiful wife looking back at him; he loved the children passionately. Because of this, Amberina and Jadrin led a sheltered, luxurious life, which in creatures of weaker character would have led to them being altogether spoiled and petulant. Amberina and Jadrin, however, were gentle, kindly souls, without any evil temperament. Quite content in each other's company, the siblings spent most of their time in the great forest on the east side of the River Fleercut, or else scampering over the rolling, bosomy hills to the west, beyond which lay Ashbrilim, the city of the king; a place where they had never ventured.

Alike as twins, even though two years separated their births, they had both inherited their mother's dark, midnight hair and lustrous eyes. Visitors to the mill-house commented on their beauty to their father, although those of more sensitive nature could sometimes not easily repress an eerie shudder whilst looking into those fathomless eyes and forest-wise faces. Friends of the miller might comment to each other, over mugs of ale, in taverns far from the mill-house, that all was not right with the miller's children.

'They spend too much time out in the moonlight,' one might say, as if to explain their white, white skin.

'And too much time in the forest.' another might add, as if to explain their mossy hair and shadowed smiles.

Sometimes, in an attempt to bring Amberina and Jadrin out into the real world, some well-intentioned neighbour might send their own children to encourage the miller's progeny to enjoy more natural childish pastimes, but the other children always went home fearful and anxious. If their parents should question them, wondering if the miller's children had deliberately frightened them, they would always answer no. Amberina and Jadrin, though strangely distant, were always polite and friendly to visitors, leading them into the forest glades and weaving their hair with flowers. No, it was not fear exactly. The children could never explain exactly what it was that made sleep come with difficulty for several nights after a visit to the mill.

It was early summer and Jadrin had just celebrated his sixteenth birthday. Soon Amberina would be fourteen years old. Their birthdays were very close together, both born under the sign of the moon and the water. After a large and cheerful tea-time, enjoyed only with the servants (as the miller had been gone to the city for some days,) the two youngsters went hand in hand, down to the reedy edge of the river, some yards south of the tall, lichened mill-house, where the stream widened into a deep, dark pool overhung with waving willows. They knelt down in the soft, damp earth and gazed into the water, not yet brilliant with the reflection of stars, but lazily roiling, dark as if with unspoken secrets. Jadrin sighed and leaned out over the pool. Amberina moved quickly to untie his hair from the black ribbon at the back of his neck, so that the raven waves, like water itself, fell to kiss the surface of the pool, floating out like weed into the dusk. 'I feel a strange heaviness about me,' Jadrin murmured in a soft, sad voice.

'It is only your own hair floating in the stream,' Amberina answered, mischievously.

'No,' her brother replied, looking up and turning to face the hills behind which the sun was still sinking in a blaze of rich colours. 'It comes from that way, I think.' He pointed.

'Then it is probably just our father coming home from Ashbrilim,' Amberina said. 'Perhaps he will be drunk again and have lost all the money he earned in the city.' They both looked at the huge, solid walls of the mill-house rising from the river upstream; as if fearful it might crumble to dust in an instant.

Jadrin sighed again. 'No, I don't think it is that either.'

'You are growing old, my brother!' Amberina sang and jumped up to dance in the pale owl-light, looking almost like the ghost of her mother; all floating white linen and midnight hair.

Jadrin smiled at her wistfully, but he could not share her joy. He gazed deep into the trees across the river, but could find no comfort in them either. After a moment, he stood up. 'I think I shall go back to the house,' he said.

His sister looked surprised. She held out her hand. 'Won't you come to the deepest, darkest glade with me?' she asked. 'The white deer gather there tonight. Perhaps they shall speak our fortunes.'

Jadrin could not tell his sister that he was no longer sure he wanted to hear his fortune, although it had been their custom to go to this place every year on his birthday. Once the deer had intimated where to find an egg-shaped quartz of power under the bank of the river. Sometimes, when the children gazed into it, they could see the lights of the city glowing within, the tall towers of Ashbrilim and the white road that led to it.

Now Jadrin shook his head and put up his hand in negation. 'I have to think,' he said and walked away from Amberina, soon lost in the half-light.

As he was climbing the bank up to the house, it happened that his father's valet, Tufkin, came down the path towards him. 'Be quick, master Jadrin,' he said, 'your father has sent me to find you.'

'Is all well at the house?' Jadrin enquired, noting the servant's worried mien. Perhaps Amberina hadn't been far from the truth in her conjecture about their father's financial affairs.

'The house still stands, aye!' Tufkin replied dryly, jerking his head towards the thick, grey walls. 'Come along.'

Jadrin followed him.

If he supposed to find his father still reeling, red-eyed from the effects of last night's drinking, Jadrin was wrong. Skimblaze the miller stood sober and erect, leaning against the stout wooden table in the kitchen of the mill-house. Jadrin noticed immediately the suppression of a cunning glance steal across his father's face. All was not well. He waited for Skimblaze to speak. The miller made several anguished noises, before turning his back on his son and saying, 'The time has come, Jadrin, for you to go to the city.'

Cool as mint, the boy replied, 'The time has come? I had no idea it would ever be due!'

'Come, come, you are nearly a man, Jadrin. What kind of education is it for you paddling about in the river and having only a little girl for a companion?'

'But why haven't you told me of this before?' Jadrin sat down. In his heart, he could feel a shred of guilt, a shred of deception, winging its way about the room like a baleful spirit. He had no desire at all to leave the riverside, the forest, or his sister, his only friend.

Skimblaze cleared his throat.'You need to learn more about life, my lad. One day all this will be passed onto you and I want to give it to a whole person, not some half-fairy changeling! You need your feet bringing down to earth.'

'You can't make me go!' Jadrin cried. He had never spoken out against his father before. 'I will hate it!'

'You're going, my boy! You're going! Tomorrow, and that's an end to it!'

'Tomorrow?' Jadrin murmured in bewilderment. 'Is Amberina to accompany me?' He asked this without much hope.

Skimblaze cast a quick, furtive glance over his shoulder. 'No. Amberina is too young. Come now, don't give me that face. You will learn to enjoy it. Travel is good for the soul. Run along now, you'd better start packing your things.' Skimblaze faced the window once more, looking out at the gently sloping bank. Perhaps he could see a faint suggestion of his lovely daughter down there, dancing lightly through the dusk, her mind far from cities and partings. Still Skimblaze could not fully face his son.

'Where am I to go?' the boy asked, in a small, husky voice.

'To the court. I've secured a place for you there. You're from a good family. Do you think I'd let you go if it was to anywhere else?'

'Have you been arranging this these last few days?'

There was a moment's silence. 'Yes,' Skimblaze said.

Jadrin climbed the curling, creaking stairs to the room he called his own. At the summit of the house, it had the smallest windows, all of ruby glass. It also felt near to the heart of the mill. Lying in bed at night, Jadrin could sense the great wooden machinery, turning, turning. The wall nearest to it, where he kept his bed, was always warm. Jadrin opened the window and gazed mournfully out over his beloved countryside. Half-heartedly, he threw a few belongings into a bag and then sat down on his bed, head in hands. He had no idea why his father should suddenly force such a thing on him, but he couldn't help suspecting the reason behind it might be connected with Skimblaze's weaknesses for good liquor and gambling for high stakes. He felt uncharitable thinking that, but the idea would not leave him. Jadrin shuddered. He was inexperienced and young, but as he watched the rising moon appear in the velvet sky beyond his window, as the wood cooled and creaked in the late evening, it could be seen, by looking at his eyes, that Jadrin would not be totally helpless out there in the unknown world.

In the morning, accompanied by Tufkin, Jadrin bid a mournful farewell to Amberina. As he leaned down from his horse, she placed a garland of woodland flowers about his neck, and offered him a velvet bag. 'Here is half of the quartz we found,' said she. 'I have the other. Guard it well, my brother, for it may help you in the world.'

Jadrin smiled and kissed the top of her dark head, already feeling a hundred years older than she. Then he lifted his horse's head with a swift command and glanced coldly at the mill-house door before cantering quickly off towards the west, Tufkin behind him.

In the doorway to the mill, Skimblaze drained the glass he held, grimaced, went back into the house and slammed the door behind him.

Amberina looked in at the kitchen window 'Why are you doing this father?' she asked.

Skimblaze sat upright in his chair, reached across the table for another mug of wine. 'You have magic, both of you,' he said, as if in explanation. 'Skills beyond the mortal man. I'm right. I know I'm right...'

Amberina shut the window without another word and went down to the river-pool. In the still, morning water, she could see an image of Jadrin riding towards Ashbrilim, his head held high like a prince.

The palace of the king stood upon a high hill at the heart of Ashbrilim. Jadrin and Tufkin rode right up to the palace gate, which were three times the height of a man, where Tufkin presented the letter he carried from Skimblaze. Eyeing Jadrin stonily, the guards let them pass through. Rarely having left his country home, Jadrin was amazed by the sights he beheld. Such opulence! The noise overwhelmed him, the bustle, the smells. He caught sight of willowy figures in splendid clothes leaning over balconies above the yard they crossed. One or two fingers pointed; he heard a stifled

laugh. It was late afternoon and the walls of all the courtyards were afire
with blooming vines beginning to release their heady, evening scent into
the air. Tufkin paused to ask directions and dogs ran between the horses'
legs as they found their way into the stableyard. Jadrin looked around,
wide-eyed, studying all the day's-end tasks being completed in noisy jovi-
ality by the well-fed servants of the king.

A tall, gaunt man in dark, voluminous clothes ducked away from a
forkful of yellow hay carelessly held aloft by a passing stable-boy, waving
away the almost disrespectfully cheerful apology. Jadrin realised the gaunt
man was heading in their direction.

'You are the miller's people?' the man asked and with a nod, Tufkin
handed him Skimblaze's letter. The man smiled. 'Ah yes,' he said, looking
up at Jadrin. 'Allow me to introduce myself. I am Galbion Floom, King
Ashalan's secretary.'

Jadrin responded politely. He and Tufkin dismounted and their horses
were led away to the stables. 'Now, boy, if you would follow me please,'
Floom instructed, indicating the way with his hand. Jadrin looked around.
Tufkin was hanging back.

'Am I to go alone?' Jadrin asked.

'It is not my place to follow,' Tufkin replied edgily, stepping backwards. 'I'll just take a tankard of ale in the servants' quarters.'

Shrugging, Jadrin curled his hand more tightly around the velvet bag
that hung from his neck on a cord, and followed the gaunt man through a
dark doorway. In silence they began to climb a winding staircase. They
climbed and climbed. Soon, it seemed, the bustle of the courtyard was left
far behind and they had entered a sleeping, ensorcelled place, deep in the
core of the palace. Jadrin's guide did not speak. They walked down long,
dusty corridors, silent but lit by bars of golden evening sunlight fighting
its way through dusty glass. More stairs.

'Is it much farther, sir?' Jadrin asked, wondering what desolate spot a
miller's son (no matter how affluent) would be given in the palace of a
king.

'No, my boy. We are here.'

Before them was an ancient, iron-studded door. Galbion Floom struggled with the heavy metal latch.

No one has come here for a while, Jadrin thought with a not altogether
unpleasant thrill of dread.

Floom had managed to open the door and was now fastidiously wiping
his hands on a large handkerchief. Without a word, Jadrin walked past
him and into the room beyond. He dropped his bag onto the floor and

dust lazily raised itself and eddied round his feet. He was in a high-ceilinged chamber, a gloomy place. The sole window was narrow and far above Jadrin's head. Only a little of the evening sunlight came down onto the wooden floor, fighting through shrouds of cobwebs and dust. 'Well!' Jadrin said, half amused, half aghast. In the shadows, he could see a mean, narrow bed, a washstand and, of all things, a spinning-wheel. Whatever else the room might contain was hidden in the darkest corners, except for several neatly twined bales of straw, which had been placed just inside the door. Jadrin looked at these askance and said, 'Well!' again. Was this some kind of joke? Was he expected to bed down in straw like an animal?

'Am I to live here?' Jadrin asked, unable to hide the dismay from his voice.

'For the time being.'

Jadrin shook his head. Dismay gave way to anger. Surely he could not be treated like this. His father's animals lived in stables more comfortable and cleaner than this.

'And are all your guests accommodated in rooms of this type?' he couldn't help asking.

There was a moment's pause before Floom said, 'You do know why you are here, of course?'

Jadrin looked at him blankly. 'I don't believe I do.'

'You are Jadrin, the miller Skimblaze's son?'

'Yes.'

Floom stroked his chin. 'And you are, as he claimed, something of a... wonder worker?'

'What do you mean?'

'A magician,' the man said irritably. 'That was the terms, I think.'

'Terms? Magician? I think you'd better explain.' Jadrin, on the whole, was a stranger to anger. Now his indignation was tinged with fear.

The gaunt man bowed, stiffly, smiling widely. 'Oh, forgive me!' he exclaimed. 'It was understood your father would have explained all this to you; the *circumstances* of your being here.'

Jadrin remained silent, numb with the horror of betrayal.

'Obviously not,' Floom continued with a sigh. He stepped over the threshold and pushed the door closed a little. 'Several nights ago, your father was involved in a... little wager. He played the king in a game of dice, making outrageous claims concerning his luck, which sadly for him, proved to be unfounded. The stakes were high. King Ashalan does not play for trinkets. Debts were incurred and subsequently, agreements reached. Your father lost everything, even the mill itself. But Ashalan is

not a harsh man. They came to an arrangement between them. The agreement was that you should come to Ashbrilim to meet your father's debts.'

'He was drunk,' Jadrin said bitterly.

Floom shrugged. 'Wine had flowed, I believe. Don't look so forlorn,
boy. I must say, the first thing your father said about you is true; you are
one of the loveliest creatures on God's earth. The other, well, that remains
to be seen, doesn't it!'

'What do you mean?' Jadrin cried. 'What else did he say?'

'No idea at all, my lad?'

Jadrin shook his head fiercely, sick with fear at what his drunken father
might have come out with.

'He thinks you can clear his debt for him. He says you have magical
powers, so great, so potent, that you can even spin straw into gold.'

Jadrin could not stifle a surprised bark of laughter. 'What?'

'Use your magic, boy! Spin your father's way out of debt, as he claims
you can. Spin this, all this, to gold!' His face creased into a caustic grin,
Galbion Floom gestured eloquently at the straw by their feet.

To spin straw into gold? Jadrin was left alone, the door firmly locked
behind him. How could his father do this to him? he wondered with
helpless dismay. Was this the education he had promised? Did Skimblaze
really think his son was the possessor of supernatural powers? No, Jadrin
decided. He suspected that Skimblaze had merely sent him to the king,
hoping (perhaps certain?) that Ashalan would be content with his beauty
alone. Surely, all this business with the straw and the spinning wheel was
some dark joke on Ashalan's part, so that when Jadrin could not complete
the task some other, more tangible, form of payment would be demanded.
This much was obvious to Jadrin, even with his limited knowledge of the
ways of men and their desires. The spinning wheel stood in a diminishing
pool of sunlight, its wheel gently rocking as if moved by an unseen hand.
Jadrin reached out and touched it. He shook his head and sat down on the
bed to wait.

Night fell. Nobody came to his door and silver fronds of moonlight
came to replace those of the sinking sun, falling over the floor, over the
skeletal form of the spinning wheel, onto Jadrin's bed. The boy sighed,
stood up and walked around the room. In a corner, he found bread and
cheese laid upon a low table next to a jug of red wine. He found a lamp and
a tinderbox. Lighting the lamp, he took some wine and began to eat the
bread and cheese. For comfort, he removed from its bag the quartz Amberina
had given to him and stared at the sharp lilac points of it, the hollow in its

centre that shivered with the brightest threads. 'Straw into gold indeed!'
he thought. 'No one, nothing, can do that. Oh Amberina, if only you
were here now.' Dismally, he breathed on the stone, thinking of Amberina
prancing, colt-like, beside the Fleercut; free as freedom itself. He felt so
alone. Straw into gold...

A shadow fell over him. Something obscured the moonlight from the
window, something that also caused the lamplight to flicker and dim. Jadrin
looked up.

'Faithless boy! I can do that!' said a voice.

Jadrin squinted at the cobwebby ledge. A spirit was crouching there,
almost featureless within a smoky veil. It hopped from the window ledge
to the floor, leaving a trail of sparkling dust in the air behind it.

Jadrin had seen spirits before. He was not afraid. 'You can spin straw
into gold?' He indicated the forlorn-looking spinning wheel across the
room.

'But of course... For a price.'

Jadrin inspected the quartz warily. Had his contemplation of it summoned the spirit? He knew the potential power of crystals. Obviously,
this particular one possessed powers he and his sister had been unaware of.
'A price. Such as?'

The spirit cavorted around in front of him for a moment, emitting
blushes of colour that made Jadrin's eyes ache. 'Something precious,' it
said.

Jadrin held out the quartz. 'This is all I have.'

The spirit glowed pink. 'No! Something more precious that that.'

'Name it.'

'I want a kiss. A kiss from your warm, warm lips. A taste of life.' The
spirit chittered and glowed and spun until the whole room was lit up like
a firework display.

'Oh, is that all?' Jadrin replied guardedly, well aware of how the very
life could be sucked from a person under the guise of a kiss.

'Just that. Nothing more. Oh, you think badly of me. You fear I will
harm you. I won't! I won't!' Its voice took on a sly tone. 'The king will
ask for more, believe me.'

Jadrin considered for a moment, looking from the quartz to the wavering form of the spirit. He felt he had little to lose. 'Very well,' he said.
'Maybe, if you can do this thing, the king will be content with gold alone,
and I can go home again. It will be a fine joke, in fact. Go ahead.'

'After you sleep,' the spirit said.

'As you wish.' Still suspicious, Jadrin went over to the narrow bed and

lay down upon it. After a few moments, his eyes became heavy and sleep
crept upon him, but not before it seemed, behind his closed lids, the whole
room became radiant as if with the lustre of gold.

In the grey before the dawn, the spirit woke him up. Beyond its pale,
gauzy body, Jadrin could see a glittering, unbelievable heap of coins piled
upon the floor around the spinning wheel. 'Now for my price,' said the
spirit, in a low, chilling voice.

Jadrin offered up his mouth for the cold, cold touch of bodiless lips,
dry as paper yet wet as grave-slime. He gasped, fighting for breath. In a
moment, the spirit leapt, triumphant, into the air, whirled around a few
times and vanished with a pop. Jadrin lay dazed upon the bed until the
morning truly came.

First, it was Galbion Floom who looked in at the peephole of the door.
Jadrin heard a gasp, then running footsteps. Soon, there was a babble
beyond the door and it was thrown wide, many brightly dressed people
bursting into the room, all talking at once. Jadrin sat up on the bed yawning. A tall young man with golden hair shouldered his way through the
chattering crowd and stared, wide-eyed, at the heaps of gold. 'What is
this?' he demanded.

'Look, sire!' Floom spluttered. 'The scoundrel Skimblaze spoke the
truth for once. The boy can spin straw into gold!'

Ashalan, king of Ashbrilim, reluctantly tore his gaze away from the
shining heaps of coins and saw, for the first, the shining thing upon the
narrow bed, whose radiance easily eclipsed that of the treasure.

'Indeed he did,' the king agreed, but in a strange and guarded tone.
He strode forward. 'Miller's son, I am most impressed by what I have seen.
Surprised too, for I thought it was you yourself that Skimblaze had in mind
to pay the debt he owed me. I did not, for one moment, really believe you
could accomplish this magic.'

Jadrin thought, 'And neither did I,' but considered it wiser to remain
silent.

Ashalan eyed the gold once more. 'However,' he said. 'Beauty does
not deceive me, neither do I always trust the evidence of my own eyes.
This may well be a fairy gold that turns to leaves within hours, or perhaps
a single spell that you and your father have worked out between you. No,
I must have more proof.' He strode to the door. His cronies shrank back,
allowing him to speak with his secretary. 'Bring more straw!' Ashalan
ordered and left the room without a backward glance.

Jadrin was in despair. Now the lonely chamber was piled high with bursting bales of straw, the spinning wheel nearly lost amongst it. All day, he sat on the bed with his chin in his hands, staring miserably at the straw. At nightfall, he took out the quartz from its bag, but without hope that he could be so fortunate twice. However, within an instant of his forming the thought, the spirit returned, once more nonchalant about the task in hand. 'And what price this time?' Jadrin enquired wearily.

'Well, that is simple. Merely this: to sleep in your arms,' it replied.

'Just that?' Jadrin asked.

'Just that,' the spirit answered.

By morning, the room was full of gold once more and Jadrin awoke feeling as drugged and chilled as if he'd spent the night under several feet of snow. He had not sensed the spirit beside him, neither did he see it leave.

To Jadrin, it seemed that Ashalan's greed was only whipped into further frenzy when he caught sight of the supposed fruits of the boy's night's work. 'Once more,' he decided (without much consideration). 'One more night of this and, I promise you, you shall never see this room again. No more spinning. It is too incredible, this talent of yours. Tomorrow, I shall make you a gentleman of the court. You shall have apartments of your own within the palace, whatever you require...'

Jadrin thought Ashalan had already had ten times as much gold as Skimblaze could have owed him. No doubt he wants to keep me around to make further use of my magical abilities later on, he thought cynically, for not once while he was speaking did Ashalan's eyes stray from the gold to Jadrin himself.

By dusk, hardly even able to find a space within the room in which to sit, Jadrin was desperate to call up the spirit again. Punctual, it materialised upon the windowsill as usual, preening its slim, glowing features with languid paws.

'Well, as you see,' Jadrin began, gesturing round the room, 'I begin to doubt whether you could ever spin enough gold to satisfy him.'

The spirit made a nonchalant gesture. 'Hmm. It would seem that way... Do you want to remain here at court, Jadrin?'

Jadrin shook his head. 'No, not really, but I can hardly go against the wishes of the king, can I?'

'Even after he has used you in this way?'

Jadrin paused for a moment to think. 'I have no choice. I doubt if my father would welcome me back if I ran away and where else could I go?'

'Oh, you are a foolish boy!' the spirit cried, as if glad of the fact, hopping to the floor, dancing in the pale rays of the moon. 'And do you wish for me to spin?'

'If you will first tell me the price this time.'

For a moment, poised as if at the brink of ultimate triumph, the shivery being glided from bale to bale, appearing to be seriously contemplating the matter.

'Mmm,' it murmured at length. 'I predict that, should I complete this task for you, the king will make you a celebrity of the court...'

'This much has been promised me, yes,' Jadrin interrupted, somewhat impatiently.

'After a while,' the spirit continued, unperturbed, 'Ashalan shall actually let himself see you. He is not a great lover of women. Perhaps this was why your father sent you here instead of your sister.'

'She is too young,' Jadrin said, wondering at the same time how the spirit knew so much of his circumstances.

The spirit shook its head. 'You are wrong. Where the lusts of the powerful are concerned, no creature is too young!'

Jadrin could sense in the spirit's words its great scorn of humankind, Ashalankind in particular.

'What is your price, then?' he asked irritably.

'The king will come to desire you,' it answered. 'I expect he will fight it for he is afraid of love and mistrusts beautiful things, but my price is that should do your best to encourage him and, when the time comes, submit to his desires. On the night that you go to his bed, you will allow me to enter your soul...'

'For what purpose?' Jadrin cried, aghast at all he had heard.

'That is not your concern.'

'But what will happen to me?'

'You will not be harmed. You will remember nothing. Agree now: yes or no? I can hear my brethren calling me from the starshine. I have little time to linger here.'

'One thing you must tell me,' Jadrin said quickly, half standing up. 'Do you intend to do the king harm?'

The spirit glowed a bright, aching white, intense as the heart of a star. 'And what do you care of that?' it asked.

Jadrin shrugged. 'I don't feel I can be part of a plot to harm anyone. It is wrong.'

The spirit spat out a stream of green sparks, which made the air smell of sulphur. 'Jadrin, he will have you and use you, as he does with all whom he desires. You are nothing to him. He would kill you as soon as look at you if you displease him. My purpose is not your concern and you must put it from your mind. I dare say, when the time comes, you'll welcome what will happen. If you are afraid that I will kill him, then fear no more. I will not, but there are things that must be done and you will help me do them.'

Then the spinning wheel began to turn, throwing off sparks of a hundred colours, like fireworks, and thundering like a galloping horse. 'Yes or no, miller's son? In the morning, if there is no more gold, you risk Ashalan taking your life to sate his monstrous greed. His moods change like clouds. He is mad and you are at risk.' The wheel spun and sang. 'Yes or no?'

Jadrin hung his head. His eyes felt hot with shame. 'Yes,' he said, and, looking up, added, 'Do it. Make the gold. I will do as you ask.'

In the morning, the great heavy door to the room was flung wide and golden coins spilled out around Ashalan's feet as he stood at the threshold. Golden light suffused his face, his long, braided hair; and Jadrin, sitting on his bed, considered that there was a certain innocence playing around the king's features. He is like a child presented with a new toy, Jadrin thought.

'Boy, you are a true magician!' Ashalan exclaimed, and ordered that all the gold should be taken to his treasury, which lay deep beneath the palace. As for Jadrin, he was led bewildered into the sunlit courtyard, where all the colourful ladies and gentlemen of the court cheered him and threw down petals to land on his hair and clothes. Jadrin held the piece of quartz tightly in its velvet bag and could not speak. He could only think of the bargain he had made and when it must come to fruition.

He was given rooms with marble floors, where curtains of heavy silk fell to the floor before the windows, and beyond them, terraces of patterned tiles overlooked the gardens and lake. He was given servants of his own to tend him, who quietly awoke him in the morning and led him to a cool bathroom to douse his skin with fragrant water, spiced with cleansing herbs. A large bird with feathers the colour of green metal lived in a cage hanging from the ceiling of his living-room and sang to him in a lilting, almost human voice.

For the first week, Jadrin was utterly dazed by all this. The food his servants brought him was richer than anything he'd ever tasted, but he could not eat. One mouthful of wine sent his senses reeling, so he lived for that time on mineral water flavoured with fruit juice, taking a small glass of warmed ewe's milk at bedtime. He did not leave his suite of rooms at all. However, this only served to aggravate the curiosity of the court, so that Jadrin was visited daily by the arrogant and elegant, the softly-spoken and seductive, all seeking to court his favour, to add him to their list of satellites. Shining people with shining names, who brought him presents, who squeezed his limbs with sharp fingers and calculating eyes, praising his talent and beauty. Of Ashalan and his immediate staff, Jadrin saw nothing. People spoke of the king, dropping his name to impress, speaking of the soirees and musical evenings in Ashalan's apartments to which only the most fashionable could hope for an invitation. Silent and awed, Jadrin could only watch these tall, affected beings strut or lounge around his rooms, feeling that he could never hope to emulate their sophistication. It seemed to him that the spirit's price would never have to be paid. He would never be drawn into the elite, exclusive circle of King Ashalan's intimate companions.

Eventually, thinking Jadrin a true adept, several ladies of the court came to ask him whether he would weave spells for them. They spoke behind concealing hands of ineffable slimness and languor, complaining of lovesickness or being the victims of envy. Some gentlemen came also, begging Jadrin to scry their futures, worried about their incomes, their wives, lovers and rivals. But, if Jadrin knew magic at all, he knew only the magic of the earth, the water, the forest. The courtiers' troubles meant little to him and he knew no spells to deal with them. However, willing to help in whatever way he could, Jadrin sat and listened, made soothing noises, and at the end of it, offered the only advice he knew. Something that had always worked for him and which he considered ample medicine for any injured soul. He spoke of the quietness of the forest, where all mundane problems lose their sting, even their form. 'Go into the trees,' he said, 'And take off your finery. Crawl down amongst the great roots and smell the earth there. Lie down beside the forest pools. Forget the city, forget who you are and breathe in the freshness. In the peace that follows, the solution to your problems may come to you.'

The palace folk were usually somewhat taken aback by this advice, but those of them who were not too lazy to take heed of it, did as he told them. Unfortunately, the forest is a dangerous place for pampered souls who are not used to it: dangerous to the body and the mind. Of the ten people who sought Jadrin's advice, three came back to talk to him again, eager to share their enlightenment, five came back to the city angry and bedraggled, having experienced nothing except discomfort, and in one case a severe chill, whilst two, a particularly dizzy pair of ladies, never came back at all. It all caused rather a controversy. Inevitably, because of this, Jadrin acquired a staunch following of supporters on the one hand and a bitterly venomous gang of enemies on the other. Rumours sprang up like fire. Jadrin was a necromancer. Jadrin was a devil. Jadrin was a saint. It could all have got ridiculously out of hand. Jadrin himself knew nothing of these rumours, locked as he was without friend or confidante in his rooms. Eventually, Ashalan himself was forced to investigate the matter.

Jadrin was summoned to the king's apartments. He went there dressed in black and bound up his hair so as to appear courtly and civilised. There was a painful, fearful beat in his chest as he followed Ashalan's servant into a small salon, where the king received visitors every morning. He sat down as he was bidden at the king's feet and Ashalan said to him, 'You must not do these things, boy.'

'Do what, sire?' he asked, in total innocence, confused as to how he'd misbehaved.

The king sighed thoughtfully. 'The people here are not like you, Jadrin. What is right for you can actually harm them, because they do not have your strength. I know that some have sought your advice, and from what I have heard, the advice you gave them was straightforward enough, and little to do with magic, but they cannot understand it, you see. And what they cannot understand will never help them. What they desire is for you to speak a few words of mumbo-jumbo over a burning censer that will make everything right for them.'

'I cannot do that, sire,' Jadrin said, with lowered eyes and lowered voice.

The king leaned forward and lifted Jadrin's chin with his hands. 'I can see that,' he said gently.

Jadrin thought: he is wiser than I imagined. He smiled gratefully and, from that moment, victim of one of the most intense magicks known on Earth, Ashalan the king lost his heart to him.

'Let us speak together,' Ashalan said. 'I have troubles of my own. Is your advice to me to lie down naked in the wild forest? Shall I find myself there, perhaps?'

Jadrin detected a note of good-humoured mockery. 'I would have thought, my lord, that you would find yourself best in the presence of all your gold,' he said boldly.

The king laughed. 'Maybe,' he said. 'After all, gold can be trusted. Its beauty never fades, neither can it become fickle...'

'But it is cold,' Jadrin said.

'True,' Ashalan agreed, 'but at least it is an obvious cold and far less chilling than the coldness that may be hidden within a human frame.'

'Then go to the forest. Take your gold with you. All of it. Lie down there with all the shining cold treasures. Eventually, you shall die, but if gold is all that you desire from life, then at least you shall die happy.'

Ashalan clearly still found this boldness amusing. 'I have heard that true magic is nothing but pure and naked truth,' he said. 'Your words convince me further. You are an artless child and yet a creature versed in wisdom. I think I shall seek your advice more often.' Laughing, he called in his secretary and ordered that refreshment be brought to them, wine and sherbets. 'Tell me of the forest,' he said and Jadrin sat at his feet and told him. 'Your words must be saved for me alone,' Ashalan instructed, 'You do not have to advise any of the pampered hens around here any more. That is my word and you must obey it.'

Wary in the soft but strengthening grip of a new feeling, Jadrin gave his word that he would.

Perhaps more subtle in the ways of love than those of accruing treasures, Ashalan courted Jadrin discretely. So discretely that Jadrin hardly even noticed it was happening. The occasional brush of fingers, the glances that lingered just a second too long: all of this the gentle but compelling language of desire. Most days, Ashalan would summon Jadrin to his apartments in the late afternoon when they would sip cordials and speak together of countless different things. Maybe the king was surprised by Jadrin's lack of knowledge in so many subjects, perhaps delighted by his innocence. Jadrin would listen, spellbound, as Ashalan spoke of far-flung corners of his kingdom. He learned about the Hell Mountains of Gashalore, those heartless crags inimical to humanity that smoked incessantly and vomited caustic showers of black ash. Reptiles with poisonous skin dwelt among the rocks, and basked in the steaming waters of the Lake of Insidious Sleep, whose toxic shores were forever wreathed in yellow fog. Jadrin, familiar only with the benign forests and hills of his childhood, was thrilled to learn of these dangerous and exotic places. And there was more. Ashalan told him about the white waters of the Fleercut further north, a treacherous torrent far removed from the lazy, feminine flow that divided the fields of Cos. In the wilder places, naked barbarians lurked beneath the spray, leaping out onto unwary travellers along the banks. Then there were the secretive desert people of Mewt, who moved their black tents with the winds. They might sell a horse to you if the offer was right—fiery, temperamental beasts that were cousins of the winds themselves—but there was always the whisper of deviltry around those people, so only the foolhardy and reckless ever approached them.

Four evenings a week, Jadrin was dismissed at sundown, whilst on the other three, Ashalan would bid Jadrin accompany him down to the Great Hall, where he would sit on a black marble throne. Dancers and musicians would come to entertain, sometimes gypsy fortune-tellers and most nights, gentlefolk would bow to seek an audience with the king himself. Haughtily, Jadrin would sit at the king's feet, his dark hair curled and perfumed, his ears, his throat, hung with black jewels, his body adorned with splendid clothes of dark, rich colours, and he would think himself content. He was not exactly sure what his role was, for he did not like to ask, but it was easy to forget about the three days he had spent in the dismal, turret room and the deal he had made with a certain spiteful spirit. Ashalan was very kind to him, and gradually the boy came to realise that the king was not the greedy, lustful fool he had once thought him to be. He was a lonely, frightened man, surrounded by sycophantic idiots, half of whom probably conspired against him. Slowly Ashalan began to trust Jadrin. 'You have brought a little peace to my life,' he said.

One evening, when the warmth of the day was being gently nudged east by a frivolous breeze, Jadrin and Ashalan walked together along the high tiled terrace that overlooked the gardens. Urns against the wall sprouted riotous haloes of yellow flowers, ivy swung in the breeze. It was an idyllic time marred only by the sound of revelry coming from the Great Hall below them, the high spiteful laughter of women, the responding drunken, male guffaws. Jadrin sensed Ashalan wince and he thought, 'In some ways you are a very weak man', and felt sorry for him.

'I do not think I was meant to be a king,' Ashalan said.

'Mmm,' Jadrin replied, noncommittally.

They had come to the wide bowl of a fountain; the water was turned off. Ashalan sat down on the brim of the pool, shredding an ivy leaf he had picked along the way. 'I will tell you,' he said. 'My father died when I was too young to understand what power meant. He thought I would be fit to follow him. I was his only son after all. There was no one else. For years, he had been trying to groom me for the role. He had me instructed in hunting and fighting and reasoning. My brain was filled with the words of kings from great times; their heroic lifetimes filled me with dread. "You must have a wife," my father said. I did not want to marry. My father ignored my protests. He procured a young wife and a set of noble, upright young men as friends. It was not enough.'

Jadrin had never heard of the young wife before, neither was she in evidence about the court. He made a carefully worded enquiry.

Ashalan sighed. 'Poor girl,' he said. 'It was no secret that she had harboured a kind of obsession for me for some time. We had virtually grown up together, for she was my second cousin. It was a liaison doomed to tragedy, I'm afraid.' He shook his head. 'I'm sorry, Jadrin, but I have no wish to speak of it further.'

The king looked so forlorn that Jadrin went and put his arms around him, not caring whether it was a disrespectful thing to do or not. At that moment, he would have dearly loved to have taken Ashalan far from the palace, far from the city, back to the quiet mill-pool and the high, stone house; a place of dark and healing. It was the first time they had embraced.

'Jadrin, I love you,' Ashalan said, a whispered confession.

Even as he savoured these words and wondered, in fact, what they meant to him, Jadrin felt the piece of quartz, still carried about his neck in its little bag, jump and grow quickly hot. The king bent to kiss him and he backed away, eyes wide.

Ashalan looked mortified. 'I have offended you. Forgive me,' he said.

Jadrin shook his head. 'No, no, you haven't. It wasn't that.' His hand strayed to the pouch at his throat and he found that it was no longer warmer than usual; there was no hint of movement. Perhaps he had imagined it. Could the spirit have forgotten about their agreement? It seemed so long ago that it was made. He sat down beside the king, confused and perhaps a little afraid. He reached up with shy fingers to trace the smile on Ashalan's mouth, and then he kissed it, absorbed it, examining the rush of pleasure this new contact initiated. In its bag around his neck, the quartz remained still and cool. Jadrin sighed and smiled.

'What is it?' Ashalan asked him and Jadrin shook his head.

'Nothing. It is nothing.'

They continued their walk in silence, going down the sweeping, white steps at the end of the terrace and into the shadowed, rustling gardens. 'I am twenty-six years old,' Ashalan said, 'I am ten years older than you, Jadrin. Perhaps I am wrong to want to love you.'

'Go down to the forest,' Jadrin said lightly. 'Lie down naked in the damp leaves and perhaps the answer to your troubles shall come to you.'

Ashalan laughed sadly. 'You are oblique and rude. Only your loveliness allows you to get away with the things you say to people.'

'I am sixteen years old,' Jadrin replied. 'I am ten years younger than you, and perhaps it is wrong for me to want to love you, Ashalan, but in all frankness I do not care about what other people think is right. Most of them are fools whose behaviour would make a demon blush. Why should we consider their opinions?'

Ashalan smiled. He shrugged. Together, they returned to the palace.

Jadrin sat on a stool in the antechamber to the king's bedroom and combed out his hair. He could see himself shining like pearl and jet in the mirror before him. His flesh tingled with the presentiment of a delicious fear. His nervousness tasted like wine. Then, interrupting his private reverie, something cold touched his shoulder. It cast no reflection in the mirror before him. He gasped and turned round quickly on the stool. There, behind him, hovered the spirit from the turret room, malicious glee scrawled across its indistinct features. 'Now!' it hissed. 'Now! Let me in! Let me into your soul!'

Jadrin stood up. 'No!' he said, flinging out his arm. 'I will not. You must ask something else of me.'

'You gave your word!' shrieked the spirit angrily.

Jadrin denied this vigorously. 'I was in no position to make such a bargain. Ashalan is not an evil man. I will not let you harm him. Tell me, what else do you want in payment?'

'Nothing,' the spirit spat petulantly. 'I will taunt you and haunt you until you do as I ask.'

'Then you will have to taunt me forever, for I never shall.'

'Hah!' the spirit snarled. 'That is where you are wrong, foolish boy. You have three days; that is all. At the end of that time, I am quite within my rights to force myself into your helpless, mortal brain and destroy you and the king together. We made an agreement, Jadrin, there is no going back now. You are bound by cosmic law.'

'And surely cosmic law is no friend of evil.'

The spirit pulsed with angry light. 'You are hardly more than a child. You know nothing of evil.'

'Perhaps not much, but enough to know it when I see it. I am young, I know that, but don't underestimate me. I know for a fact that it is always possible to wriggle out of situations like this, and I shall find the way, you can be sure of that.'

The spirit laughed. 'Brave words for a catamite, Jadrin. But I concede that you are right. You cast aspersions upon my character, but I shall prove my honesty and integrity by saving you the trouble. As you have guessed, there is a way to release yourself from our bargain and it is this. If, within three days, you can learn who and what I was on this earth, you can consider yourself free of our agreement. However, I think it extremely unlikely that you'll be able to do so. In my opinion, you are far too stupid.' It laughed again, a cruel and spiteful sound. 'See you in three days, my little friend.'

In a whirl of light, it disappeared, leaving only a trace of lingering laughter, an unpleasant smell and a cold spot in the room. Jadrin sat down again, his heart thumping madly. He stared at himself in the mirror intently for some moments before appearing to come to some inner decision. With tremor-less hand, he picked up the brush once more and ran its bris-

tles through his hair. By the time he rose and passed softly into the next
room, the cold spot had gone completely.

In the morning, Jadrin awoke in Ashalan's arms, his body trembling
to the echo of a hundred delightful pangs. The caress of mouth, the nip of
teeth, the probings of tongue and fingers, and, above all, the invasion of
spirit and body that is the most magical of all human activities—if they
could but know it—Jadrin knew. He said, 'Ashalan, I would like to visit
my family.'

And the king replied, 'Whatever you wish. I shall give you a
white stallion to ride home upon, a retinue of six liveried guards, gifts for
your kinfolk. Promise only that you will return to me.'

'Within three days, I promise.' Jadrin answered.

Once Jadrin could see the sparkle of the river in the distance, which signalled the proximity of his old home, he experienced a small, sad thrill. If
only he could live here forever beside the tumbling water with the man he
loved. That would be a life, showing Ashalan the mysteries of this beautiful land, benevolent mysteries that he felt the king had never experienced.
However, Jadrin knew that in becoming Ashalan's lover he had certainly
bid farewell to his old life forever. Ashalan would probably never see the
mill-house.

Amberina was waiting for her brother upon the road, half a mile from
the house. 'I knew you were coming,' she said.

Jadrin dismounted and walked beside her, leading his horse.

'You have such fine clothes now,' Amberina said.

'Yes. I have brought you a gown of crimson linen, sashed with gold
rope.'

'Thank you, Jadrin. Are these men your servants?' She gestured towards the six liveried riders following behind them at a respectful distance.

'Indeed they are. And do you see the girl riding behind them on the
grey pony? She is Psydre, the daughter of a witch from a far land. She was
bored of life at court, so I have brought her here to be your companion.'

'Thank you, my brother.'

'She carries a small chest of jewels to adorn your throat and wrists.'

'You are too generous, Jadrin.'

She narrowed her eyes and looked at him slyly. 'If only you had not
had to leave such a large part of yourself in the city.'

Jadrin looked at her sharply, but her eyes were twinkling with merriment.

'I am glad to see you so happy,' she said.

'My happiness is not yet complete,' Jadrin replied. 'I think I may need your help, Amberina.'

'Ah,' said she.

Jadrin had brought gifts for the entire household. Excitedly, they gathered around him in the large, warm kitchen, crying out in pleasure as the rich colours of silks and jewels spilled out over the table. Psydre, a gregarious creature, danced around the room, flinging the shining bolts of cloth around the servants' shoulders. Within minutes, they had taken her to their hearts.

Jadrin beckoned his father aside. 'This is for you,' he said, and took from his jacket a jewelled, white gold pin, which had been found deep beneath the ground and was far more valuable than all the rest put together.

Skimblaze looked at it thoughtfully as it lay in his son's outstretched palm. 'No,' he said. 'I cannot take it, Jadrin. I virtually sold you, my only son and the first-born of she whom I loved above all things, to pay off the miserable debts of my weakness. You owe me nothing but scorn.'

'On the contrary,' Jadrin replied smoothly. 'I owe you everything, father.'

Skimblaze smiled ruefully, but let Jadrin pin the jewel onto his jacket. 'And did you spin the gold?' he asked.

'In a fashion.'

'Oh, my son!' Skimblaze, unaware of all that had happened to Jadrin in Ashbrilim, drew him close, but one thing he was sure of in his heart; the boy he held belonged now, wholly, to another man.

In the evening, Jadrin and Amberina stole away from the impromptu party that was raging in the house in celebration of Jadrin's visit. Neighbours had materialised from miles away to congratulate Jadrin on his good fortune. Now, brother and sister walked hand in hand down to the riverside, where the long shadows fished the water's surface and balls of flimsy flies hung, dancing in the dusk.

'You seem taller,' Amberina mused aloud.

Jadrin did not answer. He lifted the velvet bag from around his neck and tipped out the quartz onto his palm.

'Ah yes,' Amberina said, 'I still have mine. Was it useful?'

Jadrin told her just how useful it had been, and also the situation he had got himself into because of it. 'Perhaps,' he said, 'if I'd refused the spirit's offer, Ashalan would have come to love me even though I couldn't spin straw into gold.'

'Do you really think so?' Amberina asked dryly, in a voice far wiser than her years.

Jadrin shrugged. He did not really know. 'Now, I have to learn the spirit's name, its identity. But how?'

'Perhaps in the forest...' Amberina gestured across the lazy water.

Jadrin wrinkled his nose. 'That is why I have come home, I suppose.'

'There is a place in the forest,' Amberina said, 'where the spirits gather, they that will not leave this earth or who are held here by the cruelty of their souls and their love of carnal things. You must go to this place—all pathways lead there—to see what you can learn, but it will not be easy. They can smell a living heart from miles away and will scatter if they sense you or, worse, attempt to possess you.' She sighed. 'It's not much, but I don't know how to advise you other than that. Naturally, I will come with you if you want me to.'

Jadrin took one of her white hands and pressed it against his face. 'You are more help to me than you know, but how we'll be able to conceal ourselves I just don't know. It seems hopeless.'

Amberina was just about to answer, when they were disturbed by the unmistakeable sound of low chuckling coming from the bushes beside them. The branches shook and separated to reveal the slim form of Psydre, the witch's daughter. She stood up, still laughing and pulling twigs from her hair. Amberina and Jadrin drew closer together in surprise. 'There are ways and means to everything,' she announced.

Jadrin bristled. 'Spying being one of them, I suppose?'

Psydre shook her dark, wild head and smiled with her red, red mouth. 'I wasn't spying. I just overheard. Couldn't help it, although I must confess, I am surprised to learn that it wasn't you who spun the straw into gold. Does Ashalan know of this?'

Jadrin growled and Amberina laid her hand fearfully on his arm.

'Hush now,' Psydre said sweetly. 'I can help you.'

'You?' Amberina sounded sceptical. 'Why should you want to?'

'What a suspicious little thing you are!' Psydre exclaimed. 'I don't mean you harm. You can trust me.'

'As I did the spirit in the turret?' Jadrin reminded her.

Psydre waved his comment away with a careless hand. 'Poosht!' she said. 'Come on now: listen to what I say. I can help you and I do not lie. Your sister is right, Jadrin. You must find the desecrated shrine, where the spirits congregate to emulate the ways of men. If you walk there in your flesh, you have no chance at all. No, you must leave it behind you.'

Jadrin laughed. 'Fine. Then I'll kill myself to be able to spy on the spirits. Such action seems a little extreme.'

'Do you know nothing?' Psydre asked. 'I can help your soul leave your flesh and be able to come back to it as many times as you like. It's a simple art and one that is taught to all where I come from.'

Jadrin was still a little sceptical but Amberina confirmed Psydre's words by saying that she too had heard of such abilities. 'We have nothing to lose,' she said.

'*You* don't,' Jadrin replied, rather frostily, but he agreed to let Psydre help him.

Well-guarded are the arts of the witch-women of the east. Jadrin hardly knew what was happening to him other than Psydre's soft, compelling voice seemed to lure him into infinity. She had made him lie down on the damp grass and had stroked his limbs, murmuring in a singsong voice until he was nearly asleep. Then came a sharp tug upon his spirit. For a second, he seemed to hover between sleep and waking, before leaping up with a yelp as if pulled roughly to his feet.

Psydre was smiling up at him. 'You see?' she said.

'Perfectly!' Jadrin replied. 'So what?'

'So look down at your feet, young magician.'

There, on the grass, lay the body of a pale young man, eyes closed, perfectly motionless. Jadrin recognised it as himself. He was free. His soul was really out of his body.

Amberina was on hands and knees, stunned, squinting at the spectral form of her brother's soul whom only Psydre could see with any clarity.

'Go now, Jadrin, quickly, before the moon rises,' Psydre said. 'When you want to return, merely think it so, and you will be back within your flesh.' She patted the ground beside her. 'Come, Amberina, and sit with me. Your brother must go alone. We shall have to keep each other company while I weave a protection around his body. After that, perhaps we can gaze into the pool together for some moments...'

Jadrin moved away from them, downstream, where he crossed the water and so ventured into the trees.

It was nearly morning by the time Jadrin came once more to the widest path that led out of the forest. Although he did not truly need to follow it, he was enjoying the freedom this astral movement afforded him. When the trees opened out upon the banks of the river, he thought himself back to flesh, and sat up as if waking from a dream, with stiff limbs and an aching back. Amberina and Psydre had returned to the house hours before, confident that Psydre's power was strong enough to protect the corporeal part of Jadrin left beside the river. Above the trees, behind him, the sky was flushed with pale dawn. Jadrin walked to the mill-house and let himself inside. On the kitchen table, he found a bottle of wine, which he took with him to the best parlour. Sprawled out in his father's favourite chair, he drained the bottle. By the time the servants were stirring, he was dozing, half drunk.

By midday, Amberina could contain her curiosity no more. She went to shake him awake. 'What happened in the forest?' she asked.

'I know the answer,' Jadrin said wearily, but it looked as if knowing it hadn't lightened his burden at all.

On the morning of the third day, Jadrin and the six liveried guards took their leave of the mill-house to return to the city. Jadrin said to his sister, 'Give me the other half of the quartz,' and she did so. He kissed her goodbye, inclined his head to the silent Psydre and embraced his father fondly. They spoke vaguely of reciprocal visits in the near future.

In the afternoon, some miles from Ashbrilim, Jadrin bid his companions wait for him whilst he visited a cottage set some yards back from the road amongst a snuggle of gnarled trees. The guards raised eyebrows at each other and sniffed, although none of them spoke. It was well known that the cottage was the home of a witch of less than savoury reputation. Jadrin stayed within for maybe ten minutes. When he emerged, he offered no explanation to the others, but urged that they should hurry towards the city.

On reaching the palace, without even pausing to refresh himself or brush the dust of travel from his clothes, Jadrin went straight to the king's apartments. He threw open the doors and five of the king's servants looked up in alarm. Ashalan was playing a game with counters and a chequered board with one of his courtiers.

Jadrin said, 'Send them all away!' and from the darkness in the boy's face and voice, Ashalan did so.

'What has happened?' he asked, once they were alone.

'You must tell me the truth,' Jadrin said, quietly.

'What truth? What are you speaking of?'

'Of Angeline...'

At the mention of that name, Ashalan's face fell dramatically. He was silent. He turned away.

'I shall be truthful with you,' Jadrin said, 'and my truth is that I cannot spin straw into gold. Now I shall tell you who can...'

Calmly, omitting no detail, Jadrin told the king how he had gone into the forest on the previous evening. He had followed the winding, hidden paths until he had come to the white, stone shrine, all covered in creepers and moss. There, he had lurked among the ruins, waiting for the spirits to gather. Eventually, two wavery beings had come to sit upon the tumbled stones at the front of the shrine. They were wearing forms that approximated human appearances, though their faces were terrible and their hands merely sticks of bone. Presently, others drifted through the misty ferns, coming to pluck at their companions and chitter together as children do. Jadrin had moved from cover a little. He noticed some of the shades were inclined to hover apart from the rest. He wasn't that conspicuous. Eventually one of them had said, 'One of our company is seeking justice this moon!'

And another had replied, 'Seek it? She shall have it, dearest, have it, have it!'

Then another had murmured, 'Hush now, she is here.'

Jadrin could barely differentiate between one spirit and another, but there was something balefully familiar about the blade of light that had come dancing into the centre of the glade. It danced and sang and preened, cavorting with smug merriment.

'Are you happy, dear one?' cried the spirits.

'Indeed I am!'

'And why is that, beloved?'

'Because Ashalan is to die in the arms of his whore!'

'But why, lovely sister?'

'He has my blood on his hands, my sisters, my brothers, and I desire to live once more with his on mine!'

The spirits swayed towards her like a fog. 'And how shall you do that?' they asked together.

Here the spirit grew into a great and pulsing flame. 'Quite simply,' it replied. 'Tomorrow night, I shall possess the boy, Jadrin. I shall possess his body and, through that, experience all that was denied me; the passion of the man I once loved. After that, my dears, Ashalan will experience the true, keen blade of my revenge. As he still penetrates the body that I possess, I shall take a knife and kill him! It will be very easy. Naturally, after such a terrible crime, Jadrin will have to flee the city, but then Jadrin, as he lives and breathes on this earth, shall be no more. He is too weak and no match for me. In Mewt, I think, I will discover a new and rewarding life...'

'But are you quite sure, my dear, that the boy Jadrin shall have no defence?' one of the other spirits asked.

The spirit glowed red. 'Quite sure!' it said. 'There is only one way he can defeat me but, as he will never know by whose shade he is to be possessed, there is no chance of his victory. Tomorrow night, Ashalan shall die and I shall live again. I who was once Angeline Hope DeVanceron. I who am the murdered, slaughtered, butchered, dead queen of Ashbrilim!'

Ashalan's expression of disbelief as he listened to this tale gradually changed to one of pale horror. At the end, he said, 'I did not kill her,' which Jadrin had expected and also dearly wanted to believe.

'Then tell me the truth,' he said. 'Who was this woman and why is she so bitterly seeking revenge from beyond the grave?'

Ashalan looked at the floor. It was clear he was considering memories best left forgotten. 'She was my wife,' he said.

Jadrin sat down beside him. 'Then how...?'

'I did try to dissuade her,' Ashalan butted in, slamming a clenched fist into his cupped palm. 'I told her marriage to me would be a barren, joyless venture, but she would not listen. She was obsessed. What could I do? She was a strong-willed creature and clearly intended to try and change my nature, even make me love her. A fruitless task!'

Ashalan told of how he and Angeline were married to the delight of Ashalan's father and those who had previously considered Ashalan to be a weak and sickly creature. Surely the strong and tempestuous Angeline with her fiery beauty would fill him with life and strength? Unfortunately, their relationship, which had started off badly, came to nothing. Ashalan found Angeline terrifying: a succubus of a creature, hungry and grasping. He knew his nature and refused to go anywhere near her bedchamber at night, never mind share it. This behaviour only served to stoke Angeline's pain and grief into a vicious rage. She tried to win Ashalan over, but eventually, exhausted by her efforts, resorted to extreme and desperate measures. A boy of whom Ashalan was particularly fond was found poisoned, his flesh black and burned. Ashalan knew who was responsible, but had no way of proving it. Angeline stalked the battlements crying out her marriage vows, shrieking of fidelity and the painful fate awaiting those who discredited those vows. In numerous ways, Angeline sought to cause trouble for Ashalan, especially with his father, the king. She knew Ashalan had no desire to rule, so in some undiscovered way, persuaded the old king to abdicate in favour of his son. Then she was queen and for a while the power of that position put a binding over her wounds, but it did not last.

Ashalan's original indifference towards Angeline had developed over the years into an abiding aversion. He wished her dead a thousand times a day, longing only to be free of her obsessive vigilance, her troublemaking, her carping demands. What she saw in him, he could not fathom. He was powerless to end her pain. She would not listen to reasoned argument. She would tolerate no compromise.

One night, as she had done many times before, the queen followed Ashalan to the high tower on the north wall of Ashbrilim. She knew that Ashalan was friendly with a captain of the guard there, and through her spy network had discovered the two men had arranged to meet that night. Ironically, it was not a lovers' meeting. Ashalan and the captain were good friends, yes, and with similar tastes but had never been physically close. In fact, since the episode of the poisoning, Ashalan had not been close to anyone. Angeline did not believe this for an instant. She followed Ashalan up the winding, yellowstone steps to the battlements and concealed herself among the shadows of the buttressed wall. She must have watched them for a long time, perhaps becoming disappointed, for all they did was share a bottle of wine and talk together. However, as Ashalan got up to leave, he bent and kissed his friend on the cheek. That was enough evidence for Angeline. She waited until Ashalan had gone back to the palace before leaping out of hiding. All that the captain saw was a frenzied, shrieking shape, hidden by robes, rushing towards him, brandishing a long, curved knife. He rightly presumed it meant to murder him.

Angeline did not have much time to regret her reckless behaviour. She did not think about how the captain was one of Ashbrilim's best warriors, well trained in self-defence. She had no chance. He did not know who she was. Perhaps he thought she was a mad woman from the town. After a brief scuffle, he disarmed her, but still she would not give in, frenziedly tearing at his face with clawed hands, her face unrecognisable with the insanity of her rage. Afterwards, the captain said he could not recall exactly what happened, but during the struggle, Angeline fell or was pushed over the city wall.

She did not die at once. The captain, remorseful for using violence against a woman, no matter how crazed, ordered his men to look for her body. They found her still alive, crawling brokenly among the filth and offal of the city that was thrown regularly over the walls. It was the rubbish that had arrested her fall somewhat, although both her legs were ruined. Because her face had been cut, they found her with rats clinging to her head, devouring her even as she crawled along, head wagging to dislodge them. She was clearly a mad woman, some poor wild soul, tormented by demons. It was also clear that she was dying, beyond the help of any physician. The soldiers carried her back within the walls. They never expected anyone to claim her, but made her as comfortable as they could and sat with her, waiting for her to die. No one recognised the ruined figure as Angeline Hope DeVanceron. No one, until a priest passed the lodge and the soldiers called him in to bless the dying woman. The priest lifted her hand and there, on a ring, he recognised the symbol of the house of her parents, which the soldiers had not known. A frantic search was organised and it was discovered that the queen was missing from her rooms.

She died before they could carry her home, in discomfort and filth, halfway down the main road to the palace.

'The whole business was tragic and sordid,' Ashalan said, which Jadrin thought was rather an understatement. 'None of us had realised the depths of her feelings, nor how they had dragged her into insanity.'

Jadrin thought this was rather stupid. Angeline must have had these tendencies from the beginning and in Ashalan's position, he was sure he would have identified them.

Ashalan rubbed his face. 'My father tried to persuade me to have the captain executed, because, no matter what the reason, he had killed the Queen of Ashbrilim. Perhaps I should have ordered this execution. Perhaps it was my duty, but I couldn't. You see, in the depths of my heart, no matter how hard I tried, I couldn't feel grief for her death. Secretly, I felt I owed that captain a favour, not the death sentence. Do you see, Jadrin? Do you see how terrible a creature I am?'

'You were caught in a difficult situation,' Jadrin said carefully. He was unsure how he felt about these disclosures.

'Ultimately,' Ashalan said, 'I had the captain posted to the border of Cos, where he was out of harm's way. My father never understood me, or sympathised with me at all. He made sure I was punished for what had happened in small, subtle ways, until the day he died.'

'Angeline's spirit must have been waiting for the chance to wreak its revenge,' Jadrin said, unwilling to comment on Ashalan's story. 'Unwittingly, I gave it that chance. I gave it power: my breath and my warmth. Oh, to live those few days again!'

'You sound bitter,' Ashalan said. 'I have disappointed you and it has killed our love. She has won.' He put his head in his hands.

Jadrin stared upon the king, caught in a maelstrom of conflicting feelings. In his view, the main tragedy of the story was that Angeline had obviously been very ill: no sane woman would have behaved and felt as she had done. No one had helped her. She had suffered alone, and for that Jadrin felt very sad. Still, despite the wretchedness of the story, he thought there was no excuse for the queen's spirit to continue her obsessive vendetta beyond the grave. He knew now at least that he was dealing with a mad ghost, and in some way, that gave him courage. 'Do not crumble, my lord,' he said in a cold voice. 'Angeline has not won yet. Perhaps you are to blame to some degree, but who among us acts always in complete wisdom? The fault is not entirely yours.'

Ashalan made an anguished sound. 'It is certainly my fault that she has this advantage over you. If I had been content after the first night of your spinning, this would never have happened. All she wanted of you then was a kiss. Oh, I was blind to the true gold that was in you all the time!' He put his head in his hands once more.

'Do not punish yourself with guilt any further,' Jadrin said. 'What is done, is done. Now leave me to resolve this matter, once and for all. I shall go to the bedroom. Wait here for an hour and then come after me, but no sooner, mind.'

Jadrin went alone to the king's bedchamber and drew all the drapes against the balmy evening. He lit pungent incense on a brass saucer and robed himself in white and let down his hair. From the velvet bag, he withdrew the two halves of the lilac quartz and laid them on a table next to the smoking incense. It lay like two halves of a broken egg, glowing inside, reflecting the light of the smouldering charcoal upon which burned the perfume. Jadrin stared at it for some time. Then, he sat down on the bed, calmed his mind and called to the aethers. Within seconds, the baleful spirit appeared at the window. It appeared to be a little confused. 'Let me in, Jadrin,' it said.

After a pause, the boy arose and opened the window.

'It is time, Jadrin.'

'Indeed it is.'

'If only you'd had true magic, eh?'

'If only!' Jadrin agreed.

'Well, I must give you the chance, I suppose. Have you thought of my name?'

'I have pondered it deeply,' Jadrin said. 'Would it be... Grizelda?'

'No.'

'Nanune, Riboflax, Tanteberry, Archimund?'

'No, no, no!' The spirit flickered with delight. Jadrin patiently recited every name, both male and female, that he could think of. All the while, the spirit glittered and spat light and laughed.

'No,' it said, 'none of those. You have just one more try. Your time has run out.'

Ah,' said Jadrin, 'in that case, would you, by any chance, be the shade of Angeline Hope DeVanceron, dead queen of Ashbrilim?'

At these words, the spirit shrieked wordlessly in horror, manifesting itself more definitely into the form of a gaunt, bedraggled woman, clothed in the rags of a shroud, with terrible, staring eyes. 'Sorcerer!' she shrieked.

'I am learning,' Jadrin said mildly. 'Be at peace, Angeline. You are free of flesh, so be free of pain. Why carry it with you? Fly!'

'Never! I must have my revenge, for my broken body, my broken spirit!'

'Broken long before you became queen,' Jadrin said. 'Be healed, Angeline. Fly!'

The spirit uttered a horrifying squawk and flew at Jadrin, spectral claws reaching for his face. Jadrin stepped back swiftly and picked up the broken halves of the quartz. 'If the earth cannot contain you maybe stone can!' he said and, reciting a spell that the witch at the roadside had sold him, he issued an Irrefutable Order that the spirit of the dead queen could not ignore or fight. She was sucked like smoke into the quartz, whereupon Jadrin snapped the two halves together. They sealed in an instant as if they had never been apart. For a few moments, the quartz glowed as if it contained a small flame within its heart, but by the time Ashalan came through the door curtains, it lay innocent and cool upon the table.

The next morning, Jadrin took the quartz and buried it deep beneath the garden of the palace. Over its grave, he planted three creepers of ivy to bind it into the ground. He surrounded it with scented flowers, and called upon the spirits of the earth to heal the essence of Angeline. In time, he hoped, when all that was dark had left her tortured soul, she would seep through the stone as a radiant light and soar to the celestial realm. He could do no more. But whether his actions in this regard were successful or not, the spirit of Angeline never bothered him, or Ashalan, again. But there is no doubt that what Jadrin did upon that night changed him forever. He took a little of Angeline's darkness into his being.

The Nothing Child

This story and the one after it carry on directly from 'Spinning for Gold', and retell a lesser-known Scottish fairy tale, 'Nicht Nought Nothing'. It illustrates how magic takes the path of least resistance and you should be very careful indeed when making deals with supernatural beings, especially in the choice of words used to make the deal.

As he grows older, Jadrin becomes a distinctly darker character, which to me made him more interesting. When I wrote this piece, my fascination with capricious angels was already in full flight, and Lailahel, the angel of conception, is a precursor to the fallen angels of my Grigori trilogy.

Jadrin, consort of the King of Cos, desired a son. He pondered long hours upon this vain hope, sitting among the dappled shadows on the palace terrace, pacing the marble stairs, watching the stars from pointed windows. Between them, it was impossible for two beings of masculine, physical aspect to conceive life, but neither was Jadrin composed to commit some sordid infidelity with a woman. As for encouraging Ashalan to do so, this was beyond him, beyond the hot, possessive passion of his love. There seemed no solution to his problem, yet the yearning would not leave him. He watched the palace women with their children. Perhaps he could sate this uncontrollable and inexplicable longing by adopting somebody else's offspring? He considered this idea and then put it aside. No, it was a child of the flesh that he wanted. Nothing else would do. So obsessed was Jadrin with this desire that others came to notice a dark and poisonous aura about him, violet with the intensity of his feelings. It was mentioned to the king in careful terms. Was Jadrin perhaps not quite in the full flower of health?

Ashalan questioned him, at first tenderly, then sharply, fearing some other reason for the change in behaviour.

Jadrin was reluctant to speak his thoughts aloud; surely the king would think him mad. His excuses only fuelled Ashalan's suspicions. An argument ensued. Fleeing from hostile words, Jadrin ran blindly from the more inhabited areas of the palace. When his anger had left him and his breath, clutching furiously in his chest, forced him to pause and rest, he found himself amongst a clutter of abandoned buildings, far from the rich apartments he was used to. Curiosity at his surroundings chased the bitter words with Ashalan from his mind. Entranced, Jadrin began to explore.

Some of the doorways had been boarded up, others left open to the elements, so that the winds had scoured the buildings barren. Naturally, it was the boarded entrances that interested him most. Especially that of a structure embellished with weathered, stone fetishes. Tearing the boards from their rusty nails, Jadrin forced an entrance into the building. All was dark inside, dark and silent. Jadrin's flesh prickled with excitement. 'This,' he thought, 'this is a place trod by other than mortal feet.' He was right. And, as in the tradition of magical tales, it was within that place he found a great, old book...

That evening, the court noticed a change in Jadrin. He seemed more like his old self. Not everyone present at dinner was gratified to see that he and Ashalan seemed to have settled their differences, but on the whole, the atmosphere was one of relief. Jadrin smiled secretively into his purple wine. Ashalan watched him carefully, mollified by Jadrin's apologies, but still wary. He had seen this strange and guarded smile on Jadrin's face before. It spoke of power, the kind of which Ashalan had only a cursory grasp. It made him feel as if he was sitting next to a total stranger, and someone not entirely human. It made him afraid.

Unbeknown to the king, on the night of the next full moon, Jadrin robed himself in black cloth and flowed like a vapour through the midnight gardens of the palace. He sought out a sylvan grotto, decorated with tumbled stones, that had been designed to resemble an ancient temple, artfully strung with trailing arms of ivy and convolvulus. Pale, glowing blooms exuded a secret, aching perfume into the moist darkness and above the cracked and mossy stones of the garden, the moon swam, pregnant with light in a smooth, velvet sky, sequinned with stars. Jadrin felt energy course through the fibres of his flesh. He stood upon the stones and raised his arms to the moon. The cloth fell from his back and he was an aloof and dignified courtier no longer, but a witch-boy, the creature of his childhood, he that sang the water spirits from their gnat-gauzed homes: Jadrin, as white and deadly as the hottest of consuming flames.

He conjured forth a rare and capricious angel, whose hair burned the moss at his feet, whose eyes were pale as milk, as if blind. Jadrin had memorised an ancient invocation from the old book he had found. Some of the words made his teeth ache, some made his tongue stumble and become thick in his mouth, but he persisted. The angel swayed, sometimes fading a little as if to reprimand the boy when his words slipped.

'Lailahel, angel of the night, prince of conception, I implore you...'

'Implore me, nothing,' the spirit interrupted. 'You desire a child, yet you know this cannot be under the sway of the laws of the earth mother. You are male, Jadrin; your lover is male. There can be no issue from your union. This you know.'

'This I know!' Jadrin answered defiantly. 'Yet I have summoned you, Lailahel; your power can facilitate my need. You would not have come otherwise.'

The spirit shimmered—a vagueness that could have signified amusement or displeasure. 'I have been called on pale, cold moon-nights by the fairest and most ill-favoured, the youngest and oldest of women—yet never, in my experience, have I been summoned by a boy! Maybe I can ease your difficulties, but the Goddess will not be pleased. You risk needling her wrath.'

'My Prince, I work magic, thus do I understand I must take responsibility for my actions. Make it happen. The child will be consecrated to the Goddess as soon as it is named.'

'It will not be a normal child, Lord Jadrin.'

'What is? I ask only for its body to be fair, its face to be the mirror of the moon, its mind to be swift and canny as the hounds of the Maiden.'

'So little specification?' The angel laughed; a sound both musical and sepulchral. 'Very well. I shall instruct you in what to do.'

Jadrin bowed deeply. 'I thank you, Lailahel.' He raised his head. 'So what is your price?'

The angel smiled. 'My price? By the Heavenly Spheres and all their Motes, dare I ask a price for such a boon? My price is this: nothing. I want nothing from you, Lord Jadrin.'

Jadrin frowned. 'Forgive me, but this is not the usual way.'

'Nevertheless, it is what I ask.'

'At least permit me to light a temple candle in your name and blend a sacred incense to be burned for the next three nights.'

The angel shrugged. 'If such fripperies appease you, then by no means let me prevent you from realising them. If I should ask for anything, I should ask for your silence, but, as I said, I ask for nothing.'

'You have my silence anyway. You may also have my blood, if you wish.'

The angel shook its radiant head, causing the cascade of hair to wave like weed under water. 'No need. I want nothing from you.'

Jadrin could not help but feel uneasy. He understood that there is always a price for everything and he had been fooled by sly spirits before. However, the intensity of his desire forced him to ignore any misgivings in his heart.

He knelt upon the stones and Lailahel, prince of conception, whispered instructions as to what he must do.

The moon fell to her rest and Jadrin hurried back, like a shadow, insubstantial and furtive, to the palace and his king.

On the night of the first crescent of the waxing moon, the Maiden's time, Jadrin bathed himself in salt water. Emerging from the pool dripping and stinging, he stood in the unlit bathroom of hollow echoes and slick water sounds, gazing towards the skylight, where hasty clouds muffled the stars. He closed his eyes and quickly, with a knife as sharp as a blade can be, cut the pale skin of his breast above the heart. Blood rilled eagerly over his fingers as he pressed the wound. Shaking, he knelt and lifted a silver chalice, catching a measure of the dark, warm liquid in the bowl. Inky, diluted streams ran down his body into his wet footprints. Perhaps he had cut too deep. He had not expected so much blood from a wound in that place. The air was still, watching. Magic, then. Magic. He hurried from the room, not even bothering to cover himself with a robe or towel. By the time he reached his dressing room, the wound had dried.

Ashalan slept on his back in the huge, canopied bed. Jadrin paused to regard him, filled as he always was with gratitude that such a magnificent creature could belong to him. 'Ashalan,' Jadrin called softly, a voice of the new, horned crown itself, 'look, my love, to the window, the moon.' Ashalan stirred, woken more by the invisible reverberations of the unseen blood-harp than Jadrin's words. What he saw was the willow pale, willow slim form of the witch-boy, robed now in black, whose hair was an indigo smoke, whose eyes were black as the shadows of his hair.

'It is late, where have you been?' asked the King, who could not see the dark smear upon Jadrin's breast.

'Bathing,' Jadrin replied in a strange, distant voice. He looked for a moment at the sky beyond the window. When he turned his gaze once more upon Ashalan, the king was almost afraid. Almost. His heart beat faster and Jadrin slipped between the sheets, cold and salty, feverish and hungry. If Ashalan thought it odd that his lover should whisper strange words throughout their pleasure, the heat of the moment put it from his mind. Not even when Jadrin speared himself on Ashalan's lap and screamed and screamed a hundred arcane words, his body arched and tense, his hands clawing air, did Ashalan suspect that anything was different from usual. He knew Jadrin to be a bizarre and magical creature and after three years of his acquaintance knew better than to anticipate his moods and caprices.

Spent and exhausted, he fell quickly into a contented sleep, where his dreams were innocent.

Jadrin did not sleep. He waited, lying motionless on his back, until Ashalan's breathing proclaimed him unconscious. It took only a moment then to reach down for the knife that was concealed in his discarded robe. Ashalan murmured as Jadrin drew out his arm and winced as the sliver of steel licked into the soft flesh above the wrist, but he did not wake. Into the cup, to mingle with the caking ichor already within it, Ashalan's blood dripped down. One spot fell upon the sheet. Jadrin stilled his shaking hands. No mistakes in this—no. He carefully placed the chalice on the floor, away from the heavy, swaying curtains that moved in the early morning breeze. Morning was coming through the window; there was little time. Jadrin sealed the wound on Ashalan's arm with his own saliva. Into the dressing-room then, where a small, silver dish waited beside the mirror. Jadrin smeared the surface of the dish with Ashalan's seed that he held in his body, blended it with a powder of his own essence. Blood and seed, dried over a flame, laced with wine, thickened and perfumed by the gums of karaya, tragacanth and myrrh, blended with a little warm milk; this was the basis of Jadrin's elixir. Whatever else he cast into it has not been recorded, but, by the time the sky outside was shedding its night robe for the pearl of dawning, Jadrin was slipping and darting down into the gardens once again, past the drowsing peacocks, the hanging terraces, the silent statues, to the rose garden. Here, in the yellow-rose light of dawn, he scrabbled with his bare fingers in the earth and buried the thing he had made, the blood-seed icon of desire, the egg of the dream-child. If anyone should have seen him working there, his hair and eyes all wild, they would have hidden themselves from his sight, for Jadrin in a frenzy of need was a fearsome and dangerous object to behold.

In the morning, Ashalan's servants were intrigued by the stripes of blood upon the bathroom floor, the bloody handprint upon the doorframe. Ashalan himself was somewhat disturbed to find he had cut himself in the night and that he had bled upon the sheets. Jadrin walked through the day in a daze, but there was evidence of a smile upon his face.

Months passed, the Wheel of Life turned, seasons changed. Every day, Jadrin strolled in the rose garden, trying not to peer at the rich soil in an obvious manner. He never quite stopped believing in the spell, but as time went on and the soil remained undisturbed, the daily visits became more of a habit than an eagerness. Other matters took precedence in his life. In the east of the country, near the border of Candeleen, there lived a warrior king. His tribe was small, admittedly, but he had grand designs on the territory of Cos, and his swift, cunning warriors had become adept at worrying the skirts of the eastern duchies. Flustered and irritated, the dukes had approached Ashalan together, demanding that he employ Ashbrilim's forces to quell the nuisance. Therefore, in the late Summer, Ashalan led his army away from the city to do battle.

Jadrin stood with the court on the battlements of the highest tower and watched the shining, prancing steeds kick dust from the highway, carrying the jewels of Ashbrilim's manhood towards the east. Jadrin was not overly concerned about Ashalan's safety, having worked a number of protective spells to ensure it, but he had no way of knowing how long the king would be absent, and that caused him grief.

One crisp morning when the smell of Autumn surged across the palace gardens for the first time that year, the head gardener came hurrying to Jadrin's quarters himself, begging the servants for an interview. 'Go away,' Jadrin's valet said, haughtily, 'Lord Jadrin may not be disturbed by trifles. Take your business to the Chamberlain.'

'The Chamberlain be damned!' the gardener insisted. 'I wait here until Lord Jadrin comes himself; this matter is too grave for the ears of anyone else.'

Sniffing derisively, the valet retreated and was consequently surprised by Jadrin's animated reaction to the gardener's request.

Maybe it was the turning of the season, the crescent of the new moon, but Jadrin knew that, at last, his spell had borne fruit. The gardener told, with wonder and amazement, how one of his underlings had been passing through the rose garden that very morning. A strange, mewing sound had attracted the boy's attention and there, beneath the trained branches of the grandest bush, he had seen a pale-skinned baby writhing in the dirt.

'Bring the child to me,' Jadrin commanded and the gardener hurried away, to pluck the babe from the arms of the maids in the kitchen, where they were trying to tempt it with warmed milk.

Many grisly suppositions were whispered around the palace of how some cruel wench must have buried the child, perhaps because it was illegitimate. Perhaps she'd thought it dead. Wiser women pronounced the child a changeling, too pale, its eyes too knowing to be wholly human. Jadrin, keeping secret the occult origin of the baby, made it known that he intended to adopt it. 'The king and I shall never have an heir,' he said. 'Perhaps it is this babe's good fortune to be found upon our land.'

Some secretly questioned Jadrin's judgement in this respect while others praised his charity.

The priests said, 'Dedicate the child to the Goddess quickly. If it is evil perhaps the consecration will dispel all negative aspects. The boy must have a name.'

Jadrin merely shook his head. 'The ritual must not be performed until Ashalan returns,' he said. 'It would not be right to do otherwise, however pressing it might seem. Let the king himself choose a name for his adopted son.'

The most cynical members of the court wondered how Ashalan would greet the news that Jadrin had adopted a child found buried in the rose garden as the heir to the kingdom, but they complied with his wishes and kept their suppositions amongst themselves.

A year passed and still Ashalan had not returned from the east. The boy who had no name blossomed and filled out in the arms of his wet-nurse and beneath the dark, smoky gaze of his adopted parent. True, he did not seem an ordinary child. Occasionally, the women were frightened by the intensity, the ironic humour, of his gaze; and yet, physically, he appeared normal, if perhaps a little slight in build.

'Whose soul are you?' Jadrin asked the child and in response the tiny fingers would grip air, the petal mouth smile and sigh. He had no name, and the servants, his only company, jokingly referred to him as Nothing, because it was impossible for them not to address him in some way. 'Where is Nothing?'

'Asleep on the terrace.'

'Nothing never cries.'

'Nothing has the bright eyes of a bird—a very old bird!'

Jadrin watched his magical son grow and in his heart warmed the secret of his birth, forever silent.

Ashalan and his army had a hard time of it in the east. They had ridden out to battle light-hearted and confident, unprepared for the astute organisation of the warrior king and his tribe. It was like trying to dispel a mist; swords and lances were of very little use. Here and there the ragged warriors ran, under cover of cloud and branch; shadows themselves in the night, pricking Ashalan's soldiers as they slept, loosing their horses, spoiling their water, stealing their food. Morale slumped; it was a slow business driving the enemy back, though by sheer weight of numbers it was considered inevitable by all that, eventually, Cos would have to succeed and carry the banner of victory back to Ashbrilim.

One evening, as Ashalan and his elite guard returned to their camp through a thick forest, a storm came up from the south, suddenly and fiercely. Trees above them shook leaves and sharp twigs onto the heads and shoulders of the men, rain sluiced them cruelly, wind tore their sight from them. Ashalan's stallion took a fright, being more spirited than the rest, and plunged recklessly off the path, tearing madly through dense undergrowth. All Ashalan could do was lean forward and close his eyes, trusting that the animal would quickly spend his strength and not fall. The frantic calls of his men faded behind him and he gave himself up to a nightmare of lashing branches and furious galloping. Eventually the horse burst from the trees on the banks of a raging torrent. The storm had passed but the river was swollen. On the other side, unbelievably, Ashalan could see the lamps of his camp twinkling through the dark. How could he reach it? His body ached, his clothes were torn, he was drenched and tired. As for the stallion, it was unlikely he retained enough strength to brave the fast-moving water. The camp glowed, welcoming and secure. Savoury smells of cooking meat and fresh bread drifted across to him. Ashalan tried to urge his horse forward, but he dug in his heels and wheeled about, making noises of distress.

'Either you cross the river, or we perish from cold and fatigue!' Ashalan said wearily.

The stallion would have none of it, which was more good sense than stubbornness.

Ashalan dismounted and stared miserably at the water, at the trunks of trees mashed carelessly in its foaming ribbons, the rocks that moved sluggishly downstream that had not moved for a hundred years. Human flesh would be shredded like old lace in that torrent. He sighed, hugging himself, preparing to spend the rest of the night out in the open. In the morning, he might be able to find his way back through the forest. Wistfully, Ashalan let his thoughts linger on Ashbrilim and the warm mystery of his beloved consort. Would he ever see them again.

'Why so glum, my lord?'

Ashalan turned quickly at the sound. Behind him stood a figure concealed in a hooded robe. He could not quite see the face.

'As you see, I am stranded. This damned beast took a flight through the forest. I lost my company and can't see how I can cross the river. There's no sign of a bridge.' It did occur to him that the stranger might be some creature of the warrior king, his enemy, and his hand strayed nervously to the pommel of his sword.

'No need for alarm,' the figure said, noticing his move. 'Allow me to assist you. I am a builder of bridges.'

Ashalan laughed. 'And can you build me a bridge before my fingers freeze off?'

The stranger did not laugh. 'My lord king, I can build you a bridge before you blink your eyes.'

'How did you know who I...' But Ashalan never finished the question. Even as he blinked, he beheld a shadowy shape spanning the foam, high and arched, that had not been there before. 'You are a magician, then,' he said.

The stranger shrugged. 'Of sorts. The bridge is yours, King of Ashbrilim. Why not cross it?'

Ashalan fixed the black, lustreless bridge with a narrow stare. Perhaps this man was an enemy and the bridge would dissolve to nothing when he was halfway across it, leaving him and his horse to drop helplessly into the furious swell beneath.

'Oh, do not doubt me,' said the stranger in a low, cajoling voice. 'I am no foeman of yours.'

'You are generous, my friend, but tell me the extent of your generosity. What payment do you require for this service.'

'Why nothing, king Ashalan,' the stranger replied. 'I want nothing from you. Let us just say that I have your interests at heart. What do you say to that?'

'If you want nothing then take nothing and I shall cross the bridge. I thank you sir.' Ashalan remounted his horse and with a further grateful wave to the stranger urged the animal into a canter across the sombre planks. Around them the pitchy wood groaned and creaked, below them the river tossed and snarled. Behind them, the river bank was empty and it was without incident that they crossed to the other side.

On a day of great celebration, Ashalan led his men home once more, along the wide, yellow highway from the east, to the great, gilded gates of Ashbrilim. The air was full of petals as the maidens of the city thronged the balconies, tossing handsful of bright blooms into the air to be crushed beneath the feet of the snorting horses. Two long years had passed since the army had left the city. In the end, the warrior king had been bought off rather than routed. Now everybody in the east seemed satisfied—at least on the surface. Ashbrilim gave the returning soldiers its best, shining with the last of the summer sun, giving off a heady aroma of shaded flowers and rubbed ferns.

Jadrin, with the elite of the court around him, waited on the steps of the palace, dressed in deepest blue that was the blue of midnight, with heavy, waxy blooms fixed in his hair. Behind him stood a woman holding the changeling child. Ashalan could have wept when he beheld his household. There was Jadrin, more lovely than he had remembered in his loneliest hour. There was Jadrin who came running down the steps, courtly aloofness forgotten, to reach up for his hands and say, 'My lord, you are home.' Ah, the homecoming was sweet.

Long and riotous was the feasting in the palace that day. Ashalan felt as if he was being swept along on an intoxicating wave of exotic perfume. His body was tired but it was carried high on the euphoria of his return. The fact that Jadrin carefully placed a young boy-child in his arms and, equally carefully, informed him that he now had an heir seemed only another heady facet of the glorious day. He raised the child on high and laughed, and the court laughed with him, spilling wine onto the marble floor, singing his praises. 'You are home, my lord.' Yes.

In the evening Jadrin led Ashalan into the gardens, saying, 'The boy was found here, among the roses...'

'How cruel! He seems wise for his years, such knowing eyes...'

'Yes. We thought that too.' A silence fell. They sat upon the grass, beneath the boughs of a drooping salix tree.

Ashalan began to speak of some of his experiences in the east. When he came to the tale of the strange bridge-builder, Jadrin's gaze became more intense, his expression fixed and wondering. Ashalan laughed at the end of the telling but Jadrin was silent. He stood up, his back to the king, and stared hard into the trees behind them.

'What is it?' Ashalan asked.

Jadrin raised an impatient hand. 'I... don't know. Only this. I should have thought. I should have realised. It may not be important, I don't know.'

'What? What?'

'The child. I refused to have him named until you returned.'

'So? I don't understand what you're trying to say.'

'Don't you see... the servants, they call him "Nothing"! You promised nothing. Your son is nothing. Don't you see?'

Ashalan was quite stupified by Jadrin's outburst. He uttered a small but nervous laugh. 'Jadrin, what you're saying is ridiculous! How could that stranger have known about your... adoption... when not even I knew myself!'

'There is more to it than you know, or could even guess.' Jadrin punched the air in frustration. 'Goddess, I should have realised!'

'This means nothing to me!' Ashalan said coldly. 'Perhaps you'd better explain.'

Jadrin opened his mouth to say, 'I can't' but a sudden and bitter wind swept the words from his lips. His hair blew across his eyes and he heard Ashalan swear in surprise. All the trees rustled furiously around them. The air smelt of acrid smoke and stale flowers. 'No,' Jadrin said.

'Such a welcome!' said a ringing hollow voice.

Ashalan turned to follow the direction of Jadrin's gaze and beheld the same cloaked figure who he had encountered on the banks of the river back east.

'Lord Jadrin,' the figure said in a silky voice, 'would you give me any less welcome than you gave the king when he returned? After all, I granted you your heart's desire.'

'Who is this?' Ashalan demanded, cold on the inside with a sick dread.

'Tell him, Jadrin,' said the angel.

'It is Lailahel, prince of conception,' Jadrin replied.

'I have come for my payment,' said the angel.

'You asked for none.'

'I asked for nothing.'

Jadrin sighed deeply. 'It is plain to me what you really want. You tricked me.'

Lailahel laughed. 'Nothing is a magical child, Jadrin. More my son than yours. Both of you promised him to me; you can't deny that. He does not belong with you and your kind.'

'Very well.' Jadrin took a deep breath. 'Tomorrow. Give us until tomorrow.'

'As the cock crows. No more.' And without further manifestation of any kind, the angel vanished.

Ashalan had no more than looked on in horrified disbelief; now he demanded an explanation. Feeling he no longer owed the angel anything, including silence, Jadrin told him the whole story. At the end of it, he stood back, expecting Ashalan's rage, but the king merely shook his head and held out his arms. 'Beloved,' he said, 'you are a dreaming romantic boy.'

Jadrin's body stiffened in affront. 'I am no longer a boy and there was nothing romantic about what I did. When Lailahel returns tomorrow another child shall be in Nothing's place. Nothing shall be in the temple being consecrated to the Goddess!'

And so, long before dawn, Jadrin carried Nothing to the creamy-stoned temple. He roused the priests, who sleepily shuffled into the Hall of Naming and lit the candles and incense.

'Hurry,' Jadrin said, glancing through the windows. Only grey light showed outside.

They named the child Jadalan, for his parents, and crowned him with myrtle leaves. Surely no malefic entity could touch him now. Jadrin knelt before the altar and entreated the Goddess to protect the child. Perhaps he had done wrong in invoking the angel, but it had been done for love and without evil intent. Feeling reassured, Jadrin went back to the palace, leaving Jadalan in the care of the priests. At dawn, the angel came to him in his sitting-room.

Jadrin was holding a child on his knee, a happy, bonny creature. 'Then take him,' Jadrin said and held the child out, turning away as the angel's glowing fingers closed around the plump, pink body.

'You had your wish, Lord Jadrin,' Lailahel said, 'and several years' enjoyment of it too. Think yourself blessed that I concurred with your desires at all!'

'Forgive my ingratitude,' Jadrin replied curtly, 'but I can find no comfort in your words. Just take the child and go.'

Lailahel put the child onto his back and flew up through the ceiling, manifesting himself on another plane of existence. There was quite a journey ahead to the angel's palace of light, but travelling through the aether is an intense pleasure in itself and time means nothing there. Pausing to rest, Lailahel put the child down upon a glittering crystal rock.

'Well,' it said, 'Soon you will be a long, long way from the place you know as home. Do you wonder what your parents are doing now, little nothing child?'

'I know what,' the child said frankly. 'My mother will be feeding the hens behind the kitchens and my father will be putting new loaves into the oven.'

With a horrified howl, the angel realised that he had been tricked. Furiously, he cast the child back into the world of men, some yards from the city gates. 'Find your own way home!' it boomed. 'And tell Lord Jadrin I will be back at sunset!'

'It was a mistake,' Jadrin said mildly when Lailahel returned.

'Mistake? Don't try my patience. Don't try to tell me you don't know your own child, Lord Jadrin!' The angel glowered, emitting a poisonous aura of brown and livid red.

Jadrin shrugged. 'Nothing is very similar indeed to the baker's son. I was distraught at losing him, blind with grief. The child you want is playing with the dogs on the terrace. Take him, take him.'

'You should apologise for the inconvenience you have caused me,' said the angel in a peevish voice. 'Otherwise, I could cause all of your hair to fall dead upon the floor and blind you forever, grief or no grief.'

'I am mortified!' Jadrin clutched his throat, a picture of wounded innocence.

Lailahel experienced a pang of satisfaction that such a beautiful creature had formed the magical child he intended to abduct. 'Very well. Have no fears for the boy, Jadrin. He shall grow in power and magificence far more than he could have done under your care.' And in a whirl of light, Lailahel, formless and spiralling, swept out of the window and across the terrace. A black haired boy sat upon the chequered, marble tiles whispering to a pair of panting, grinning hounds. Light enfolded him, warm and strong as hands. Still giggling, the child was borne aloft, tossed onto the angel's back and away.

This time, they travelled overland; fields and forests passed beneath them as they rushed towards the sinking sun. Lailahel listened with pleasure to the delighted cries of the child as the world flashed by beneath them. However, a faint but persistent niggle of doubt caused him to sigh, 'You will soon be far from the world you know, little nothing child. Do you wonder what your parents are doing now?'

'That's easy!' responded the child precociously, 'My father will be waiting on table in the king's apartments while my mother mends lace in the butler's parlour.'

Only the fact that he was prince of conception and thus, in some ways, a patron of children, prevented Lailahel from hurling the unfortunate boy to the ground and hurtling straight to Ashbrilim to raze the palace to the ground. He swallowed his fury and with a graceful curl, skimmed around and flew back the way he had come.

Jadrin and Ashalan, as the child had predicted, were indeed sitting down to enjoy their evening meal. The light had not yet vanished from the sky when all the long, arched windows of the dining-room burst asunder and the angel Lailahel gusted into the room. With frightening calm, he strode over to the table and placed the butler's child among the tureens of vegetables. 'Your servant may be missing this,' the angel said dryly.

Jadrin attempted to bluster some reply but the angel raised his hand and shook his head.

'I don't want to hear your excuses, Lord Jadrin. There is only one thing to be said and it is this. Unless the real child of your blood is brought to me immediately, I shall be forced to shake this magnificent and historic building to rubble and then curse you and your beloved king with a dreadful plague, which you shall unwittingly spread to all your subjects before dying a particularly painful and undignified death. I hope I've made my intentions clear.'

'I don't think there can be any doubt as to your determination,' Jadrin said in a choked voice. He turned to Ashalan. 'We have no choice. We will have to give up our son.'

'You should never have done this, Jadrin,' Ashalan said. He called for the butler. 'Your son is returned to you,' he said. 'Have no fear, we appreciate the service you did for us and you and your wife may keep the gold we gave you. Be thankful that events have turned out this way. Now, be so good as to have your good woman bring out Prince Jadalan.'

With great sorrow, Jadrin handed his son to the angel, who smiled and said, 'In future, have the good sense to adopt some earthly child, Lord Jadrin. I believe there are plenty of them about. Good evening to you!' And with a spiral of blinding effulgence, he whisked the child onto his back and flew away, towards the red sky of the west.

As they streaked between the rosy clouds Lailahel felt to compelled to ask, 'What do you suppose your parents are doing now, little nothing child?'

Prince Jadalan curled his perfect little white fists in the angel's streaming hair and said, 'You know very well, Lord Lailahel. They will be grieving my loss and perhaps ordering somebody to sweep up the glass in their dining-room.'

Thus, with a deeply satisfied laugh, the angel looped and wheeled and disappeared from the world of men taking Jadalan the changeling child with him.

Living with the Angel

There are echoes of the androgynous Wraeththu in this story, probably because it was written while I was working on 'Enchantments of Flesh and Spirit'. At the time, I was pondering deeply the concept of gender and identification, although probably wouldn't have thought of it in those terms. I must have been playing with these ideas when I devised Variel's fate in this piece, because if I had followed the premise and theme of the previous two stories in the sequence, it wouldn't have happened. I don't want to say more than that in the introduction, because it will give the plot away.

Lailahel, prince of conception, lived in a far and mystical realm, high above the souls and aspirations of mankind. His home was a wondrous palace, wrought of light and sound, where every room had a mysterious tale to tell and strange aethers roamed the tall, echoing corridors.

Jadalan, the abducted son of the King of Ashbrilim, was very impressed with this new home. Because he was only a child, because he was only half-human and because of the angel's potent power, the memory of his old life soon began to fade. Away went the vision of green fields stretching beyond the city walls. Away, the sight of rolling forests to the north, skirting the great purple mountains where the night eagles lived. Forgotten too, were the faces of Jadalan's parents; the witch-boy Jadrin and the king himself. Estranged from the lands of men, Jadalan became more angel than human.

Now, sometimes angels stretch and stretch so far that they release a portion of themselves into new reality. Lailahel had done this once and had formed for himself a son of his own—though son is not really the word for an angel child. As all angelic creatures, they are neither one gender nor the other, but something of both and sometimes nothing of either. Lailahel's child was named Variel. He was pleased to have a companion, especially one as strange and unethereal as Jadalan. Wherever Jadalan walked in the palace, things came into being as if he called them from the air. Variel could not do that and was delighted when Jadalan made him dogs and jewels and bizarre furniture. 'It was there all the time,' Jadalan would say.

'But no one can make them real like you can,' Variel would reply.

They played together in the crystal fields beyond the palace, where ferns the size of houses swayed and sang to them. Jadalan learned all about the spirits that live beyond the senses of a human and how to call them up and speak with them. The air always smelled of jasmine in that place and at night the sky became a deep, rich purple, but there were no stars. Jadalan slept in a bed of sighing mist and ate from bowls of honeyed ambrosia whenever he was hungry. Lailahel, genuinely fond of the boy, taught him many arcane things and would brush out his hair with the sparks that flowed from his fingers. Jadrin's childhood, therefore, was nothing other than idyllic, but Lailahel was careful to teach the boy about the dark side of existence; misery, loss, privation and pain. The angel knew that if the boy remained ignorant of these things he could only ever exist as a powerless half-creature. However, Jadalan's journeys through such experiences were always necessarily those of the mind and he would always wake up to the soothing light of his wondrous home and the cries of his nightmares would fade away to mere lessons in his head. Nonetheless, he learned and grew to be a wise yet joyful sixteen year old, with more angel in him than he'd ever have had growing up in the gardens of Ashbrilim. As he grew in wisdom, so he grew in beauty and eventually because of the close proximity in which they existed, Jadalan and Variel fell in love. Neither of them particularly understood what they were feeling because they were very innocent and neither of them had any idea what the strange sensations in their bodies could mean or how they could be satisfied. Lailahel noticed their growing closeness with unease. He knew that if they discovered the pleasures of the flesh, they might want to leave and form their own astral palace. Lailahel would no longer have control of either of them. Caught up in a maelstrom of jealousy that had more than one cause, Lailahel decided that Jadalan would have to leave the palace of light. Variel was of his essence; the angel could not bear to lose him.

One morning soon after this revelation, Lailahel said to Jadalan, 'You are nearly a man, or as close to a man as you can get, therefore the time of testing has come. You must undertake a series of tasks, which, if you fail them, will mean you'll have to return to the world of men.'

Jadalan looked horrified. In many ways, he had lived an idle life.

'It may sound hard,' Lailahel said, 'But believe me, it's for the best. Beyond the blue fields of the north, you will find a single stone sticking from the ground at the boundary of my lands. It is the last stone of the spire of a buried temple. By sundown tonight, you must have excavated that temple or else be cast out into the world of men, where you will be cold and the light may burn you.'

Miserably, Jadalan trudged down the blue fields until he saw the stone that Lailahel had spoken of. Using a spade, which he'd manifested into being on the way, he tore at the crumbling, fragrant, crystalline soil, but as fast as he dug a hole the crystals fell back into it. The land was too dry, the

spade too small. By the time Variel came down the field to bring him a
lunch of ambrosia, Jadalan was in despair, clawing at the ground with his
bare hands. 'Oh Variel, tonight I must leave here,' he cried. 'As fast as I
try to dig up the temple, it is covered again. There's no hope.'

'Don't fret,' said Variel. 'Go over to that hill and lie down and rest.
You'll get nowhere if you're tired. Perhaps I can think of a way to help
you.'

Jadalan and Variel went to the hill and sat down together. Jadalan ate
his dinner and then collapsed on the short, alien turf, exhausted by his
work. As soon as he saw this, Variel got to his feet and went back to stand
by the temple stone. He held out his arms and cried out to the sky,

'All ye beasts of field and stone,
All ye beasts of woodland throne,
Attend me now and dig this earth,
Bring the temple to rebirth.'

And in a great flash of blue light, strange creatures hastened out from
the trees of glass and metal, burrowed up through the crystal soil and flowed
round Variel's ankles like a sea of fur and spines and fluff. He directed
them to their work and, by the time Jadalan stretched and yawned and sat
up on the hill, in the valley there stood a magnificent, gleaming temple.
Jadalan knew that Variel had done this for him and ran down the hill to
take the angel's child in his arms. 'You have saved me,' he said and kissed
Variel on the mouth. It was an impulsive gesture and one they had not
thought to try before.

However, Variel was afraid of experimentation. 'We must return to
the palace,' he said. 'Lailahel will be pleased that you have passed the first
test.'

This, of course, was not altogether true. Lailahel suspected that Jadalan
must have had some kind of outside help but it never crossed his mind that
Variel might have had anything to do with it. 'You will find tomorrow's
task just as simple, I'm sure,' he said silkily. 'To the west of the palace is a
lake that is seven miles long and seven miles wide. Your next task is to
drain it so that I may walk in the ruins of an ancient angelic city that used
to stand there.'

Jadalan was again filled with alarm. At daybreak, after a mostly sleepless night, he set out for the great, still lake to the west of the palace. In the
weird, morning light, it appeared as a polished, silver tray. Surely, some
liquid other than water lay there. Jadalan went to the shore of the lake.
White sand of fragrant resin crunched beneath his feet to release a pungent
perfume that made his head ache. The lake was absolutely motionless—

and vast. He sat down in the sand and rested his chin on his fists to stare helplessly out over the object of his task. He had no magic strong enough to deal with it. By tonight, he was sure, he would once again be treading the rough earth of the world of men, homeless and unwanted.

After a while, Variel came down to the lake, bearing a pitcher of milk for Jadalan's refreshment. 'As you can see, I've made very little progress in draining the lake,' Jadalan said scornfully and with a dismal, humourless laugh.

'Don't worry,' Variel replied. 'Drink this milk and lie down to rest on that bank of wild myrrh-moss over there. Perhaps I can think of some way to help you.'

Gratefully, Jadalan did as he was told. The milk made him sleepy and presently he fell asleep.

Then, Variel went to stand at the edge of the lake and raised his arms to the sky, calling out over the shining surface,

'Silver beasts of foam and wave,

Attend to me, my friend we'll save,

Drain the lake and drink it dry,

Reveal the city to the sky.'

Immediately, the calm, mirror surface of the lake began to stir. Fish of every shape and size swam up through fissures in the lake-bed from other water-ways, underground rivers, and hidden oceans. Being angelic by nature they swallowed the liquid of the lake and took it with them back to their shadowy aquatic realms, far beneath the ground. And in its place, the ancient city stood revealed, purple weed clinging to its ragged spires, its proud avenues choked with silt and stones. Jadrin awoke and ran to the edge of what was now an enormous crater. 'Variel, how did you do it?' he exclaimed.

'It was done because it had to be done,' Variel replied. 'Let us return to the palace, so we may tell Lailahel.'

'If first I may kiss you again,' Jadalan said.

Variel looked surprised. 'Well, if you want to, then you may.'

Jadalan put his arms around the angel child, and thought about how slim he was, how fragile. He took a handful of Variel's silver hair and thought about how fine it was, how pure and fragrant. 'Variel, you are beautiful,' he said. 'I could never tire of looking at you.'

'Tire, maybe not. But Lailahel will lock me away if we don't return home. It is late.'

'Are you afraid of me in some way, Variel?'

'Perhaps I am. After all, you are an earthly creature.'

'Then maybe I should return to the place where I came from!' Jadalan cried, surprised at the pain those words inspired. He ran away from Variel, up the swaying fields towards the palace. I belong nowhere, he thought. I am neither man nor angel. What am I? Is there anywhere I can truly belong?

Lailahel could not disguise his agitation when Jadalan summoned him to a western window of the palace and showed him the drained lake and the city that lay there instead.

'I would advise you to wait until the mud has dried before you attempt to walk the streets of that place,' Jadalan said, trying to be helpful. 'It looked very deep and smelled most unpleasant.'

'Don't presume to lecture me, boy!' Lailahel snapped. 'So you completed the task?'

Jadalan looked away. He found it very difficult to lie. 'The task is completed, yes,' he said.

At this, Lailahel gripped his arm with talonned fingers. 'You don't fool me! By the elements, you surely have the blood of Jadrin in your veins. A minx, a trickster, like him! Who helped you, boy? Who drained the lake for you?'

'I did it myself!' Jadalan cried, feeling his face grow hot.

Lailahel appeared to withdraw into an icy tranquillity. His temper sloughed away. 'Very well. Tomorrow, complete the last task or it's back to the earth for you! In the centre of my neighbour's garden is an image of the Tree of Life. I want you to climb it and bring me back a pearl from the crown you will find in a nest at the top of the tree.'

'Your neighbour's garden?' Jadalan repeated in a small voice.

'Just so,' replied the angel.

Jadalan went directly to his room, threw himself on the bed and wept. He knew that Lailahel's neighbour was a crusty demon of truculent and unreasonable nature, who guarded his land with basilisks and cockatrices, who devoured first and asked questions later. Even before he reached the Tree of Life, Jadalan knew his task was doomed. He realised that Lailahel really meant to kill him, and in a flash of insight saw the tasks for what they were. Lailahel had no intention of testing him, he could see that now. 'He only wants to be rid of me,' Jadalan thought miserably. 'It is because I am half human.' There was no alternative but to leave the land of angels immediately and find his way to the world of men himself. Perhaps there, he could find a secluded corner in which to meditate on his woes until death took the hand of age and left him lifeless. The thought of solitude gave him some comfort. Lailahel had spoken of earth as a crude and uncomfortable place, but Jadalan now remembered the dreams he had once had of green fields and shady glades in creeping forests filled with the bright eyes of woodland beasts. Let the angels keep their stark, beautiful purity; he would go to the land of his fathers. Only the thought of leaving Variel caused any real pang in his breast. As he packed his most treasured belongings, he kept seeing the huge violet eyes of the angel he loved. He saw the smile, the hair, the quickly moving hands. No matter! Hardening his heart, Jadalan crept from his bedroom and tiptoed down the misty corridors of the palace, out into the purple night, where moths the size of dinner plates flickered and glowed among the curling branches of a grove of maiden trees and the road shone white and hard towards the north. Jadalan walked through the night, past the temple he'd been ordered to excavate, past the boundary of Lailahel's lands. As he walked, he found he was weeping and that his body was aching for a final embrace. But he was alone under a moonless sky and no one heard him.

In the lilac morning, Variel awoke and hurried down to the gleaming terrace where he, Jadalan and Lailahel were accustomed to break their fast. Only Lailahel was seated at the table sipping a distillation of amber crystals and staring with unreadable expression out towards the mud-limned city where the silver lake had once stood.

'So where is Jadalan?' Variel asked. 'Have you set him another task?'

Lailahel turned a speculative eye towards his son. Maybe there was a note of sarcasm in Variel's voice that morning that was not usually present. 'As you ask—yes,' the angel replied stiffly.

'What is it this time?'

'What business is it of yours?'

Variel shrugged. 'Curiosity only.'

'Someone has been helping the boy, I'm sure of it. Therefore, I consider it more prudent to keep to myself what I've asked him to do this time.'

'Forgive me,' Variel said smoothly, 'but I fail to see why these tests are necessary. Hasn't Jadalan been as much of a son to you as I am?'

'A son to me, but what to you?' the angel raged suddenly.

Variel was taken aback. 'A brother,' he replied, 'what else. I'm very fond of Jadalan and it upsets him that you should test his loyalty or his suitability to remain here like you're doing.'

'Variel, you are blind! I should send you too to the world of men to learn a little common sense. Jadalan desires you. He will violate your mind and body if he remains here. Don't speak! Just think about my words. He will bring the crudity of humankind to our dreaming land. I won't have it.'

'What if he completes the tasks?' Variel said quickly before Lailahel could silence him.

The Angel of Conception stared long and narrowly at his son who, though small beneath his father's gaze, stared back bravely. 'If he completes the tasks?' Lailahel laughed. 'If he does that, he can have you. He can have you across my own dinner table if he likes! If he completes the task! Hah!'

And with that, Lailahel drained the rest of his amber liquor and swept back into the palace of light.

Variel sat trembling for a further pleat of light and shadow. Lailahel had left a lot of his rage behind, which lingered over the table like a pungent smoke. Variel was concerned for Jadalan, suspecting that this final task would be the hardest of all. He realised that Jadalan would have no hope of completing it without his help. Sighing, he rose and glided into the palace, gazing at the marvellous things that Jadalan had wrought for them. Climbing the white crystal stairs, he went to Jadalan's room, hardly daring to hope that he would be there, but perhaps to gain some clue as to where Lailahel might have sent him. The room felt very different than it usually did. This was because Jadalan had left a fume of grief and despair in the air—alien aromas to the palace of light. It also felt very empty. Variel sat on the bed and absorbed the atmosphere. After a few minutes, he gave a short gasp and shot to his feet. A cursory search confirmed his fears; Jadalan had gone. He had not gone to complete the task either, but just to wander away and find some corner in which to grieve. All this Variel gleaned from the air of the room, but one thing he could not grasp—what the task had been. He must know! If he could complete it himself then he could find Jadalan and bring him back. Hadn't Lailahel himself said that Jadalan could stay if the task were completed? Hadn't he? Almost in a panic, Variel ran from room to room, trying to glean some clue, some pervading atmosphere, some phantom word or sigh that could tell him what he needed to know. There was nothing. Eventually, he paused in the salon where Jadalan had told Lailahel the lake had been drained. Naturally, the angel had been prudent enough to clean the atmosphere in the place; he wanted to be sure there was no way anyone could discover Jadalan's final task, but he had forgotten one thing. On the far wall, almost obscured by a heavy curtain, hung a large, oval mirror. This was one of Jadalan's creations and Lailahel had admired it, which was why it now hung on the wall. Variel passed through the room like a ghost himself and he heard the mirror whispering as it revolved the images it had absorbed over the past few days in its cold, glass soul. Variel paused and stared at the bright surface. Only his own reflection stared back. 'Tell me,' he said. 'Is Jadalan in there? Is he?'

'Demon tree,' the mirror whispered. 'Crown of the tree. A pearl. A pearl...'

'Demon tree?'

'The tree of life. Its image.'

'A pearl from the crown? Is that what he asked for?' Variel could not believe his ears. Sabbalom, their neighbour, was notoriously solitary. It required aeons of negotiation even to secure a social visit, never mind permission to climb the image of the Tree that hung over his lawns. Variel was not sure whether even he could complete such a task. He sighed. Sure or not, it would have to be done. Why? He kept on staring into the mirror. He had lived for an age in this place before Jadalan came. Why risk danger just to keep him here? Couldn't life resume its old pattern now? Variel considered. He thought about the barren days that would ensue without Jadalan's bright company; the absence of his humour, the absence of his beauty. 'I would rather travel the world of men myself to find him,' Variel thought. 'My father's house is a wasteland without him.' Thus a decision was made and without further hesitation, Variel transformed himself into a spiralling column of light-shot mist and whirled up and away towards the demon's garden.

Jadalan had come close to the edge of the angel's kingdom. Ahead of him, a golden gate hung in the sky, flanked by winged sentinels holding drawn swords. The gate was so vast that he felt he could touch it, but it was some leagues off yet. Jadalan put down his bag of meagre belongings and stared back up the road for a moment. He could no longer see any of the shining dwellings of the angels, only a strange, flat plain of sparkling stones. Here the dominion of Earth crept over the threshold and the magical stuff of angelic creation drew back its toes in distaste. Jadalan allowed himself to shed a few last tears of farewell. His vision was blurred by them to the extent that it seemed a shimmering vortex spun along the road towards him. Jadalan blinked and the rushing spiral was still there. He made a sound of distress and picked up his bag to run and run. He was sure it was Lailahel coming after him and he feared for his life. All misery was forgotten in that moment of stark desire for survival. He began to run, but the sparkling stones of the road had become slippery beneath his feet so it seemed that, as if in a dream, he could not go forward at all. The rushing wind was nearly upon him and, uttering one last despairing, defiant wail, Jadalan fell to his knees, covering his face, letting the vortex engulf him. But then there was no cold, furious embrace but only a sudden stillness and a voice he knew saying, 'Jadalan, Jadalan, get up. Get up quickly.' The voice was almost unrecognisable because of its hollow ring of fear but he could tell it was Variel.

The instant relief and joy that recognition gave him soon subsided to a more bitter, spiteful human reaction. 'You should not follow me, Variel,' Jadalan said. 'I am returning to the land of my fathers as Lailahel wants, and if you were truly honest with me, you'd say you wanted too.'

'Don't be a fool, Jadalan!' Variel said, surprised.

'I won't return! I can't!'

'I know that. Neither can I. Look.' Variel held out his hand and uncurled the long, pale fingers. In his palm rested a single, enormous, perfect pearl in which the colours of the universe shifted and writhed. Variel looked at the light of it reflected in Jadalan's face.

'The pearl. You took it.' He looked at Variel. 'Why?'

'I'm not sure. It seems senseless, I know. When Sabbalom comes cursing over the wall, Lailahel will know that it was me who took it. I've exiled myself. For you. It's senseless. I don't know why. I thought I could sneak in and steal it and bring you back. We could have said you'd taken it yourself and everything would have been alright. I must have been out of my mind. The place was crawling with sentinels who kicked up such a cacophony when they saw me that Sabbalom himself came out onto the lawn. He saw me and was furious. He will know who I was, I can't go back. You must take me with you.'

Jadalan looked wretched. 'No, Variel, I can't do that,' he said. 'You'd hate it and then you would hate me. Say I bewitched you, anything, only go back to your father's palace. I beg you.' He had clenched his fists helplessly in front of him.

'How strange you are, Jadalan. You don't want me to go back at all,' Variel said. 'Nor am I going to.'

'I'm human, you're an angel. You'd pine for your home. Please. Go back. Let me go.'

'No. I don't want to live here without you. I can change. I can live in the world of men. Others have done it. I want to be with you, Jadalan.' He held out his arms and wrapped Jadalan in them. Then Jadalan was lost and could not have sent Variel back for all the freedom in the world. They clung to each other, tiny as pins on the wide, glittering road, with the great gate of creation hanging over them.

'Come,' Variel said. 'Lailahel will follow, I'm sure of it. We must go.'

Jadalan kissed him one last time and picked up his bag. Together they walked towards the gate, swiftly, not looking back. After a few steps Jadalan said, 'What is that odd noise, Variel?' He made to turn and look behind them, but Variel hissed.

'No, don't look, don't look! It is just a breeze passing over the stones, nothing more.' They increased their pace.

'Variel,' Jadalan said in a low, tense voice. 'I am filled with fear— filled with it! What is that noise?'

Variel clutched his arm, bringing pain. His face was almost translucent, his eyes wide and completely black. 'Don't look back, don't say what you think it is. There are just soul birds flying above us, that's all. Quick! Quick!' They were almost running. Hot air blew the hair up on their heads and a whistling scream penetrated through the wind; a scream of fury and potency.

'Variel, it's him! It's Lailahel!' Jadalan screamed, unable to keep the name inside him any longer.

'Then run! Then run! Then run!' Variel replied, and half swooping, half running, he dragged Jadalan along the road, which roiled like smoke beneath them, a writhing black shadow between them and the gate.

Jadalan felt tears of sheer terror sting his face. He could hardly see the Gate now and swore he could feel the hot breath of the avenging angel on the back of his neck.

Suddenly, Variel pulled him to a halt. 'Keep going, Jadalan,' he said, 'I shall distract Lailahel in some way. I will come to you. Keep going.'

'No,' Jadalan croaked. 'You won't. Lailahel will kill you. Let's keep going—together...'

'Hush, no time for that, no time at all. Run. I love you. Run.' And Variel let out one shuddering gasp of breath and blew Jadalan up the road.

Jadalan wailed and waved his arms, calling out, until Variel disappeared into the black smoke. His voice came faintly to Jadalan's ears or maybe into his mind. 'I'll come to you, I promise. But you'll only know me if nobody else touches you in love before I come. Otherwise your memory of me will fade completely. Take care, Jadalan, and wait for me!'

Then the black mist enclosed Variel completely. The Gates of Creation creaked open and Jadalan was sucked, head over heels into the world of men.

Variel stood small and straight upon the road, facing the approach of Lailahel, with Jadalan's wails fading behind him. All he had as protection was the pearl from the Tree, and his knowledge of such things was far from all-encompassing. Lailahel appeared as a black storm, eyed with golden orbs of anger. The raging column paused in front of Variel, its spinning decreasing until the tall, slim form of the angel could be seen hovering within it. 'What are you doing?' he asked in a reasonable voice.

'I am following Jadalan to the world of men,' Variel replied. 'You cannot stop me Lailahel. I have made up my mind.'

Lailahel uttered an indulgent laugh. 'A pretty show of loyalty, dear child, but woefully misplaced! Do you realise what will happen to you in that place?'

'Nothing worse than the emptiness I'll feel should Jadalan go from my life.'

'Such loneliness would be a boon in comparison! Foolish child! If you turn from our world and live upon the Earth, you will become mortal as they are, doomed to age and die. But neither will you become one of them. You can't. Neither man nor woman can you be, and they will fear you because of that. They will cast you out and pelt your body with stones, a body that will be an abomination to them, because they will not understand it. They will desire you and loathe you. And as for your beloved Jadalan, well, under the light of his own sun you will appear as a demon to him, a creature of darkness. What is translucent and holy here in our lands will become freakish clay beneath the sun. Follow him, Variel, and you condemn yourself to a misery as eternal as mortal life can be.'

Variel hesitated. Then he said, 'You lie,' in a small, uncertain voice.

Lailahel laughed. 'Lie, do I? In your heart you know that I do not. Come home with me. If you desire closeness then I can give it to you, but do not turn to mortal beings for that—ever. They will destroy you, as they destroy all things they do not understand. And, it must be said, he could never give you pleasure, Variel. It is beyond his capabilities. Stay with your own kind. Come home.'

Variel still hesitated. He stared hard at Lailahel, whose golden eyes were impenetrable as the metal itself. 'I shall have to see this for myself,' he said at last.

'You won't be able to return if everything goes black. You do know that, don't you?'

'I gave him my word I'd follow.'

'They expect us to break promises. We are angels, unpredictable and contrary. Forget him, Variel. Come home.'

'In my mind, I see the sense in your words, Lailahel, but my heart is telling my mind to be silent. I love Jadalan. I must follow him, for good or bad. I have no choice.'

Then Lailahel grew in stature until the image of him filled the whole, glowing sky. He turned the sky livid violet with his fury. 'I will not let you go, Variel. You are my son.' And poisonous tendrils of semi-solid fume snaked towards him.

Variel screamed, unsure of what to do. He found that he had tossed the pearl from the crown of the Tree of Life high into the air, where it spun and spun, a single bright mote against the shadows of the angel's rage. The pearl contained the sum of all knowledge, a blinding ache that burst into the air of the land of angels, a thousand, thousand sharp thrusts of light and meaning. In an instant, Lailahel was given the vision of Variel, bound and helpless, chained in the palace of light and the light was gone from him. He was given the vision of himself suffering the pain of love unrequited as Variel watched the windows for a Jadalan who could never return. All life would be sterile should Lailahel force Variel to return home. With a wail that equalled Jadalan's in despair and wretchedness, Lailahel was sucked inside the vortex of his own ire and disappeared with an eery hiss in the direction of the palace of light.

Variel was left upon the road, alone. He turned around. Above him the giant sentinels spread their wings and drew back the Gates that he should pass. He flew towards them. They did not look at him directly. Variel followed Jadalan into the world of men.

Jadalan meanwhile had emerged from the realm of angels in the land of Cos and, as fortune was with him, very close to the city of Ashbrilim, the home of his parents. It was early morning there and Jadalan found himself walking along a wide, dusty road with fields on either side. He stared at the marvels of the mortal world; the jewel colours of the trees and grasses and flowers, the impossible hue of the morning sky as the sun rose in the east. Horses galloped through the dew, mad with the joy of simply being alive. He walked and walked, and, as the hour drew on, came across other people setting out for their day's work in the fields, the markets, the villages. At noon, he paused by a well to drink and a pretty girl with green eyes and a brown dress offered him a cup of milk instead. She took him to her cottage and fed him and then offered him more than food or drink. 'Kiss me,' she said, pouting prettily. 'I've never seen a lad more handsome than you.'

'I can't,' he replied, smiling.

'And why's that? Spoken for, are you?'

'In a way. I'm waiting for an angel.'

The girl laughed good-humouredly and pestered him no more. Jadalan could tell she thought him strange, perhaps mad. He left the village, still heading west. By late afternoon, the spires and turrets of Ashbrilim could be seen like a mirage in the sky. Jadalan asked an old man scything grass by the road, 'Is that the city of King Ashalan?'

'It is,' the old man replied.

'My parents live there. I'm going home,' Jadalan said and the man nodded and smiled; perhaps he too saw a madness there.

Jadalan wandered the streets of Ashbrilim, eyes wide, steps dragging with fatigue brought on by the assault of stimuli to mind and senses. A thousand brutish odours filled his nose, far removed from the vague perfumes of the land of angels. Everywhere colour and noise whirled around him, indecipherable to his alienated condition. He was almost blind, shaking and nauseous by the time he reached the gates of the palace. The reason for his being there was fading fast in his memory; his body was unable to cope with the drastic differences. Out in the country, those differences had been pleasant, challenging, new. Here in the city, they were cruel and overwhelming. The close proximity of thousands of human souls and human bodies oppressed him; he could sense all their petty cruelties and jealousies, all their dark secrets. Jadalan sank wearily to the ground, leaning upon the closed gates. Never had he felt so ill.

Then, with a shattering burst of noise, the gates were thrown wide open, causing the wilting Jadalan to cringe further towards the dirt, hands to ears, his stomach churning. Loud shouting and laughter, and the sound of horses' hooves sounded from within the courtyard. Jadalan crawled to the side, just in time to avoid being trampled by a group of riders trotting smartly out into the city. Jadalan squinted. Shapes blurred before his eyes. He did not know it was Ashalan himself, setting off for an evening's hunting in the forests and fields beyond Ashbrilim's walls. Dogs swarmed around the horse's feet and it happened that one of them was the puppy with which Jadalan used to play, in those days before the angel came. Time moves in a strange way between the worlds. Though Jadalan had been away for many years in angelic terms, only eight seasons had passed in the land of Cos. If Jadalan had returned a different way, or on a different day, it might have been that he'd come back to a place where his family had been dead for years. It might have been that the city itself had fallen to dust. There was no way of knowing. He'd been lucky and the dog that he had petted as a baby recognised his scent, broke away from the pack and bounded up to him, tail wagging wildly. Before Jadalan could move, the animal had covered his mouth with affectionate licks, the touch of love that Variel had warned against, thus effectively destroying any vestiges of memory that Jadalan had retained of the recent past. He lay back in the dust with the dog nuzzling his face, eyes staring vacantly at the sky. Ashalan noticed the commotion and sent one of his aides to see what the dog was doing.

'Why sire, it is a lad,' the man said.

Ashalan dismounted and went to see for himself. It was as if Jadrin himself lay there, stupidly gazing, but a Jadrin of even finer aspect and ambience.

'The boy is ill,' someone said. 'Perhaps diseased.'

'Have someone take him into the palace,' Ashalan said.

'Is that wise, sire?'

'Have someone take him into the palace.' The king's tone was not to be argued with.

In this way, Jadalan returned home, but without the capacity to say who he was or what had happened to him.

Because of his beauty, he was taken to the royal apartments, bathed and laid in a soft bed. Ashalan had even considered that this was some relative of Jadrin's come to seek him out, but Jadrin claimed no recollection of such kin. He watched the boy coolly as the servants tended to his body. He felt he ought to be angry at the way Ashalan had brought him in; it was obvious why, and yet, some part of him, deep within, was drawn to the pale stranger. 'Perhaps I find him attractive myself,' Jadrin thought and yet, it did not feel that way. When the servants had finished, Jadrin sent them away. He stood and stared at the boy lying there. 'Yes, he looks like me,' he thought. 'How odd.' A vague memory stirred, of a moonlit bathroom and blood, black in the moonlight, pooling on the floor. Jadrin shuddered and the boy opened his eyes. They were the colour of violets.

'Who are you?' Jadrin asked and the boy struggled to speak. 'Who are you? Who are you?' Jadrin had leaned right over him, his voice filled with a tremor that could have been fear. Then a whisper: 'Who are you?'

The boy sighed. 'I don't know,' he said. 'I am no one. I am nothing.'

Jadrin found himself pressed against the far wall, one hand to his mouth. He dared not think. He dared not hope. Nothing.

Jadalan recovered slowly, but his mind seemed almost empty. He wandered, pale and lovely, through the corridors of his parent's palace, sat with them to eat, smiled and nodded at their friends, walked in the gardens with his arm through Jadrin's, became beloved to them. Jadrin suspected who he might be, but never voiced his thoughts. Perhaps Ashalan too had some intimation of the boy's identity, but a weird kind of fear kept the king and his consort from discussing the matter. Jadalan simply was. He was with them and they were fond of him. People seemed afraid of the boy so Jadrin named him Ailacumar, which was a deity name, seldom used by the populace, but which represented the god in his aspect of wandering youth. Ailacumar hardly ever answered to his name. There seemed within him a deep and secret sadness. He slept for most of every day and though he smiled, would never laugh.

Variel came to earth in the middle of a forest. He crouched shuddering, beneath the branches of a giant oak, his gossamer angelic robes torn to shreds, his amber skin bruised and scratched. For a while, he could not remember who or what he was, why he was there or where he had come from. The earth claimed him. Stupid with terror, senseless to a degree even more than Jadalan had been, he was unaware of urine pooling beneath him, melting the last of his clothing. He had come to earth and its coarseness claimed him instantly, as if resentful of his aetheric origins. Learn reality, She said. Feel pain and fear; piss yourself. By nightfall, under the softer caress of the moon, Variel stumbled painfully along a forest track. The ground beneath his feet tore his flesh, even the light of the moon burned him. He was unprepared for a visit to Earth. Lailahel was experienced and knew what precautions to take, how to modify his form. Variel was virgin and ingenuous and the Earth mocked him.

Eventually, he found shelter in a byre at the edge of the forest. Lights burned in a farmer's cottage nearby, but he was too terror-stricken to seek aid there. Animals moved patiently in the musty darkness and he lay down in the hay, shivering himself to sleep. There were no thoughts of Jadalan, not even any thoughts of home, just a bewildered and helpless vacuum in his mind. All he desired was rest and warmth.

In the morning, the farmer's daughter came to milk the cows in there and found him. She ran shrieking to the cottage. 'There's a dead person in the byre, Papa!'

The farmer, his sons and his wife hurried out to see. They thought he was a girl at first, until they carried him back to the cottage and saw the finely formed organ between his legs. The farmer's wife made a sign to protect herself from spirits. 'It's a man-woman,' she said. 'A faery messenger.'

'We must put it back where we found it,' one of the sons said to his father. 'Its people will come for it.'

'It's near dead,' said the daughter. 'I'll fetch a blanket.'

As the family debated what to do with their unearthly visitor, Variel groaned and writhed and opened his golden eyes. The family gasped as one, which under other circumstances would have been comical. Variel put his hands over his face and made a terrible sound of despair. Bravely, the daughter went and wrapped the blanket round his shoulders.

'Who are you?' asked the mother.

Variel stared up at them helplessly. Their odour, their physical strength, their animal forms virtually made him feel sick. He shook his head and closed his eyes, hot tears squeezing between his lids.

'Are you of the faery?' asked the farmer, gruffly.

Variel shook his head. He could not speak.

'Obvious what this creature is,' said one of the sons proudly. 'A freak. Probably from one of the travelling fairs. Probably got lost, and separated from its people. Is that right, stranger?'

Variel could sense these people desperately wanted answers about him. He was weary, sick and afraid. He nodded his head. It seemed the best thing to do. And they accepted that.

The farmer's daughter's name was Phoebe. A kind-hearted soul, she took Variel into her care, nursing his constantly solidifying physical form back into health. Variel simply lay on a low cot in Phoebe's room, staring at the far wall for three days, watching the sunlight and the moonlight cycle and slide and feeling himself change, become clay. He lay there thinking about what his angelic father had told him and how all those words were becoming truth. He was conscious of the heaviness of his body, the unwieldy solidity of his flesh. He could smell himself beginning to emanate the animal odours of humankind. He could feel all that was magical about himself draining away.

On the morning of the fourth day, Phoebe woke before dawn as usual to attend to her chores and then, as sunlight burned away the grey, came to bring Variel a bowl of cereal foamy with warmed milk. Previously, Variel had been unable to stomach more than a mouthful, so Phoebe was rightfully surprised as she watched her unearthly charge heartily consume half of the bowl before clutching his stomach with a groan. 'You feel better today then,' she said, eyes round as coins. Variel had not spoken to her yet. She had to sit down when he said,

'Yes. In a way, I think so.'

What a strange voice this person had. 'What are you?' Phoebe asked. 'What is your name? Where do you come from?'

Variel remembered what Lailahel had told him about humans pelting him with stones and thinking him a freak. He was unsure of what to say and merely opened and closed his mouth a few times.

'You are afraid,' Phoebe said. 'Don't be. You are among friends here. We will not harm you or send you back, if that's what you're afraid of.'

'No one can send me back,' Variel said, and told her his name.

Phoebe seemed content with that for the time being and offered him some of her youngest brother's clothes to wear.

The family gathered for breakfast and, for the first time, Variel joined them. The kitchen was dark and pungent. Dogs and cats continuously put their paws onto Variel's lap where he sat, begging food. Variel was afraid of them. He was less than an animal in this world, for even animals knew the way of things here and how to behave. He was also uncomfortably aware of the curious glances cast his way, disgusted by the brutish table manners of Phoebe's male relations. Even though Phoebe tried to encourage him to drink a glass of apple juice, he dared put nothing in his mouth, for fear of bringing it right back onto the table.

At length, Phoebe's father pushed his plate away, uttering a resounding belch of satisfaction and announced, 'Mother, it is not right that wench, strange as she is, should be dressed up as a boy. See to her togs and have Phoebe show her the chicken runs.'

Thus Variel learned that in this world at least he was destined to be a she, however odd, and from that moment it was true that things became easier for him.

So Variel learned the lore and customs of working the land. She found that, after a while, it came as a natural and enjoyable thing to do. She did not mind the long hours or the hard toil and found her new human body became less of a burden as time went on. With Phoebe's encouragement, she began to take care of her appearance, and took joy in the lissom athleticism of her form. Slim as a whip she was, sinewy as a boy and fast as a hare. She could wrestle with Phoebe's brothers and not be bested, she could fell a tree with the heaviest axe and still be a fey, languid beauty in the lamplight at dinner. The family came to adore her and could not remember what the days had been like before the flame of Variel's presence had come to warm their home.

Variel could not believe that the world of men could offer such pleasures as she now beheld. The miracle of life, the changing banner of the seasons, delighted her and filled her with awe. As an angelic being, isolated in the realms of light, she'd had no thought for the Great Goddess of the Earth. Now, Variel embraced her as did all the farming families in the community.

One night she and Phoebe went down to the pool hidden in a sunken spinney in the farthest paddock. It was the night of the full moon and

Phoebe wanted to bathe naked in the waters to entreat the Goddess for the powers of attraction. There was a young lad working for a neighbouring farmer for whom she'd developed a craving. Variel was happy to comply with her friend's wishes. Indeed, she looked upon Phoebe as a sister now. As she sat on the bank of the pool, watching the farmer's daughter raise her wet, pale arms to the sky, Variel reflected on how long she had been in this place and for the first time was visited by a pang that reminded her of Jadalan. He seemed a creature of her dreams nowadays, an insubstantial idea that bore no relation to her life as she now lived it. Her past life had become similarly unreal. Now she was a young woman, with a young woman's needs and feelings, if not possessed utterly of a young woman's physical form. This was what the Goddess had decreed and Variel considered that the Goddess was indeed a benevolent Being to have so tolerated her on the Earth. It was almost as if she'd been rewarded. How wrong Lailahel had been and yet, how right, too.

Phoebe came swimming to the water's edge. 'You seem thoughtful, Variel. Are you all right?' she asked.

Variel smiled. 'I was thinking of my father,' she replied.

'Do you miss him?' Through veiled remarks made by Variel, Phoebe had gleaned Variel had been found in such a distraught condition because of being exiled from home by her angry parent. It was a subject they rarely discussed, for Phoebe sensed it gave Variel pain to think about it.

Variel wrinkled her brow. 'Miss him? How odd. I never thought of it that way. I suppose I do, but there's no point grieving. I'll never see him again.'

'What was he like?' Phoebe asked carefully. From Variel's dreamy expression she was thinking the father must have been a wild and handsome creature.

'He was an angel,' Variel replied, laughing. 'I was an angel too, and he kicked me into the world of men.'

Phoebe laughed too. 'You are a strange one, Variel. Your sense of humour is peculiar at times.'

Variel frowned. 'No, I lied. I was not kicked into the world of men. It was my choice. I loved a man. I followed him. But now it's like a dream.' She turned and stumbled away from the water, one hand to her eyes, the other blindly reaching forward.

Perplexed and concerned Phoebe scrambled from the water, her wet skin gleaming like silver, and hurried after her, not even pausing to dress herself. 'Variel, stop! Come back!' She ran after the swiftly marching Variel and laid a restraining hand on her arm.

Variel spun around, shaking her arm from Phoebe's hold. 'Am I human, am I?' she demanded angrily.

Phoebe was frightened and confused. Had Variel gone mad? 'Of course you are,' she soothed, and then remembered the weird, shimmering body she had found in the byre, the odd sexuality of it, the alien feel of it. 'You are *now*,' she amended.

Variel snarled. 'Don't be so sure!' she snapped and then with another lightning change of expression began to cry and raised her face to the moon. 'Goddess, what am I? Can I truly live here in contentment? Am I worthy of such a thing? Or will I one day petrify and shatter and break like a crystal shard? Oh, help me! Help me!'

Phoebe was concerned that one of her brothers on his evening chores might hear the commotion and come to investigate. She dragged the protesting, wailing Variel back into the hollow, where the night breeze ruffled the surface of the pool. The water grasses rattled as if the Goddess herself was concerned at what was happening. 'Get into the water!' Phoebe ordered, tearing Variel's clothes from her back. 'Come on: hurry! Get into the water!' Above them, a vast, pale moon sank towards the trees at the edge of the meadow.

Shivering and weeping, Variel removed the petticoats and undergarments that were gifts from Phoebe's mother. 'Do not look at me,' she said.

Phoebe turned away her face. She did not look back until she could hear Variel splashing into the pool. Crouched down below the surface, only Variel's face showed above the water, her eyes wide and black, her white-gold hair floating around her head like wet silk.

Phoebe stepped into the pool and held out her hands, of which Variel took hold. 'Pray,' Phoebe entreated. 'Pray, Variel, pray! Don't lose it all. Gain more! Pray!'

Phoebe's hands ached from the iron grip of Variel's weirdly strong limbs. Tears squeezed from between Phoebe's eyelids with the pain. The water felt like ice around her legs and stomach. Everything hurt and Variel's face was pinched into an ugly expression of helpless pleading, of determination, of angry strength. Suddenly, with a final agonising squeeze of her hands and a shuddering gasp, Variel threw back her head and, releasing Phoebe from her grip, raised her arms to the sky. With a fluting peal of triumph, Variel rose up from the water, her wet hair clinging to her body, and Phoebe backed, splashing towards the bank, wiping her face. It was as if she beheld an embodiment of the Goddess herself. From between the strands of Variel's encompassing hair, proud, blooming breasts jutted like perfect fruit; an area that had been rather devoid of swelling before. The waist curved in as if carved from perfect wood and, as Variel strode through the water to the bank, Phoebe could clearly see that there was no longer the slightest evidence of masculinity between her legs.

Wild-eyed, Variel stood upon the bank. 'I have been answered!' she cried, fists clenched and raised above her head.

Phoebe scrambled up the bank. She could not speak. She knew she had witnessed some kind of miracle but it had been so awesome, so strange, she was unsure whether gods or demons had been responsible for it.

The next morning, Phoebe was awoken by a chilling cry from Variel's bed. In an instant she hurried to her friend's side, throwing back the blankets, fearing some reversal of last night's event. There was no need to worry. Clutching her stomach, Variel struggled from the bed, where the bottom sheet was stained with red. There could be no mistake. Variel was truly a woman. The Goddess had visited her with the indelible mark of femininity. As the earth, as the beasts, as the birds themselves, Variel was one of the Goddess's creatures now. A fertile female. It was then that she knew it was time for her to seek the city of Ashbrilim.

The family were hardly pleased that Variel wanted to leave them. At breakfast, she told them she must seek the city of the king. She was grateful for all the help they had given her, and one day hoped to reward them for their troubles, but she knew she had a destiny and had to fulfil it.

'What business do you have in Ashbrilim?' asked Phoebe's father.

'I must find the man I love,' Variel said. 'I made a promise.'

Reluctantly, the family gave her provisions and fondly wished her farewell. Phoebe wept openly and begged Variel to return to her one day. This Variel promised to do, if she was able. She too was sad to leave her friends, who had given her so much, but she had a purpose and could not deny it.

For many days and nights, Variel travelled to Ashbrilim. Along the way, she questioned people about Jadalan. 'Does the king have a son?' she asked.

'Of sorts,' she was told. 'Though some say he is not quite of this world.'

Variel was then sure that Jadalan had found his way home. She had only to present herself at the palace for them to be reunited.

However, once in the city, Variel quickly discovered that a common person simply could not walk in through the gates of the palace. She spoke to the guards on duty at the main entrance and said she had come to see Jadalan, the son of the king.

'There is no such person,' said one of the guards. 'The king's son is Ailacumar.'

Another guard laughed. 'Perhaps she has come to offer herself as a bride to the prince! There's enough of 'em flocking here for that!'

'Then she should get his name right,' said the first. 'We were told that Jadalan died as a babe. The new son is Ailacumar. Be off with you, wench! Look at you. You're no friend of royalty.' The guards clearly thought Variel was mad.

Variel pondered the situation until nightfall. Then, because she was more agile than a human could be, she climbed an ancient oak next to the high wall that surrounded the palace gardens. She crawled along a wide limb that hung over the garden and dropped down onto the wide lawn beneath. The palace gleamed before her in the moonlight. She could see guards stationed around it. For while longer, she must think and plan.

At the back of the palace was an orchard at the end of the kitchen garden. Variel made her way to this place and climbed into an old apple tree, next to a clear pool of water. Here, she went to sleep and trusted that her dreams would advise her.

In the early morning, the head gardener's short-sighted daughter passed by the pool and looked into it. She saw the reflection of Variel's face in the water and mistaking it for her own, said, 'Why, how beautiful I am! I should not be working in the garden. I shall ask my father to go to the king at once and tell him that I am the true bride he seeks for the hand-some boy he calls a son, who sighs and sleeps so much.'

Variel had been woken by these remarks and looked down in wonder. She meant to speak, but the girl hurried off before she could do so. A short while later, just as Variel was considering climbing to the ground, the gardener's wife happened to be passing and she also paused to look into the water. As her daughter had done before her, she mistook Variel's radiant reflection for her own—the daughter had inherited short sight from her too. 'Well, look at me!' she declared. 'I am beauty itself! Why should I be married to a mere gardener? I will go to the king at once and tell him I am the true bride he seeks for that boy he calls a son, who sleeps so much and speaks so little.'

A short time later, as the gardener went into his house for breakfast, he was faced with his womenfolk, who he could only presume to be demented. There they were in the kitchen, putting on finery and talking about being so beautiful they must wed a prince. To him, they looked the same as they always had. In between arguments with each other about who was the most beautiful and fit to become a princess, they told the gardener about

how they'd seen their reflections in the pool that morning. Suspecting
capricious magic at work, the gardener went himself to investigate the
matter. He saw the beautiful face in the pool and looked up, spying at once
the young woman hiding among the green leaves.

'Are you a witch?' he asked her.

'No,' Variel answered. 'I am a lady from a far land, and I have come to
see the prince.'

'Get down,' said the gardener. 'You are charming my womenfolk in
strange ways, and it must not be.'

Variel climbed down out of the tree. 'Thank you, sir,' she said. 'You
are most kind not to report me to the guards. Will you favour me further
and tell me more about the talk I've heard, that the prince is to be married?'

Because she was so beautiful, and the gardener was charmed by her in
a different way to the women, he told her that Prince Ailacumar was so
listless, his parents had been advised by the palace physicians to find a
bride for him, in the hope that vivacious female company might coax him
from his lethargy. 'Girls and women from all quarters of the world have
come to the palace,' said the gardener. 'And now, I have heard, King Ashalan
and Lord Jadrin have chosen a suitable bride. The wedding takes place
very shortly.'

'Will you help me?' Variel said. 'I am the prince's one true love.'

The gardener stared at her, 'I should think you mad,' he said, 'but I
have never seen a girl like you.'

'If you'll take me to the prince, you'll not regret it,' Variel said.

Sighing, the gardener nodded and took her into the palace. They went
to the room where the royal family took their breakfast, and here Jadrin
and Ashalan sat with their adopted son, whose head was sunk on his breast
in slumber. Variel recognised him at once as the one she loved. Also seated
at the table was an exotic princess from a far land, who was indeed very
beautiful, but she might as well have been a horse for all the notice Jadalan
took of her.

'What is this?' King Ashalan demanded as the gardener ushered Variel
towards the table.

'This young woman claims to know the prince,' he explained.

'Indeed!' said Jadrin. 'You must tell us all you know of him, girl.'

But Variel barely heard Jadrin's words. She rushed to Jadalan's side
and knelt beside his chair. 'Hear me,' she said, 'I have come to you as I
promised I would. Awake and look upon me.'

Jadalan did not stir, but uttered a soft sound as if his dreams were pleasant.

Variel knew then that some creature must have touched Jadalan in love before she'd come to him, and that all memory of her had faded from his mind. Part of him was lost, perhaps, in the land of angels.

Variel took hold of his hands and no one stopped her. Jadalan's parents and his prospective bride looked on in curiosity and perhaps some hope that this stranger could awaken the prince. Variel began to sing, 'For you I raised the city dead, for you I drained the lake, for you I took the pearl of life with both our lives at stake. For love of thee, beloved one, I fell for love of thee. And to this world I came a girl, your one true love to be.'

When Jadrin heard this song, he asked Variel what she meant, for their son had not spoken of any of these things to his parents.

Variel looked at him and said, 'Three times I completed the tasks that Jadalan had been given by my father, Lailahel. He is my one true love, but now he will not awaken or speak to me. I have travelled here in vain.'

'Jadalan!' Ashalan exclaimed. 'How is this possible? Our son was hardly more than a baby when he was taken from us. We dared not hope this person might be him.'

'This is your son, Jadalan, have no doubt,' Variel said. 'Time passes differently in the land of angels. And I was an angel's son, banished from my father's realm for daring to love a human.'

At once, Jadrin jumped out of his chair and went to his son's side. He put his arms around Jadalan and kissed his face and told him to awaken.

The sound of his name drifted through the fog in Jadalan's mind and he opened his eyes. The first thing he saw was Variel's face and she leaned forward quickly and kissed him upon the mouth. At her touch, Jadalan's memory returned completely, and he stood up, drawing Variel to her feet also. It quickly became clear that the exotic foreign princess would not become his bride.

Jadalan and Variel were married very soon after, and lived long and interesting lives. Jadrin never again resorted to conjuring magical beings to grant his desires, and used his own magic to stay young for many years after Ashalan had gone to his grave an old man. Of the angel Lailahel, nothing was heard again.

The True Destiny of the Heir to Emiraldra

This story is a reinterpretation of the old Scottish fairy tale, 'Tattercoats'. In this retelling, I have been somewhat kinder to the stubborn old grandfather than in the original story, where he is ultimately condemned to a life of isolated misery.

The unadulterated versions of the old tales are often quite grim, and the majority of them have been cleaned up and sanitised to make them suitable for children. But the original versions provide a rich vein of inspiration for writers of fantasy, and there are now dozens of collections of retold fairy tales aimed at adults.

The goosegirl or gooseherd is a character that appears regularly in the old tales, and quite often they have magical abilities. The goosegirl in this story is a witch who plays a magical flute. There are echoes of 'Cinderella' in the riches to rags to riches aspect of the tale and the harsh treatment meted out to the main character before they end up with the prince. Oops, is that a plot spoiler? Well, this is a fairy story, so it's hardly a secret how it's going to turn out.

There was once a grand lord who had built his castle on a high cliff overlooking the sea. The castle was named Emiraldra and was a happy prosperous place. The vines grown in the vineyards produced the finest wine in the land of Cos. The sheep in the fields of Emiraldra produced the finest, softest wool, and all the corn was the plumpest, most golden ever beheld. Lord Thaldocred was a fair and generous employer. He had a wife and daughter whom he loved more than anything. However, one dark, windy day the wife of Lord Thaldocred succumbed to a fierce fever and within days she had wasted away and was dead. The Lord was beside himself with grief and only the comforting attentions of his beautiful daughter Shilalee, sustained his will to live. 'Think now, father,' she said sweetly. 'Though my mother is gone from us, her life was one of fullness and happiness. Now she has gone to a higher place, where one day, we shall all be together again. Let us remember her with pleasure and not sadness.'

Thaldocred held his daughter close. 'You are all that I have now,' he said.

In the Spring, when the first buds were appearing upon the trees, a travelling carnival came to the lawns of fair Emiraldra. People with bright clothes, white flashing teeth and dark mysterious eyes came to knock on the castle doors. Thaldocred would have preferred to send them on their way (with perhaps a small gift, for he was not a mean man), but Shilalee begged him to let the wanderers set up their carousels and gaily-coloured stalls upon the green. People could come from all the nearby villages, she argued gently, and it would be a happy time for all; an assurance that the gaunt winter of death and unhappiness had passed. Thaldocred, as putty in his daughter's hands, relented. Shilalee herself, dressed in green with her long dark hair plaited with spring flowers, went to supervise the arrangement of the carnival. It was then she caught sight of the gypsy boy, Brackeny. Like her, he had long dark hair and a ready smile. Like her, he was lithe and slim, but where her eyes were dark brown, his were moss green and half hidden between thick black lashes.

Shilalee first saw him sitting upon the steps of a caravan, playing upon a reed pipe. It was as if he played to her alone. At first intrigued and attracted, by the time evening came again to the land, her interest had thickened to love. She desired Brackeny more than anything she had ever wanted before. Here was the prince she had so often dreamed of in her cold virgin bed. Such beauty could never been seen in the land around Emiraldra. They spoke together, drawn by their similarities. He told her: 'I will bring you unhappiness. I cannot stay here.'

But she replied firmly that only a few days spent in his company would be worth the heartbreak of separation. Because she was indeed lovely and bright, and a pleasure to be with, Brackeny became her lover; the first she had known. Shilalee was careful not to let her father discover what was going on, for she knew that had he known, his anger would be dangerous for Brackeny. She was Thaldocred's little girl; only he would be given the privilege to decide when, and by which man, she would be taken as a wife.

When the time came for the travellers to move on, and she had bidden a sorrowful farewell to the beautiful gypsy boy, Shilalee was obliged to keep her grief to herself. And that was not all.

In the cold, dark months of deepest Winter, just as the time when Thaldocred was reminded most of death, Shilalee fell to the ground, crying out in pain. For a long time, she had been trying to conceal the fact that she was with child; now her time was upon her. Delirious with fear, anger, incredulity and the impotent lust for revenge, Thaldocred watched helplessly as the single remaining object of his affection writhed and screamed in agony. It was in a dark, heavily curtained room that was over-heated from the effects of a blazing fire, and too stuffy from the smell of human blood, the heaviness of human pain. Here, as minutes passed into hours, Shilalee fought to deliver her child. Women bustled, candles guttered and spat; outside the wind howled. By morning, a pale watery sunlit morning,

Shilalee lay pale and lifeless, staring upon the bed. Close by, mewing in a rough cot, her infant son gave voice to life.

From the moment of his birth, the child became the focus of Thaldocred's hatred. If it was not for this pink mindless scrap, the father reasoned, then his beloved Shilalee would still live. How could she have kept such a thing from him? In rage and pain, he paced the chamber, occasionally throwing bleak glances towards the child. Then, in cold, colourless fury, he ordered that the boy be sent down to the servants' quarters. 'Doubtless there is some barren wench who may want it,' he said.

Shilalee's old nurse, aghast at such callous sentiments, gathered the child in her arms. She looked round the dark, grand bedroom and shook her head. The child was quiet against her breast. Sighing, she took him to her own quarters in the east wing of the castle. Because she had loved Shilalee's mother and Shilalee herself, she devoted herself to caring for the child. Of all those who lived in Emiraldra, she alone had had some intimation of what had transpired the previous spring. Because of this, she named the baby Brackeny, for his father, and as he grew older, the child called her Mussy, which was not quite mother, and not quite nurse, but something in between.

Brackeny's childhood could have been sublime and happy, but there was a change in the air of Emiraldra. All the love had gone from the place. Thaldocred, unable to give proper vent to his grief, had become cruel and petty, seeking solitude, shunning his old friends. The servants, hapless victims of this changed, nit-picking personality, inevitably took it out on Brackeny. Like Thaldocred, they felt that he was to blame for everything, and consequently tried to make his life a misery. They also welcomed the opportunity to treat a member of the aristocracy as cruelly as they'd always dreamed of doing. They gave him nothing. His grandfather gave him nothing. All his clothes were cast-offs and hastily assembled rags, patiently gathered by his beloved Mussy. Because of this, the servants called him Tatters, and the name stuck. Mussy tried to shield him as best she could from their abuse, but one particularly spiteful, grudging individual, the steward of the castle, went carping to Thaldocred about how Mussy was keeping the child in seclusion in the east wing and how they desperately needed extra help in the kitchen. Hadn't Thaldocred himself promised the child to the servants on the day of his birth? As if the mere mention of the boy's existence gave him pain, Thaldocred waved his hand quickly and told the man to do as he wished with the child; he did not wish to hear of it. Mussy could not argue with that. Every filthy, most tiring job in the castle was given to Tatters. It was forgotten by nearly everyone that he was the gentle Shilalee's son; her memory itself seemed forgotten. As Thaldocred had become bitter and cruel, it seemed all his household followed suit, but far from becoming a down-trodden weakling, the boy Tatters seemed to rise above it, letting unpleasantness waft over him like a swift-moving stream. Mussy knew that this was the heritage of his gypsy father, like his dark skin, his dark green eyes, his thick black hair. Nothing could mar the blossoming beauty of Tatters; not grime, not privation, nor even hostility and cruelty. He had a ready smile and every evening, when he returned to the draughty rooms he shared with Mussy in the east wing, he would essay to make her smile. 'Times are hard, my lambkin,' she would say, and the boy would reply,

'It is just like Winter, Mussy. All Winters are hard. We must wait for the Spring.' He possessed an eerie optimism about his estate.

Mussy had told him at quite an early age about his parents. She had also tried to explain about his grandfather, but it seemed beyond the child's comprehension; he wasn't interested in hearing about it. Shilalee had been entombed within a grand mausoleum in the castle grounds. Tatters liked to go there, whenever he could sneak away undetected, hoping that his mother could see him. Sometimes he was sure he could feel her there. Her likeness in cold marble was often warm to the touch and her stone face was sad. Tatters told her not to mind too much about things. He was too full of life to care deeply about what the people of Emiraldra thought of him. They called him bastard, changeling. Most of the time, he felt like a different creature altogether; not even human. The shrilling of the servant women, the kicking and pinching and cuffing of the men, could not touch him. Sometimes he could barely understand their language.

And so the grandson of Thaldocred grew up. Only Mussy kept a reckoning of his birthdays, but by the time he was eighteen, many of the younger female servants began to change their attitude towards him. Their sharp teasing became laced with a different kind of tension. For, from being a beautiful child, Tatters had grown into a beautiful young adult, tall and clean-limbed, lithe as a forest cat, and swift as an eagle. Tatters was not interested in the eyes of the women. He sensed them as pungent, hot and heavy-breathing things, whose spirits were mouths and hunger and nothing else. He felt contaminated near them. But it was not just the women who were aroused by him. Once, one of the stable lads, who had been harbouring the desire for some time, jumped him in the dusk as he walked back to the east wing. Tatters was afraid for the first time. The only other living being who had touched him was Mussy and this was clearly different. He could not understand what was happening, only that he must get away. The man breathed filth and hunger into his ear, fighting to open his clothes. Tatters was disgusted. He held his breath. He fought back, blindly, wildly, and the man fell away, coughing. Tatters saw an erect phallus protruding from the man's clothes. He did not understand and later, Mussy was loath to explain. She told him to be wary of people, which he took readily to heart.

In the Spring, following Tatters' eighteenth birthday, a young woman came to the back door of the castle, seeking employment. She was an odd, skinny creature, boyish and wild-looking, with wise eyes. Something about her infuriated the steward at once, but then he was a man who bitterly resented any intimation of intelligence or beauty in others, whatever their age or gender. It had happened that the lad who had looked after the geese had died in the hard winter from a fever of the lungs. Somebody new was needed to take over his duties. The wages were insultingly low, the hours long and many other household chores were included in the employment. The steward grudgingly told the girl about this, pointing out that she hardly looked strong enough to take the job on. Smiling, the girl thanked him and said that appearances were deceptive, and she really was very strong indeed; she was happy to accept the job. Her name was Charlaise and she was a traveller.

One day, Tatters was walking in the fields beyond Emiraldra. He was supposed to be gathering mushrooms for the evening meal, but had so far been unlucky in his search. As he walked, he became aware of a strange, lilting sound wavering distantly in the air around him. He followed it. Breasting a hill, he caught sight of a large flock of geese in the valley below. Sitting on a stone with lifted knees, a slim figure, dressed in green and brown, was playing on a wooden flute. Tatters walked down into the valley, drawn by the sound. He could not be sure whether the seated figure was male or female, for while the clothes seemed male, something about the body within them didn't. He rarely listened to the servants' chatter and hadn't heard about the goose girl. As for Charlaise, she was usually long gone from he castle grounds by the time Tatters awoke in the morning, and she came indoors long after he had fallen, exhausted, into bed. She had been waiting to meet him, however.

As he approached, she stopped playing and turned her face towards him.

'Don't stop,' he said. 'It was the sound of the earth, and such sounds are few in Emiraldra.'

'I can play for you any time,' she answered. 'You must be Brackeny.'
Tatters had almost forgotten his true name. He nodded, a little confused. 'It's been a long time since I was last called that.'

Charlaise smiled, raised the flute to her lips, and played a few haunt-
ing notes. The geese were all looking at Tatters as if resenting his intru-
sion. They bustled around the stone where Charlaise sat.

'Your wait will not be in vain,' she said, gazing into the distance.

Tatters thought she must mean the mushrooms. He spoke about not
being able to find any.

Charlaise laughed aloud. 'Dance for me,' she said, and played a merry
air.

Tatters' limbs could not disobey the summons of the music. He danced
and the geese danced with him. White feathers floated up around him into
the air.

Time passed like a dream, and hundred thousand images seemed to
flash through Tatters' mind. He saw places he had never seen.

By the time Charlaise took the flute from her lips once more, the sun
was high in the sky. Tatters sank to the ground, exhausted. 'I shall be late
now,' he said.

'Then you'd better be going,' Charlaise answered nonchalantly.

'But the mushrooms...' Tatters looked around himself, helpless.

'Look properly, then you shall see,' said Charlaise.

Tatters left her and scrambled up the hill. In the next field, he came
upon a carpet of white mushrooms, which he was sure hadn't been there
before. As he picked them, he heard the sound of Charlaise's flute, drifting
idly as if from far away. It was in this manner that she educated him about
life.

Tatters came home from the fields to great excitement. Everyone was chattering, standing idle at their tasks. As usual, nobody would answer his
questions when he asked what had happened, so he went in search of Mussy.
He found her plucking herbs in the garden.

How old she looks now, he thought, and was pierced by a cold dart
that was presentiment of the time when she would no longer be on this
earth. Who would care for him then? He ran to her side. 'What's happening, Mussy?'

'Ah,' she answered, straightening up, a hand to the small of her back.
'Today a messenger came from the house of Duke Orvember. Oh, such
finery he wore! It brought back memories of happier times.' Mussy's face
took on a dreamy expression. 'Why, I remember when your grandfather...'

'What was the message?' Tatters interrupted quickly, to bring her back to earth.

She looked at him askance. 'There is to be a great celebration. Duke Orvember thinks it is well past the time for his eldest son to marry, so he has organised a Great Event, to which all the nobility are obliged to take their daughters. Orvember will himself choose a bride for his son. Such was always the way at one time, of course. Everyone of importance will be there. It will be a splendid occasion.' She sniffed. 'Your grandfather has been invited.'

'Oh,' said Tatters. 'Do you think he'll go?'

'Who can tell?' the woman sighed. 'Come on, boy, give me your arm back home. My back is as stiff as a quill.'

On their way back to their rooms, Tatters told Mussy about the goose girl. 'She is very strange. Her music showed me many peculiar things.'

Mussy gave him a shrewd glance. 'Perhaps it would be better if you stayed away from her. Remember you mother got mixed up with an enchanting traveller, and look what happened to her!'

'But I have no friends,' Tatters said, stung. 'I like her. She doesn't frighten me. I can hardly get into the same kind of trouble as my mother, can I?'

'Just keep your wits about you, that's all,' Mussy advised. 'Come now, lad, there's no room for a dour look like that on your bonny face.'

He smiled at her and she mussed his hair. Together, they walked into the castle.

Much to everyone's surprise, Thaldocred, far from flinging the gilded invitation from him in disgust, seem actually nudged from his apathy by it. As if throwing wide the windows of his soul, long unaired, he ordered that a fine new suit of clothes be made for him. Some vestige of happiness appeared to have been kindled in his heart. He occasionally smiled at people.

Encouraged by what she thought might be a change of heart in her master, Mussy summoned her courage and one evening as Thaldocred ate his dinner alone, she crept up to his seat and made a brave request. Her heart was pounding, she could barely speak. 'Could you not take the boy Brackeny with you to the Occasion, milord? He is such a fine young lad and will do you credit.'

Thaldocred dabbed at his mouth fastidiously with a napkin. 'I have no living relatives,' he said stiffly. 'And have no reason to take a servant with me to the house of Duke Orvember.'

Mussy backed away, aggrieved by his cold tone. She did not tell Tatters what she had done.

Every day now, Tatters sought out Charlaise's company. Very soon they became fast friends. He found her easy to talk to and much of what she told him was full of mystery and magic. Whenever he danced to her music, it was as if his mind filled up and overflowed with happiness and a strange, earthy wisdom. He learned many things, such that cannot easily be put into words. Now, she would dance with him often. Together, they travelled to distant places in their minds, and the music was their vehicle. 'You must go to the Great Event at Duke Orvember's castle, Charlaise said.

'Don't be silly,' Tatters replied, but Charlaise did not laugh.

Tatters had never spoken to his grandfather. He had caught sight of him on occasion, but always in the distance. Thaldocred did not come to the part of the castle where the servants lived. Tatters never thought of the lord as his relative, and did not even want to.

Some days after her first request of Thaldocred, Mussy felt she must try again. Surely, there must be some way of reconciling the lord with his grandson? Life was far too short to create such misery. Mussy was sure that in Tatters Thaldocred could find happy memories of his wife and daughter. She sought him out in the stable-yard one afternoon, and asked again. 'Could you not take Brackeny with you to Duke Orvember's, my lord?'

'No. Leave me alone.' He mounted his horse.

Mussy realised the futility of pressing the point and departed.

The whole countryside was filled with the bustle and excitement of the coming Event. People came from afar, all flocking to the town, Skylander, where Duke Orvember's castle reared proud and glittering above the River Musk. Often, colourful strangers could be seen upon the road, which passed the castle Emiraldra, riding in outlandish carriages and accompanied by slaves in silk. Merchants, gypsies and fortune-tellers were drawn to the area.

It all unnerved Tatters a little, who was used to calm and tranquillity in the air of the land.

Charlaise mocked his feelings. 'Change, it is the wine of life.' She played sharp, sweet notes on her flute.

Tatters shook his head. 'I, for one, will be glad when they all go home again,' he said glumly.

Charlaise laughed. 'You must go to Skylander, Brackeny.'

'Why?'

'Because of your nature, your true self.'

'And what is that, Charlaise?'

The girl pulled a wry face and blew a series of low notes on the flute. 'Don't you know?'

'Do you?'

She laughed. 'I know everything. I know justice when I see it, especially of the most apt and poignant kind.'

Tatters often misunderstood, or did not understand at all, a lot of what Charlaise said. Sometimes he thought she was teasing him, pretending to know so much about himself that he did not.

One day, as Tatters danced to Charlaise's music, beneath the hanging willows on the banks of the river, he became convinced he was being watched. Charlaise stopped playing, and the only sounds were the murmur of the water and the occasional call of a bird. Tatters saw a tall, shiny horse standing among the trees. 'Someone is there!' he cried, pointing.

'Indeed there is,' Charlaise agreed, without looking. She looked at her flute with a smile and then played a low, tuneless melody.

The hidden rider urged his horse forward and Charlaise said, 'Have you lost your way, traveller?'

Tatters saw a well-dressed young man, who smelled of pampered living.

'I am on my way to the castle at Skylander,' said the traveller.

'Then you must be going to the Great Event,' Tatters said, walking forward. He touched the velvet nose of the nervous horse, who snorted into his palm.

'I suppose I am,' the young man said.

'Break your journey,' Charlaise suggested. 'Take food and wine with us.'

Tatters turned to her quickly, for they had no food or wine, but to his astonishment there on the grass was a white cloth, heaped with tempting country fare.

'Why, thank you,' the young man said, and jumped down from his horse.

Tatters pursed his lips. Clearly, Charlaise had some interest in this person.

The traveller asked their names.

'This is Brackeny,' Charlaise said and raised the flute to her lips once more.

As she played, Tatters said, 'And she is Charlaise. She is a witch.'

'Is she?' The young man laughed. 'Call me... Willow.' He was looking at the trees. Tatters wondered if that was his real name. Willow took off his hat. Beneath it, his hair was the colour of green-gold. Tatters was impressed by Willow's appearance. Previously, he had considered Charlaise and himself to be the only beautiful people in the entire world.

'Offer our guest some refreshment, Brackeny,' Charlaise said, breaking off her tune for a moment.

Tatters did so. As Willow chewed the food and swallowed the wine, he looked from one to the other of them. 'Are you related?'

'No,' Tatters said.

'Yes, we are,' Charlaise interrupted. 'I am his cousin once removed.'

Tatters smiled. What else would she come out with?

'And where do you live?' Willow asked.

'In the...' Tatters began, but again Charlaise interrupted him.

'That is not your affair, stranger. It is most discourteous of you to ask.'

Willow smiled ruefully and raised an eyebrow. 'Forgive me, my lady!'

Charlaise inclined her head. 'You are forgiven, Master Willow.'

'Well!' Willow leaned back upon the grass and crossed his feet. 'I could not have wished for a better outcome to my day! There I was, hopelessly lost, and I come upon by accident two radiant beings of the fields, who are clearly *both* witches!' He sat up. 'I must say I've never come across people like you before in these parts. Are you travellers?'

'We are all travellers upon the road of life,' Charlaise said. She had been playing a series of monotonous notes, but now the tune picked up, first lilting, then sharp and shrill, then drifting once more. Tatters ate one of her illusory cakes and found it very satisfying. Willow's eyes were glazed. He was listening to the music.

'It is very hot,' he said. 'I feel... light-headed.'

'Take our guest into the shade of the trees, Brackeny,' Charlaise said, and it seemed that even as she spoke the music did not falter at all. 'Take him beneath the hill.'

Tatters helped the young man to his feet and led him beneath the branches of the willows. Now they could not see Charlaise at all, but her music still reached them, clear and strong. Willow put his head in Tatters' lap; his eyes were closed. Tatters could not help but take a lock of the green-gold hair in his fingers.

'I am very tired,' Willow said. 'I have travelled a long way upon the road of life, perhaps, or upon the road of stone. It is all one to me. I am tired, yet strangely I cannot sleep. Perhaps if you could stroke my brow?'

Tatters complied without pause, thinking, how strange that we can do this. How strange to touch another's flesh and want to do it. This person is alive. He breathes as I breathe, he thinks as I think, yet we are worlds apart. I cannot know his thoughts, and yet our skins are touching. How strange.

The music was deeper now; it felt as if dark clouds had drawn across the sun. It was as if Tatters and the man were in a dark green room, closed away from the world. A cool breeze shifted the leaves.

'Lie down beside me, Brackeny,' Willow murmured. 'I am cold now and need your warmth.'

Tatters curled his arms around him.

'You are a witch,' Willow said, and began to kiss him.

Tatters was intrigued. He did not find the experience unpleasant. In fact he was surprised to find his body responding in several unaccountable ways. As the music played beyond the leaves, Willow and the boy moved together to the rhythm, the heartbeat of the earth; and the rich, dark smell of the earth rose, just as slowly, around them.

Charlaise sat on the grass, gazing into the distance, her eyes smiling. Not until she heard Tatters cry out in delight and Willow's answering moan, did she stop playing. In the silence that followed, a dim peal of thunder came from the south.

'I must go now,' Brackeny said, and sat up in the room of leaves.

'I must see you again,' Willow told him.

Brackeny reached for his clothes. 'There is no point. You are obviously a person of high rank, while I am... well, there is no point.' He went out into the darkening sunlight. Charlaise smiled at him.

Some moments later, Willow followed. 'Come to the Occasion at Skylander,' he said to Brackeny.

'No, for one thing I have nothing suitable to wear.' He indicated his ragged clothes and bare feet with a scornful gesture.

'That doesn't matter. Come as you are. It is important.'

'And make a fool of myself? No. Anyway, I'll not be welcome, fine clothes or not. You know nothing about me.'

'Don't be bitter, Brackeny,' Charlaise said. 'He'll be there, Master Willow. Have no fear.'

'What?' Brackeny blustered.

Charlaise smiled at Willow. 'Go in peace, sir. I promise he'll be there.'

Brackeny and Charlaise parted on rather bitter terms, or at least on Brackeny's part. 'With your magic, you will make a fool of me!' he said angrily, but half his anger was deep and heartfelt sadness.

'With my magic, I have made a lover of you—a loved one. You must trust me.'

'What? When you lie so much? Are you really related to me, Charlaise?'

'Yes,' she replied calmly. 'I am your cousin once removed, as I told you. Your father sent me.'

Brackeny was momentarily silenced by this, but still unsure whether or not to believe her. 'What else have you made of me, Charlaise?' he asked in a low, troubled voice.

'I have given you your true self,' she answered.

Brackeny went back to the castle.

At Emiraldra, the first servant who caught sight of him called, 'Hey Tatters, clean the yard, you lazy numskull!'

Totally out of character, Brackeny walked up to him and floored him with a single blow. 'I am Brackeny,' he said. 'Brackeny. Don't forget it.' Then he cleaned the yard.

That night, in the small mirror in his room, Brackeny examined his body for outward changes. What was I doing? He wondered. Was it just Charlaise's music?

He ran his hand down his lean, hard chest, his skinny flank. It brought an echo of gentler, more tender caresses that made his loins ache. He thought of Willow with a sad and wistful sigh. He thought of the slim body, the gentle mouth, the sensitive eyes that had smiled for him alone. He felt that all of it was beyond him, because he was only a servant. Out of reach; a bright star visible beyond the prison bars. At best, all he could be was a man like Willow's whore, something to be kept hidden away, something to be ashamed of. He could not tell Mussy what had happened, but he knew that from now on he would no longer answer to the name of Tatters. He had gained an obscure kind of self-respect. He had made a statement against those who despised him.

Unknown to Brackeny, that evening Mussy tried once more to change Lord Thaldocred's mind. She was incensed enough to say, 'You can't go on living in the past, my lord. Brackeny is living, here and now. He is Shilalee's flesh, her blood. By denying him, you deny not only yourself, but Shilalee as well.'

Thaldocred thought about this. Then he could not help but think of

Shilalee on the bed upstairs, writhing, legs spread, screaming like a slaugh-tered hog. He thought of her blood, her death that had been without dignity of any kind. He shook his head. 'I am sorry. It may be that you are right and I am wrong, but I am getting too old for change. If I die wrong, then I die wrong. Please don't mention this matter to me again. Now go.'
She did so.

The following day, Thaldocred rode away from Emiraldra towards Skylander. He took with him an armed escort of three men. The servants commented on his good mood. He had ordered that they hold a celebration of their own that evening. Now, a huge bonfire was being built in the yard. For once, nobody went out of their way to be unpleasant to Brackeny. Still feeling confused and dazed, he decided to go and find Charlaise. He was not sure whether she meant him ill or good, but she was still the only person he could talk to about this matter.

He found her in he place he had first seen her, sitting on the grey stone, playing her flute. She smiled when she saw him. 'Today, we go to Skylander,' she said.

'Oh, Charlaise!' Brackeny cried, horrified, thrilled, full of dismal hope. 'Why?'

'To watch all the grand ladies and gentlemen arriving at the gate of the castle, of course. Aren't you inquisitive about which lovely girl will be chosen as the Bride?'

'Not really. Are you sure that is the only reason we're going?' Brackeny's question was scornful, but in his chest, his heart began to pound. Though he knew it would be wise never to see the man he knew as Willow again, he also knew that he would not be able to resist trying to.

'That is all,' Charlaise sang, and swinging her long, brown hair, she sprang from the rock and began to dance towards the road. Brackeny fol-lowed. Half of him knew he shouldn't but still he went. Behind them, the geese called mournfully, although they did not leave the stone.

'Are you really my kin?' Brackeny asked as they walked.

'I am,' she answered. 'You were named for your father, you know. Though he had to leave here, Brackeny did not forget you. He knew Shilalee was with child. He knew when you were born and how you grew. He cares for you very much.'

'If that is so, why doesn't he come and take me away?' Brackeny asked. 'Why does he let me stay in Emiraldra with people who dislike me.'

'It is not your destiny to be a traveller,' Charlaise said, gravely.

'You have not answered me. What is my destiny? To be a fool, an outcast? To be offered love serves merely to illustrate the shortcomings of my existence.'

'What will be, will be,' Charlaise declared enigmatically. 'Come now, Brackeny, lift your knees. We shall dance for fifty paces.'

By the time they reached the town, evening had come. Skylander was lit by a thousand lamps and everywhere was music and activity. Charlaise led the way to the gates of the castle, shouting lewd replies to those who called out to her in the markets. She greeted strange people with slanting eyes and gaudy, beribboned clothes. Brackeny followed meekly. He scanned every face, looking for Willow. At the gates, a guard stepped out in front of them. 'Hey, what do you two think you're doing?' he demanded roughly, barring their way with his pike.

In reply, Charlaise merely lifted her flute to her lips and played a quick, merry tune. The guard's face went strangely blank; he stepped back.

Charlaise went first into the castle. 'Where are we going?' Brackeny asked, but his voice was slurred. He felt drowsy; everything around him looked indistinct. Charlaise was playing one of her most powerful musics. Brackeny followed her without question, blindly. They came at last to a great hall, approached through a black colonnade. The hall was filled with light and sound, and many richly-dressed people, who were all twittering and preening and drinking wine. Dozens of young ladies simpered together, looking coyly towards the three thrones at the end of the hall. There the Duke Orvember sat with his wife and eldest son. Perhaps he was already surveying the livestock that had gathered for his inspection. One to be the Bride.

Charlaise knew that by the end of the evening, when more wine had flowed and the sense of competition had heated up, the simpering would turn to sneers, the demure conversation to slander. 'Shallow creatures!' she announced, and took her flute from her lips.

Until that moment, both she and Brackeny had been rendered invisible to other people by the magic of the flute. But the instant the music stopped, both of them materialised out of thin air, slowly, like a gossamer veil falling. There was a sudden hush around them, then a wave of gasps, followed by a wave of subdued laughter. Everyone gawped in surprise. Was this a joke? Glancing towards the Duke, some were not sure whether to laugh out loud or not. In the middle of the room, stood two unlikely figures. One a slim, boyish girl, dressed in man's clothing, and the other a tatty ragamuffin, with bare feet and holes in his pants. Both of them appeared in need of a good wash and brush-up. Perhaps they were entertainers.

Coming out of a daze, Brackeny blinked and looked around himself. In shock and horror, he realised where he was. He felt trapped. On all sides, hostile faces were closing in. He could feel their eyes boring into him, into the very core of his soul. Brackeny looked at Charlaise in despair. She had betrayed him. Was she pleased at his misery? She must hate him as much as all the others. She was mad. His father could not possibly have sent her to Emiraldra. In that moment, he was filled with anger at the world, at his estate, at the looks the people gave him, how they judged him for his appearance. They were all ugly, in spite of their fine clothes and perfumes. He pulled himself straight. 'Take a good look!' he said loudly, in a clear voice. 'For I am as rich on the inside as you are on the outside and, I might add, as poverty-stricken without as you are within.'

Sparing not a glance for Charlaise, without even looking for the one he knew as Willow, Brackeny made to shoulder his way from the crowd.

'Wait!'

Brackeny froze.

'Would you leave these people after delivering to them only half the lesson?'

Brackeny turned and there was Willow, but this was a man who was dressed in black and silver, who wore a silver crownlet upon his green-gold hair, and who had the emblem of the Orvembers emblazoned across his tunic. 'Thank you for coming,' he said.

'It was not my doing,' Brackeny replied stiffly, not really surprised to discover Willow's true identity. He could not resist stealing a glance at Charlaise. She stared at the floor, smiling in a secretive fashion.

'Won't you join me, sir?' the Duke's eldest son asked with a bow.

Brackeny looked at the faces that were hungry with curiosity around him. He nodded. 'I would be honoured.'

The Duke's son led him to the great, carved thrones at the end of the Hall. Brackeny saw Duke Orvember staring at them with an expression comprising dread and apprehension. His wife, a contained creature, merely kept one eyebrow raised permanently in surprise.

The Duke's son faced the crowd. 'I am Persilian, eldest son of this house, and I would speak.' He looked to his father for permission. Orvember raised a cautious hand, but his eyes were pleading for constraint on his son's part.

Persilian took Brackeny's hand in his own and another ripple coursed around the hall. 'For two years,' he began, 'I have been travelling the land, learning, I hope, a little about life. It was on my mind to find myself a wife during these travels, but of all the ladies I met, there was not one who did not look at the world through a narrow window. There was physical beauty to be found, oh yes, and I am not ashamed to admit that in many cases I took advantage of the undisguised offers of fulfilment that were made to me. But beauty of the soul, ah, that is a rare thing, and I was not lucky to come across it once, in either man or woman. As you know, my father called me home. He spoke of celebrations, of events, of taking matters from my hands. "I shall find you someone to love, Persilian," he said and that, as far as he was concerned, was that. Coming home, I lost my way in the fields beyond Emiraldra and it was there, virtually on my own doorstep, that I found the soul with whom I want to spend the rest of my life. I have found true beauty and I do not have the slightest intention of forsaking it.'

And then, in full view of everybody, he took Brackeny in his arms and kissed him. The stunned silence that followed seemed unbreakable. Brackeny could see Duke Orvember, sitting with his head in his hands, staring, mortified through his spread fingers at Persilian. Beside him, his wife stared at the floor, her hand over her mouth and Brackeny had the clear impression that she was trying hard not to laugh. Eventually, the Duke managed to find his voice.

'You speak bravely, my son,' he said, 'but one thing I feel compelled to mention. Where do you intend to find heirs? One would suppose that a union between two males could only be without issue?'

His dry tone produced the ghost of a titter around the hall.

'You are right, father,' Persilian agreed. 'We have two courses of action. One is that Brackeny and myself leave Skylander without further embarrassment to yourself, and seek a position in the court of King Ashalan, who himself has a male consort. In view of our predicament, I feel sure we would be made welcome. The other is that you accept whom I have chosen. You have other sons, after all. I will make one of my nephews my heir.'

Duke Orvember made an impatient, harried sound. 'All right!' he said hurriedly. He was clearly not oblivious of the light in which he would appear to King Ashalan should Persilian carry out his threat. 'One thing I shall say in order to dissuade you from this course, Persilian, and I am bound by honour to say it, though it may sting your ears and those of this good company a little.' He looked at Brackeny steadily. 'To be the consort of the Duke of this Duchy is a less than simple task. It cannot be compared with life in the fields or upon the road. It requires the skills of a person who is born to the role. You, boy, are clearly not of that ilk. I am unconvinced you could cope with such a station, or indeed that you would enjoy it. Now, while love blooms with its freshest petals, such things as duty, routine and order are easy to overlook, and rightly so. But once the first blooms have been shed and the firm fruit must grow, then what once was once looked upon as endearing ingenuousness may become an irritating lack of education, a fault. What was once intriguing and new may become an embarrassment. In the court of a king, or indeed a mere Duke, you will be at best a novelty, at worst a fool.'

In the silence that followed, Brackeny looked at Persilian and let go of his hand. Like a blight, the curses and kicks of the servants of Emiraldra seemed to howl, to rise and buffet round his head. As he had feared, all he could ever be was Persilian's plaything. Brackeny backed away from the thrones, shaking his head. Persilian held out his arms in dismay. And then strong hands were on Brackeny's shoulders and a gruff, loud voice was in his ear, reverberating around the hall.

'Stop this!' it growled. 'Would anyone dare to repeat that? Would anyone dare to insult the future lord of Emiraldra?'

A gasp hissed around the room and Brackeny turned his head. It was his grandfather, Thaldocred, who had spoken, Thaldocred's fierce dignity that had echoed round the room. 'This is my grandson,' he boomed. 'In rags, because my heart has been in rags. Since the day his mother died I have denied him, but no more. Let no man say that he is not fit to rule with Persilian in this house. Nor let any man judge them for what they believe. This is my grandson.'

'And my beloved,' Persilian added dryly.

At this, Duke Orvember threw up his hands. 'Well, ladies,' he said. 'Let the music continue. Let there be dancing once more. Enjoy yourselves as best you can. It seems the matter is out of my hands. There will be no matchmaking tonight.' With a wave of his fingers, he bade the orchestra to play and servants moved once more among the crowd bearing trays of wine.

And so, Brackeny's destiny was fulfilled. He was united with the one he loved and reconciled with his grandfather. Persilian's servants gave him splendid clothes. He washed his face and hands and feet. Tatters was gone for good. When he emerged once more into the hall to take his place at Persilian's side, he searched for Charlaise among the crowd. There were so many questions he wanted to ask her. How much had she known? Had his father before him loved, and been loved, by men? But even as he searched, he knew that Charlaise had gone. If she'd had a mission, she'd completed it.

In the night air, Brackeny fancied he could hear a faint echo of her magical flute, a mournful tune, a sweet farewell, but he could not be sure. If she was ever seen again in that land, it is not recorded.

My Lady of the Hearth

This story first appeared in 1998, in 'Sirens and other Daemon Lovers' edited by Ellen Datlow and Terri Windling (Harper Prism). I've always been fascinated by cat-headed deities, in particular the Egyptian goddess Bast. I reinvented Bast for the Magravandias trilogy, making her a goddess of the land of Mewt and renaming her Purryah.

This story is in Pygmalion vein, as the protagonist prays to the goddess to create his perfect woman – in this case from his cat. One of Aesop's Fables, 'Venus and the Cat', also greatly influenced and inspired this story. The man gets his perfect cat wife, but ultimately she cannot forget her origins. I'd always loved that old tale, and thought about what it would really be like to have one of your cats turned into a human by divine agency. Knowing my cats as I do, I could only foresee great problems, and if you threw sexual desire into the equation it could all get a bit tricky.

The most beautiful women in the world have a cat-like quality. They slink, they purr; claws sheathed in silken fur. In the privacy of their summer gardens, in the green depths of forests, I believe they shed themselves of their attire, even to their human flesh, and stretch their bodies to the sun and their secret deity. She, the Queen of Cats, is Pu-ryah, daughter of the Eye of the Sun; who both roars the vengeance of the solar fire and blesses the hearth of the home. Given that the goddess, and by association her children, has so many aspects, is it any wonder that men have ever been perplexed by the subtleties of females and felines? Yet even as we fear them, we adore them.

When I was young I had a wife, and she was a true daughter of Pu-ryah. It began in this way.

When my father died, I inherited the family seat on the edge of the city, its numerous staff, and a sizeable fortune. The estate earned money for me, administered by the capable hands of its managers, and I was free to pursue whatever interests I desired. My mother, whom I barely remembered (for she died when I was very young), had bequeathed her beauty to me: I was not an ill-favoured man. Yet despite these privileges, joy of the heart eluded me. I despaired of ever finding a mate. Thirty years old, and romance had always turned sour on me. I spent much of my time painting, and portraits of a dozen lost loves adorned the walls of my home; their cold eyes stared down at me with disdain, their lips forever smiling. It had come to the point where I scorned the goddess of love; she must have blighted me at birth.

It was not long past my thirtieth birthday and, following the celebrations, my latest beloved, Delphina Corcos, had sent her maid to me with a letter, which advised me she had taken herself off to a distant temple, where she vowed to serve the Blind Eunuch of Chastity for eternity. Her decision had been swayed by a dream of brutish masculinity, in which I figured in some way—I forget the details now.

The banners of my birthday fete still adorned my halls, and I tore them down myself, in full sight of the servants, ranting against the whims of all women, to whom the security of love seemed to mean little at all. The letter in all its brevity was lost amid the debris. I dare say some maid picked it up in order to laugh at my loss with her female colleagues.

Still hot with grief and rage, I locked myself in my private rooms and here sat contemplating my hurts, with the light of summer shuttered away at the windows. Women: demonesses all! I heard the feet of servants patter past my doors, heard their whispers. Later, my steward would be sent to me by the house-keeper, and then, after hearing his careful enquiries as to my state of mind, I might consider reappearing in the house for dinner. Until then, I intended to surrender myself entirely to the indulgence of bitterness.

In the gloom, my little cat, Simew, came daintily to my side, rubbing her sleek fur against my legs, offering a gentle purr of condolence. She was a beautiful creature, a gift from a paramour some three years previously. Her fur was golden, each hair tipped with black along her flanks and spine, while her belly was a deep, rich amber. She was sleek and neat, loved by all in the house for her fastidiousness and affectionate nature. Now, I lifted her onto my lap, and leaned down to press my cheek against her warm flank. 'Ah, Simew, my sweet angel,' I crooned. 'You are always faithful, offering love without condition. I would be lucky to find a mistress as accommodating as you.'

Simew gazed up at me, kneading my robes with her paws, blinking in the way that cats show us their affection. She could not speak, yet I felt her sympathy for me. I resolved then that my time with women was done. There was much to be thankful for: my health, my inheritance and the love of a loyal cat. Though her life would be shorter than mine, her daughters and their children might be my companions until the day I died. Many men had less than this. Simew leaned against my chest, pressing her head into my hand, purring rapturously. It seemed she said to me, 'My lord, what need have we of sharp-tongued interlopers? We have each other.'

Cheered at once, I put Simew down carefully on the floor and went to throw my shutters wide, surprising a couple of servants who were stationed beyond the window, apparently in the act of gathering flowers. I smiled at them and cried, 'Listen for my sorrow all you like. You'll not hear it.'

Embarrassed, the two prostrated themselves, quaking. I picked up my cat and strode to the doors. 'Come, Simew, why waste time on lamenting? I shall begin a new painting.' Together, we went to my studio.

I decided I would paint a likeness of Simew, in gratitude for the comfort she had given me. It would have pride of place in my gallery of women. I arranged the cat on a crimson cushion, and for a while she was content to sit there, one leg raised like a mast as she set about grooming her soft belly. Then, she became bored, jumped from her bed and began crying out her ennui. I had made only a few preliminary sketches, but could not be angry with her. While she explored the room, clambering from table to shelf, I ignored the sounds of falling pots and smashing vases, and concentrated on my new work. It would be Pu-ryah I would paint; a lissom, cat-headed woman. Simew's face would be the model.

Pu-ryah is a foreign goddess. She came to us from the east, a hot land of desert and endless skies. She is born of the fire and will warm us, if we observe her rituals correctly. I had no intention of being burned. My brush flew over the canvas and I became unaware of the passing of time. When the steward, Medoth, came to me, politely mentioning that my dinner awaited me, I ordered him to bring the meal to the studio. I could not stop work.

I ate with one hand, food dropping from my fork to the floor, where Simew composed herself neatly and sifted through the morsels with a precise tongue. Medoth lit all my lamps and the candles, and even murmured some congratulatory phrase as he appraised my work. He made Pu-ryah's sign with two fingers, tapping either side of his mouth. 'The Lady of the Hearth will be pleased by this work.' he said.

I turned to wipe my brush. 'Medoth, I had not taken you for a worshipper of Pu-ryah.'

He smiled respectfully. 'It comes from my mother's side of the family.'

I laughed. 'Of course. She is primarily a goddess of women, Medoth, but perhaps because she knows the ways of her daughters so intimately, she makes a sympathetic deity for those who suffer at their hands.'

Medoth cleared his throat. 'Would you care for a glass of wine now, my lord?'

I worked until dawn, given energy by the fire of she whose portrait I made.

Simew lay on some tangled rags by my feet, her tail gently resting across my toes. Sometimes, when I looked down at her, she would wake and roll onto her back to display her dark golden belly, her front paws held sweetly beneath her chin. She seemed to me, in lamplight, more lovely than any woman I had known, more generous, more yielding. If I were a cat, I would lie beside her and lick her supple fur with my hooked tongue, or I would seize the back of her neck in my jaws and mount her with furious lust. This latter, inappropriate thought made me shiver. Perhaps I had drunk too much wine after my meal.

As the pale, magical light of dawn stole through the diaphanous drapes at the long windows, I appraised my work. Fine detail still needed to be added, but the picture was mostly complete. Pu-ryah sat upon a golden throne that was encrusted with lapis lazuli. She was haughty, yet serene, and her eyes held the wisdom of all the spheres, the gassy heart of the firmament itself. She gazed out at me, and I felt that I had not created her at all, but that the pigment had taken on a life of its own, and my own heart had imbued it with soul. I had depicted her with bared breasts, her voluptuous hips swathed in veils of turquoise silk. Her skin was delicately furred and brindled with faint coppery stripes. Her attenuated, high-cheek-boned face had a black muzzle, fading to tawny around the ruff, then white beneath the chin. Her eyes were topaz. Around her neck, I had painted a splendid collar of faience and gold, and rings adorned her slender fingers. Her claws were extended, lightly scraping the arms of the gilded chair. Behind her, dark drapery was drawn back to reveal a simmering summer night. I fancied I could hear the call of peacocks in the darkness beyond her scented temple, and the soft music she loved so much. Her taloned feet were laid upon flowers, thousands of flowers, and their exotic perfume invaded my studio, eclipsing the tart reeks of pigment and solvent. She was beautiful, monstrous and compliant. If I closed my eyes, I could feel her strong arms around me, her claws upon my back. No woman of this earth could compare.

Weary but content, I went out into my garden to sample the new day. Dew had conjured scent from the shrubs and gauzed the thick foliage of the evergreens. Simew trotted before me along the curling pathways, pausing every so often to look back and make sure I was following. I felt at peace with myself, at the brink of some profound change in my life or my heart. Delphina Corcos seemed nothing more than a thin ghost; I could barely recall her face. Let her deny her womanhood and seek the stone embrace of the Eunuch. The day itself was full of sensuality, of nature's urge to procreate. The woman was a fool to deny herself this.

Simew and I came to the water garden, where a low mist lingered over the linked pools. Simew crouched at the edge of the nearest pond, her whiskers kissing the surface of the water. I gazed at her with affection. 'Oh, Simew, how cruel it is we are separated by an accident of species! If you were a woman, we might walk together now with arms linked. I might take you in my arms and kiss you.'

The fire of the goddess ran through my blood. As the sun, her father, lifted above the trees to sear away the mist, I spoke a silent prayer to Puryah, declared myself her priest. Yet, in her way, she was a goddess of carnality, so how could I worship her alone, without a woman to help express my devotion?

I pressed my hands against my eyes, and for a while all the grief within my heart welled up to smother my newfound serenity. I had riches, yes, and a loyal feline friend, but I was essentially alone, devoid of a companion of the heart, with whom I might make love or talk about the mysteries of life.

Then I felt a soft touch upon my arm, gentle fingers. Alarmed, I dropped my hands and uttered a cry of shock. I beheld a young woman, who backed away from me, her eyes wide. She crouched down before me, utterly naked, her skin the colour of honey, her body hunched into a position of alertness.

'Who are you?' I demanded, while within me conflicting emotions made war. My male instincts were aroused by the surprise of finding a naked girl in my garden, but she was still an intruder. What was she doing there?

The girl held up her hands to me, and now her expression was pleading. She shook her head slowly from side to side. Her face was small and heart-shaped, utterly enchanting.

'Speak!' I said, 'or I must summon my staff to evict you.'

The girl's face was puckered with anguish. She shrugged her shoulders in an ophidian motion, which seemed to indicate impatience, then touched her mouth with her fingers. I realised she could not speak.

I reached down and took her forearms in my hands, lifted her to her feet. She did not seem at all ashamed at her state of undress, and I could not help but admire the trim conformation of her body. 'Are you lost?' I asked her.

She smiled then and shook her head. It was a fierce smile, quite without fear, and a strange tremor passed through me. She held my gaze without blinking, pushing her long amber hair back behind her ears. Then, she dismissed me from her attention and held out her arms before her, twisting them around as if to examine them for the first time. After this, she shrugged and began to walk away from me. Aghast, I called out and she paused and glanced over her shoulder, before resuming her walk back towards the house. I felt that she knew this place well, but how? I think perhaps it was at that moment I realised Simew was nowhere to be seen. A chill coursed through my flesh. No! I called her name, scanning the trees and bushes, but of course it was my lovely visitor who turned her head to answer the call.

Pu-ryah had heard my prayers and answered them. As I had dedicated myself to her, so she rewarded me. Simew had been transformed into a woman, the most lovely woman I had ever seen. I caught up with her by the cloister that flanked the back of the house, and here took hold of her arm.

'We must be discreet,' I said. 'The servants must not see you undressed.'

She shrugged again, as if to imply she would concur with my wishes, but didn't really care whether someone saw her or not. I went into the house before her, and led the way back to my private chambers, checking round every corner beforehand to make sure the coast was clear. In my rooms, I turned the key in the lock, and leaned against the door to gaze upon this magical creature. She stood in the centre of the room, looking around in curiosity. The world must appear very different to her. Then she turned her attention upon herself, and began to stroke her body in long, slow movements. She raised her hand to her mouth and licked it. I was entranced by her, my cat woman.

'You can no longer wash yourself,' I said. 'The human body is far less supple than a cat's.'

She gave me a studied look, as to contest that remark. Her mouth dropped open and expelled a musical, feline cry. She was not mute, then. My flesh tingled.

She slunk towards me, her eyes half-closed. I heard her purring. When she was very close, she butted her head against my cheek, uttered a chirruping sound. I seized her in my arms. She wriggled away, still purring, and ran nimbly to my bedroom. I followed her and found her crouched on all fours, on the bed. She turned round in a circle a few times, before collapsing gracefully in a curving heap, peering up at me seductively through a veil of hair. The invitation was unmistakable. I approached her and she rolled onto her back, as was her custom. I reached down and stroked her belly, conjuring louder purrs. Her skin was softly furred by tiny, transparent hairs. I ran my hands up over her firm breasts and she arched her back in delight. Emboldened, I continued this tactile investigation, sliding my fingers down between her muscled thighs. All I found was welcome. Lust overtook me and I tore off my robes. Simew positioned herself on all fours once more, her glistening vulva displayed provocatively, her hands kneading the bed clothes before her. When I entered her, she screeched; her whole body became rigid. Never had coupling been so swift for me.

Afterwards, she did the most astounding thing. I watched in silent amazement as she contorted her body without apparent difficulty and set about washing her private parts with her tongue. Then, she cleaned herself all over, licking her hand to reach more inaccessible areas, unable only to attain the back of her neck. I lay in a stupor beside her, aroused once more by her bizarre behaviour. When she came to lie against my side, purring, I laid her on her back and took her that way. Her desire was kindled instantly and she appeared to enjoy the change of position.

Throughout that day, I taught her many tricks of the art of love. The servants came to my doors, but I would not allow them entrance. No doubt they thought I had succumbed to melancholy once more. But then, they must have heard the howls and grunts emanating from the bedroom, and drawn their own conclusions, upon which it is better not to dwell. Simew could not help but sound like a cat when throes of delight overtook her.

How she loved the sexual act. I had always suspected cats were masters and mistresses of carnality, but now, with Simew transformed physically into a human, while retaining feline sensibilities, I had no doubt. She was quite impossible to sate. The more we coupled, the more hungry she became. I remembered that the member of a male cat is barbed, and people say that during feline copulation it is only when he withdraws from the female's body, thus tearing her delicate flesh, that she finds satisfaction. I had no wish to hurt my beautiful lover, but how could I provide her with what nature had denied me? Eventually, her agitation became so great, I put my fingers inside her and raked my nails along the slick flesh. She uttered an ear-splitting howl and lashed out at me, her body bucking. Within her, powerful muscles gripped my fingers and warm liquid flowed down my wrist. Then, as the convulsions subsided, she lay quiet, her eyes half closed, a soft purr rippling from her throat. I felt exhausted.

When I stood up to go to my bathroom, I found my body covered in scratches, welts and bites. My member seemed to have shrunk back into my body in an attempt to escape my lover's demands.

Weak, I drew my own bath and lay there for some time, blinking in the steam. I had never felt so utterly complete. The sexual urge had been drained from me. I had filled Simew's cup to the full and now my vessel was empty, but the experience had exhilarated as much as sapped me.

I knew that I could not keep Simew a secret, nor did I want to. I had no women's clothes for her and this must be attended to before anything else. As I went back into the bedroom, drying my tender flesh with a towel, I gazed upon her lying amid the tangled sheets, her damp hair spread around her shoulders. She was sleeping now, but for how long? I dared not leave her alone, because Simew was accustomed to having the run of the house. If I locked her in my chambers, it was likely she would awake and then howl at the door until one of the servants came to her aid. Medoth had keys to my rooms. He would no doubt be summoned to let the cat out. It had happened before in my absence. I dared not think about the consequences of that.

In the end, I woke her with a gentle caress and told her we must go out of the house and purchase garments for her. As always, she appeared to understand my every word, although I sensed she was not altogether pleased with my suggestion. I remembered the occasion when a previous lover of mine had bought her a jewelled collar, and the manner in which that gift had later been found shredded under the dining-table, its expensive gems scattered by playful paws.

I dressed her in one of my own robes, using sashes to create a suitably fitted garment. Simew growled a few times as I made her hold out her arms to assist my adjustments. I bound up her hair as best I could, then led her from my chambers. Medoth had clearly been lurking nearby, and now came forward to hear my orders. Without explaining the presence of the oddly-dressed female at my side, I demanded my carriage be made ready for a trip to town. Discreet as ever, Medoth bowed and obeyed my word.

The trip was not without its awkward moments. The proprietress in the dress shop we visited seemed to accept my story of a visiting relative having had an accident with her luggage, but unfortunately Simew was unable to behave in the way that women usually do while purchasing clothes. The noises she made, the attempts to bite from her body the gowns she found most offensive, plunged the staff of the establishment into silent horror. I laughed nervously and explained she had an hereditary affliction of the mind. At length, the proprietress suggested frostily that we take one set of garments now and that the rest might best be examined and tried on in the privacy of my home. Someone from the shop would be sent round the following day. I understood her desire to get rid of us, because several other customers had already vacated the premises in alarm at Simew's behaviour. Spilling coins from my purse into the tight-lipped woman's hands, I agreed readily with her suggestion and Simew and I fled the shop. She was dressed now in a simple gown of soft green fabric, and wore emerald slippers on her feet. The outing had been a trial, but at least my lover was now dressed.

In the carriage on our way home, I tried to explain to Simew that it might be best if she remained silent in the presence of other people. Clearly, I had a lot of work to do with her regarding etiquette and good manners.

The story I concocted for the servants was that Simew was a distant cousin of mine, who had arrived in the night, having escaped a brutal father. I could do nothing but provide sanctuary, and indeed had even extended my services to offering her marriage, so that she would be forever safe from paternal threat. The servants were all stony-faced as I told them this story, and it was Medoth who ventured to tell me my cat was missing. I think he guessed the truth at once, because Pu-ryah was his goddess, but he did not voice his suspicions to me.

So the transformed Simew became part of my household. I decided that once I had trained her enough to be presentable in company, we would be married and all of my friends in the city would be invited. To the servants, I repeated the story that Simew—who I now called Felice—had been ill, because of the treatment she'd received from her father. Her mind was slightly damaged, but it could be cured, and patience and love were the medicines she must receive. Because she was still essentially Simew, it didn't take long for the household to learn to love her. Everyone became conspirators in my plan to transform this wild girl into a young woman of society. To her, I think it was all a game. She was playing at being human and thought it was hilarious to ape our behaviour. She learned to laugh, and it was the most thrilling expression of joy any of us had ever heard. It brightened every corner of that vast house; she was like an enchanted light buzzing through its halls and chambers. No one could have overlooked her cat-like habits, but they were prepared to tolerate and then to change them.

The portrait of Pu-ryah was hung in the main hall, and Simew would often stand before it, staring into that feline face, as if remembering with difficulty the days when she had looked the same.

One of the strangest things about Simew the woman was her incomparable clumsiness. As a cat, she had always seemed a little heavy on her feet, and no fragile things had ever been safe in her presence, but now she seemed unable to enter a room without knocking something over. At dinner, wine glasses were spilled with regularity, quite often onto the floor. Medoth arranged that a servant equipped with a pan and brush was always stationed near the door. We got through so much glassware and crockery that eventually I bought Simew a set of her own, crafted from gold. These, she could not break by accident. It took a while to teach her to eat using cutlery. She found that these implements simply delayed the consumption of food and would sometimes lash out and me and growl. I pointed out that a young lady of breeding would never eat food directly from her plate without even the agency of fingers. 'Simew,' I murmured one night, with fraying patience. 'You are here to be my wife. The Lady herself has arranged it. I'm doing all I can to keep my side of the bargain, please oblige me by keeping yours.'

Then, she laughed and shrugged. 'All right,' she seemed to say, but there were still lapses.

Neither could she take to immersing herself in water to bathe. The shrieks and clawing that occurred when we tried to enforce it became too much, and eventually we had to compromise. At morn and eve, her personal maid would clean her body with a damp sponge. This she tolerated—just. The maid was often scratched.

It was also difficult to accept Simew's gifts, which invariably she brought up from the cellar or in from the grain store. I would hear her muffled chirruping as she made her way to my studio, and then she would fling open the door with a dramatic gesture of her arms. A mouse, or even a rat, would be hanging from her mouth. It was worse when they were still alive. Her eyes would be shining and she'd run to me and drop her prey at my feet. I suppose she expected me to eat it with gratitude. It took some weeks to rid her of this habit, and I ached to see the sadness my disapproval conjured in her eyes.

She loved perfume though, and I indulged her craving for it. Scent was like a religious tool for her. She never wasted it, nor mixed aromas but, after her bathing routine, chose with care which perfume to wear. This she would apply with economy to her throat and wrists, lifting her hand to her nose to take little, contented sniffs from time to time throughout the day. It was an adorable habit.

At night, she would be waiting for me in my bedchamber, clothed only in delicious scent, purring softly in her throat, kneading the pillows. She rarely offered herself to me submissively now, but grabbed me bodily and threw me down onto the bed to begin her pleasure. I taught her technique perhaps, but she taught me something more powerful—the instinctual sexual drive of an animal. I realised that cats had their own beliefs and that sex was very much a part of their devotion to their spiritual queen. They had a language we could not understand, that functioned nothing like a human tongue, but it *was* language. In time, during our lovemaking I too began to make the sounds and Simew displayed her approval with purrs. Pu-ryah was always very close to us in our bedchamber.

Simew the cat, the house mourned. The housekeeper decided she must have stolen or killed, and I went along with this idea, but my grief could not have been that convincing. Perhaps no one else's was either, for as time went on I have no doubt that more than one of my staff suspected my new love's origins and then passed their suspicions around, but we all had to pretend.

Eventually, I decided that Simew was ready to present to society. The household was put into a frenzy by the preparations for our grand marriage. My friends already knew I was betrothed to a mysterious distant relative, and more than a few had been most insistent about meeting her—especially the women—but I had remained steadfast in my refusal. 'She has been very ill,' I said. 'She cannot yet cope with social occasions.'

'I have heard,' one lady remarked at a soiree, 'that she was locked by her brute of a father in a cellar for years on end. Shocking! Poor dear!'

I inclined my head. 'Well, that is an exaggeration of her trials, but yes, she has suffered badly and it has affected her behaviour.'

'How dreadful,' another murmured, touching my hand. 'You are so good to take her under your wing in this way.'

I could not say that had I possessed wings, it's unlikely I would still have been there to accept their sympathy.

I do not know what my friends expected when they finally met 'Felice', but I know the experience amazed them.

Our nuptial banquet took place on an autumn evening. During the day, we had undergone a quiet wedding; a priest from Pu-ryah's temple had come to the house to officiate at a ceremony that had been written especially to accommodate my bride's inability to speak.

In the early evening, Simew's maids dressed her in splendid gown of russet silk. Her hair was twined with autumn leaves of gold and crimson and I adorned her neck and wrists myself with costly ornaments of amber, topaz and gold. She appeared to be as excited as any of us at the prospect of being introduced to my friends.

I waited downstairs to receive our guests as they arrived, while Simew underwent the final primpings and preenings in our chambers. I wanted to present her once everyone had gathered in the main hall. I wanted them to see her descend the stairs in the caressing lamp light.

Ultimately, the hour arrived. My friends were clustered in excitement around the stairs, and I signalled one of the maids to summon the new mistress of the house. I continued to exchange pleasantries with the guests and it was only when the assembly fell silent that I knew Simew was among us. I turned, and there she stood at the top of the stairs. I shall never forget that moment. She was the most radiant, gorgeous creature ever to have entered the hall. My heart contracted with love, with adoration. She stood tall and serene, a half smile upon her face, and then with the most graceful steps slowly descended towards the company. I heard the women gasp and whisper together; I heard the appreciative, stunned murmurs of the men.

'May I present my wife,' I said, extending an arm towards her.

Simew dipped her head and glided to my side. She smiled warmly upon the gathering and together we led the way in to dinner.

Bless my love—she behaved with perfect decorum as the meal was served. Nothing was tipped over or broken; she ate modestly and slowly, smiling at the remarks addressed to her. Those sitting nearest to me lost no time in congratulating me on my fortune. They praised Simew's beauty, grace and warmth.

'You are a lucky fellow,' one man said with good-natured envy. 'All of us know you've nursed a broken heart more than once over the past few years, but now you have been rewarded. You've earned this wondrous wife, my friend. I wish you every happiness.' He raised his glass to me and I thought that I must expire with joy.

The meal was all but finished, and Medoth was supervising the clearing of dessert plates. Soon, we would all repair to one of the salons for music and dancing. Simew loved to dance; I was looking forward to showing off her accomplishment.

Then, it happened. One moment I was conversing with a friend, the next there was a sudden movement beside me and people were uttering cries of alarm. It took me a while to realise that Simew had not only vacated her seat in a hurry, but had disappeared beneath the table. For a second or two, all was still, and then the whole company was thrown into a furore as Simew scuttled madly between their legs down the length of the table. Women squeaked and stood up, knocking over chairs. Men swore and backed away.

Again stillness. I poked my head under the tablecloth. 'Felice, my love. What are you doing?'

She uttered a yowl and then emerged at full speed from beneath the other end of the table, in hot pursuit of a small mouse. Women screamed and panicked and, in the midst of this chaos, my new wife expressed a cry of triumph and pounced. In full sight of my guests, she tossed the unfortunate mouse into the air, batted it with her hands, and then lunged upon it to crack its fragile spine in her jaws.

'Felice!' I roared.

She paused then and raised her head to me, the mouse dangling, quite dead, from her mouth. 'What?' she seemed to say. Tiny streaks of blood marked her fair cheek.

At that point, one of the ladies vomited onto the floor, while another put a hand to her brow and collapsed backwards into the convenient arms of one of the men.

I could only stare at my wife, my body held in a paralysis of despair, as my guests flocked towards the doors, desperate to escape the grisly scene. Presently, we were left alone. I could hear voices beyond the doors, Medoth's calm assurances to hysterical guests.

'Simew,' I said dismally and sat down.

She dropped the mouse and came to my side, reached to touch my cheek. I looked up at her. She shrugged, pulled a rueful face. Her expression said it all: 'I'm sorry. I couldn't help myself. It's what I am.'

And it was, of course. How wrong of me to force human behaviour on the wild, free spirit of a cat.

The news spread rapidly. I told myself I did not care about the gossip, but I did. For awhile, I was determined not to abandon my position in society and attended gatherings as usual, although without my wife. I felt I should spare her any further humiliation. Whenever I entered a room, conversation would become subdued. People would greet me cordially, but without their usual warmth. I heard remarks through curtains, round corners. 'She is a *beast*, you know, quite savage. We all know he's an absolute darling to take her on—but really—what is he thinking of?'

I was distraught and blamed myself. Simew should have remained a secret of mine and my loyal staff. I should have kept her as a mistress, but not presented her publicly as a wife. How could I have been so blind to the pitfalls? We had never really civilised her. I know Simew sensed my anguish, although I strove to hide it from her. She fussed round me with concerned mewings, pressing herself against me, kissing my hair, my eyelids. The staff remained solidly behind her, of course, but she was not their responsibility; her behaviour could not affect them. The terrible thing was, in my heart I was furious with Simew. Public shame had warped my understanding. I suspected that she knew very well what she'd done at the marriage feast, but had wanted to shock, or else hadn't cared what people thought of her. She had despised them, thought them vapid and foolish, and had acted impulsively without a care for what her actions might do to me. My love for her was tainted by what I perceived as her betrayal. I wanted to forgive her, but I couldn't, for I did not think she was innocent. I made the mistake of forgetting what she really was.

One night, she disappeared. The staff were thrown into turmoil, and everyone was out scouring the gardens, then the streets beyond, calling her name. I sat in darkness in my chambers. I had no heart to search, but sought oblivion in liquor. Steeped in gloomy feelings, I thought Simew had gone to find herself a troupe of tom cats, who like her had been turned into men by the imprudent longings of cat-loving women. No doubt I, with my over-civilised human senses, could no longer satisfy her. She would return in the morning, once she thought she'd punished me enough.

But she did not return. Days passed and the atmosphere in the house was as dour as if a death had taken place. I saw reproach in the faces of all my servants. Dishes were slammed onto tables; my food was never quite hot enough. One evening, my rage erupted and I called them all together in the main hall. 'If I don't see some improvement in your duties, you are all dismissed!' I cried. 'Simew is gone. She is not of our world, and I am not to blame for her disappearance. Her cat nature took over, that's all.'

They departed silently, back to their own quarters, no doubt to continue gossiping about me, but from that night on, some kind of normality was resumed in the running of the house.

After they had left, I went to stand before the portrait of Pu-ryah, resolving that in the morning, I would have it taken down. I heard a cough behind me and turned to find Medoth standing there. I sighed. 'If she is a mother, she is cruel,' I said.

Medoth came to my side. 'You put much into that work, my lord. Some might say too much. It has great power.'

I nodded. 'Indeed it has. I thought I could brave Pu-ryah's fire, but I was wrong, and now I am burned away.'

'Your experiences have been distressing,' Medoth agreed. He paused. 'Might I suggest you make a gift of this painting to the temple of the Lady? I am sure they would appreciate it.'

'Yes. A good idea, Medoth. See to it tomorrow, would you?'

He bowed. 'Of course, my lord.'

I began to walk away, towards my empty chambers.

'My lord,' Medoth said.

I paused and turned. 'Yes?'

He hesitated and then said. 'One day, you will miss her as we do. She only obeyed her nature. She loved you very much.'

I was about to reprimand him for such importunate remarks, but then weariness overtook me. I sighed again. 'I know, Medoth.'

'Perhaps you should acquire another little cat.'
I laughed bleakly. 'No. I don't think so.'

I did see Simew again. After some years had passed, she came back occasionally, to visit the servants, I think. Sometimes, I found fowl carcasses they had left out for her in the garden. Sometimes, alone in my bed late at night, I would hear music coming from the servants' quarters and the joyful peal of that unmistakable laugh. To me, she showed herself only once.

It was a summer evening and dusk had fallen. I went out into the garden, filled with a quiet sadness, yet strangely content in the peace of the hedged walkways. I strolled right to the end of my property, to the high wall that hid my domain from the street beyond. It was there I heard a soft chirrup.

A shiver passed through me and I looked up. She was there, crouching on the wall above me, her hair hanging down and her eyes flashing at me through the dusk. She was clothed, I remember that, in some dark, close-fitting attire that must be suitable for her nocturnal excursions. Where was she living now? How was she living? I wanted to know these things, and called her name softly. In that moment, I believe there could have been some reconciliation between us, had she desired it.

She looked at me with affection, I think, but not for very long. I did not see judgment in her eyes, for she was essentially a cat; an animal who will, for a time, forgive our cruel words and unjust kicks. A cat loves us unconditionally, but unlike a dog, she will not accept continual harsh treatment. She runs away. She finds another home.

My eyes filled with tears and when I wiped them away, Simew had gone. I never married again.

Night's Damozel

This story first appeared in 1998 in Interzone magazine in the UK. It has a similar theme to 'My Lady of the Hearth', in that the protagonist falls in love with a woman who is not entirely human. I wrote this story with Eloise Coquio, and the plot derives from an idea Lou had concerning a man obsessed with poisonous flowers. I liked some of the surprises Lou invented for the tale, the serpentine twists and turns. Sympathies for the characters wind this way and that, like a serpent over the sand; nothing is certain. Lou had clear and vivid images in her head, but was looking for a story structure. We workshopped the ideas, and Lou wrote some of them down as a first draft. I then did the bulk of the writing, added dialogue and so on.

Like many characters I've written about in short stories, I think that Xanthe, the femme fatale of this tale, has a bigger story to tell. I hope that one day she makes an appearance in another story or novel. I do wonder what she's getting up to at the moment, because it's bound to be something intriguing!

On the morning of her arrival, Samuel wandered out into his garden. Already the sun was blistering and the still, clammy air threatened later storms. He walked along the shaded walkways where, as it dripped through the dense canopy of leaves, the burning yellow light turned to cool amber. His heart felt too large within its cage of bones. Where was the joy with which he should be greeting his new bride? Standing in the sunlight, he shivered.

Samuel was a quiet man with few friends, and those who had somehow stuck to his life since childhood now lived far away. He saw them only once a year, in early summer, when for a month he would travel overseas. His life was marked only slightly by the presence of others; he had a single servant, a bad tempered woman named Hesta, who lived on a nearby farm. She visited him daily, but Samuel rarely saw her. He left her coins as wages once a week and consumed her indifferent cooking with neither relish nor disgust.

Few other visitors ventured up the long, tree-shuttered driveway to the house, yet Samuel never felt lonely. He had companions. His garden was full of them: nearly a hundred different species of rare and exotic plants. They were his passion. They spoke to him without words, and listened to his most secret confidences without interrupting. They indulged him with gifts; dark, sticky fruit and flowers whose petals felt as soft as the skin of children. Their names were beautiful: Dancing Bride, whose spray of small white blooms concealed a bitter nectar that stopped the heart; Severia, whose juices thinned the blood so effectively, a simple scratch might result in slow death; Lady Anne's Pearls, whose dull-bloomed berries nestled in a grey-green nest of prickled leaves, and whose taste was sweet yet paralysed the lungs. There were many more languishing in darkness beneath the evergreens, hugging their secret lives to themselves, or wantonly sprawling over the lichened walls of the sun garden. Often Samuel would lie among them and inhale their narcotic scent until his head throbbed and pulsed. During his annual travels, he had gathered his dark ladies from every corner of the world. But this year, he had journeyed to the hot land of Mewt, where he'd cut for himself a different kind of flower, and soon she would be here.

Samuel's steps were slow, even dragging. He wondered how he would tell the green ladies of his wife's arrival. He should have spoken before, but had sensed the displeasure his news would invoke. They would be anxious, for they were used only to his company.

There was a queen to Samuel's kingdom and her name was Night's Damozel. Her velvet blooms, of imperial purple, reared on tall, slender necks from a coronet of long, silver-furred leaves. Her pollen could be deadly, yet to one familiar with her charms, it imparted a sweet euphoria. Samuel had long acquaintance with the Damozel and spent many a balmy evening with his head in her royal lap, inhaling the sparkling dust that drifted down from her open hearts. Now, he came again to her court in a grove of ancient yews. Little sunlight reached her, yet her bower was always temperate. Her maids of honour were a riot of cobalt ground poppies. Swollen bees hung drunkenly above her blooms, droning low and deep.

Samuel knelt before her, his head bowed. He felt the sun reach down with attenuated fingers between the needles of the yews and touch his neck. He told the Damozel his news.

He had first seen Xanthe in twilight, standing above him on a balcony at the villa of one of his acquaintances. Framed by tall, sputtering candles, she had been holding a long-stemmed glass to the side of her face, gazing out at the dark sea beyond the villa gardens. The ocean breeze lifted tendrils of her hair and they coiled around her face and shoulders like questing vipers. She was lovely: tall, slender, her body swaying slightly as she meditated upon the approaching night. Samuel's heart was at once captivated for he saw within this woman a similarity to the green ladies who populated his garden. Like them, she seemed remote, silent, rooted to the spot.

On the terrace near the cliffs, where a host of people mingled, and food and wine grew damp and warm respectively in the heavy air, he sought out his hostess, a duchess named Sythia. She stood at the centre of a group of guests, amusing them with gossip. Samuel sipped his wine and made what he hoped were discreet enquiries about the woman on the balcony. Sythia smiled conspiratorially and led Samuel to one side. 'You speak of Xanthe. You like her? Of course you do. She is charming. A temptation to many men.'

Samuel, unused to such direct words, felt himself grow hot. 'She is interesting,' he replied, which was exactly what he felt.

Sythia's smiled widened. 'You would like to meet her, of course.'

Samuel was irritated by Sythia's demeanour. He knew the people who thought themselves his friends had despaired of him ever finding a mate. Well-meaning older ladies had often told him he was a well-favoured man and had many admirers, but once he saw the women whose eyes he'd caught, he had to flee. They seemed so pink and fleshy, so clumsy. Now, his fumbling enquiries about Xanthe would soon be known to all the company. The morsel of information would be relished as much as the rare, salty shell-fish that lay dismembered on the duchess' table.

'In truth, I know very little about the lady,' Sythia confessed as she cut through the throng of guests that cluttered her garden. 'I met her at a soiree some weeks back, and like you, felt my curiosity stir. Nobody knows her. She is an enigma, and a lovely complement to any gathering. I have invited her here three times already.'

Sythia paused beneath the balcony where Xanthe still contemplated the scenery. The duchess called her name and, languidly, Xanthe directed her attention towards the sound. Her face remained expressionless. 'My dear,' said Sythia, in a voice of constrained excitement, 'would you come down here for a moment. There is someone who wishes to meet you.'

With neither words nor smile, Xanthe put down her glass on the rail of the balcony and descended the steps that flanked the house, her movements precise yet elegant. Then she stood before them, towering over Sythia, looking Samuel directly in the eye. She was dressed in a long, finely-pleated garment, the colour of ripened corn, that clung to her body like scales. Her dark, straight hair hung lustrously over her shoulders. Her skin appeared dusty, and Samuel instinctively knew it would feel smooth and dry to his touch. He wanted to shrink from Xanthe's overt scrutiny, yet simultaneously wanted to drown in her unwavering gaze.

He could no longer remember how Sythia had affected introductions. His memory had discarded any words that had been exchanged beyond that initial overture, but he could still recall in detail the smashing of the sea below, and the scent of the night-blooming vines, and Xanthe's private smile as she observed, through her dark, slanting eyes, his developing infatuation.

In a dry, barely interested kind of way she apparently decided to collude in his desires. Later that same night, after most of the guests had retired to bed, or else had fallen where they stood among the empty glasses, she led Samuel to a bare promontory and here, beneath the swelling moon, discarded the sheath of her dress, to reveal a long, sinuous body whose flesh was cool yet supple. She had no inhibitions whatsoever, although Samuel, being devoid of experience in these matters, wondered whether all women were so open in this regard.

There followed a week of intoxicated passion, of fever and of joy. In the mornings, Xanthe would leave Samuel's bed and go to sun herself upon the balcony, kneading into her skin fragrant oils that were absorbed almost immediately to leave a matte sheen. In the afternoons, while the other guests dozed after lunch, she and Samuel would walk into the nearby town, and drink cold, tart wines beneath the shade of awnings outside sleepy inns. She did talk of herself, of her dreams and expectations. Her voice was low, husky, with a slight lisp. Her family were rich, she told Samuel, and she was an artist. She was amused by Sythia's patronage, but was happy to enjoy the benefits of the friendship. 'I love her house,' Xanthe said. 'The rocks around it retain such heat.'

At the end of that week, Samuel had made up his mind: he wanted Xanthe as a wife. One afternoon, as they paused in their daily walk at a shore-side inn, he became emboldened by wine, and took hold of her hands across the table. 'Xanthe, be my bride.'

She looked at him inscrutably for a few moments, then said, 'If you like.'

Just a few days later, they married in a small, mountain temple, and afterwards Sythia threw a banquet in their honour. Then, Xanthe had returned to her family estate to organise the packing of items she wished to transport to her new home, while Samuel had travelled back across the sea to his homeland of Tarbonnay, where he would prepare his demesne for her arrival.

'And today she comes,' Samuel told the Damozel. 'I pray you will love her as I do.'

The afternoon had dulled and seemed to fall silent; the bees had tumbled away, and not even a leaf stirred in the bower. Then, as Samuel raised his head, the sun reappeared from behind a cloud and the Damozel's stately blooms turned slowly away from him. She seemed to gaze haughtily at the sky.

'Fear not, my lady,' he murmured. 'My consort will attend you as I have. She is eager to meet you and tend you. She will be a mother to you. It is a wife's duty to love all that her husband loves.'

The sun rolled behind the first black cloud of the approaching storm, and stayed there. First the Damozel, then her handmaidens, slowly bowed their heads once more and stared at Samuel with the blind eyes of their velvet hearts. He had never lied to them before.

Samuel did not bother to make any special effort over his appearance to greet his new wife. He spent a few hours tending his plants, then, pausing only to wipe his hands on a dirty rag, bound back his long hair with a piece of twine, and positioned himself in his gloomy study to await Xanthe's arrival. His eyes skittered with discomfort over the disarray in the room, as if becoming aware of it for the first time. Perhaps he should have hired a team of cleaners to prepare the house for her arrival, but it was not his habit to fuss about his environment. After the last of his parents' retainers had left, complaining the house was too large for so small a staff to cope with, he had never engaged anyone but Hesta, who in fact did very little for her money. Still, domestic matters would be Xanthe's province. He smiled to himself. He had never considered that particular benefit of taking a wife.

After Xanthe did not arrive at the expected hour, Samuel started to feel impatient. Rain began to fall heavily upon the garden, which did not improve his mood. Hesta presented herself at the doorway of his study. She was a large woman with resentful eyes. 'Is she here yet?' she enquired rather disrespectfully.

'No,' Samuel answered shortly. 'Prepare a cold supper and leave it in the kitchen.'

Hesta grunted and departed, perhaps relieved she would not be required to stretch her culinary talents for the benefit of a new wife.

Samuel waited for the storm to pass, then went outside, where the air was cool and damp. He resolved to walk down the long, winding driveway and if Xanthe had not made an appearance by the time he reached the road, he would lock the gates. It was as if the events of his recent holiday had been a dream, a pleasant dream, but one ill destined to continue. Now, it seemed inconceivable that Xanthe, with her foreign air, would settle successfully in his home. He must have been bewitched in Mewt; lulled by the hot, perfumed air and the long, lazy nights.

At the gates, Samuel put his hands upon the wet, rusty rods and peered down the road that led to the nearest town. He saw her then, walking ahead of a wagon like a common farm girl. She wore a sun-coloured, loose dress that brushed her ankles, and her face was shadowed by a wide-brimmed hat. She walked languorously, clearly in no particular hurry to reach her destination. Sometimes, she paused to sniff a road-side flower or turned to say something to the wagon driver. Not until she'd nearly reached Samuel's gates, did she look ahead, notice him and raise a languid hand to wave.

'You are late,' Samuel said churlishly.

'Yes,' she agreed and came forward to lay a cool hand on his arm. 'Open the gates then, Samuel, so the wagon can carry my effects to the house.'

The wagon heaved past them; it was not heavily laden. Xanthe hooked her hand through Samuel's arm and they strolled up the driveway behind the wagon. Their feet crunched upon gravel that was softened by clumps of dark moss. 'This is a rich and fertile land,' she remarked, 'but I trust it is not too cold in winter. I thrive only in heat.'

Samuel ignored these words and snapped. 'You are now the lady of this house, Xanthe. You should have hired a proper carriage in the town, rather than arrive here on foot like a slattern.'

Xanthe laughed and squinted at him sidelong. 'Why, Samuel, you look like a farm-hand yourself. There are seeds in your hair and dirt beneath your nails. Cheer up. Don't be irritable just because I chose to enjoy a walk and acquaint myself with the land. I am here now.' She leaned over and kissed his cheek.

Her touch kindled heat within him. 'This is your home now, my love. We shall be happy here.' The dream took on flesh once more.

Xanthe uttered an appreciative murmur as the house appeared around a bend in the drive. The garden at the front was rather neglected; a sweep of waving grasses, hedged by willows. The house itself lay like a sleeping lizard in its grounds; a grey sprawl of wings, buttresses and towers that had formed over the generations from architectural additions by Samuel's ancestors. It was scaled with a myriad tiny windows and its walls were lazily uneven, corseted with immense wooden beams. The late afternoon sun, still watery from the storm, washed the lichened walls with rusty light and gilded the window panes. 'So warm,' Xanthe breathed. 'So warm.'

The heat of summer, however, seemed not to have penetrated the hall of the house, and here the air felt uncomfortably cold and damp. The house smelled of its own age - once a familiar, comforting odour to Samuel, but now somehow repellent. He noticed his wife shiver a little. 'The place needs a good airing,' he said lamely. 'It was shut up while I was away.'

Xanthe glanced at him, but made no comment, even though Samuel could guess she thought the house had been neglected for rather more than a month. The wooden panels of the hall, which once had burned with the sheen of bees' wax, now looked dull and sticky. The floor tiles were obscured by years of accumulated mud, trampled in by Samuel from the garden. Xanthe ventured forward cautiously, apparently examining her surroundings.

Samuel called, 'Look out,' but it was too late. Xanthe had stepped into a tray against the wall and had scattered its contents.

'Oh, I'm sorry, I've spilled all your seeds,' Xanthe said, adding pointedly, 'I didn't see them.' She bent to brush them up but Samuel hurried to her side and stopped her hand.

'Don't touch it, my love!'

Xanthe frowned. 'Why not?'

Samuel took her hand in his. 'It's poison. A hazard of living in the country, I'm afraid. We have a problem keeping these old places free of vermin.'

'Vermin,' said Xanthe, flatly, straightening up.

'Mice,' Samuel explained. 'Even rats—not that they often come this far into the house, of course, but the cellars, the old larders... I have to keep poison down.'

Xanthe raised an eyebrow. 'Don't worry. Rodents don't scare me. They are too small to inspire fear.'

Samuel smiled at her. What an admirable quality in a woman, this fearlessness where vermin were concerned. He'd always believed women screamed and fainted at the mere mention of them. He led her through the dark passages of the house, into the old kitchen, where he suggested she should wash her hands. Xanthe went to the great, white sink—which was not as white as it could have been—and turned on the cold water tap. 'Poison is dangerous,' she said. 'We might have children one day, Samuel. Why haven't you got a brace of good cats to deal with the problem?'

Samuel did not wish to mention that the poisons growing in his garden were lethal to dogs and cats, while at the same time oddly attractive to them. The thought of children made him go momentarily cold. He imagined little hands reaching for the tempting, deadly fruits. He laughed too heartily and made a feeble joke that animals did not like him.

'Do they not?' Xanthe said coolly, looking for something on which to wipe her wet hands, and finally opting for the front of her dress.

As the sun sank, they went into the dark, dusty dining-room and there consumed the modest repast that Hesta had left for them; cold meats, cheese and thick, heavy bread. Samuel had found a bottle of wine that had not gone off, but it was thick and red - nothing like the light, acid wines he had enjoyed with Xanthe in Mewt. Afterwards, Samuel showed Xanthe around the more habitable areas of the house, finally leading her to his bedroom. Xanthe's nose wrinkled fastidiously, but she seemed relieved to discover that at least the sheets were crisp and clean. Spiders bred in the dusty, faded folds of velvet drapes around the bed, and the windows were opaque with grey-green grime. Samuel had made a small effort at decorating the room, however, and had filled a number of huge, antique vases with garden flowers—not the children of his ladies, but some lesser blooms left over from the days when his mother had tended the estate. Xanthe sat on the bed and said, 'I may have to make changes here, Samuel.' She leaned back on stiff arms and looked around herself. 'You've had dire need of a homely touch, it seems.'

'You may do what you like to the house,' he replied.

Xanthe nodded and silently smiled. Standing, and fixing him with her slanting eyes, she peeled away her dress. Samuel went to her, eager to touch her smooth skin once more, to breathe in her intoxicating scent. Pulling away from him, she walked, naked, to the window and wiped the glass. The moon was rising above the trees, sailing high. Xanthe struggled to open one of the windows and, at last, with a scraping creak and a fall of dead insects and spider webs, it released its hold on its frame. Xanthe stood tall, taking deep breaths. Samuel put his hands upon her smooth, bare shoulders and kissed the cool flesh. She buried her fingers in the thick velvet drapes and sighed like the night.

Below them, in the pale moonlight, the flowers had turned their heads towards the ground. But for the rustling of rats in the grass, the gardens were silent.

The following morning after breakfast, Samuel took his new bride into the garden behind the house. He had decided there was no point in delaying a certain crucial introduction, although his heart beat fast.

Xanthe stepped down the shallow steps led to the lawn and shaded her eyes. 'It is so bright out here after being inside. The house needs light, Samuel.'

Samuel took her elbow in a firm yet gentle grip and ushered her over the grass to the first walled garden. Herbs grew here, surrounded by granite pathways. In the centre was an ancient grey sundial, almost like an altar. Beyond the herb garden, steps led down into a shaded avenue of stately poplars, with lawns to either side, bordered by mature roses of dark red and startling white. Behind them, lush green ivy tumbled over crumbling walls.

Xanthe examined her surroundings with apparent pleasure, complimenting Samuel on the variety of the plants and the secluded mystery of the linked gardens. 'Is that water I hear?' she asked. 'Oh, Samuel, do you have a water garden?'

Breaking away from him, she ran down a pathway, her swift body dappled by sunlight. Samuel was forced to run to keep up with her, slightly annoyed by her wilfulness.

He found her by the fountain, where a voluptuous stone mermaid held up her hands to release a stream of cold, clear water. The pond was greened with the leathery saucers of water-lilies. It was surrounded by a circular path, around which grew a tall juniper hedge. Samuel once again slipped a hand beneath Xanthe's elbow. His voice was hushed. 'This way.' He put a finger to his lips.

Xanthe frowned quizzically, but did not speak. She went compliantly into the yew walk that led to the court of the queen. Samuel saw her studying the strange plants that grew in the gloom, some with long, white heads like trumpets and others with purple spikes. Later, he would regale her with their secret histories. Then, the narrow opening in the hedge was ahead, and he allowed his new bride to go before him.

Night's Damozel reared imperially in her green bower. Xanthe paused at the entrance to this hidden garden, and Samuel heard her draw in her breath. She seemed almost shocked. He hurried past her, smiled encouragingly and urged her forward. 'Come, come, this is who I've been waiting to show you.'

Xanthe's eyes were wide; it made her look peculiarly sinister. 'It is a creature of enchantment,' she breathed, and then flicked him a narrower glance. 'Where did you get it?'

'A corner of the world,' Samuel whispered, 'but hush. Stand before her, but not too close. Her pollen is toxic.'

So the new bride was introduced to the queen. Their beauty seemed to complement each other; both so tall and still. Samuel could not detect any sense of rivalry or pique in the Damozel, but perhaps the presence of another human being stifled his communication with the flower.

'I can see,' Xanthe said softly, 'that all other flowers in your garden are but a screen for this priceless bloom. You keep her secret, of course.' She nodded gently to herself. 'But that is only right.'

'Well, I wouldn't go so far as to say...'

'No!' Xanthe interrupted. 'I can see the truth of it. Thank you for bringing me here.'

Samuel felt oddly uneasy. He wasn't sure what reaction he'd expected from Xanthe, but it wasn't this.

As they walked back to the house, Xanthe was silent. Samuel asked her what she thought of his garden.

'It is a wonderland,' she said. 'Your haven of myth and dream.' A certain gleam in her eyes made Samuel wonder whether she'd divined the nature of his relationship with some of the more narcotic plants. He did not like her thinking that. She seemed to be laughing at him.

It is my hobby,' he said stiffly. 'I have spent a lot of time on it.'

She smiled. 'Oh yes, I can see that. I have some small knowledge myself, for my father is something of a horticulturer.'

'Really.' This was news to Samuel.

'Indeed. I think I can say that although you cultivate many rare species, there is only one of true value—your maiden of the night. The others may be seen commonly in many Mewtish gardens.'

'Is that so?' Samuel felt nettled, annoyed that someone who herself had confessed to having 'small knowledge' would dare to comment on the value of his collection. It would take some getting used to—living with someone else, who was full of opinions of their own. Still, she was indeed beautiful, and he was gratified she shared his respect for the Damozel. He bent down to pluck a delicate blue flower, a species of orchid. 'This reminds me of you. It is named Velenia, after a bewitching woman. This flower is yours, my love.'

Xanthe took the bloom and stared at it bemusedly. 'It has thorns, tiny thorns,' she said, twirling it in her fingers. By the time they reached the sundial, her fingers had begun to itch and sting. She dropped the flower on the lawn.

At mid-day, Hesta arrived for work, and disappeared with Xanthe into the kitchens. Samuel felt strongly that he was excluded from their domain, but was relieved that Hesta seemed not to resent his new wife. Later, he questioned Xanthe on how Hesta had behaved. 'We will have an understanding,' Xanthe replied. 'She is a strong-willed woman, who expected trouble, I think, but I trust she is as pleased with me as I am with her.'

This answer seemed ambiguous, but it was clear Xanthe did not intend to expand upon it. Samuel, a stranger to the ways of women, reluctantly accepted that it was beyond his comprehension.

On the morning of the second day, Samuel said to Xanthe, 'You have brought the sun from Mewt with you.' By ten o-clock, the gardens had begun to simmer in the heat.

'Aah, this is the weather I like,' sighed Xanthe, padding on bare feet out from the house to the lawn.

Samuel glanced at the sky. A heatwave, or worse, a drought, would mean a lot of work for him in the garden. All the plants would need to be kept watered. He felt exhausted. Tonight, he must try to get more sleep.

Xanthe on the other hand seemed full of energy. She made her way to the sundial garden and there composed herself on the ancient grey flagstones, fanned by the scent of baking herbs. At noon, Hesta stamped out from the house, carrying a tray of refreshment. Samuel, working on a flower-bed nearby, saw her disappear into the herb garden. She did not come out for some time. It was strange how Xanthe seemed to have cultivated a friendship with the dour Hesta so quickly. They seemed unlikely companions.

As the weeks passed, this friendship developed. Xanthe apparently encouraged Hesta into cleaning some of the rooms, because the house became a lighter, airier place that smelled of scent and polish. Xanthe seemed to respect that Samuel needed time alone with his ladies, for she rarely went into the garden after sundown, having spent most of day sunning herself by the sundial. She really was quite a lazy creature, but her presence inspired Hesta to work hard, despite the uncomfortable heat, which seemed now to have invaded even the shadiest corner of the house.

Samuel was concerned by the persistent lack of rain; the more delicate of his plants were already beginning to suffer the effects. Fortunately the shady bower of Night's Damozel seemed to suffer the least, and it was here where Samuel concentrated his greatest efforts at keeping the soil moist. He always watered the Damozel in the sultry evenings, and after his task was complete, disrobed himself, confidant he would not be disturbed. Then he would lie down on the drenched leaves of the Damozel, while a mist of dream dust shimmered down from her open hearts. Sometimes, in his intoxicated state, Samuel could almost believe that the Damozel was indeed a female of flesh and blood. A spirit lived within her, who manifested into his dreams as a soft-fingered lover. It was as if he had two wives; one of the sun and one of darkness. The night was so serene and comfortable, whereas the scorching day made him irritable and anxious. In these tranquil moments, Samuel found uncomfortable thoughts forming in his head.

Had he made a mistake in bringing Xanthe here? She was lovely, but a foreigner, and despite their weeks of passion in Mewt they had very little in common. She was here now, installed. He would have to live with her forever. Yet she was compliant, soft-footed and unobtrusive. The only changes she had made to his life had to be seen as positive. Why did these doubts come to plague him? All the while, a soft drift of pollen fell from the blooms of the Damozel, like words into his ears.

As the summer scorched the lawns, Xanthe basked in the herb garden, while Samuel toiled to keep his ladies alive. The work was really too much for him, the garden too large. At first, as he struggled around his domain carrying heavy buckets of water, he thought Xanthe might offer to help, but when no suggestions were forthcoming, he stomped over to the herb garden, intent on complaining. Wasn't a wife supposed to assist her husband in all his duties? He found her lolling prostrate in the sun, soaking up its heat like a reptile. At his approach, she rolled onto her back on the flag-stones and squinted up at him. Her dress had fallen from her shoulders, where her skin was dry as paper and studded with tiny pebbles and strands of moss. 'You are sweating on me, Samuel. What is it you want?'

'Some help.'

She frowned. 'To do what?'

He gestured angrily. 'My garden is dying and you just lie here all day, every day. Help me carry the water.'

Xanthe laughed and raised herself onto her elbows. 'You want me to help? What on earth for? Get a boy from the town, or one of the farms. You surely can't expect me to lug carriers of water about.'

'You know I don't want strangers here.'

Xanthe shrugged. 'You are a fool. Keep your dark lady secret, by all means, but there's no reason why some local boys shouldn't attend to the rest of the place.' She smiled. 'Samuel, I am not a big, strong man and that's what you need for this. See sense.'

'What about Hesta? Get her to help me.'

Xanthe shook her head mildly. 'No, the garden is not Hesta's province. She has too much to do about the house.'

'I noticed!' Hesta's hours had increased over the weeks, as had her wages—at Xanthe's insistence. It was as if the women were somehow building a new house around him that no longer belonged to him.

'Are you complaining that I have turned your ruin of a house into a home?' Xanthe said, her voice cool.

'No, no...' Samuel wanted to abandon the conversation. He backed away from his wife until the hedges hid her from view. Pausing beyond them, he heard her sigh, then imagined she just settled herself back to drowsing, dismissing him from her mind.

Disgruntled, Samuel sought the sanctuary of Night's Damozel's bower. He couldn't help unburdening himself of sour thoughts about his wife. 'Sometimes, the mere sight of her makes me angry,' he confessed. 'Yet she is exquisite—submissive and calm. What she said about hiring boys from the village was right, of course, and yet...' He shook his head. 'There is something wrong. Something.' The queen of his garden listened patiently. She alone seemed unaffected by the heat. Around her, her maidens lay swooning on the soil.

Later, when he returned to the house, Xanthe was there with her serpent smile and cool, welcoming hands. 'Samuel, we must not argue about petty things. Of course, I shall ask Hesta to give you an hour of her time every day. I'm sure she won't mind.' She bathed his brow and kissed his finger-tips. She was his wife, his beauty. He felt ashamed.

Now, every day, Hesta, apparently without grudge, tramped back and forth from the kitchen to the gardens with water. She was a strong, steady worker, but even her help was not enough to slake the thirst of the parched soil.

'The garden is dying,' Samuel told Xanthe in anguish. 'I am helpless.'

'There is more to life than gardens,' Xanthe said. 'And anyway, what is lost can be regained. Your precious Damozel won't wither. I know you make sure of that.'

Samuel did not like her tone. She often seemed to make innuendoes about his relationship with the Damozel, but not enough for Samuel to challenge her outright. He wondered whether in some way Xanthe actually enjoyed watching him panic as his ladies succumbed to the drought. Perhaps she was jealous.

Every day, Samuel examined the rat-traps he kept in corners of the house to augment the poison trays. For the past few weeks, he'd been surprised to find all the traps empty, although on one occasion he'd thought he detected a smear of blood, some hairs. It was strange there were no kills. Had the vermin become wise to his precautions, or was the continuing hot weather responsible?

He mentioned it to Xanthe, who replied, 'Are you complaining? I'd have thought you'd be glad to see the back of them.'

Again, that sharp tone, an implied criticism. 'But they are not gone completely,' Samuel said, 'I hear them walking beneath the floor-boards at night. Don't you?'

Xanthe shrugged. 'I hear many strange things. This is an old house. What do you expect?'

Anger burned through him. He wanted to strike her. Relations between them were becoming more frequently tinged with what Samuel perceived as sniping comments, yet at the same time, he found his desire for Xanthe increased. His lovemaking became urgent and unsophisticated although Xanthe remained unruffled by his lust. Samuel always felt drained and exhausted afterwards, usually falling into a deep sleep within minutes, while he suspected that Xanthe remained awake for hours. More often than not, he would wake in the morning with a pounding headache, as drained and groggy as if he had hardly slept. The heat was oppressive; he felt weak and sickly.

As the weeks of summer rolled on, it seemed that Xanthe's initial interest in renovating the family pile had been short-lived. Hesta, no longer confined to scrubbing away the past in the house, was now Xanthe's constant handmaiden, sitting beside her in the herb garden, shelling peas for dinner, or skinning rabbits. Xanthe's sole occupation was to lie in the sun, and when she entered the house at night, she seemed to burn with her own light. She and Hesta murmured together. Samuel could hear their soft tones in every corner of the garden, and occasionally a husky laugh. Hesta brought gifts for Xanthe from the farm, some of which were distinctly strange: a dish of goat's milk, what appeared to be a withered umbilical cord, some dried poppy heads, a dead bird. Samuel supposed this was some traditional thing that his mother must once have enjoyed with the local women. One day, in the kitchen, he said, 'She seems to think you are a cat.' He gestured at the milk Hesta had left out in a dish on the table.

'No,' said Xanthe emphatically, 'she does not. The milk is for my hands and arms.' She began to rub it into her dry skin.

'But the other things...' He wrinkled his nose in distaste.

Xanthe examined him blandly. 'Alkanet root, poppy seeds, feathers? They are ingredients for a herbal concoction. I have trouble with my skin.'

Samuel shook his head. Xanthe increasingly unnerved him. She was attentive in their shared bed, but during the day seemed distant and indifferent. Also, Samuel noticed that she rarely seemed to drink. It was unnatural. As he watched her dipping her pointed fingers in the milk, he had to suppress a shudder. It was more than being unnerved; he felt a wave of revulsion.

Xanthe looked at him, alert, as if his mind was her garden in which to walk. She smiled at him, perhaps with a hint of cynicism. He felt dizzy; the heat was getting to him. There was so much to do, yet he had little energy. Xanthe had come into his domain and had made it hers. She had brought searing equatorial heat with her, and both he and his garden were withering in it. She will be the death of me, he thought.

That evening, Samuel wearily carried water to the Night's Damozel's bower. Her blooms reared into the darkness, releasing a drizzle of shimmering pollen. He held out his hands to it, let it run over the backs of his hands. Xanthe left dust wherever she lay. In the mornings, their bed was full of it, a pollen of her own, faintly soapy against his fingers. Groaning, he threw himself into the lap of the Damozel's leaves. 'Help me,' he said. 'I am invaded!'

The Damozel could not speak. She only gave him visions. As the pollen settled over him, seeped down into his lungs and melted through the pores of his skin, he saw Xanthe stealing through the house at noon, when all was still and drenched in heat. He saw her stoop over the rat traps and take the soft corpses from them. He saw her eat. In his stupor, his stomach roiled. She had what she wanted: this house, these gardens. She would turn them into a barren desert where her unnatural hunger for heat could be indulged. She was a witch who influenced the weather, killing all that he held dear. Hesta was her creature now; bewitched and pliant. What a fool he had been.

The blooms above him looked like fairy faces. He fancied he could almost see thin lips mouthing silent words. 'Listen, my beloved, listen...'

Later, Samuel crept in from the garden, and went to the room where his wife lay slumbering. He stared at her for a few moments, noticing the faintly luminous sparkle on her skin, which might be an effect of the oils she used. He dreaded the powdery touch of her flesh against his own, yet when he slid beneath the covers beside her still form, he could do nothing but take her in his arms, inhale her strong, musky scent. She had that power over him. He resented it. Do not think. Act now or it will be too late. Carefully, he rolled her onto her back. She made a small sound, but did not wake. Her lips were slightly parted.

Samuel dribbled a shining stream of motes down into Xanthe's mouth. The Damozel's pollen could be rubbed into the skin, inhaled or ingested, the latter being the most effective method. The gate of dreams or the portal of death: only long acquaintance with the lady made that distinction. A dust glistened faintly at the corners of Xanthe's lips; Samuel covered them with his own, her body with his.

The funeral cortege milled around the front of the house. There was Sythia, imported from her summer home of Mewt, holding a scrap of black lace to her eyes. She was surrounded by others of her tribe, profligates, counts and divas, debutantes, artists and concubines. The majority of them had been summering at Sythia's estate, and once the news of the death had arrived by swift courier, the group had flocked to accept the invitation to the funeral. They were a mass of tall, nodding feathers and rustling costumes of black silk. Jetty horses stamped and snorted before the hearse, tossing their girlish manes, their hooves polished to a sheen. The day should have been overcast and grey, the trees weeping tears of rain. Clouds should have occluded the sun. The brightness and heat of late summer seemed an affront to the occasion, and several ladies were already feeling weak in their tight stays.

Sythia spotted a tall figure emerging from the shadows of the hall and swept up the worn front steps. 'Oh, but I shall ride with you in the foremost carriage. What a distressing time, for you, dear heart. How terrible. How cruel.'

Xanthe paused to pull on a skin-tight pair of black gloves. She inclined her head coolly. 'I shall be grateful for your company, Sythia.' Together, the women descended the steps, and the mourners drew apart to give them passage.

On the boat over, one of Sythia's friends had divulged an alarming revelation. Although information concerning Xanthe was scant in Mewt, the informant had discovered that Samuel's death occasioned the fourth time Xanthe had been widowed. 'It seems, my dear,' the confidant had said dryly, 'that the lady has a distressing propensity for losing husbands.'

'Sad coincidences,' Sythia said coldly, for she admired Xanthe greatly.

'Perhaps so,' the companion said, 'but this is certainly the shortest marriage of her history. The other three husbands at least survived the wedding for several years.'

'You should not say such things,' Sythia retorted. 'That is how ugly rumours start.'

Her friend raised an eyebrow. 'But I heard this from the second cousin of her last husband, who was Cossic. What do you think the talk of the coast is at present? There were rumours already. Some have said that Samuel had the spectre of death at his shoulder even as he spoke his marriage vows.'

'I won't countenance this nonsense,' Sythia said. 'Xanthe is a lovely woman. She comes from a rich family, and lacks for nothing.'

Now, as she climbed into the sombre carriage, with Xanthe so self-possessed beside her, suspicions flitted across Sythia's mind. The widow seemed very little marked by grief. Her eyes were clear, her face set in its usual enigmatic expression. 'It was very thoughtful of you to wait so long for the interment, my dear,' Sythia said. 'This heat...'

Xanthe flicked her a glance. 'Poor Samuel has no family. It was the least I could do to gather his friends for this occasion.'

'But three weeks...'

'The coffin is sealed,' Xanthe said. 'And we have stored him in the cellars, which are cool.'

Sythia shuddered. The frank details seemed indelicate. 'Of course, we came as soon as we could.'

Xanthe patted Sythia's hand. 'I know. Please don't trouble yourself.'

Sythia paused for a moment, then said, 'The contents of your message were scant. How exactly did Samuel die?'

Xanthe closed her eyes for a moment, the first signal Sythia had seen that the widow suffered any twinge of emotion. 'This may be distressing for you to hear,' she said, 'but the truth is, Samuel has long been addicted to intoxicants extracted from certain exotic plants he grew at the estate. I'm afraid he poisoned himself unwittingly.' She seemed to sense her companion's troubled thoughts and fixed her with a guileless stare. 'The family doctor from the town has identified the plant responsible, and we made upsetting discoveries in my husband's study—equipment to distil the essence of the plant, and so on.'

'Oh,' said Sythia inadequately.

Xanthe sighed. 'I have little luck where husbands are concerned, it seems.'

'You poor creature,' Sythia murmured, but still her heart beat fast.

At the graveside, while the mourners sweated uncomfortably in their ornate costumes, Xanthe stood cool and tall, staring down into the gaping earth. She seemed at least melancholy.

'What will you do now?' Sythia asked her as they returned to the house. 'Come home to Mewt?'

'No,' Xanthe answered. 'I shall remain here for a while at least.'

'Alone?'

Xanthe smiled. 'Yes. Alone.'

In the humid evening, Hesta reverently sponged Xanthe's skin with milk. The moon was rising behind the trees and the gardens lay in silence. There were no rats out there, nor in the house; no small creatures at all. All the guests had gone.

Xanthe rose from her bath and Hesta wrapped her in a towel. 'I will never marry outside my own kind again,' Xanthe said.

Hesta made a small, comforting sound. 'It was not your fault, my lady.'

Xanthe shook her head. 'This time... this time, it seemed so right. He accepted me as what I am, did not question my behaviour.' Her voice was low and uninflected, her gaze steady. She glanced down at Hesta. 'But what I am has followed me from Mewt. It was waiting here, but twisted.' She sighed and touched her belly. 'It is time now for me to settle this matter.'

Hesta dropped a small curtsey. 'I will await you, ma'am, in the kitchens.'

Xanthe smiled. 'I will not be long.' She clad herself in a long sheath of fabric, the colour of the moon, opalescent and oily. She glided through the house and out through the long back windows, down across the yellow lawns, past the sundial, the mermaid fountain, deeper, deeper into the garden to the court of the queen. In the outer courts the ladies of venom lay desiccated in their beds, petals strewn around them like papery jewels. Xanthe paid them no attention.

The queen, Night's Damozel, still reigned in her bower, despite the fact that Xanthe had denied her water for three weeks. Her leaves had withered and the tall stalks of her flowers were wrinkled like the skin of a crone. The purple flowers were splayed open, like dying tulips, revealing black and golden hearts. Xanthe crept through the yews on silent, naked feet and stood before her.

'Greetings,' she said. 'We have commerce to conduct, you and I.'

A single, damaged petal fell from one of the flowers, and the stillness of the night was absolute. Xanthe began to circle the central bower. 'Your lover is dead, and your minions have either perished or retreated into a death-like sleep. How much longer will you stand, dark lady? I admire the way you cling to life, even though half your roots are now nothing more than lifeless twigs.'

Night's Damozel seemed to shudder in the moonlight and another petal fell.

'Come forth,' Xanthe hissed, her eyes like slits, her elegant hands clenched into fists at her sides. Her narrow body swayed before the Damozel, and her will pulsed out of her like steam.

Again the plant convulsed.

'Do you hear me?' Xanthe said. 'I order you to come forth. If you savour life, then obey me. If not, I shall trample your crippled body into the earth. I am not afraid of you, dark Damozel, for my poisons are greater than yours.'

The image of the plant seemed to ripple, and a stream of vapour exuded from the earth. It coiled at ground level, and then puffed upwards,
resolving at last into an indistinct, female figure.

'But you must show me more,' Xanthe said. 'I do not believe this
wisp, this ghost!'

The emanation gradually became more solid, until it was clear that a
strange woman stood upon the withered leaves of the Damozel. Her skin
was pale with purple shadows. Her heart-shaped face was alien, horrifying, yet peculiarly alluring. She had barely a nose to speak of and her eyes
were feathered slits.

Xanthe shook her head. 'He never had the power to conjure you, did
he,' she murmured, 'but then he knew so little of what he had.'

The Damozel fell to hands and knees upon the soil, her pale downy
hair falling over her face. She looked starved, nearly dead.

'You know I could have come before,' Xanthe said, 'and perhaps you
were waiting for me. If I had succumbed, would Samuel still be alive?'
She put her head on one side to study the spirit of the flower. 'I could
destroy you now,' she said. 'And should. Poor Samuel. He sought to kill
me with your pollen, and woke in me the instinct to survive. What could
I do but strike? I had no choice, for my nature overcame me. Didn't you
think of that? I found him dead upon me. You are a jealous mistress, lady,
but I know your measure.'

The spirit of the Damozel lifted her head. Her eyes wept an indigo
steam.

Xanthe extended one slim foot until it nearly touched the Damozel's
fragile, splayed fingers. 'I have loved and lost too many times, but in
Samuel found peace. In his innocence and inexperience, he lacked the brutal qualities of men who awake the beast within me. Noxious flower, you
have destroyed my haven, for now I am alone again!'

The Damozel's fingers flexed in the dry soil.

Xanthe folded her arms. 'In my land, you are known by a different
name, Ophidia. You are the serpent flower. They say in Mewt that the
serpents who doze among your leaves give you the gift of their poison. It is
said that this is how you able to concoct your seductive venoms.' Xanthe
laughed coldly. 'We know better, don't we?'

The spirit raised its head and opened its mouth, the interior of which
was black. No sound came out.

'Oh, you are parched, of course,' Xanthe said. 'Do you choose death or
life, dark lady? You see, I am merciful. I give you that choice.' She
squatted down before the spirit. 'As I know your kind, Ophidia, you must

know mine. We have a long history between us. I walk the land, but you cannot. You are the cauldron of venom, and I am its channel. Together we become greater than our separate parts. You have killed my love, and made me all that I sought to forget. So, we must revive the ancient contract. Refuse me, and you die.'

The Damozel's eyes were black holes in her pale countenance, without expression. Then, with painful slowness, she attempted to crawl to Xanthe across the crumbling soil.

Xanthe smiled to herself and stood up, retreating a few steps. She gestured with both arms. 'Come, come to me, serpent flower. Get to your feet.'

Stumbling, the Damozel lifted her body erect. It seemed she was unused to it, for her limbs moved awkwardly. There was a hunger in her posture, in the curve of her spine.

Xanthe put her hands upon the mushroomy flesh of the Damozel's arms and lifted her as if she were a child. Xanthe opened her mouth wide and lifted her tongue. In the moonlight, two dark glands that leaked an inky liquid extended over her lower teeth. Even before the Damozel's lips met her own, a spray of venom jetted out of her mouth, smelling of burned feathers. 'I know you,' Xanthe hissed. 'Take my bane.'

The house was cool now, a shadowy sanctuary from the sun. The gardens below simmered and seethed in the last of summer's heat; the grass now parched and crisp, the flowers brown and withered. Xanthe looked out upon the garden from her bedroom window as Hesta busied herself stripping the sheets from the bed. Summer was breaking now. It would not be long before the cold came creeping across the land, bringing with it the desire for sleep.

'My lady,' Hesta said.

Xanthe turned and found the woman holding out the folds of white bed-sheet to her. They were filled with a fibrous dust. 'Yes, it is time.' She stroked her swollen belly, where the heart of a daughter beat and grew. Xanthe's kind rarely had sons. She took some of the dust in her fingers, then let it trickle away. Her skin itched, and now her face looked grey and tired.

'It has been a long summer,' Xanthe said. 'I will be glad to cast it away.'

She removed her dress and went naked through the house, down long stairs, through the drawing-room and out into the sunlight, moving stiffly. The desiccated lawn crunched beneath her feet. In the herb-garden, the

soles of her feet burned against the flagstones, yet her face registered no
pain. Deeper now, into the court of the queen. The bower thrived in a
tropical lushness, and a single flower remained in the midst of the Damozel's
leaves. Here, Xanthe lay down upon the soil. She closed her eyes and
arched her back, her brow wrinkled in a frown. She touched her throat,
and then pressed one fingernail, the colour of dried blood, against her flesh.
The skin parted with a soft popping sound. Slowly, she drew the nail down
her body, opening herself up like a flower. Pollen drifted down from the
Damozel; the last of it. No blood beaded along the deep scratch in Xanthe's
flesh. The skin simply lifted away, like old paper, crumbling with age.
Beneath it lay clean, virgin skin already coloured a deep honey gold, glistening as if kneaded with rich oils. Softly, the last petals of the Damozel
fell down upon Xanthe's body and veiled her eyes.

The Face of Sekt

This story first appeared in 'Grotesques: a Bestiary', 2002, edited by Thomas Roche and Nancy Kilpatrick (Berkeley).

As 'My Lady of the Hearth' involved a reinterpretation of the Egyptian goddess, Bast, so this story introduces Sekt, the Mewtish version of the lioness-headed Sekhmet. I set the story in the land of Jessapur, which is mentioned only briefly in the Magravandias Chronicles. It was inspired by the mystery-steeped land of India, which is such a wonderful and colourful place – even in this reality – it could have been invented by a writer of fantasy. The Hindu religion is as old as that of the Pharaohs in Egypt, the main difference being that the Hindu rituals and ceremonies have survived and still thrive to this day, while those of the Egyptians are mostly forgotten, or are recorded only in fragments. India has inspired a great many writers, and I was eager to explore Jessapur. In this story, Sekt is a foreign goddess, imported by conquering invaders, but shaped by the land to which she has become native.

This is a fairly recently published story, but I wanted to include it here. I have reinstated some paragraphs that were cut from the 'Grotesques' version.

I am the lioness. I speak with her voice. I look out through her eyes. I am she. I doze in the hot bars of sunlight that come down through the temple roof. I breathe in the scent of flowers. Priests come to me and ask questions so I will talk. It doesn't matter what I say, because all the words of the goddess have meaning. They sing to me to improve my humour. 'Oh mighty one, sheathe your claws of gold. Let your eyes shine with the summer light. Blaze not our hearts from us with your gaze. Let your voice be soft, oh snarling one. Be kind to us.'

'Know me,' I answer in a purr and stretch out my body on the tiles.

They prostrate themselves and then, Meni, the high priest will raise himself before the others. 'Oh mighty Sekt, beloved of Aan, queen of fire, lady of the red flower, hear our petitions.'

Aan, I might mention, is my husband, whom I have never met. He lives in another temple somewhere. They say his face is beautiful, but the chances are I will never find this out for myself.

'Speak,' I say, yawning.

And they do. The questions are too tedious to relate. I have to let my mind go blank so the answers will come. Say this prayer, do that ritual task, cast scent, rake the sand, spill blood. It's all they want from me.

The crown of the goddess covers my head, my face, and rests upon my shoulders. It is fashioned from beaten leaves of gold, shaped and painted. Wearing it, I resemble the black basalt statues of the goddess that line the courtyards and populate the darkest niches of the temple: lioness-headed women. The mask was put upon me in my fifteenth year and comes off rarely. No one may see the true face of the goddess. My handmaidens withdraw from my chamber before I remove it to sleep.

There are no mirrors in my chamber, none of Mewtish gold nor Cossic glass. If I looked upon myself I might die, for once I was human and the body that carries this goddess is still that of a woman. It is frail. I dare not even touch my face for fear of what my fingers might explore. When the mask was put upon me, Sekt entered my flesh. I was changed somehow. I wash myself in a sacred fountain, so that only the water may touch my face and hair.

I have lived this divine life for nearly ten years. The time before that is hazy in my memory now. I remember being a child and the smell of dust in the heat. I remember looking down at my bare dusty toes, and somewhere a voice is scolding me for being wayward. But the name they called, I can't remember that at all. She doesn't exist any more. I am Sekt. I am she.

At one time, our land was a province of the sacred kingdom of Mewt and although those empire days are but distant memories, our culture is still saturated, if subtly, with Mewtish things. Our major religion is one of them. Taskish monks might still swing their bells in their high, lonely eyries of peaks and draughts, but down here where the sun beats relentlessly, we are devoted to the goddess, Sekt, the Mewtish lioness deity. Originally, she was a goddess of war, whose fierce countenance gazed down from the banners of Harakhte the conqueror. One of the first things he did here in Madramarta, capital of Jessapur, was build a temple in Sekt's honour. That temple still stands and has been added to over the years, to create a great sprawling complex near the edge of the city. It is a labyrinth of immense chambers, full of shadows, and tiny shrines where a priestess might mutter in the dark. It is called the Sektaeon. Back in the days when Harakhte sought to rule the world, the daughters of native high caste families were first taken into service here. The most beautiful and noble women became her new priestesshood in this country. One the eve of the great festival of Sekt, a woman came from Akahana, the Mewtish capital. Her name was Senu, and she was the High Priestess of Sekt. Senu selected the girl who would become the goddess' avatar in Jessapur. A mask was fashioned in the semblance of Sekt and, with great ceremony, it was placed over the head of the girl, rarely to be removed, and never in public. From that day onwards, the girl was called Sekt also. She wore the golden face of a lioness, always proud, always snarling.

Sometimes, as I am lazing in my garden, I wonder whether that first goddess-made-flesh put up a fight. To the noble families of Madramarta, the abduction of their daughters must have seemed a terrible thing. Women of their caste would never have been expected to serve others, and what is the avatar of Sekt but a servant of both the people and the goddess? Sekt was a deity of war and retribution, far different from the gentle divine mothers and concubines my people knew and loved. Sekt would have none of them. The native deities were weak, servile, and yet the paradox was that to be worthy of the goddess, our women had to become all that she was alleged to despise. We had to serve her without question.

This does not mean I resent my calling. As a representation of Sekt on earth, I am above such petty feeling. I am privileged above all other women. I have no secret yearning to escape the temple, or even this mask. I can bask in the sun all day if I want to. I don't have to think. So, why bother? Long ago, my people embraced Sekt as a national goddess. At first, this may have been through fear, but later because they saw her power to work for them. Once they were herded into Sekt's temples and shrines, newly built and gleaming among our ancient hills, she turned her face towards them. She listened to their prayers, and very soon afterwards Harakhte was killed in battle by the king of Cos, and the Mewtish empire fell. Jessapur regained her independence. She has never lost it since. I like this irony. I believe Sekt loves us.

Every day, priests and priestesses in fire red robes walk the temple from end to end, renewing the magical seals over every entrance, however small. This is to keep the ancient spirits at bay, the djinn of the arid wilderness beyond the city and its fertile girdle of land. The djinn are born of fire and are therefore attracted to a goddess of that element. They desire also to wear flesh, and who better to steal a body from than a priest or priestess of fire? Sometimes, I think the djinn are long dead, and the precautions are only tired old ritual, but at other times, when the wind blows hot through the long reaches of the night, I hear a voice from the wilderness, in my heart rather than my ears, and it unnerves me.

Meni, my high priest, came to me this morning, in my solarium, which is actually a shady, green place. He glided between the lush trees and plants, dappled by the sunlight that found its way through the waving fronds of the vines. I was reclining upon some cushions, surrounded by lionesses, who lay licking their paws at my feet. We were being serenaded by the water garden. The rivulets conjured different notes as they ran through the various mechanisms hidden among the ferns. I was not in the best of moods as, during the night, the wind had blown with exceptional passion from the wilderness, carrying with it a scent of burning meat. I had turned restlessly, woken up from a dream of smoke. The darkness in my chamber had seemed watchful, almost sly. A flavour of the haunted night remained with me. I wondered whether it was a portent, and perhaps it was, for the high priest clearly hid a certain agitation beneath his serene and flawless countenance.

Meni stood before me and bowed. 'Your reverence, there is a matter for your attention.'

I have nothing to do most of the time, so it really perplexes me why every possibility of action seems only an irritant. 'Oh, what, Meni? Can't you see to it?'

He bowed again. 'Your reverence, it is a matter of importance. King Jaiver himself has requested that you turn your divine face towards it.'

'What matter is it?'

'It concerns the Prince Reevan. He has a malady.'

One of Sekt's aspects is a goddess of plagues, but she is equally adept at averting human illness. 'I shall burn a pouch of incense for the boy and direct Sekt's healing force in the direction of the palace.'

Meni paused. 'It is rather more than that,' he said. 'The king has requested your presence.'

That made me sit up. 'Indeed?' I did not have to go. I was a goddess, who obeyed no one, yet I was intrigued as to why the king desired my physical presence. Was the prince so desperately ill? But that did not make sense. The most ailing of royals were generally carried to the temple, where they could be nursed by the priestesses, close to the presence of Sekt. 'What is the nature of this malady, Meni?'

He shrugged. 'I have not been told, your reverence. All I know is that Jaiver humbly requests your presence and has already made an sizeable donation to the temple treasury.'

'Then prepare my litter.'

Meni bowed and departed, and presently a retinue of servants came padding to my garden, where they attended to my needs. They washed my hands and feet, and rubbed the palms and soles with red ochre. They applied cinnamon perfume to my wrists and throat, and veiled me in scarlet voile from head to foot. Beyond the temple, I would be concealed behind the curtains of my litter, but sometimes in the labyrinth of the city, strange winds can arise, which might blow the curtains apart. We have to take precautions so that common people never behold the face of the goddess.

The tasselled litter was carried by four eunuch priests. Before it marched a dozen priestesses in the red and gold robes of Sekt. They scattered petals of scarlet poppies before my path. At the head of the procession, Meni rode upon a beautiful nut-coloured horse. Behind my litter strode three priests who also acted as my bodyguards. And behind them was a company of neophyte priests and priestesses, on hand to collect any spontaneous donations onlookers might wish to make.

Thus, we processed through the faded grandeur of old Madramarta. I love my city, although I rarely get to see it. It is a like a ghost of what it used to be, yet still beautiful. The ancient palaces are now tenement buildings full of low caste workers, or else they have been turned into bazaars. The temples of forgotten gods stand rotting amid jungled gardens. In the dusty streets, forlorn peacocks trail their tails in the dirt, crying plaintively for the ordered landscapes of their ancestors. Everywhere there is evidence of a past opulence, now lost. As a province of Mewt, we prospered, for the Mewts loved the idea of sacred blood—such as the ichor that runs in the veins of our aristocratic families—and honoured our country. They were not harsh governors and shared with us their knowledge of arts both occult and scientific. Now, in a time of independence, internal politics ravage the heart of Jessapur. The lowborn have turned our palaces into warrens. They spit on the idea of divine providence and seek power for themselves. The king still reigns, but just. His palace is a citadel.

We passed through the first series of gates and towers, into open park land, where pale deer run. In the distance, we could see the ghost of the white palace shimmering in the heat. It is called Jurada, which means home of the high god. Only as you draw close to it can you tell it is not a mirage. Trefoil lakes surround it, and mock temples, and ornate gardens. Even though so many of the ancient houses have fallen into disrepair, Jurada still gleams as if new. It is said the entire remaining wealth of the country is divided between the upkeep of the temple of Sekt and that of the royal palace.

My party had to walk for nearly an hour along a shady avenue to reach Jurada. We came to a halt by a pool full of exotic fish in front of the main entrance. A scrum of servants ran out from the cool depths of the hall and laid down a carpet of ferns for me to step upon. I was offered saffron water and a piece of sugared coconut, which I accepted with grace. Meni went ahead of me into the palace and the rest of my retinue surrounded me protectively. The priestesses sang in rapturous high voices while the priests hummed an accompanying undertone. I put my sacred feet upon the ferns and walked the short distance to the hall. I left scarlet footprints.

The king was waiting for us in his throne room, which seemed a little inappropriate to me. I felt we should have been conducted directly to the royal family's private apartments, where the prince must lie in his sick bed. Was this a subtle affront? I was alert for strangenesses. A memory of my dream of smoke came back to me. Queen Satifa was present, magnificent in cloth of gold with a diadem of emeralds upon her regal brow. She sat on a golden throne beside the king, who was surrounded by courtiers in dark robes, the magi who counselled him. The chamberlain, chief conjuror over this clutch of demons, stood imperiously to the left of the king's throne. There was no sign of the crown prince, nor indeed of any of the other royal children or wives. The king's expression was grave.

He inclined his head to me, as I did to him, my hands raised, palms together before my breast. 'Oh mightiness, you have called for me. How may I aid you?'

The king made a nervous, abrupt gesture with one hand. 'I am grateful for your presence, revered lady. My concern is Prince Reevan. He is sorely afflicted.'

'Take me to him. I will assuage his hurts.'

'It is not that simple.'

I narrowed my eyes slightly, although no one would be able to tell because of the mask. All they'd see was the snarling face of the goddess, dimly through my veil. 'Please explain the difficulty, your mightiness.' I glanced at the queen. Her head was lowered. She would not look at me.

'A demon has possessed him,' said the king.

I paused. 'A demon, mightiness?' This would explain, then, the reluctance to bring the prince to the temple.

He looked slightly uncomfortable. 'Yes. That is the diagnosis.'

'By whom, may I ask?' I turned my head towards the vizier so he'd be sure I was looking at him.

'A wise man has come to us,' said the king.

'A wise man?' I said haughtily. Who was it making diagnoses of royal ailments— indeed possessions—before I? 'Are you sure his appraisal of the situation is sound? There are old legends concerning possession by demons, but now our more enlightened understanding is that, in most cases, when people were said to be hag-ridden, they were in fact afflicted by a malady of the mind. You must tell me, your mightiness, of your son's symptoms.'

'This I will do,' said the king. 'Then you may see him and reach your own conclusion. But first, I must inform you of the events that led to it.'

Eight days before, I was told, news had come to the court of a master magician who was creating something of a stir in the tea rooms of the more affluent corners of the city. His illusions, it seemed, were so convincing they could inspire terror, obsessional devotion and dark hatred. He claimed he could drive people mad with his magic, mad for love or envy, mad for despair. The illusions themselves were so astounding, so beautiful, that many were moved to tears. One man said he was transported back into the most golden day of his childhood, when he had become aware in his heart of the spirit of the sky—a moment he had never recaptured. Another man spoke of how his long-broken heart was healed of hurt as the woman who'd sundered it came to him and asked for his forgiveness. There were many stories such as these. It was all illusion, of course, but it touched people, and word of it came to the king. 'Send for this man,' he'd said. 'Let him show the court his expert trickery.' And so the magician was sent for.

As I was told this story, I could picture the man's charlatan's garb, all flouncing colourful robes and extreme hand gestures. I listened patiently while the king described the wonders this paragon of tricksters performed for the court. 'It was all the usual fare and more,' he said. 'Not only could he make serpents dance to the music of a flute, but they would come out of their baskets and choose dancing partners from among the ladies. Then they would turn somersaults, before tying themselves into a complicated knot and flinging themselves back in their baskets.'

I nodded. 'Mmm.'

'Then, he filled the air with flowers that turned to bubbles when you touched them. He made a servant boy climb up a rope he flung into the air, and which stayed there taut. The boy came down again and told us all of a magical land he'd found at the top, where the sky was red and the trees were bright yellow. The magician then took the hand of my old mother and turned her back into the girl she'd once been. The effect lasted for over an hour, and my mother has not stopped weeping since.' The king raised his arms. 'I have never beheld such wondrous magic. He is a powerful man indeed.'

'Indeed. Does he have a name, this man?'

'He calls himself Arcaran.'

'I see. How is his arrival connected with your son's illness?'

The king tapped his lips with restless fingers. 'Ah well, the two events go together but not in any way you'd imagine. On the morning I sent for the magician, Reevan seemed out of sorts on awaking. He felt tired, listless. He could barely move. When my physician examined him, Reevan spoke of bad dreams, a night during which he had been hunted by demons through a strange and terrifying landscape. The experience had exhausted him. The physician proclaimed Reevan had a slight fever, which had caused hallucinations in the night. The prince was given a posset to soothe him.

'But the illness only became worse. It was as if his life was draining away, and it happened so quickly. In the space of a day. I decided Reevan must be sent to the temple, but Arcaran intervened at this point. He came into the sick-room, unbidden, and there made a terrible hissing noise, all the while drawing symbols in the air around him. I was naturally aghast and affronted and about to order him out, but he said to me, "Great king, you are familiar with the stinging salamander?"

'I can't remember how I answered this bizarre and inappropriate question, but Arcaran raised his hands against my bluster and said, "There is a stinging salamander on your son's back. It is feeding upon him."

'I could see no such thing and said as much, although I remember my flesh went cold.

"Oh, it is there," said the magician, "it is an elemental being, the cause of the prince's torpor. It must be removed, and quickly, for it is already laying eggs."

'When I heard these words, I went utterly cold. It was as if I could smell something foul in the room, something evil.'

The king shook his head, and would have continued, but I decided it was time to interrupt this preposterous narrative. 'Eggs? Salamanders? Perhaps it is time I saw the phenomenon for myself.' I paused. 'I trust no action has yet been taken to remove this alleged elemental?'

The king shook his head. 'Indeed not. Arcaran was most insistent that your aid should be sought first.'

'How polite of him,' I said. Quietly, I wondered why the charlatan showed such consideration.

Accompanied only by his vizier, King Jaiver led Meni and I to the prince's bedchamber. Here, dark drapes were drawn against the heat of the day, so that the light was brownish. I saw the boy lying on golden pillows, covered by a thin tasselled blanket. His body gleamed with sweat, but I sensed that should I touch him, his flesh would be cold. I could tell at once that this was more than a fever, but I could not credit the idea of unseen parasites.

I walked around the bed for a few moments, sniffing the air. The strange thing was that I could not smell sickness. The air was dry and faintly redolent of smoke. They had been burning an acrid incense in there. I forcibly repressed a shudder. 'I really think he should be moved to the temple,' I said. 'He needs light and air.'

'But the demon creature,' said the king. 'You should not carry one across the threshold of the Sektaeon. Surely that would be dangerous?'

I made my voice cold and harsh to indicate my patience was fraying. 'I and my priesthood are quite capable of dealing with any eventuality.'

The king bowed. 'Great lady, we have no choice but to obey your word, but I have to say that your decision distresses me greatly. In the temple of fire, the elemental could acquire great strength and take what is left of my son's life.'

'You must trust me,' I said.

Then, a faint hiss and a dry rattle emanated from one of the dark corners of the room and a man emerged from the shadows. He had, of course, been present the entire time, but for whatever reason had concealed his presence until now.

He bowed slightly and extended his arms in an expansive gesture. Such theatre! 'Great lady, you must not take the boy into your temple.'

I put as much sneer into my voice as I could muster. 'Ah, you must be the *physician* who diagnosed the case. Your presence is no longer required. I am here now.'

The magician stole forward. He was not garbed in the flamboyant robes I'd expected, but in dark, close-fitting garments, such as those worn by nomad warriors of the wilderness. 'You are sceptical,' he said mildly, 'and that I understand, but perhaps if you and I could be alone with the prince for a short time, I could show you the nature of the affliction.'

'Now is not the time for illusions,' I said briskly. 'We can all see the prince is gravely ill. Now, if you will step aside, my priest will carry his highness to my litter.'

'No,' said the magician, and for brief moment his strange dark eyes burned with an amber spark. He held my eye for a while, almost as if he could see through my mask, and during that time it was as if he and I were the only people in the room. I had never encountered such an intensity of gaze. Within it, I saw passion, fire and knowledge, but also a fierce kind of tragedy. It shocked me.

'I am an illusionist, yes,' said the magician softly, 'but not just that. There are times for illusions and there are not. I am aware of the distinction, lady.'

I hesitated for a moment, then said, 'Leave us. Everybody.'

There were murmured assents from the king and his vizier, but forthright protests from my high priest. 'Your reverence,' Meni said in a strained voice. 'Is this wise?'

I turned my head to him. 'There is nothing to fear. Please, leave. I will call you shortly.'

Alone, Arcaran and I faced each other across the bed, where the prince moved feebly, uttering sighs.

'I appreciate this,' said the magician, 'You will...'

I interrupted him coldly. 'Do you know who I am?'

He frowned briefly, then bowed again, smiling. 'You are the avatar of Sekt, the goddess on earth.'

'Yet you speak to me with little respect. It's clear to me that the king dances to your tune. Who and what are you? Why are you here? What is your aim in this?'

He continued to smile, apparently unflappable. 'I appreciate your curiosity and concern. Here are the answers you seek. I am what you perceive me to be. I am here because I was summoned. My aim in this is to heal the prince.'

It was clear he sought to charm me, yet there was something—*something*—utterly compelling about this man. Merely being in his presence seemed to inform me he had seen many wonders of the world, that he possessed great knowledge. Perhaps he too wore a mask. However, I would not let him win me over that easily. 'You prey upon the rich,' I said. 'You dupe them of their riches with your illusions.'

He grimaced, head tilted to one side. 'That is a sour depiction of my profession, but not without some basis of truth. Still, I am a creature of many facets. Not all of them are based upon deception.'

I made myself totally still. 'Show me this parasite, then. No tricks. The truth.'

Without further words, he leaned over the prince and gently turned him onto his stomach. He drew down the blanket. Reevan's flesh appeared sallow in the dim light, the sharp ladder of his spine too close to the surface of his skin. The magician lifted the prince's hair from his neck. 'Look closely,' he said. 'To see it, focus beyond the prince's skin. Try to look inside him.'

'I am not easily suggestible.'

'This is no illusion. Do as I say. You are Sekt. You must be able to see this creature.'

For some moments, I concentrated as he suggested, blurring my sight until my eyes watered. Then, it came. I saw nothing with my physical sight, yet, in my mind, I sensed pulsing movement, many legs and a pres-

ence of malevolence. If it had a form at all, it was a filthy smoky suggestion of a shape. I drew back, uttering an instinctive gasp. Even then, I was
aware of the power of suggestion. This did not have to be real, simply
because I'd perceived it, yet there was no doubt an evil odour of malice
oozed upwards from the bed. It was like being in the presence of a crowd
of people, who all hated me utterly. I made no comment, confused in my
own thoughts.

'You see?' said the magician.

'I *see* nothing,' I replied carefully. 'But I sense something. This may, of
course, be an illusion emanating from you.'

'It is not,' said the magician softly. 'Come now, great lady. You are
Sekt, a goddess. The goddess perceives all, does she not?'

It came to me swiftly then how wrapped up I was in the trivia of
mundane life. I lived fully in the corporeal senses, lolling around in the
sun, uttering the first words that came into my head. And yet I was supposed to be divine, to see and sense all. Perhaps I had been too much the
lazy lioness. 'There are ancient rituals in the temple library,' I said slowly,
'which are designed to deal with possession by bodiless entities. It would
perhaps do no harm to perform them.' I stood up straight. 'I must summon my priest.'

'No, said the magician.

'It is not your decision.'

'I have another suggestion. Will you hear it?'

'Very well.'

'I have travelled in many lands and have seen many strange things.
My knowledge has been gathered from every corner of the world. I have
seen cases such as this before, and once a fire witch taught me how to treat
the condition. The prince is afflicted by a spirit of the wilderness, a creature of fire. The people of this city have mostly abandoned the old ways,
and while, in some respects, this ignorance has weakened the ancient spirits, in other ways it has made the people vulnerable to them. They have
forgotten how to protect themselves, how to fight back.'

I remembered the dreams I had had, the smell of burned meat around
the temple. 'I have always believed that new gods drive out the old. Sekt
is mistress here now.'

'Yes, a goddess of fire. She is not that different. Like calls to like.
What reason would she have to drive out her own denizens, only because
they are known by a different name? This is why *you* can remove this
parasite. In a way, it is your servant.'

I stared down at the prince. If this was true, I felt no kinship to the thing on the boy's back. I could barely sense it. I realised then that the priesthood of Sekt had lost a lot of their magic. We were fat and domesticated lions, dozing by pools, licking our paws. Where was the lioness of the wilderness, breathing fire? Did she still exist within me? I had no doubt the magician had also thought these things. Perhaps he despised me for what I was; a mask with nothing behind it. 'What was the suggestion you had to make?' I said.

'That you and I take the prince out into the wilderness, where I will teach you what the fire witch taught me.'

'Why to the wilderness? Why not here?'

'We need the elements around us. We need to tap their power. Too long have you hidden behind stone, my lady. I am offering you a great gift. If you are wise, you will take it.'

'You are importunate!' I snapped. 'I am Sekt.'

'Are you? Then banish this creature of fire now. Take it by the tail and toss it from the window.' He stood back with folded arms, appraising me.

I was breathing hard. My veil fluttered before my face. Meni would never allow me to venture out into the wilderness alone with this man. He would not let me be so foolish and, if necessary, would physically restrain me. Yet there was a wild desire for me to take what the magician offered me. I sensed he spoke the truth. I wanted to be alone with him, buffeted by hot winds beneath an ardent canopy of stars. I wanted to conjure fire spirits, be the lioness of the desert. 'It would be regarded as unseemly for me to venture out with you alone,' I said.

'Do they watch you so stringently?'

'Are you suggesting deception? How will you spirit the prince from his bed without detection?

He smiled and I realised he was beautiful, like the sky is beautiful, or the raging of a storm. I had met no one like him before. 'Remember what I am,' he said.

'When? How?' I asked, breathless.

'Tonight,' he said simply. 'Why delay? Will you be able to get away?'

I thought about the sleeping temple, the dozing guards, the great air of torpor that hung over its colonnaded halls from dusk until dawn. I could slip like a wraith from shadow to shadow, leap the wall like a lioness, land without making a sound.

'I know what you are,' he said. 'You are a goddess, yes, but are you not also a woman? Are you not also a lioness? You crave adventure, even the hunt. You crave the ecstasy that freedom brings. Indulge yourself, my lady. Who will ever know?'

He was a friend to me. I had known him many lifetimes. In the night, in the wilderness, he would be a black lion, gliding at my side.

Once the king and Meni returned to the prince's bedroom, I told them that I would perform the ancient rituals the following evening. I would need a day to prepare. Meni seemed a little bemused by my decision, and I knew that later he would quiz me about it, but he was loyal and did not voice his concern in public.

Outside the palace, back in my litter, I felt dizzy, almost sick. What was I doing? How had I become so infected with these alien feelings? The magician had conjured illusions for me, but I knew they could be real, because they did not involve magical ropes, phantom flowers, or even bittersweet memories. They were possibilities, a revelation of what could be. I had never craved freedom, yet now it seemed the most heady thing on earth. I had never felt the stirrings of desire for a man, nor even curiosity, yet here it was, hot and burning in my belly. I should have known then, sent word to the king, had the magician drowned or beheaded. Yet, instead, I lay back among my cushions, swooning like a lovesick girl.

I could not wait to dismiss my servants from my presence this evening. The air was full of a tension only I could feel. Candle flames bent into a wind that was not there. Incense smoke curled to the side. Even now, I entertain a dangerous hope. I think of Aan, the husband I have never met, he whose face is beautiful. Has he found some way to escape his temple? Has he come to me wearing the face of a man? How can I think such things? And yet, I do not find myself thinking about the fate of Prince Reevan, or even what the magician will show me tonight. I think only of his face, of being near him, of the vast expanse of wilderness around us, the infinite sky above. I run my fingers over the mask that shrouds me. The gold feels hot like fevered skin. I feel it might crack like the skin of a serpent and then I will slither out of it, reborn. If he does not wither before me, he is the one, but dare I take that chance?

At each hour, boy priests sing litanies to the goddess and her heavenly entourage. At the hour after midnight, when only the young priests are awake, I slipped from my bed, took up the mask and placed it over my head. I dressed with speed and covered myself with a dark hooded cloak that I wear to walk through the gardens in the rainy season. As an afterthought, I clasped around my neck a golden chain, from which hung a lion's eye stone, striped dark crimson and gold. Perhaps instinctively, I sought to provide myself with some kind of protection.

The temple was so quiet, and yet I thought I heard in the distance a rumble of thunder. For a moment, I wondered whether I would ever return there and such was my excitement that at the time I did not care.

It was as if I were invisible. I hurried past the open doors, beyond which lay sleeping servants. I undulated like smoke past guards who lounged at their posts, their eyes wet slivers that looked only upon dreams. The gardens were held in a humid caul of air. Lionesses sprawled beneath the trees, some upon their backs with their paws curled over their chests. I ran among them and none stirred. Lightning scratched across the night, but there would be no rain. The sky was a robe of stars.

Then the garden wall was before me. I yearned to leap it, but it would not be necessary. Flights of steps run up to the top of the wall at regular intervals, so that guards can patrol it, or else temple staff might sit there and watch the life of the city. I chose one of these flights at random and ran up it, then stood for a while on the wall, looking down. The city was spread out ahead of me, a mass of dim glows and hulking shadows. Now I must jump, for there were no steps on the other side of the wall. It looked so far, yet I knew it was not. I glanced behind me, fearful for a second that someone was watching me, but the temple and the gardens were still and silent, as if enchanted. I drew in my breath and leapt.

I landed on all fours on the short wiry grass and, for some moments, felt I should continue my journey in this manner, that I had discarded the body of a woman altogether. Then I stood up and saw that, yes, I still had arms and legs and that running on all fours would be both ungainly and slow. Quickly, I ran to a grove of tamarinds near the road, which was a glaring pale ribbon in the darkness. The wilderness was very near. I had only to follow the road for a short time, then take a narrower track to the east. The wilderness is always there around us. If people should abandon the city, it would soon revert to a strange and tangled waste, dry and tough and desert-coloured.

I had arranged to meet Arcaran at the edge of the waste, by a forest of broken towers, which were all that remained of an older city than ours. Their shattered fingers cast eerie shadows on the ground and I was sure that ghosts lingered there. For a while I could not find the magician and ran about in circles among the looming ruins. Then he stepped out of the shadow of a tower in front of me. He was a creature of night, yet I could see his face clearly; its sculpted planes, the faintest breath of dark beard about the jaw.

'I am here,' I said, 'where is the prince?'

'I have hidden him in the ruins. I thought you were not coming.'

'Take me to him.'

'We must venture further from the city. We are too close here.'

Prince Reevan lay with his head resting on a broken column. He looked young and vulnerable, his eyes staring blankly at the stars. I thought for a moment that he was dead, then he made a small sound and a thread of drool fell from his lips. I was alarmed by his condition and knelt at once to place my hands upon him, but Arcaran cried, 'No, don't touch him.'

'Why?'

'The parasite could transfer itself to you. We are not yet prepared.'

I stood up. 'Then we should proceed quickly.'

Arcaran lifted the prince in his arms and began to walk away through the ruins. I followed, looking about myself. I did not feel afraid or, if I did, the sensation felt pleasurable. It did not cross my mind that I was essentially, despite my title and status, a young woman alone with a strange man far from my sanctuary. I had always believed I was a goddess, but in truth did I really possess a goddess' powers? I did not know how to smite a man if he should attack me. I did not even know how to defend myself with human strength. Yet there I was, following him. It seems senseless now.

Beyond the ruins was a rocky valley, surrounded by high spiky cliffs. We went down into it and there I saw that a fire had been built and already lit, flames leaping hungrily at the sky, shedding showers of sparks.

The magician laid the prince down on the ground and I awaited the preparations for what I was convinced would be some arcane ritual. As he arranged the prince's limbs, the magician said, 'I have spent a lot of time in Mewt, my lady. I have visited the great temples there of Sekt and of her sister, Purryah, the cat goddess. The priests revealed to me some of their knowledge. It is a wisdom that never came here. For a century, your people have had an incomplete belief system.'

'The original priestess of Sekt in Madramurta was trained by Senu, High Priestess of Akahana,' I said. 'How do you know what we have or have not learned?'

'I know because you are unaware of what to do now. A true avatar of Sekt would know.'

'And so, presumably, do you.'

He nodded, squatting before me, his long, expressive hands dangling between his knees. 'I do, and I will tell you, but it may alarm you.'

I stood stiffly before him, wondering what would be said and whether it would be true.

'You must expel the breath of Sekt into the boy,' said the magician. 'You must conjure it. Do you know how?'

I wanted to answer that I did. I wanted him to think I was something more than just a mask, but I couldn't answer, because I didn't know.

He ignored my silence and said, 'First you must remove your mask.'

'No! It is forbidden. I may only do so when I'm alone. You should know that.' But, in my heart, that leap of hope.

He looked at me steadily. 'The mask should be removed for certain types of work. This is one of them. Don't you know why you are masked?'

'Because I am the goddess and her presence in me has changed me. I am too terrifying to look upon. I would wither you.'

He laughed softly. 'It would take more than that to wither me. Do you think you are hideous beneath it, a gorgon to turn me to stone?'

Again, I could not answer. 'It is the law,' I said.

He stood up and came towards me. He drew back the cloak of my hood and put his fingers against the hard skin of the mask. Beneath it, I burned. It was I who was turned to stone. 'I can see your eyes,' he said. 'I can see your mouth. You wear this mask to contain your power. The high priestess in Akahana wears hers only for state occasions, but you are bridled here, held back.'

I felt I would die from suffocation. I could not breathe. The mask constricted me. I was more aware of its presence than I'd ever been.

'Take it off,' he said. 'I am not afraid. Nor should you be. Claim what is yours, what you've never truly had.'

My hands moved automatically. I had no choice. He took a step back and watched me as I lifted the mask from my head and shoulders. Immediately, the wind felt too hot on my skin. My hair was lifted by it. His expression did not change. I felt exposed, impotent. Was all of my courage contained within the mask? I had no strength now. He came towards me, put his hands upon my face. I expelled a cry for his touch burned me. 'I know you,' he said. 'I have always known you.'

Some instinct made me pull away. I glanced down at Prince Reevan and saw that his entire body was covered in a crawling black smoke. It was as if he was being devoured by a swarm of insects. The magician's face looked black too, yet his eyes burned wildly. They were blue now, yet surely only a moment ago, they'd been dark?

'Don't be afraid,' he said. 'Accept. You can see now, *truly* see.'

I gulped the searing air. My eyes were weeping tears of flame. 'The prince,' I managed to burble.

The magician laughed and with a flick of his hand, made a gesture.

'The brat doesn't matter. He is only a decoy. Watch.' At once, the enveloping darkness rose from the prince's body into the air. He cried out, his limbs jerked. 'It is done,' said the magician. 'Simple. The salamander was my creature. I put it there. It was you I wanted. It was always you.'

I backed away from him, incapable of thought, of rationalisation.

He stalked me. 'You people are pathetic,' he said. 'You were given a power you could have developed. You did nothing but lie complacently in the temple until the power fell asleep from ennui. I can wake it, lady. It is already mine. I have come for you. Do you understand? For all it has atrophied, something was created here in Jessapur. I smelled it. It drew me. You are more than Senu ever could have been, yet you do not know it.' He drew himself up to his full height and it seemed to me as if his flesh was smoking. I could smell charred meat again. His eyes were smouldering blue flames. 'Do you know what I am?'

I knew. Part of me, a part of me that should have been greater, had always known. 'Djinn!' I said. Hungry, envious of flesh, full of guile.

'They let me in,' he said. 'You let me in. Look at you. A gargoyle. The mask has more life in it.'

I put my hands to my face and all I could feel was a frozen snarl, made of ivory. I had the wedge-shaped muzzle of a cat, a cat's sharp teeth. If ever I had been a normal woman, now I truly was a semblance of Sekt, lioness-headed, a statue made flesh. Hideous. Monstrous. This was the secret the mask had hidden. Now, the lioness had been released, but she had no strength. She had been domesticated.

'You have the potential power of the red fire, the white fire,' said the magician, 'that which is stronger than the orange fires of hearth or altar. You are most powerful free of your mask, lady, but also, paradoxically, most vulnerable.'

Arcaran made a sudden movement and grabbed hold of my arms. It was strange because there was no substance to him. He was smoke, yet I could not escape him. From the waist down he had transformed into a boiling column of darkness. He dragged me towards the fire and I could hear the song of the sparks. The flames leapt higher as if in anticipation. 'We shall be one,' he said. 'I shall have Sekt's essence. You do not deserve it.'

He was never flesh, I can see that now. Even his body was an illusion. He wanted mine, and the gift of fire that lay slumbering within it. To him, I was naïve and stupid, a posturing child with no true understanding of the goddess' power. Perhaps he saw himself as a denizen of Sekt and sought to reclaim her, release her. But most of all, he wanted my body. I knew that when I returned to the temple, I would no longer be me, and that a prince of djinn would hold sway in the hallowed precincts. No one would ever guess.

The flames licked at my clothes. Soon, it would be over. I could not help but fight, even though I felt my predicament was helpless.

Then she moved within me. I felt a flexing in my muscles and bones, a great sense of outrage. A voice roared from my throat. 'I am Sekt!'

I breathed in the flames, and expelled them in a gust of blood red sparks. Arcaran uttered an inhuman scream and fell backwards into the fire. The leaping hot tongues enwrapped him and he lay there staring up at me in fury. I snarled at him and he snarled back, but he was no longer the one in control. 'Do not presume,' I growled. 'Don't *ever* presume.'

Then I turned my back on him and put my hands against my face. I was no longer snarling. I felt pliant flesh, slightly furred. The golden mask stared up at me from the ground. It was a lifeless thing. I sensed him move behind me and turned round. He looked like a man again, a beautiful man, although his long hair was smoking.

'You cannot have this flesh,' I said. 'It is mine. I have provenance over this land.'

'Sekt,' he said, 'you misunderstand. I sought only to wake you.'

I snarled at him again. 'Fool! I know what you sought—a way into my temple, and thus to create your own reign of fire over the land and its people.'

'It has already begun,' he said. 'You cannot stop it, but should join with me. Look at this land. It is dying. The divine kings are shorn of grace and power. My influence smokes through the streets of Madramarta, inspires its slaves to revolt.'

I shook my head. 'You are deluded. You were banished once, because you could not, or would not, help the people of Jessapur against their conquerors. You have no true might, only a sneaking creeping insolence that finds a home only in the hearts of the ignorant and debased.'

'The greatest changes will always be born in the darkest gutter,' said the magician. 'What happens in a noble court or an enclosed temple affects only the privileged few. That is not change, but indulgence.'

'Perhaps there is some truth in your words,' I said. 'But now the people have me. I will serve them here as I serve them in Mewt. I always will.'

'Brave words,' hissed Arcaran. 'It is most likely that all you will do is fall asleep again. You need my influence.'

I snarled and stamped my foot, and the ground shook for a great distance around us. 'Smite you!' I hissed.

He raised his hands. 'I am already smitten, as you pointed out. Is there to be no peace between us?'

'There cannot be. You cannot be trusted.'

His face twisted into an evil leer. 'Go back to you temple, then. Be alone. But rue this day, Sekt. Remember it. It will haunt you.'

I stared at him unblinking for some moments, then turned away. I went to the prince, who lay unconscious near the fire and lifted him in my arms.

'Sekt,' said the magician. 'You cannot contain me. You will return. You will call for me. You know you will. Like speaks to like. I woke you.'

For some moments, I considered his words, then carefully placed the unconscious prince back on the ground. Arcaran was sitting amid the flames of the fire, the most beauteous sight I could imagine, the most treacherous. I lifted the lion's eye pendant in one hand and held it up before my face on its chain. 'I will never be without you,' I purred. 'I both love and hate you, and will hold you forever against my heart.'

He grinned at me, confident.

I dropped my jaw into a smile and spoke in a voice of command. 'I call upon the light at the centre of the universe!'

'What are you doing?' said Arcaran. The smiled had disappeared from his face.

'Great powers, attend me!' I roared. 'Hear now the voice of Sekt! Give me your power of compulsion'

'No,' said Arcaran. The features on his face had begun to twist and flex.

'Yes,' I answered softly, then raised my voice once more, arms held high. 'By the power of the creative force, I compel you, prince of djinn. I command you. Enter into this stone. I am Sekt, queen of fire. You will obey.'

A searing wind gusted past me, pressing my robes against my body, lifting my hair in a great tawny banner. Sparks fountained out of the fire. Arcaran expelled a series of guttural cries and his body writhed amid the flames. I do not know whether he felt pain or not, but very swiftly, he reverted to a form of smoke. I sucked his essence towards me, then blew it into the lion's eye pendant. It felt hot for some moments, and glowed with an eerie flame, then it went cold and dark. I placed it back against my breast once more. He would always be with me, but contained, a genie in a stone.

I lifted the prince once more and glanced down at the golden mask lying nearby. Already ashes from the fire had drifted over it. I would not wear it again. There might be another mask, and sometimes I would wear it, but it would be of my own design and I would don it through choice.

It seemed my altercation with the djinn had taken only minutes, but as I walked back towards the ruins, I saw that already the light around me was grey with dawn. Soon the pink and gold would come, the morning. As I walked, I breathed upon the prince's face. His eyes moved rapidly beneath their closed lids. He would recover swiftly from his brief ordeal. I had breathed the white fire into him. He was mine. I would make a true king of him, for all the people.

Near the temple, I passed a peasant woman with her children taking fish to the market. When I drew near, they fell to the ground before me, their hands over their heads. 'I am Sekt,' I said to them. 'Look upon me.'

The woman moaned and uttered prayers, but even so, raised her head.

'You are blessed,' I said. 'Carry word to the city that Sekt walks amongst you. She is unmasked and awake. Remember her face.'

Now, I am home. I can sense Meni awaking in his chamber. I will go to him, show myself to him. I am Sekt.

The Island of Desire

This is the most recent of all the stories and was only completed for this collection. I began writing it a couple of years ago, with the idea of sending it to the editors of one of the adult fairy tale collections, but for some reason I lost the thread of the story and couldn't be bothered to finish it. Coming back to it after so long with fresh eyes has given me the inspiration I needed to write the end.

The story is based upon the fairy tale 'The Twelve Dancing Princesses', and also another old Scottish tale, 'Kate Crackernuts', which shares a similar plot. In the first story, the hero is male and solves the mystery to free the princesses from their enchantment, but in 'Kate Crackernuts', the protagonist is female and it is she who frees an ensorcelled prince from the fairy realm, where he is drawn to dance every night. I liked the idea of a male victim and a female rescuer, so used it in 'The Island of Desire'.

There is often little logic in fairy stories, and even as I wrote this I wondered why and how, in all versions of the tale, no one ever works out what the wayward royal children get up to at night. Lone strangers, usually knights, keep vigil and succumb to sleep, but why on earth doesn't the king move his daughters/son to a public room, or a different town, or wherever, to seek to break the enchantment? Why doesn't he have a gang of soldiers stationed outside the bedchamber, who can come rushing in the moment they hear strange sounds? Still, if sensible actions like this were taken, half the story would be gone, or at least made more difficult, and the mystery would probably have been solved long before the enterprising adventurer reaches the palace. I think that wrestling with this problem was what caused me to abandon the story in the first place, so decided the only way to complete it was to go with the fairy tale logic.

Again, as with other short story characters, I can see the possibility of writing more about the lady Maris. She is an adventurer, and this is only one of her adventures.

The land of Skyripi is blue and mauve: that was my first impression. The tall, slender trees have softly-furred leaves that are more silver-grey than green; plants grow there like nowhere else in the world. Their foliage is dark purple, the most sombre tones of deepest cyclamen and the green of winter ivy. I rode in on the King's Highway from Cos, whistling through my teeth to my horse, looking for all the world like the happy wanderer I was. Two nights before I had met a fair knight beside the road, and because he looked doleful, I had invited him into my tent and there, after some persuasion, divested him of his armour. As we lay upon my furs he asked me where I was going, and I told him I would go where my nose led me. Every morning, I sniff the air and follow the scent most pleasing.

He said to me, 'Dear lady, would you like money, for I know where there's some to be earned.'

I answered that of course I would.

He told me then to go to the city of Rappernape, where the king was in need of a good soul to help him with a family problem.

'What kind of family problem?' I asked, demonstrating the muscles of my fighting arm.

The knight put his long fingers over my wrist. 'No, it requires cunning and stealth, but there is a cost. Some have died already.'

I did not like the sound of it, but was intrigued. The knight went mysterious on me, and would say only, 'From what I heard of the oracle at the pool, drink nothing, speak nothing and you will be invisible to their eyes.'

Of course, he was no ordinary knight, as I discovered when I woke in the morning, and found only a strange, grey-skinned elemental sitting on my chest. 'Do not go in by the canal road, but the iron road,' he said, and flew out of my tent, uttering a scream, which I hoped celebrated repletion and not something more sinister.

I came to a fork in the road, and there was a hag plaiting hemp in the dust. 'Is this the way to Rappernape?' I asked her and she nodded.

'Which is the best road to take?'

She indicated to the left, 'That is the canal road', and to the right, 'that is the iron road. They are both roads, and the distance to the town is equal down either one.'

I thanked her and rode down the right hand fork, trusting that my elemental lover had not played a trick on me. The iron road was hard beneath my horse's feet and around it there was a feeling of intensity. The taste of blood was in my mouth. When the twin spires of the city's cathedral were visible above the trees, a creature stepped into the road ahead of me. It was not beautiful, and disturbingly human in appearance, although its face was a nightmare of tusks and warts. Most fighters would slaughter such a beast on the spot, but I have travelled through many strange lands, and have learned from the wise men and women who lurk in their darkest corners that no creature should be judged on appearance alone. 'Greetings,' I said, pulling my horse to a halt, which was difficult for his strong-

est urge was to flee the apparition before us. 'You are blocking my way, so
I presume you want something of me.'

The creature snuffled a little and I supposed he might be thirsty, so
offered him a drink from my leather. He took it and was clearly delighted
to discover I did not keep water in it, but something more potent. 'A
witch gave me that,' I said. 'By all means, finish it.'

The creature did so, then grunted, 'You are going to the castle of the
king.'

I nodded. 'There is a problem there, I understand.'

'Many have died without solving it,' said the beast. 'The soft-skins
know not the ways of the land.'

All non-humans have this attitude. They think we are inferior, and in
many ways they are right. But what they fail to recall is that humanity
rules the world, whilst they are consigned to desolate spots and the unreal
realms beyond enchanted gateways. From what the beast had said, I determined that the problem was supernatural in origin. The creature would
give me no further information, so I bid him farewell and carried on into
town.

The king seemed eager to meet me, and I was presented to him in his
great hall that very afternoon. He asked me my name and I told him,
'Maris.' My full name is Marissa, but I dislike the simpering implications
of it, and only my parents, who have never been happy with the life I've
chosen for myself, now use it.

'You are an adventurer,' said the king, a statement loaded with judge-
ments. They always need us, but never do they lose their opinion that we
are somehow undesirables.

'Life to me is an adventure,' I said reasonably. 'I look for problems and
attempt to solve them.'

The king pointed outside the window to where a number of headless
bodies were impaled on spikes in the courtyard beyond. 'They too shared
your philosophy.'

'Why are they dead?' I asked clearly, not letting apprehension colour
my voice.

The king sighed. 'It is the price for failure. I resent having my raised
hopes dashed. It is unfair and must be punished.'

There was a certain neat, if grim, logic to this. 'So what is the problem?'

'My sons,' said the king. 'Calobel and Cataban. They are twins. A
year ago they succumbed to a strange ailment and are now listless and pale.
Every morning, they lie upon their beds fully dressed, even though they

disrobe the previous eve. Their boots are worn through and their hands tremble. Guards stationed outside their rooms see nothing. Heroes, knights and adventurers have kept vigil by their bedside, but can never stay awake— hence the dangling corpses.'

I nodded, frowning earnestly in sympathy. 'I can appreciate your exasperation in this matter. I would like to apply myself to solving the conundrum.'

The king sighed. 'Nothing would please me more. I will give you three days to succeed, and if you fail, you will join the others hanging outside.'

He was not a lenient man, it seemed.

The queen herself took me to her sons' apartments in the castle. She wrung her hands continually, muttering that she did not like to think of a woman undertaking this task, as it would grieve her to see me dangling in the courtyard. I assured her she should not worry. Privately, I mulled the situation over in my head. Sorcery was the obvious cause of the sickness. I was surprised none of my sorry predecessors hadn't worked this out and sought magical aid.

The sight that greeted me in the bedroom of Calobel and Cataban is still with me. They lay upon their bed, their black hair draped across the pillows like unravelled elven silk; hints of purple shining among the black. Their skin was translucent, their eyelashes long against their poreless cheeks. They were the most beautiful youths I had even seen and I yearned at once to touch them. They appeared to be asleep.

'It is always this way,' whispered the queen. 'They lie in an enchanted swoon waking only at sundown to take their meals. Then they are instilled with a feverish animation and make plans to go out riding or to walk the fields. But their excitement does not last and within an hour they are once again apathetic on their bed.'

I shook my head. 'Hmm. May I examine them?'

The queen assented, and I approached the bed. First I checked for the marks left by vampires and succubae, finding none. I attempted to wake the youths, to no avail. I smelled their breath to learn if any of the major sleeping sicknesses infected them, but their breath was sweet. Too sweet for individuals who lay in continuous sleep—I would have expected their humours to be sour. There was no sign upon them of enchantment and no tokens hidden around the chamber. The queen explained that several wizards had inspected the rooms before, and certain magical precautions had been taken, but none had worked. I admit I was perplexed. All I could do was perform the vigil and make sure I stayed awake. Now, I wished I hadn't given away all of my witch's potion to the creature on the road, for its effect was to keep one awake for days at a time.

'I must sleep now,' I said to the queen. 'Have your people wake me before sundown.'

The queen bade me sleep upon a couch in the adjoining sitting room, and here I willed myself to refreshing sleep. At the appointed hour, a maid shook me awake.

Calobel and Cataban were still slumbering when I entered the room, but as the last slanting red rays of the sun lifted from their bed to finger the wall above, their eyes opened in unison. They looked at me immediately, and never had I been transfixed by so dark a gaze.

'Will you tell me what you do each night?' I asked them, and they smiled at me like cats, secretive and deceitful.

'My lady, we sleep,' they said. 'We dream.' Their voices were of different timbres, but other than that they might have spoken through a single, shared throat.

I had to ask a difficult question. 'Is your father the king?'

They nodded. 'He is.'

They did not, to me, appear completely human, but that might have been the effects of the enchantment, for the moment I saw their eyes, I could sense a hex hanging about them like an odour. They slithered from their bed in nightshirts of soft linen that fell enchantingly down their shoulders, revealing the milk of their flesh. At first glance they were effeminate—and indeed their dark charms were like those of many a sorcerous female—but I quickly realised they were otherworldly, like elf children, sinister and deceptively frail in appearance.

'We must eat,' they told me, brushing past me like a storm of feathers, towards a table by the window where various platters lay heaped with food.

'I shall sit in this chair,' I told them, pointing to a seat beside their bed.

'As you wish, dear lady,' they replied and looked at one another with a smile.

I expected trickery and have to confess I did not feel wholly confident. Many had failed before me, some of whom had no doubt possessed cunning equal to my own.

As their mother the queen had predicted, the youths ate heartily and then discussed what they would do for the evening. I listened to their conversation carefully, alert for any strange nuance of tone, or innuendo of speech. All seemed normal. They wanted to ride their horses into the forest and even moved towards their dressing room to equip themselves accordingly, but even before they crossed the threshold, they began to yawn and rest their heads upon each other's shoulders. 'Perhaps tomorrow,' said Cataban. As one, they fell onto the bed.

I stood looking at them for some time. Their breath was even, their pose relaxed. I must not sleep, clearly, but what bewitchments might come stealing through the night to rob me of that resolve? I sat down in a wide seat beside their bed, and put my chin in my hands. The moon rose outside casting eerie shadows about the room that moved slowly across the bed. Periodically, I arose and paced the chamber. The air was full of expectation, as if unseen presences stooped in the corners of the room, holding their breath. Beyond the high windows, I heard the king's guard intone the calls of the watch, as the night ticked on. Presently, even that fell silent, and it felt as if only I was awake in the entire world. Unaccountably, my heart had begun to race. I fancied that some unheard music vibrated the air that my ears could not detect, but that my heart could hear. I had an urge to tap my feet, my fingers, even though not even the whimper of a dog broke the silence of the waiting night. Never had I felt more wide-awake.

Then, a sigh came from the bed, and I saw the princes writhe out of sleep like twin serpents upon a heated rock. They blinked, wiped back their loose hair from their eyes, and stared at me inscrutably. I did not speak, but stared back. Hadn't my elemental told me not to speak? They clicked their fingernails and advanced upon me.

'Here, pretty lady,' lisped one. 'Come stroke my hair.'

Another slithered across the floor on his belly. 'Are we not beautiful? Don't you want to touch us?'

They were lovely, yet hideous. An invisible steam seemed to seep from their pores that lulled the senses and brought back the most poignant memories of joy. I lived for a moment in some idyllic summer of my childhood, when all the world was mine and I celebrated the true, innocent freedom that is lost to us through maturity. Oh, to taste that emotion so many years on. It was like wine, or stronger, like the blooms of a narcotic lotus. Now I could see how others had failed before me. Knights had slumbered in this chamber, neglecting their duties, but it was not a slumber of the mind. Their hearts had leapt into the realm of dreams, and there they stayed. The room seemed to fade before my eyes. I felt cool fingers on my knees, and smelled a fragrance of cut grass and carnations. They wrapped me in their hair, breathed snatches of alien words into my straining ears. I was caught in the music of their soft laughter, drowning, drowning.

Then they offered to me the cup.

I saw it hanging before me, independent of their hands: a crystal chalice full of a deep blue liquid. 'Drink,' they said to me. 'Be a child once more and run over the endless hills. Run with the deer, the hare. Feel the winds of immortality cut the years from your body.'

I could smell it: a scent like envenomed nectar. My mouth watered. I wanted it so badly: to forget, to be back there, without scars of mind or heart or body. I took the cup from the air, and heard them laugh. 'Enjoy,' they cried and I knew they were moving away from me. All that existed was the cup, cold between my palms.

I cannot say I think myself superior to any of those who challenged the darkness before me. There is no doubt that many men and women of calibre had sipped from that deadly vessel in my place, perhaps far nobler than I: stronger, wiser and more clear-headed. Perhaps there comes a time when a chink in the universe opens up, and a blinding clarity comes through. It is chance, I think, not design. Whatever, something closed my lips as my nerveless hands lifted it to my mouth. It was as if another dwelt inside me, crying 'no, for pity's sake, no!' I wanted to drink—there is no doubt of that—and on another night or perhaps only a few minutes earlier or later, I would have done. But that moment was mine. Somehow I had earned it, and the cup stayed trembling at my lips. I like to think it was the influence of my elemental lover, calling me back from the abyss.

Beyond the phantom chalice, I could see, as if through a veil, the princes standing beside their bed. One of them clapped his hands, and slowly the bed slid to the side. The canopy above it swayed and creaked, and an opening in the floor was revealed beneath it. The twins paid me no more heed, perhaps seeing only the cup at my lips. Presently, with a swish of hair and a flash of pale linen, they disappeared into the opening in the floor. I held my breath for fully a minute, then gently set down the chalice on the bedside table and rose to my feet.

I was afraid, but it would have been foolish not to be. Beneath the bed, a stairway appeared to lead down into the deepest regions of the castle. There was a smell of earth and a cool, damp breeze rose up from the dark hole. Cautiously, I stepped onto the top stair. I could sense no movement below me; the princes had descended quickly. I imagined their feet had not touched the cold stairs: they had glided down like phantoms. What commerce could they have in the dungeons of their father's domain? I shuddered, thinking of unholy feasting and the cries of weak, dying prisoners. But the stairs did not emerge into the filthy vault I expected—they continued to plunge into darkness. What little moonlight had seeped into the hole was now eclipsed. My heart hammered against my ribs, and my eyes strained to see some glimmer of white below. On several occasions, I paused, thinking it would be better if I retraced my steps and sought to escape the castle undetected. Only a terrible fate could await me here. But perhaps some lingering essence of the princes' charms, or a fume from the deadly chalice, encouraged me deeper.

After what seemed an hour of slow descent, I walked into a wall ahead. The stairs had ended. Feeling with outstretched fingers, I encountered to the right what appeared to be the entrance to a passageway or room. There was in fact a door, which opened at slight pressure from my fingers. A cold blue light engulfed me immediately, which sent me reeling back into the stairwell. After a few moments, my dark-adapted eyes adjusted, and I saw that a bare chamber lay before me, lit by tall white candles, which emitted the strange cyan radiance. At my feet lay two discarded skins; the night robes of the princes.

Opposite me was another door, upon which was carved the grinning head of some otherworldly creature. I knew that whatever lay beyond that door was personified by this carving, something bestial and corrupt. The princes had thrown away their mundane trappings; who knows what they had transformed into? Venturing onward might bring me to the same conclusion experienced by all my predecessors: death or perhaps worse. Doubt and fear yelped at my heels the entire distance of the chamber, and then my hand was upon the door and slowly it opened to my touch.

Beyond it lay a vast cavern, lit by knobs of greenish yellow radiance atop carved posts. I stood upon a stretch of black, mica-starred sand at which lapped the sluggish waters of an oily lake. A single boat carved a route across it; even from a distance I knew the princes sat within it. The place was otherwise deserted. Looking up, I could see far overhead a forest of polished stalactites. Gnarled posts of stone rose from its waters like ancient markers. It was like the entrance to the land of the dead.

I walked along the shore following the direction the princes' boat had taken, wondering how I could possibly keep close to them. The lake was a maze of stalagmites and I had no doubt that soon the twins would be lost to my view. Then, rounding an outcrop of rock, I came across a rotting jetty to which was tied a small rowboat. I exalted for only a moment, because I soon saw that a creature clad in black rags was crouched in the prow, its manner proprietorial. 'Is this boat for hire?' I asked it.

Twiggy, clawed fingers pushed back its tattered hood to reveal a leathery face with only slits for a nose and a lipless mouth, rather like a bat. Sparse hair grew along its brow. It regarded me thoughtfully for a few moments, and then shifted restlessly upon its haunches. 'Might be,' it lisped.

I offered it a coin, which it sniffed and bit. Presently, it snuffled loudly, then gestured at the simple bench seat in the middle of its vessel. 'Where going?'

I climbed aboard and pointed at the vessel on the lake, which was fast disappearing between columns of stone. 'To wherever that boat there goes.'

The creature nodded, as if this was a reasonable destination. It waved its skinny arms in the air, and the boat launched itself from the sand. Without the agency of oars or rudder, it began to nose its way after the vessel ahead.

The journey wasn't long. After only half an hour or so, stronger light began to show through the forest of stalagmites and eventually the pillars of stone thinned out, until the lake was as clear and unmarked as a black mirror. Ahead loomed a festival of lights and music; an island reared from the still water, and here it seemed was the princes' destination. I have never heard music like it, nor shall again. It was fast and merry, yet strangely morbid; a blend of wailing pipes and hammering drums. I could see a host of figures cavorting about on the shore of the island. 'What is this place?' I asked the creature guiding the boat. 'Who lives there?'

It did not seem to think there was anything amiss in me not having this information already. There seemed little caution about strangers in this subterranean world. 'It is the palace of the Ambertrantes,' it replied.

'And what are they?'

'Those who call themselves rulers of this realm.' The creature spat carefully into the black waters.

'You would contest their claim?'

The creature shrugged. 'No. I am never invited to the island, though.' It eyed me beadily. 'Perhaps you, madam, could take me with you.'

'I am not invited either,' I replied. 'Perhaps we should land the boat somewhere discreet.'

Behind the great palace lay a stretch of shadowy beach, where abandoned gazebos fell slowly to dissolution. Several figures sat apart from each other, their heads in their hands. They seemed not to notice our approach. Since my guide seemed so amenable, I told it why I was there. 'Am I in danger here?'

It seemed not to understand the question.

'Will the Ambertrantes or their guests hurt me?'

Again, puzzlement.

Sighing, I tried once more. 'What happens here?'

The creature's thin mouth split into a grin. 'Much, much. All pleasures. You will be welcome, yes.'

'Wait for me here,' I said. 'And I will pay you more coins.'

The creature nodded, its eyes glinting with greed.

So I stepped onto the shore, where the sand was all of crushed sapphires. The land was lit by an eerie radiance that seemed to emanate from the palace itself: an edifice that clawed the air, both splendid and deformed. A hundred styles of building, from all corners of the world, seemed to comprise its towers, walkways, domes, colonnades and courtyards. Its walls were of polished porphyry and onyx. Silk flags hung from poles of gold, their tassels as soft as human hair. I heard laughter in the air, both manic and sublime. I heard the sound of many feet running. My nostrils were assailed by a thousand competing aromas, some exquisite, some foul. I walked up a wide flight of steps that led from the beach. Around me, emerald green peacocks pecked a sward of scarlet grass. One fell out of a tree as I passed and flapped drunkenly in a swirl of shed feathers at my feet. I saw that all the trees had trunks of gold and silver, and their leaves were made of jewels. Lanterns swung in a breeze I could not feel, and once a woman ran past me, arms stretched out ahead of her, screaming in hysterical delight. No one paid me any heed. There were too many people around for a single stranger's presence to make any impact, perhaps—but I sensed the elemental's words were correct and none could see me. Wine flowed from fountains, down into the mouths of those who lay in the pools beneath them. Narcotic fumes oozed from cubes of incense that smouldered in human skulls. I saw men and women of incredible beauty, like glaciers or naked flames. All were dancing, dancing. As I passed into a great ballroom, lit by a hundred crimson chandeliers, I saw then the princes I had followed. They were dressed in indigo velvet, strung with icy diamonds. Their eyes seemed to be filmed with milk; they danced. This was the land of gratification. I wondered how the princes had found entrance to its heady domain.

Invisible, I strolled among the revellers. No one could see me. They were all like statues come to life; physically perfect, but strangely devoid of souls. I sat on a chair at the edge of the hall and watched for some time. Then I rose and went back out into the gardens and thence to the shore. Before climbing back into the boat, I broke off a small twig from one of the trees and concealed it beneath my jacket.

'That is stealing,' said the boatman. 'The Ambertrantes won't like that.'

'Take me back,' I said. 'Tomorrow night I will need your services again.'

'If you return, they will kill you,' said the beast.

'It is a risk I will take,' I said, 'and not your concern. You will get paid regardless.'

Shrugging the boatman guided the boat across the dark lake to the farthest shore.

Back in the princes' bedchamber I hid the jewelled twig amongst my belongings, then composed myself on the couch that stood against the wall. To be sure, I was fast asleep by the time Calobel and Cataban came stealing back up the dark stairway, although I awoke as they got into their bed. I could hear them whispering together, laughing softly. No doubt they thought I would soon be a dead woman.

The following morning, the queen came to the princes' chamber and enquired how my night had been. I stretched and yawned and told her I was well pleased with what I'd learned.

'You were asleep,' said she, her face pinched with suspicion.

'I have three days,' I said. 'Trust that at the end of this time, all secrets will be known.'

That night, the princes once again enacted what they supposed to be their deception upon me, and once again I only pretended to drink the draft they gave to me. As before, I uttered no word. This time, I followed close upon their heels as they descended the stone steps, and as before, they could not perceive my presence with their eyes. However, at one point, in the darkness, I trod upon the hem of Calobel's nightshirt and he hissed to his brother. 'All is not right. Something has pulled at my robe.'

'Rats,' said Cataban. 'That is all.'

In the antechamber at the bottom of the stairs, they discarded their nightclothes and dressed themselves in the velvet suits similar to those they had worn the previous night. The clothes were waiting upon pegs in the wall, and there was no sign of the discarded nightshirts they'd left there the last time. Once in their finery, they opened the door upon the dark shore.

Following them out, I stumbled a little and sent a litter of stones flying. Again, Calobel said, 'All is not right. Did you hear that noise?'

'A distant firecracker from the palace grounds,' said Cataban. 'Stop fretting.'

I watched them climb into their boat and then hurried to where the little warty boatman was waiting for me. This time I had brought him more coins to keep him sweet.

I followed the princes as before, into the palace of light. Again, it was filled with a throng of people, dancing and running about and shrieking hysterically. The princes danced like lunatics, drinking strange ichors from crystal chalices, much like the one I had been offered in their bedchamber. This night, I stayed a little longer, and at some point the princes disappeared. I didn't see them go and ran out in a panic to the gardens, worried they'd gone home early and would discover I wasn't where they thought I'd be. But their boat still rested against the shore, where they'd left it. I went back into the palace and searched as many rooms as I could enter, but there was no sign of them. Dawn must not now be far away, so I knew I must return to my boatman, but as I was leaving the palace, I heard a lady say, 'The Lord and Lady of this house spend too much time with the princes Calobel and Cataban. They are neglecting all those of us who worship at their feet.'

Her companion, a handsome man dressed in armour, said, 'Fear not, my lady, for after tomorrow the princes will be no more. The time has come for their dance to reach its climax.'

How I wished I could interrogate these people, but of course it was not possible. As I left the palace, I took one of the crystal goblets from a table. It was a beautiful thing and hidden fires lurked within its facets.

In the morning, again the queen came to question me and once again I assured her that soon the mystery would be solved. I wasn't yet sure myself how I would solve it, because what I'd heard the previous night had hardly been encouraging, but I was not without hope.

Later, as I followed the princes on their nocturnal excursion, I took with me my sharpest blade.

This time, I stuck close to Calobel and Cataban, to make sure I did not lose sight of them. They were beautiful to behold, but that night, it seemed a dark shadow hung over them. Their movements were more languid, their eyes unfocused. They had the look of creatures hypnotised by a snake.

Long past the midnight hour, I saw the princes glance at one another. Cataban nodded his head and Calobel took his brother's hand. They left the ballroom through a curtained doorway, and I went after them at once. We passed through many chambers, in which scenes of great excess were enacted like bizarre theatrical productions. I was in a strange frame of mind, neither disgusted nor delighted. Neither was I afraid. It was as if I'd drunk the waters of forgetfulness, and walked in a drugged state.

Finally, I followed the princes into a chamber lit by fire-pits of blue and green. Long-backed lizards baked themselves upon steaming stones, and salamanders crawled in and about the unearthly embers. Otherwise, the chamber appeared empty. The princes danced together, to music only they could hear. Once we'd walked under the arch that led into the room, all sound from beyond was cut off, as if someone had closed a door of lead upon us. Then, Calobel stopped dancing, his body shaking. 'Brother, there is someone here with us,' he said.

Cataban frowned. 'No, no, they have not yet come.'

'Not *them*,' the other urged, 'but someone else.'

I held my breath, standing utterly still. Their milky eyes looked directly at me, yet I knew they could not see me. I was not part of this world, but like a phantom in it.

'There is no one,' Cataban said, and turned a slow pirouette on the spot.

My heart ached to see them caught in this weird thrall. They were two of the beautiful sons of the world, and did not belong in this place of dark hedonism. Even as I began to plan what I could do to save their souls, there was a great crash in the room, like someone striking an immense gong. It was the clamour of swords, of thunderbolts. The princes began to dance maniacally, as if their lives depended on it. The sight was at once grotesque and arresting. Hair spun and writhed and limbs described jittery arcs on the air. They were but puppets and someone had just tweaked their strings.

The light in the room grew more intense, and I saw a wall of heavy drapery peel away to either side. Beyond it was stark white radiance, and against it two silhouettes, one male, one female. Their costumes were magnificent, high collars rearing behind their heads, spiked with black feathers. The woman took the hand of the man and together they strolled down a shallow staircase into the room. 'My pets,' said the woman, in a voice like the bells that shake at the ankles of dancing girls.

'Pleasing,' said the man.

They were very tall, their skin of a strange bluish tinge. Likewise their hair was stroked with cobalt flashes and their eyes shone like sapphires. Demons, I thought, and took an unconscious step backwards. The princes meanwhile threw themselves about the room in a frenzied manner. The woman laughed and clicked her fingers. 'Dance, my pretties. Dance for me.'

The feet of the princes were but a blur, and their faces were agonised.

This was an enchantment of great potency, and the only ones deriving pleasure from it were the demons.

'How well they dance,' said the demoness to her companion. 'It seems almost a shame to quench their flames.'

'There will be more such as they,' said the demon, 'for is it not our magic that makes them so lovely?'

'I think I love them,' said the demoness, 'and if I didn't love you more, I would crush the jewelled leaf of a tree and mix it in a chalice of smoke and fire with your blood. Then the enchantment would be ended, and there would only be they and I to explore new possibilities upon our island of desire.'

'You love me more,' said the demon. 'The children of the earth are your playthings, my dear, and your sustenance. If we do not quench their flames, our work would be in vain, and that beauty you enjoy so much would wither. Then this would become the island of despair instead.'

'Food,' said the demoness, staring sadly at the dancing princes. 'They seem so much more than that.'

'But they are not,' said the demon. 'They have danced for us for many seasons to tenderise their essence. Now, they are ready to delight us.' He clapped his hands and called the princes' names. At once, they became still and stood with drooping heads in the centre of the room, held in trance.

The demons glided towards them, and each took a prince in their arms. I expected them to be vampires and suck blood, but instead, they began to bite the princes' flesh. I realised then they would consume the youths alive. There was no time for me to consider my actions. I unsheathed my blade and leapt into the centre of the room. The demons did not anticipate this and I beheaded them in a trice with swift strokes of the weapon. The princes were barely nibbled, and still stood lethargically before me. I gathered up the heads of the demons and tore down some of the draperies in the room in which to wrap them. Even as I was doing this, strange sounds reverberated through the palace: low hoarse screams and the crash of timbers. I realised that, in destroying these creatures, I had set about the destruction of their sorcerous domain. There was no time to waste. I could not risk speaking to the princes, because that would break my protection of invisibility and, in any case, it was doubtful whether they'd be able to hear me. With the heads slung over my shoulder, I took an arm of each prince in my grasp and dragged them, stumbling, from the room.

Outside, the palace was in chaos. Huge lumps of ornate plasterwork were falling from the ceiling, walls were collapsing and draperies were aflame. Panicking revellers were running this way and that, shrieking madly, and were in such a state of horror and alarm they had no time to notice me. Still, I was aware that the demons must have defences about the place, so dragged the princes as quickly as I could to the gardens. It was difficult to proceed because the island itself was sinking back into the dark lake. Explosions lit the air around the palace, and I could see that far above, there were only rocks covered in fungus and no sky.

The boatman was agitated to the point of being difficult as I tried to shove the princes into his boat. 'My vessel is too small,' he said. 'We will sink.'

'Then take the other boat!' I said. 'The one the princes use.'

'It will not obey me,' said the boatman. 'I cannot steer it.'

'Then we risk a sinking!' I snapped. 'Hurry up! When this island submerges, there will be a maelstrom and any boatman foolish enough to be hanging around here then can think of drowning whether the boat is too heavy or not!'

Grumbling, the boatman saw the sense of what I said and he began to urge his little vessel back across the lake. It was a perilous journey— terrifyingly slow, because the boat was so burdened, and the waters roiled and churned around us. Many times, I was sure I'd have to swim to shore, and wondered how I could save my own skin and still bring the princes back to their parents. Looking back towards the island, I could see people fleeing to boats around the shore, and even as I watched, whirlpools began to spin and sucked some of the unfortunate wretches down beneath the surface of the lake.

Oblivious, Calobel and Cataban lolled on the floor of the boat, their heads upon each other's shoulders. They missed entirely the final great spectacle as with a huge roar, a burst of sparks and filthy spray, the island disappeared completely, taking most of those floundering around in boats with it.

When we finally reached the other side of the lake, I was exhausted with anxiety and could see the little boatman was also near the end of his strength. Whatever nether creature he might be, he had served me well these past nights. It seemed he realised this for himself.

As he dragged the boat to shore, he said, 'Never mind the fine glitter-ing coins you have given me, lady. Now, my employment is at an end, for there will be no one to transport and nowhere to transport them to. There-fore, I am seeking new employment, and it has occurred to me how well I have worked for you, and that a brave adventurer should have a companion to see to her needs and to lend his brains when she requires an intelligent mind to aid her. I proudly offer you my services.'

I observed him for a few moments, then said, 'Help me with the princes, creature. We shall see.'

'I can do far more than guide a boat. I have great magics.'

'Just help me get these boys back to their beds.'

In the morning, as usual, the queen came to the bedchamber. I had already made some preparations and was ready for her. Calobel and Cataban lay stupefied upon their beds and indeed now looked close to death, for their breathing rattled in their chests. The queen glanced askance at my new servant, whose name I'd learned was Gart.

'My sons look the same to me,' said the queen. 'And now you will hang. I had entertained great hopes for you. It is a great pity.'

'I have solved the mystery,' I said. 'There will be no hanging. Have the princes conveyed to a room where you and your husband can watch me break the enchantment.'

Frowning at me, the queen nodded her head. 'Very well, but I think you are misleading yourself.' She gestured at Gart. 'What is that beast?'

'My servant,' I said. 'We should make haste. It appears the enchantment is finally sucking out the princes' lives.'

Even as I spoke, I was aware of strange movements within the bundle of cloth that lay on the couch, and which the queen had not noticed was leaking unsavoury fluids. I had a suspicion that the demons might still have power even without their bodies.

Calobel and Cataban were carried on litters to the great throne room, where the king had convened all his courtiers. I stood before him and he said, 'Is it plain to me that you have failed where all others have failed. What is the purpose of bringing my sons here? Soon, you will dangle in the courtyard.'

'Indeed I will not,' I said. 'I have followed your sons for three nights to a subterranean realm, where they have danced the night away. They were ensorcelled by demons, who sought to devour their life force.'

'Rubbish!' exclaimed the king. 'This story is preposterous.'

'In this place,' I said, 'the trees are made of gold and silver, and their leaves are made of jewels.' I took from my jacket the jewelled twig.

'A bauble,' said the king, 'a pin for a lady's hair.'

Sighing I plucked a tiny leaf from the twig and put the rest of it back in my jacket. 'In this place, they have magical artefacts and here I have a chalice of smoke and fire.' I withdrew the goblet from my jacket and held it up for all to see. A few courtiers around the chamber made soft sounds of surprise, for indeed the chalice was a beautiful thing, glinting with eerie flames within its depths, around which threads of purple smoke drifted and writhed.

'Conjuror's tricks!' declared the king. 'Any witch could have made you that.'

'This place was ruled by two demons,' I said. 'And these I slew to rescue your sons, who but for me would now be dead.'

'They appear near dead in any case,' said the king in a hostile tone. 'And where are the demons you spoke of?'

'Here,' I said and taking the bundle from Gart who stood behind me, I unwrapped it and threw its contents onto the floor. They rolled to the foot of the king's dais.

The entire court let out cries of horror, for in this world the demons were not beautiful. Their facial features writhed and sneered and they uttered abominations.

The king stood up. 'My sons are dying,' he said, staring with wide eyes at the rolling heads. 'Does this count as success?'

I said nothing but took out the goblet from my jacket once more and crushed the tiny leaf in my hand. These fragments I put into the goblet. At my signal, Gart lifted one of the demon heads, which protested greatly, and squeezed some black blood from the stump of its neck into the goblet. I mixed the potion with my fingers, then went to the princes to administer it, all the while praying to every god that existed that this would work.

The princes drank the foul juice I poured between their lips and for some moments moaned piteously upon their litters. Then Calobel sat up and said, 'Papa, Mama, what are we doing here?'

At once, the entire court broke into tears and cheers and everyone began to clap loudly at my success. The queen ran to her sons and embraced them. Now, though still comely, they looked like ordinary young men, yawning and stretching and wondering where they were. I doubted they would remember any of what had happened to them, which was probably just as well.

'Take these demon heads,' I said to king, 'and convey them to a place where you must light a brazier. Throw salt into the flames and then burn the heads. In this way, they will be utterly destroyed. Then, we shall talk about my reimbursement for this task.'

'You are an astounding woman,' said the king. 'Name your price and I will gladly pay it.'

So, there it was. The mystery solved, the enchantment broken. If I'd entered the city along the canal road, I might not have succeeded, and if I'd not heeded the elemental's words, I would have certainly failed, but I pay attention to omens and advice, so I was instead a heroine, heaped with rewards and praise. The king and queen were most insistent I should marry one of the twins and become a princess, but however handsome the princes were, they were tainted in my eyes, and anyway, I had no desire to live a fat, contented life. Instead, I summoned my new servant, Gart, who was proving himself more every day to be an entertaining and resourceful companion, and we rode out of Rappernape on fine horses with full purses. Perhaps for some weeks, we will enjoy the countryside before finding new adventures. Even the strongest, most quick-witted heroine deserves a holiday now and again.

Storm Constantine has been writing since childhood. In 1985 she began work on the first of her Wraeththu trilogy, *The Enchantments of Flesh and Spirit*, which was quickly accepted and published in 1987 by Macdonald Futura in the UK. and TOR in the US. Since then she has published 13 more novels in the UK and US, and one exclusively US story collection from Stark House Press.

Her most recent work includes the Grigori trilogy, a series of novels about fallen angels, published in the US by Meisha Merlin, and the Magravandias Chronicles, an epic fantasy in Gothic style, the second volume of which, *Crown of Silence*, has recently been published in the US by TOR. She is currently working on a new Wraeththu trilogy, to be published by TOR.

Lately, Storm's writing has turned to books on psychic developments (*The Inward Revolution*), an exploration of ancient feline deities (*Bast and Sekhmet: Eyes of Ra*), and updated ancient astrology (*Egyptian Birth Signs*).

On her way to becoming a successful short story writer and novelist, Storm has also managed a rock band, worked in experimental video, exhibited and sold her own artwork and became co-editor, with Eloise Coquio, of *Visionary Tongue*, a dark fantasy magazine.

She lives with her husband, Jim Hibbert, and nine cats in an historic part of the English Midlands, close to ancient hunting grounds and far from the industrial dark of the black country.

If you enjoyed this title, you might enjoy the following from

STARK HOUSE PRESS

0-9667848-2-0 **INCREDIBLE ADVENTURES**
by **ALGERNON BLACKWOOD** $16.95

Fantasy stories that defy categorization from the author of "The Willows."

0-9667848-1-2 **CALENTURE**
by **STORM CONSTANTINE** $17.95

Fantasy novel set in a world of floating cities

0-9667848-0-4 **THE ORACLE LIPS**
by **STORM CONSTANTINE** $45.00

Signed/Numbered/Limited Edition hardback collection of the author's stories

0-9667848-3-9 **SIGN FOR THE SACRED**
by **STORM CONSTANTINE** $19.95

Fantasy novel about the search for an elusive messiah

If you are interested in purchasing any of the
above books,
please send the cover price plus $3.00 U.S. for the 1st book
and $1.00 U.S. for each additional book to:

STARK HOUSE PRESS
1945 P STREET
EUREKA, CA 95501
(707) 444-8768 * griffins@northcoast.com

NAME _____

SHIPPING
ADDRESS _____

_____

_____

VISA/MC# _____ EXP. _____

BILLING
ADDRESS _____
(if different) _____

_____

ORDER 3 OR MORE BOOKS AND TAKE A 10% DISCOUNT!